THE ULTIMATE CONSPIRACY

W. A. Harbinson started to uncover the nightmarish truth about Unidentified Flying Objects (UFOs) in the research for his international bestseller *Genesis*. Now he has taken that groundbreaking work and expanded it, going back decades to create another astounding epic. *Inception* is a terrifying story based on documented historical fact that reveals what is really known about UFOs while it holds readers spellbound with a breathtaking thriller about organized evil, global conspiracy – and the secret future of our world . . .

INCEPTION: THE FIRST BOOK OF THE EPIC TERROR SERIES *PROJEKT SAUCER*

About the author

W. A. Harbinson has been a journalist, magazine editor and TV scriptwriter. Born in Belfast, Northern Ireland in 1941, he left school at fourteen, studied mechanical engineering, then joined the Royal Australian Air Force. While serving in the RAAF, he drafted his first novel, *Instruments of Death*. In 1980 he completed the classic *Genesis*, the epic novel of the world's most fearsome secret that became the inspiration for the *Projekt Saucer* tetralogy. (*Inception* is chronologically the first novel in this sequence.) Harbinson lives in north London with his wife and two children.

Inception

W. A. Harbinson

PROJEKT SAUCER: BOOK ONE

NEW ENGLISH LIBRARY
Hodder and Stoughton

First published in Great Britain in 1994
by Hodder and Stoughton
A division of Hodder Headline PLC

A New English Library paperback

10 9 8 7 6 5 4

British Library Cataloguing in Publication Data

Harbinson, W. A.
Inception. – (Projekt Saucer Series; Book 1)
I. Title II. Series
823.914 [F]

ISBN 0 450 61750 5

Typeset by Avon Dataset Ltd, Bidford-on-Avon

Printed and bound in Great Britain by
Cox & Wyman Ltd, Reading, Berks.

Hodder and Stoughton
A division of Hodder Headline PLC
338 Euston Road
London NW1 3BH

For
Howard and Vicki Moore
and
Julia and Nicola
My favourite Muswell Hillbillies

AUTHOR'S NOTE

In 1980 my 615-page novel, *Genesis*, based on a mass of research material, became a cult best-seller on both sides of the Atlantic. It remains in print to this day.

Reviewing the novel on its initial publication in the United States, *Publishers Weekly* said: 'Harbinson has drawn so heavily on factual material and integrated it so well into the text that the book begins to read like non-fiction . . .' This conclusion was drawn by other reviewers, and over the years I received many letters from readers who obviously thought the same and begged me to tell them which parts of the book were fact and which were fiction. For the record, then, here are some facts.

Before writing *Genesis,* while researching a different novel altogether, I obtained through the Imperial War Museum, London, two short articles that attracted my attention. One was a routine war report by Marshall Yarrow, then the Reuters special correspondent to Supreme Headquarters in liberated Paris. The particular cutting I had was from the *South Wales Argus* of December 13, 1944. It stated: 'The Germans have produced a "secret" weapon in keeping with the Christmas season. The new device, which is apparently an air defence weapon, resembles the glass balls which adorn Christmas trees. They have been seen hanging in the air over German territory, sometimes singly, sometimes in clusters. They are coloured silver and are apparently transparent.' The second article, an Associated Press release published in the New York *Herald Tribune* of January 2, 1945, illuminated the subject even more. It said: 'Now, it seems, the Nazis have thrown something new into the night skies over Germany. It is the weird, mysterious "Foo fighter" balls which race alongside the wings of Beaufighters flying intruder missions over Germany. Pilots have been encountering this eerie weapon for more than a month in their night flights. No one apparently knows what this sky weapon is. The "balls of fire" appear suddenly and accompany the planes for miles. They seem to be radio-controlled from the ground, so official intelligence reports reveal . . .'

Official 'Foo fighter' reports were submitted by pilots Henry Giblin and Walter Cleary, who stated that on the night of September 27, 1944, they had been harassed in the vicinity of Speyer by 'an enormous burning light' that was flying above their aircraft at about 250 miles per hour; then by Lieutenant Edward Schluter, a fighter pilot of the US 415th Night-Fighter Squadron based at Dijon, France, who, on the night of November 23, 1944, was harassed over the Rhine by 'ten small reddish balls of fire' flying in formation at immense speed. Further sightings were made by members of the same squadron on November 27, December 22, and December 24.

While no official designation of the Foo fighters was offered, most reports indicated that they appeared to be under some kind of control and were certainly not 'natural' phenomena. Indeed, according to a London *Daily Telegraph* report of January 2, 1945, RAF pilots were describing them as 'strange orange lights which follow their planes, sometimes flying in formation with them, and eventually *peeling off and climbing*' (author's italics).

According to the Italian author Renato Vesco, in his book *Intercept – But Don't Shoot* (Grove Press, 1971), the Foo fighter was actually the German *Feuerball*, or Fireball, constructed at an aeronautical establishment at Wiener Neustadt. It was a flat, circular flying machine, powered by a turbojet, and used during the closing stages of the war both as an antiradar device and a psychological weapon designed to disturb Allied pilots.

In any event, sightings of the Foo fighters tailed off and

ceased completely a few weeks before the end of the war.

The next wave of UFO sightings occurred in Western Europe and Scandinavia. From 1946 to 1947 many people, including airline pilots and radar operatives, reported seeing strange cigar- or disc-shaped objects in the skies. On June 21, 1947, Harold Dahl reported seeing saucer-shaped objects flying toward the Canadian border. Three days later Kenneth Arnold made his more famous sightings of saucer-shaped objects over the Cascades, also flying toward the Canadian border.

These and subsequent sightings led to speculation that both the Soviets and the Americans, utilizing the men and material captured in the secret research plants of Nazi Germany, including those at Peenemünde and Nordhausen, were developing advanced saucer-shaped aircraft.

Were such speculations based on facts?

It would certainly seem so.

During the early 1950s, a former Luftwaffe engineer, Flugkapitän Rudolph Schriever, then resident at Hökerstrasse 28 in Bremerhaven-Lehe, West Germany, claimed that in 1941 he had designed the prototype for a 'flying top,' which was test-flown in June 1942. In the summer of 1944, with his colleagues Klaus Habermohl, Otto Miethe, and an Italian, Dr Giuseppe Belluzzo, he had constructed a larger version of his original prototype. Then, in the East Hall of the BMW plant near Prague, they redesigned the larger model, replacing its gas-turbine engines with an advanced form of jet propulsion.

An article about Projekt Saucer was later published in the indispensible volume, *German Secret Weapons of the Second World War* (English-language editions published by Neville Spearman, London, 1959, and the Philosophical Library, New York, 1959) by Major Rudulph Lusar. It included reproductions of Schriever and Miethe's flying-saucer drawings.

According to Lusar, the flying saucer consisted of a 'wide-surface ring which rotated round a fixed, cupola-shaped cockpit.' The ring consisted of 'adjustable wing-discs which could be brought into appropriate position for the take-off or horizontal flight, respectively.' Also developed was 'a discus-shaped plate of a diameter of 42 meters (138 feet), in which adjustable jets were inserted.' The completed machine had a height from base to canopy of 32 meters (105 feet).

Schriever claimed that his 'flying disc' had been ready for testing in early 1944, but with the advance of the Allies into Germany, the test had been canceled, the machine destroyed, and his designs either mislaid or stolen. His story was, however, contradicted by alleged eyewitness Georg Klein, who later stated to the German press that he had actually *seen* the test flight of the Schriever disc, or one similar, on February 14, 1945.

Doubt may be cast on Klein's date, because according to the War Diary of the 8th Air Fleet, February 14, 1945, was a day of low clouds, rain, snow, and generally poor visibility – hardly the conditions for the testing of a revolutionary new kind of aircraft. Nevertheless, according to author Renato Vesco, the test flight of a machine called the *Kugelblitz*, or Ball Lightning Fighter – which was rumored to be a revolutionary kind of supersonic aircraft – was conducted successfully over the underground complex of Kahla (near Nordhausen) *some*time during February 1945.

Did the United States then become involved in flying saucer projects?

The short answer is: yes.

Evidence for US involvement surfaced with information about the US Navy's Flying Flapjack, or Flying Pancake. Designed by Charles H. Zimmerman and constructed in 1942 by the Chance-Voight Corporation, the Flying Flapjack, or V-173, was an experimental, vertical-rising, disc-shaped aircraft that used two 80-hp engines. A later, more advanced model, the XF5U-1, utilized two Pratt and Whitney R-2000-7 engines of 1,600 hp each. It was rumored to be over 100 feet (30 meters) in diameter and to have jet nozzles – resembling the 'glowing windows' seen on so many UFOs – arranged around its rim.

It was built in three layers, the central layer being slightly larger than the other two. As the saucer's velocity and maneuvering abilities were controlled by the power and tilt of the separate jet nozzles, there were no ailerons, rudders, or other protruding surfaces.

In appearance it was remarkably similar to those reported by so many UFO witnesses.

The US Navy claimed to have ceased working on the Flying Flapjack project in 1947 (the first version, the V-173, is stored with the Smithsonian Institution), but US involvement with saucer-shaped aircraft did not stop there.

The reports that started the modern UFO scare – the Dahl and Arnold sightings of 1947 – both stated that the saucers flew back toward the Canadian border. On February 11, 1953, the Toronto *Star* reported that a new flying saucer was being developed at the Avro-Canada plant in Malton, Ontario.

Both the US and Canadian governments vehemently denied involvement in any such project, but on February 16, after freelance photographer Jack Judges had taken an aerial photograph of a flying saucer resting outdoors in the Avro-Canada plant in Malton, the Minister for Defence Production admitted to the Canadian House of Commons that the firm was working on a 'mock-up model' of a flying saucer, capable of flying at 1,500 miles per hour (2,400 km/h) and ascending vertically. Shortly after this announcement, the president of Avro-Canada wrote in *Avro News* that the prototype being built was so revolutionary that it would make all other forms of supersonic aircraft obsolete.

The aircraft's official name was the Avro-Car.

According to official statements, the Avro-Car was tested in 1960 and subsequently abandoned as a failure. (The prototype is now on display for all to see at the Army Transportation Museum at Fort Eustis, Virginia.) However, while the Canadian and US governments have insisted that they are no longer involved with flying saucer construction projects, there are many who believe that they are lying and that the Canadian, British, US, and even Soviet governments are continuing to work on highly advanced, saucer-shaped, supersonic aircraft based on the work done in Nazi Germany.

Those who believe in this are often quick to point out that of the original Projekt Saucer team, Habermohl was captured by the Russians and taken back to the Soviet Union, along with over six thousand German technical specialists of all kinds, to work on similar projects; Miethe went to the United States with Wernher von Braun and other German rocket scientists and ended up working for Avro-Canada, in Malton; and Rudolph Schriever insisted right up to his death, in the late 1950s, that the Soviet Union and United States were both working on flying saucer construction projects based on material captured during the war.

For the purposes of my fiction, I have utilized many real-life people, including the mysterious John Wilson and the Nazi SS generals Artur Nebe and Hans Kammler.

The term 'real-life' is used in regard to John Wilson only in the sense that during the first modern UFO sightings – the Great Airship Scare of 1896–97 – when airships of unknown origin and advanced design were reportedly seen, and landed, all over the United States, the man whom most witnesses reportedly spoke to had introduced himself simply as 'Wilson' and claimed that his airships had been constructed in Iowa and Illinois.

He was not seen or heard of after the great scare ended – though C. C. Akers, former sheriff of Zavalia County, Texas, to whom Wilson had referred when speaking to one of the witnesses, claimed that he *had* known a Wilson who was of 'a mechanical turn of mind' and 'working on aerial navigation and something that would astonish the world.'

Regarding the SS general Artur Nebe: While he was placed on a Nazi 'death list' in 1944 and disappeared shortly after, his death was never confirmed. Many felt that he had simply fled for his life. As for General Hans Kammler, his history with the SS and the V-2 rocket program is well documented, but what became of him after he disappeared from Germany in April 1945 remains a mystery to this day.

These are some of the facts supporting the fiction of the original *Genesis* as well as *Inception*.

Ponder them wisely.

W. A. Harbinson
London, 1990

CHAPTER ONE

The sun was still rising over the barren prairie near Roswell, New Mexico, when the Model T Ford, towing a trailer and churning up clouds of dust, approached the flat plain of Eden Valley, followed by a vintage black touring sedan.

Parked by the wooden shelter near the steel-webbed tower that soared sixty feet above the desert floor, with her knees propped up on the steering wheel of her car and her notebook resting on them, Gladys Kinder chewed on her pencil, watched the distant caravan approaching, then nodded thoughtfully and started to write. She began positively.

Well, folks, what an era it has been! First the Civil War, then the Industrial Revolution, and now the Age of Science and Technology. And what advances have been made in the past few years! Michael Faraday explored electrical induction, Joseph Henry made startling advances in electromagnetism, Bell devised the telephone, Morse the telegraph, Edison the incandescent lamp, Heinrich Hertz detected radio waves, Marconi produced the wireless communicator, and other scientists are presently revolutionizing our concept of the essential elements of matter and the behavior of light-waves – all in the space of a few years!

And this very day, just before we hail the bright and shiny New Year of 1931, our very own scientific genius, Robert H. Goddard, is about to launch his latest liquid-fueled, instrument-carrying, gyroscopically controlled rocket from the desolate plain known as Eden Valley.

Eden Valley! An appropriate name – since what is being created here could well lead to a world changed beyond our wildest imaginings.

A strange and terrible beauty is being born here in Roswell, New Mexico . . .

She studied what she had written, not pleased with its awkward mixture of the folksy and the academic, then looked up again as the caravan approached the steel-webbed launching tower and braked to a halt.

As the dust subsided around the vehicles, Gladys gazed around her to take in some background details, then hurriedly jotted down what she had seen:

From where I sit, which is close to the rocket's launching tower, the snowcapped El Capitán Mountain rises from the foothills near the southwestern horizon. To the east are the sunlit slopes of the Caprock and, beyond them, the Staked Plains, where the Comanche Indians, Spanish explorers, and even Billy the Kid roamed not long ago . . .

Temporarily blocked and deciding to fill the rest in later, she put the notebook and pen back into her shoulder bag. As she looked up, five men stepped down from the two vehicles, casting long shadows on the desert floor.

She instantly recognized the forty-eight-year-old Goddard from his stooped walk and thin, tubercular body. He did not like journalists, did not approve of her being there, and so stared directly at her, his brown gaze intense over his mustache, before turning away to give instructions to his small group of mechanics and machinists.

Wilson wasn't among them.

Surprised, Gladys slid her knees off the steering wheel and looked south across the flat plain, hoping to see him driving toward her. Thwarted, she returned her gaze to the front in time to see the crew unwrapping the long bundle that had been covered with quilts and oilcloth and trussed down on the back of the trailer towed by the Ford.

Once it had been unwrapped, the men lifted Robert H. Goddard's latest rocket out of the trailer bed.

It was a slender cylinder, about eleven feet long and nine inches in diameter, complicated with various tanks and tubing. One of its stabilizer vanes was painted bright red. The men carried it with considerable care to the sixty-foot launching tower, which had been guyed by cables and anchored in concrete.

Henry Sachs, the crew chief and instrument maker, and Al Kisk, Goddard's brother-in-law, climbed the tower and fastened cables to the striped rocket to hold it steady until its moment of release. Meanwhile, on the ground below, two of the mechanics, brothers Lawrence and Charles Mansur, reeled wire out from the tower to the control shelter that had been constructed about a thousand feet away from the launching tower and buttressed with sandbags. Then Lawrence headed out into the desert with his recording telescope and stopwatch while Charles walked up to Gladys and grinned nervously at her.

'No journalists are supposed to be here,' he said. 'Goddard's not pleased to see you.'

'Wilson told me I could come,' she replied.

'Oh, did he, indeed?'

'Yes.'

'So where's Wilson?'

'I was going to ask *you* that.'

'I don't know,' Mansur said. 'I don't know anything about that damned Wilson. No one does, Gladys – except maybe you.'

'And Goddard.'

'Goddard swears he's just an old friend.'

'Then that's what he is.'

'He sure has a lot of priority for someone who's just an old friend and claims to know nothing about aeronautics.'

'So it goes,' Gladys said.

'You're a damned good journalist, Gladys. You've got eyes

and ears. You know damned well we resent him.'

'Why?'

'Why ask, since you know?'

'I only know what I'm told, so tell me.'

Mansur shook his head from side to side, grinning sardonically. 'All I can tell you is that *I* don't know a damned thing about Wilson. I don't, my brother doesn't, none of the other crew members do – and what Goddard knows, he's not about to discuss. In other words, Wilson is a mystery – he's just here as Goddard's friend.'

'Doing what? The cooking?'

'Very smart, Miss Kinder.'

'So, *what*?'

Mansur shrugged. 'Again, I don't know. All I know is that Wilson appeared out of nowhere about six months ago, that he's been tight as can be with Goddard since then, and that the two spend a lot of time in Goddard's workshop, doing God knows what. According to Goddard, we're not supposed to talk about Wilson. As far as the public's concerned, Wilson doesn't exist. And as far as *we're* concerned – by which I mean Goddard's crew – Wilson has a mysterious hold on Goddard, with the master doing what the student bids. And he also has you in his bed – so what else do you want to know?'

Gladys smiled. 'Wilson's about sixty years old. Who the hell are you kidding?'

'Well, Gladys, you're thirty-five. And Wilson doesn't *look* like a sixty-year-old. He looks about your age.'

'Gee, thanks, Charlie!'

'Dammit, Gladys, you know what I mean.'

'Yes, Charlie, I do.'

What Charlie meant was that while Wilson was at least twenty years older than Goddard and claimed to be working for him, the general feeling among the crew was that he had somehow, surreptitiously, taken charge of the rocket project and was pulling all the strings behind the scenes. Charlie believed that because Gladys slept with Wilson, she must know more about him than anyone else; but she didn't.

As a journalist for the Roswell *Daily Record*, as well as Wilson's mistress, she had been unable to resist asking him more than once about his past. She'd learned only that he had an aeronautical background, had never been married, and was the least emotional man she had ever known.

He was a mystery, all right – and most mysterious of all was the fact that although he worked constantly in Goddard's workshop, he had never once attended an actual rocket launching and had even insisted that if she, Gladys, wanted to keep seeing him, she had to ensure that his name was not mentioned in connection with Goddard's work.

And God knows, she *did* want to see him again. She needed to share his bed, was addicted, even against her better judgment, to what he could give her there. And what he gave her there was something that sometimes shamed her – a sexual heat in which love had no place because he could not conceive of it.

He certainly wasn't a warm man, not impelled by finer feelings, but his very lack of emotion was what made him so good in bed, so patient and controlled, more exciting as a lover than most of those she had known.

And he was sixty years old . . .

'You're not really involved when you do it,' she'd once told him. 'You treat it as a functional endeavor, a mere form of release. You're not involved on any other level – least of all emotionally.'

'Count your blessings,' he'd replied with his familiar, slightly superior smile. 'It's because I'm not involved that I can control myself until you're satisfied.'

'You make me feel like an instrument of masturbation.'

'That's what sex is,' he said.

No, not an emotional man – certainly not a romantic one – yet it was true, as he had said, that his functional approach to the act of love was what made his loveless sex so exciting. He could keep going for hours – sometimes it seemed forever – and came to orgasm only when she begged him to do so.

Thus his coldness, while depriving her of affection, made the sex something special.

She had certainly needed it. He had come to town at the right time. Gladys had been born and raised right here in Roswell, the only child of farming parents, and had married too young to a man who, though decent in his way, had bored her to tears. The marriage had been a disaster, coming to grief on a bed of stone and producing no children. But when, five years ago, her husband had died of a heart attack, followed soon after by the death of both her parents, Gladys had felt that her life was falling to pieces and took refuge in drink.

The drink had dulled her pain and shock, but also released her from inhibitions, and she had taken up with a string of different men, most of whom disappointed her. She toughened up pretty fast, developed a pragmatic outlook, and charmed the proprietor of the Roswell *Daily Record* into trying her out as a journalist. It was the best thing she'd ever done, giving her a sense of her own identity, and she'd buried the disappointments of her life in her work for the paper. She became a strong, independent woman easily bored, quick with her tongue, and discovered that a lot of men didn't like it and so shied away from her.

Not that she gave a damn – she didn't want to marry again. But then Wilson had come to town, looking to work with Goddard. Since, when Gladys met him through Goddard's assistant, Charlie Mansur, he'd made it perfectly obvious that he was intimidated by no one, she'd thought him a breath of fresh air and become involved with him.

It was not a romantic relationship, but it certainly had its moments, and she enjoyed the sex and found Wilson intriguing – a real mystery man. So, she was well pleased.

Returning to the present, Gladys looked away from Mansur as another car pulled up and Goddard's blond wife, Esther, climbed out with her camera and equipment. Henry Sachs filled the rocket's tanks with gasoline and 'lox,' or liquid oxygen, as Goddard greeted his wife. When Sachs had finished, Goddard checked the rocket's controls, connections,

14

pressure tanks, and aluminum-sheathed oxygen tank, waved to Larry Mansur in the distant observation post, then returned to the protected control shack with his wife and Sachs.

'Do I have to join them?' Gladys asked.

'No,' Charlie replied. 'You're far enough away to be safe, no matter what happens. But *I* have to join them.'

'You don't want me to get near Goddard, right?'

'Right, Gladys. Goddard's already mad that you're here, so I won't tempt the fates.'

'Thanks, Charlie.'

'Okay, then.'

Charlie returned to the buttressed control shack as Esther Goddard put her camera on its tripod and pointed it through a hole in the shelter wall. Goddard looked at his watch and started counting off the seconds, letting the pressure-generating tanks build up to two hundred pounds, and eventually, after what seemed to Gladys to be an eternity, gave the order for the ignition to be fired.

Gladys knew he had done so when, from her vantage point well away from the launching tower, she heard a roaring noise and saw flames shooting out from the base of the rocket. The rocket shook violently as if about to blow about, lifted up slowly, reluctantly, then gained speed and suddenly shot out of the tower and soared toward the sky.

It climbed vertically, in a straight line, then veered south. It kept climbing as it headed south, at about a thousand feet, then ascended even higher, caught the sun as it leveled out at two thousand feet, then curved down again and raced toward earth. Its parachute didn't open, so it came down too fast, screeching and whistling, obviously out of control. It crashed into the sands of the desert about half a mile away, exploding in a great cloud of sand, its pieces scattering everywhere.

One of the men whooped with excitement, another bawled, 'The goddamned gyroscope!' and Henry Sachs had jumped into the touring sedan and was heading toward the scene of the crash even before the cloud of sand had settled down.

Gladys looked at Goddard, where he stood behind the

shelter, talking to his wife as she carefully checked her movie camera. The great scientist was actually smiling, which meant that most of the test had been successful – but then, when he glanced over his shoulder at Gladys, his mournful face registered disapproval that she was still there.

Not wanting to push her luck, and mystified by Wilson's absence, Gladys started her car and drove back across Eden Valley, heading south, toward Roswell.

Goddard's Mescalero Ranch was located on eight acres of land, three miles northeast of Roswell. As Gladys pulled up in front of the sprawling pueblo-style ranch house surrounded by scrubby trees and desert, she was struck again by the incongruity of Goddard and his rocket team being there, so close to the legendary Pecos River, where the men still wore blue jeans, high-heeled boots, and broad-brimmed hats, where the pioneer trails still cut through the nearby town to the borders of Mexico, and where the natives still talked about the exploits of Billy the Kid and other legendary, local desperadoes. She knew that Goddard had chosen this spot because he needed a relatively high region free from fog, and with a minimum of rain and snowfall – but even so, as she climbed down from her car and walked toward the house, the thought of rockets soaring over this barely modernized territory seemed slightly unreal to her.

She didn't actually go to the house, but instead went to the frame machine shop near it, where she guessed Wilson would be, as that's where he had slept during his stay here. After glancing automatically at the small static frame and concrete trough, called 'the bathtub,' located a hundred feet away and used for testing the rockets, she entered the unlocked machine shop and found Wilson kneeling on the floor by the cot he slept on.

He was packing his suitcase.

Shocked and confused, Gladys sucked in her breath – a sound loud enough to make Wilson stop what he was doing and look up at her.

His eyes were as blue as the sky above New Mexico, bright with an icy intelligence – and unnervingly steady.

'Hello, Gladys,' he said quietly.

'Hi,' she replied.

'You're back earlier than I'd expected.'

'So I see.'

He glanced down at his suitcase, smiled thinly, then closed the case and stood up to gaze steadily at her.

'I'm leaving,' he said.

Gladys closed her eyes, feeling sick to her stomach. Chilled by the flat tone of his voice, she knew he meant what he said.

'Open your eyes,' he said. 'Don't be childish. You always knew this would come. How did the test go?'

She opened her eyes and tried to see him for what he was. His hair was silvery, his face handsome but ascetic, and although he was sixty years old, he looked twenty years younger.

She only knew what he looked like.

'The test went okay,' she said. 'There was some problem with the gyroscopic controls, but otherwise it was fine . . . You were going to run away without telling me?'

'Yes,' he replied.

'Why?'

'Because I didn't want any arguments. I told you that someday I'd be going – and today is the day.'

'I didn't think you'd actually—'

'I'm not responsible for what you think – only for what I say. And I told you that one day I'd be leaving and going alone.'

'God, Wilson, you're hard.'

'You've known that since you've known me.'

'I think I'm going to have to sit down.'

'Help yourself,' Wilson said.

She took the chair at Goddard's old writing desk, next to his lathe and workbench, lit a cigarette, exhaled a stream of smoke, and squinted through it at Wilson. He was a tall man, as thin as his smile, and his blue gaze was steady.

'Okay,' she said, 'so you always told me you'd leave

17

someday. But I still didn't think you'd go this way – deliberately sending me out where I'm not wanted and then sneaking away.'

'I told you: I didn't want any arguments.'

'It's human to argue.'

'To be human is to err.'

'We *are* lovers, Wilson. That must count for something.'

But he merely shook his head, arguing an academic point. 'No,' he said, 'I'm afraid it doesn't. At least, not for me. The only thing that matters to me is my work -- as I've told you repeatedly.'

'Yes, Wilson, you've told me repeatedly. I just happened to think you might not mean it.'

'I always mean what I say.'

Gladys's heart was racing and she felt desolated, but when she saw the icy glint in his eyes, she knew it wouldn't mean much to him. He would leave her as some people disown their pets – and he would never look back.

Accepting that, she was able to protect herself by becoming professional.

'You're a strange bird, Wilson.'

'You're free to think so.'

'I'm not the only one who thinks so. Goddard's men *all* think you're strange.'

Wilson smiled mockingly. 'What can I say to that? I'm not responsible for the thoughts of petty minds. What they think is irrelevant.'

'They think you're the genius behind Goddard.'

'They're wrong: I was learning *from* him.'

'They think you know more about rockets than you let on – and that only Goddard knows how *much* you know.'

Wilson simply smiled again. 'I have to go now, Gladys.'

'Does Goddard know you're going?'

'No.'

'Is this how you say good-bye to *him*? To a genius with whom you've worked for six months? Is this how you thank him?'

'I thanked him by working for him for free. Now that I've

learned what I need to know, I've no reason to stay here.'

Shocked again at how truly cold Wilson was, Gladys blew another cloud of smoke and watched it spiraling in front of her.

'So what did you need to know?' she asked him.

'What Goddard could teach me.'

'About rockets?'

'Yes.'

'And what did you need to know that for?'

'That's not your concern,' he said.

She looked intently at his blue eyes, trying to find what she had missed, but saw only a luminous intelligence, beyond rancor or warmth.

'If you're so concerned with rocket technology,' she said, 'why not stay with Goddard?'

'Because this country always betrays its great scientists – and will soon betray Goddard.'

'Does that mean you're going abroad?'

'Yes.'

'Where to?'

Wilson smiled. 'To where my own work will be appreciated.'

'And where's that?'

'I can't tell you.'

'I'm a journalist. I can find out.'

'It won't help you.'

'I can also find out just who you are.'

'That won't help you either. Now I've got to be going.'

He picked up his suitcase, gazed down at her, smiled thinly, then walked out, not even kissing her good-bye. She had pride, but her heart betrayed her and she jumped out of Goddard's chair, then hurried to the doorway of the machine shop and looked into the morning sun.

Wilson climbed into his battered Ford, turned on the ignition, waved at her as if he were just going for a short trip, then drove toward the town of Roswell, with its pioneer trails and still-burning legends, to disappear into his unknown future and leave her all alone again.

'God damn you!' she whispered.

CHAPTER TWO

Ernst Stoll's heart was racing with anticipation when he saw his girlfriend, Ingrid, already seated at a table by a window in the Kranzier Café, Berlin. Feeling resplendent in his new SS uniform, almost like a movie star, he leaned over to kiss Ingrid's cheek, lightly stroked her short-cropped blond hair, then sat facing her and took hold of her hand.

'You look lovely,' he said, meaning it. His excitement was raised by the pale beauty of her face, which was emphasized by her wide-brimmed black hat, black jumper, and string of pearls, all meant to match the new black coat she was wearing. 'And that coat suits you perfectly,' he added, 'Did you get it in Paris?'

'No,' she said with a gentle smile. 'Right here, in the Kurfürstendamm. Parisian fashions are frowned upon these days, so I made sure it was German. *You* look handsome in your brand-new uniform – black suits you as well – though I still wished you'd stayed with the Reichswehr, instead of joining the SS.'

'Let's have coffee and strudel,' he suggested, deliberately changing the subject, not wanting this particular day to be spoiled with even a small disagreement. 'Yes?'

'Yes, Ernst.'

He called the waitress, gave her the order, then glanced out at the busy corner of the Unter den Linden and the Friedrichstrasse, its snow turned to slush by the many cars and pedestrians. When he returned his attention to Ingrid's green gaze, he was overcome by his love for her.

21

'You look excited,' she told him.

'It's seeing you,' he replied.

'No, Ernst, I don't think that's what it is. We both know what it is.'

He was grateful that she realized and didn't mind too much. Today was January 30, 1933. It would be a memorable day for Germany and already it was starting. Right now, Hitler and Göring were in the Chancellery with von Papen and Hindenburg, and the street between the Kaiserhof and the Chancellery was crowded with people. Before the day was out, Hitler would be the Chancellor of the Third Reich. A new era was dawning.

'I didn't expect to see you today,' Ingrid said. 'I was surprised to get your message. I thought you'd gone home for the fortnight.'

'I couldn't miss this day,' he told her. 'And my parents understood. My father still doesn't approve, of course – he thinks I've betrayed my middle-class origins – but my mother recently joined the National Socialist Party, in secret, which I think is amusing.'

'I don't,' Ingrid said. 'A divided family isn't amusing. Your beloved National Socialist Party, which has already divided the country, is now dividing individual families. Do *you* think it's amusing?'

'I didn't mean it that way,' Ernst said, feeling a little embarrassed.

'No, I'm sure you didn't,' she said with soft sarcasm, then, perhaps realizing how she sounded, gently changed the subject. 'So, how *is* your family, Ernst?'

At that moment, the waitress returned with their coffee and strudel. 'They're fine,' Ernst said, pouring the coffee from the pot and thinking of his family home in Heidelberg, a grand house with fine gardens on the lower slopes of the majestic Odenwald. 'Father's sold his architectural firm and seems happy to have moved out of Mannheim – and Mother likes it as well.'

'I'm glad,' Ingrid said, 'though I'm also glad that I saw the old house in Mannheim before it was sold – the house you were brought up in. There aren't many like that these days.'

Ernst knew what she meant. His father had been one of the most successful architects in Germany – his work conservatively based on neo-Renaissance and the 'safe' classicism of Ludwig Hoffmann – and his house in Mannheim, where he had spent most of his life, was a spacious residence built around an elaborate courtyard and guarded by wrought-iron gates. Within that imposing home, Ernst had been brought up to treat as perfectly natural enormous neo-Gothic rooms, French furniture, Empire upholstery, fireplaces faced with valuable Delft tiles, glittering chandeliers, maids with white caps, black dresses, and white aprons, and even butlers in purple livery with gilt buttons. Certainly, as Ingrid had noted, there weren't many houses like that these days – but the very opulence of the lifestyle is what had driven Ernst away from it and into the National Socialist Party, thus outraging his father as well as upsetting Ingrid.

He couldn't explain what attracted him to Hitler because he wasn't too sure what the appeal was. He only knew for certain that he'd been swept up in a tide of enthusiasm generated by his fellow students, first in the Institute of Technology in Munich, then in the University of Berlin, where he had been studying rocket technology under Professor Karl Emil Becker.

If he'd had any doubts at all about National Socialism they'd been swept away when, during his final semester at the university, he had attended an address that Hitler had delivered, in the Hasenheide Beer Hall, to the students of Berlin University and the Institute of Technology.

At first not impressed by the Charles Chaplin look-alike in a plain blue suit, who started speaking almost shyly in that dirty, gloomy beer hall, Ernst had soon been mesmerized by the rising passion of his rhetoric. He was astounded to find himself bawling and clapping with many other students in a spontaneous outburst of enthusiasm. A few days later, unable to forget that mesmeric performance, he had joined the

NSDAP; then, a few months after that, he dropped out of the university to join the army as a commissioned officer with the Weapons Office. When recently offered a transfer to the elite SS, he had been thrilled beyond measure.

'You're looking very thoughtful,' he said to Ingrid, who was staring straight at him in her disconcerting manner.

'I was thinking what a pity it is that you dropped out of university in order to look handsome in such a uniform. You wanted to be an engineer, Ernst, and now you're a policeman.'

'A soldier,' he corrected her, perhaps too firmly. 'The SS isn't the Gestapo. Please bear that in mind. The Gestapo is the Secret Police organization, run by Göring. SS stands for *Schutz Staffel*, or Guard Detachment, and the SS, created by Himmler, is Hitler's personal bodyguard – not a secret police force.'

Ingrid shrugged. 'It's still sad, Ernst. And I still don't understand why you did it, apart from naïveté.'

He felt a flash of anger, but tried to conceal it. 'As I told you before, I joined the army because I wanted to be a *rocket* engineer, and the army is the best place to do that.'

'That much I understand.' She brushed the blond hair from her green eyes, gazed out at the busy corner of the Unter den Linden and Friedrichstrasse, then returned her quizzical gaze to him. 'But I still don't understand why you then had to join the SS, which, whether a police force or Hitler's personal bodyguard, is not the place for a promising young engineer.'

'Because,' Ernst lied blatantly, 'it is the elite of the army and I only want to be in the best. It's as simple as that!'

In fact, what he couldn't explain to her was the bitterness he had felt ever since being rejected by the German amateur rocket society, the VfR, whose members included not amateurs, as the title implied, but most of the leading rocket experts of the day.

Also known as the Spaceship Travel Club, the VfR had come into being in 1927 when a group of brilliant space-travel enthusiasts had taken over an abandoned three-hundred-acre arsenal, which they called their *Raketenflugplataz,* or Rocket Flight Place, in the Berlin suburb of Reindickerdorf, from where they actually shot some crude, liquid-fueled rockets skyward. Intrigued by the success of the VfR, which by 1930 included rocket experts Rudolf Nebel, Willy Ley, Hermann Oberth, and Klaus Riedel, the Ordnance Branch of the army's Ballistic and Weapons Office, headed by General Becker, had appointed Captain Walter Dornberger to create a rocket-development project at the army's firing range at Kummersdorf, about fifteen miles south of Berlin. It was now widely assumed by those involved with rocketry that as soon as Hitler came to power (which he almost certainly would today), the VfR would be disbanded by the Nazis and become part of the Kummersdorf program.

Ernst had desperately wanted to be part of the VfR, irrespective of who controlled it. After his rejection because of his lack of practical experience, his bitterness had been made more acute when Wernher von Braun, a fellow pupil at the university, had been accepted.

Thus, when Ernst was persuaded by a friend that working with the SS technical intelligence group would at least give him the opportunity to keep in touch with the rocket program and perhaps, in time, even give him authority over it, he had not been able to resist asking for the transfer.

'Listen,' he said to Ingrid, covering his anger with a broad smile and taking hold of her hand again, 'I can't wait any longer. Let's go and see what's happening at the Chancellery. There's bound to be a decision soon – and I want to be there when it's announced.'

Ingrid's smile, though still loving, was also slightly mocking. 'You want to be a part of history, Ernst?'

'Yes, Ingrid, I do.'

She acknowledged his enthusiasm with a defeated shrug of her shoulders. 'Then let's go, Ernst!'

As they hurried along the snow-covered Unter den Linden, past its elegant shops and many pedestrians and the noisy flow of traffic, Ernst glanced frequently at Ingrid's flushed face, its beauty now emphasized by the raised fur collar of her black overcoat and broad-brimmed hat. He loved her dearly, though they often disagreed, particularly when they talked about politics and general morality. They seemed opposites, then.

She came from a good family in the wealthy Berlin suburb of Wannsee – but she didn't believe, as he did, in the National Socialist Party. She was a liberal, like his father, believed in her own class, and could not be convinced that Hitler would create a new, better Germany. Even now, when they were supposed to be in love, she and Ernst fought a lot about the issue, which wounded him deeply.

As they approached the corner of Berlin's finest shopping street and heard the sudden roaring of the crowd that had filled the Wilhelmstrasse, Ernst knew that they had just missed the announcement he had wanted to hear. Nevertheless, he practically dragged Ingrid around the corner, into the Wilhelmstrasse, where, between the Kaiserhof and the Chancellery, the great crowd was tramping the snow to slush and roaring approval.

Stopping by the Ministry of Justice, facing the Presidential Residence, Ernst received confirmation from a jubilant fellow citizen that Hindenburg had resigned and Adolf Hitler had just been sworn in as Chancellor of Germany.

Ernst whooped with joy, swept Ingrid up in his arms, and spun her around on the pavement.

'*Wunderbar!*' he exclaimed.

Any doubts about love or compatibility were swept away in the fervor of the rest of that memorable day. Ernst had no sooner released Ingrid from his embrace than he saw Adolf Hitler standing upright in the back of his open-topped car as it crept slowly through the mass of people in the Wilhelmstrasse, taking him back to the Kaiserhof. Shouting himself hoarse like all the others, Ernst watched his hero being driven past, then embraced Ingrid again, kissed her passionately, and realized that the excitement was contagious and finally getting through to her.

Excited, they went for lunch, got drunk on beer and schnapps, then took a room in the Adlon Hotel, where their faces were known. They made drunken, passionate love, uninhibited by doubts, and Ernst thought that he would die in Ingrid's body, with its smooth, burning skin, perfect breasts, and sublime, pale-white legs. They broke apart drenched in sweat, breathing harshly, exhausted, and he felt that he had died and been reborn and could never stop loving her.

'You're magnificent,' he told her.

Then he had to leave to take part in the torchlit parade that spelled the end of that great day.

Darkness was falling on the city when, with thousands of other troops, all in uniform and with many wearing their swastikas, Ernst started marching from the Tiergarten. Accompanied by the beating of drums and the blare of martial music, they passed under the Brandenburg Gate, and then continued down to Wilhelmstrasse, where hundreds of young men were hanging from the railings or perched like birds in the trees.

Raising his voice with those thousands of others in the 'Horst Wessel Lied' and other patriotic songs, Ernst soon found himself in the torchlit darkness outside the Presidential Palace, where a weary Hindenburg raised his hands in salute. Then the crowd moved to the Reichchancellery where, to Ernst's immense joy, Hitler appeared at a window to look down fondly on his men and acknowledge with a smile their triumphant chanting of 'Heil, Heil, Sieg Heil!'

Hitler smiled and raised his right hand and the massed troops roared acknowledgment. Then Hitler went back inside and Ernst lowered his gaze – away from that lighted window, from the fluttering red and black flags, from the torches that had formed a river of fire in the Wilhelmstrasse . . . and saw Ingrid emerging from the crowd, her eyes bright with excitement, her arms outstretched as the drums continued pounding and the noise became deafening.

She threw herself into his arms and clung to him as he stroked her light-blond hair.

'Oh, Ingrid!' he said passionately. 'A great day! The future is ours! Let's get married at once!'

'Yes!' she whispered, clinging to him, part of him. 'Yes, Ernst, let's do it!'

Their hearts beat like the drums.

CHAPTER THREE

'Yes,' Mike Bradley said, thinking about Gladys Kinder instead of the facts as he gazed out the window of General Taylor's office at the other buildings being constructed on the sloping green fields of Langley Field, Virginia. 'I told him we were about to form a National Advisory Committee on Aeronautics and were considering a team that would include him and other aeronautical geniuses, such as Charles Lindbergh and Orville Wright – and the legendary Robert H. Goddard *still* showed no interest. He just doesn't give a damn.'

'Why?' Taylor asked pragmatically.

'Because he doesn't trust anyone,' Bradley replied with a frustrated shrug of his broad shoulders, remembering the polite, suspicious voice he had heard over the telephone, when he had called from his office on Wall Street. 'Reportedly he patents every damned thing he invents, is notoriously secretive and uncooperative with his fellow scientists, feels that many of his ideas have been stolen by them, notably those in Germany, and will take help only from organizations like the Smithsonian Institution, which lets him do whatever he wants. In fact, he's even refused the assistance of the California Institute of Technology Rocket Research Project and has been relying instead on the inadequate funding of Clark University in Worcester, where he teaches physics when he's not working on his rockets.'

'Though according to Charles Lindbergh,' General Taylor pointed out, 'whom I met here just yesterday, Goddard *has* recently accepted some other help.'

'True enough,' Bradley said. 'With Lindbergh's recommendation he was recently able to get a Guggenheim Foundation grant for $2,500, which enabled him to leave Clark and return to Roswell, New Mexico.'

Where Gladys Kinder lives, he thought. He'd been unable to stop thinking about her since their brief meeting. *It's ridiculous,* he thought. *You're being ridiculous. She's just a sharp-tongued lady from a cow town and you're imagining things.* Though he couldn't help wondering . . .

'Is that where he was when you phoned him? Back in Roswell?'

'No,' Bradley said. 'He hadn't returned there yet. He was still at Clark.'

'If what you say is true, he thinks that if he joins our proposed National Advisory Committee on Aeronautics, he'll have to share his precious ideas with us.'

'That's my bet,' Bradley said.

General Taylor smiled laconically. 'Sounds like a burgeoning crackpot,' he said.

'But a brilliant one, General – and one you could do with on your side. Since a major function of the committee will be to assess the military possibilities of aeronautical developments around the world, a man of Goddard's background and reputation would be invaluable to you – not only for his technical knowledge, but also as a public relations weapon.'

'Well, we'll just have to get along without him.'

'I guess so,' Bradley said.

The sound of hammering from outside momentarily distracted the general and made him glance out the window. Following his gaze, Bradley saw some men in coveralls kneeling on the roof of the adjoining building as they expertly nailed down some more beams. When these buildings were completed, they would house the new National Advisory Committee on Aeronautics as well as a branch of the too-informal army air force intelligence. General Taylor was currently the head and Bradley was an increasingly enthusiastic, but unofficial, agent of the intelligence unit.

'It's interesting that he should be so concerned with German rocket development,' the general said, returning his thoughtful gaze to Bradley, 'since that's also what *we're* concerned with right now.'

'The Pentagon isn't,' Bradley replied. 'Since the White House has adopted an isolationist stance regarding Europe, there's no Pentagon interest in German weaponry.'

'I can't speak for the whole of the Pentagon, let alone the White House,' Taylor said, 'but I think I can say with confidence that we in military intelligence *are* concerned with the growing militarism of Germany – particularly since Hitler was elected chancellor. It's not our belief that America will be involved in European politics per se, but there's certainly been enough concern to cause the air force to informally gather information on aeronautical developments in Hitler's new Germany and, especially, on any further developments regarding the—' The general glanced down at the notes on his desk. 'The *Verein fur Raumschiffart,* or VfR,' he read, then looked up again

'Right,' Bradley said. 'The German amateur rocket society.'

'It's wonderful,' the general said with a slight, sardonic smile, 'how bright boys like you can bring back such interesting information from their vacations in Europe.'

Bradley knew what the general was getting at. He had been a highly decorated pilot during the Great War who had left the service in the mistaken belief that he was becoming too old for it and needed a more settled life. So, he studied law, married Joan, had two kids, Mark and Miriam ... As a successful lawyer, specializing in the drafting of complex agreements between government departments and civilian aeronautical research establishments, he had become increasingly bored with Wall Street and started calling his old military buddies to ask them for work, official or otherwise, that was more important and exciting.

Convinced that matters in Europe would eventually lead to another world war, he had used his Ivy League Wall Street friends to build up strong connections in Washington, DC, and

London. Eventually he managed to convince the army's chief of staff, General Douglas MacArthur, to let him embark on an unofficial intelligence-gathering trip to Europe, in the guise of studying international laws relating to aeronautics.

During that trip, in 1932, aided by some old friends who were now with the well-organized British Intelligence Service, he had traveled extensively and reported, in particular, on the growing militarism of Germany. What he had seen there had shocked him and made him fear for the free world. He no longer shared his own government's confidence that America could stay out of Europe – certainly not if the National Socialists, under Hitler, got what they wanted – and upon his return to the United States had insisted in his lengthy report that the country must prepare itself for inevitable involvement in another world war.

While his report had not been taken seriously by the White House, since then General Taylor had used him as an unofficial agent between Taylor's army air force intelligence branch and British intelligence, as well as a legal adviser, general administrator, and headhunter for the soon-to-be formed National Advisory Committee on Aeronautics – which is why Bradley had made his recent, unsuccessful trip to Robert H. Goddard in Roswell, New Mexico.

'But why would our air force be interested in a bunch of amateurs?' General Taylor now asked, after a thoughtful pause.

'Because they're not amateurs,' Bradley told him. 'The *Verein fur Raumschiffart* was founded in 1927 and soon included most of the rocket experts of the day, including Hermann Oberth, Max Valier, Rudolf Nebel, Willy Ley, and Klaus Riedel.'

The general gave a low whistle of respect. 'That's some bunch of scientists,' he said. 'What were they up to?'

'We know that a number of small liquid-fueled rockets were fired from their testing ground in the Berlin suburb of Reinickerdorf. Then, in April 1930, Captain Walter Dornberger was appointed to the Ordnance Branch of the German Army's

Ballistics and Weapons Office, headed by one General Becker. Dornberger was to work on rocket development at the army's Kummersdorf firing range, approximately fifteen miles south of Berlin. Two years later the VfR demonstrated one of their liquid-fueled rockets to Dornberger and other officers at Kummersdorf.'

'I'm surprised I haven't heard of this,' Taylor said, sounding slightly aggrieved.

'Maybe that's because recently, with Hitler's support, the Gestapo moved in and overnight the VfR ceased to exist as a civilian organization.'

'But it's now being used by the army.'

'Right. A lot of its members, including the reportedly up-and-coming Wernher von Braun, were taken under Dornberger's wing and began working at Kummersdorf in strict secrecy.'

'Ah,' the general said softly, 'so *that's* why our air force is concerned!'

'Damned right,' Bradley said. 'And if they knew what I just learned in Roswell, they'd be even *more* concerned.'

'And what was that, Mike?'

'Since Goddard was so damned suspicious and frosty over the phone,' Bradley explained, thinking again of Gladys Kinder and feeling distinctly guilty, 'I visited Roswell in order to interview those who had known him there – his engineers, the local townsfolk, and so forth. Anyway, over the week I spent there, I became increasingly concerned with the fact that Goddard, with so little assistance either financially or from fellow scientists, had managed to make such extraordinary advances in rocket research. Then, shortly after the final launch, I was introduced to a woman—'

'I won't tell your wife that,' the general interjected.

Bradley grinned, as if appreciating the joke, but immediately he was consumed by the guilt he had been trying to keep at bay ever since his meeting with Gladys Kinder.

The proprietor of the Roswell *Daily Record* had put him in touch with her. They'd met in the bar of his hotel. He was instantly intrigued by her air of worldly cynicism. In the course of a conversation about Goddard's rocket team, he'd become uncomfortably attracted to her, which she had soon realized.

She had passed a few mischievous remarks to that effect and actually managed to make him blush.

She was tall and lean and had a head of short-cropped brown hair, which made her seem slightly mannish, and gray eyes that were disconcertingly steady over a full-lipped, sardonic smile. She had been wearing a long, belted dress, with high-heeled boots and a Stetson hat. He, in his gray suit, portly and not too tall, in his mid-thirties and starting to show it – though thankfully he still had his hair – had felt soft and pampered in her attractively casual presence.

You didn't meet women like that in New York – and besides, he just *liked* her.

Now, when he recalled her and also thought of his attractive, good-humored wife, Joan, who lovingly looked after their home and children in Connecticut, he felt as guilty as if he had had an affair, which he certainly had not done.

He had simply been tempted, that's all . . . So why should he feel guilty?

'The woman, Gladys Kinder,' he continued uneasily, 'was a journalist for one of the local papers, the *Daily Record*. When I said I'd spent the past week checking up on Goddard and his old launching grounds in Eden Valley, she told me that two years ago she'd had an affair with another physicist who'd stayed with Goddard for six months, spent most of that time working and sleeping in Goddard's machine shop, and was considered by most of Goddard's men to have been very influential on Goddard's work. Those facts were later confirmed in my discussions with some of the rocket team.'

Even now, as he spoke to the general, Bradley thought it odd that the mention of Gladys Kinder as Wilson's mistress should make him feel slightly resentful and, perhaps, even jealous. It was too ridiculous for words, but he couldn't deny the feeling; and when he recalled her sly smile in the hotel's gloomy bar, her droll mockery of his obvious confusion in her sensual presence, he was irresistibly seduced by her image and wanted to see her again.

Crazy. Just crazy . . .

'*What* was this woman's name?' the general asked, picking up his pen and staring with what Bradley, in the guilty panic of his thoughts, imagined was accusing intensity.

'Kinder,' Bradley replied, feeling a helpless stab of desire and its bed partner, guilt. '*Gladys* Kinder.'

'Kinder,' the general murmured, writing the name down. '*Gladys* Kinder,' he emphasized, as if deliberately tormenting Bradley. 'Mmmm . . .' he murmured, studying the name thoughtfully before putting his pen back down, looking up again, and saying 'So, what about him?'

'Pardon?'

'The physicist that the Kinder woman told you about.'

'Ah, yes . . .' Bradley gathered his thoughts together. 'Miss Kinder told me that when the physicist had left for good after the rocket launching of December 31, 1930, Goddard had confessed to her that his mysterious, temporary assistant was a, quote, *genius*, who had helped him develop many of his more notable innovations, including liquid-fueled, self-cooled motors, gyroscopes for guidance and control, lightweight fuel pumps, and reflector vanes to help stabilize and steer the rockets. The guy's name was John Wilson.'

'Interesting,' General Taylor said, writing that name down also, then popping some gum into his mouth and starting to chew, 'but I can't see what relevance all this has to Adolf Hitler's Germany.'

'Well, I can't be too sure of this,' Bradley replied, 'but I *do* have my worries there.'

'Don't tease me, Mike.'

'Well, for a start this John Wilson's a complete mystery. No one at Roswell knew where he came from, Wilson wasn't about to tell them, and even *Goddard* swore he didn't know anything about him, other than the fact that he was extraordinarily knowledgeable about physics and aeronautics, just turned up at the ranch one day, showed Goddard some of his own drawings, and then asked if he could help him with the rocket project. As for Wilson's journalist friend, Gladys Kinder—'

He couldn't avoid the name, and it brought back all his guilt.

'—even though she was his mistress during that six months, she learned only that he had an engineering background and loathed the US government for reasons that he never explained. She also learned, just before Wilson's abrupt departure, that he intended leaving the United States for good and going to a country where people like him and Goddard would be appreciated, instead of being treated as cranks.'

There was more loud hammering from outside and General Taylor, after wincing, said, 'I can't stand this goddamned noise, Mike. Do you fancy a walk?'

'Sure,' Bradley said, feeling trapped with his recollections of Gladys and glad to escape. 'Why not?'

They left the office and walked outside, where the noise of the workers was even louder and the sun shone over the flat green fields. Relieved to feel the fresh air, Bradley followed the general away from the skeletal buildings and their many workers, down toward the banks of the Potomac River.

'So where do you think your mysterious genius, this Mr Wilson, went?' General Taylor asked, striding across the grass and glancing keenly around him.

'A lot of the German engineers,' Bradley said, 'including Wernher von Braun, revere Goddard and are known to have based their work on his ideas. Our mysterious John Wilson would certainly have known that – and would also have known that while here, in the United States, Goddard's theories were being treated with contempt, Germany was spending fortunes on rocket research that was, by and large, based on his work.'

'So you think this Wilson went to Germany.'

'I don't think it – I know it. I checked yesterday with the Immigration Department and learned that one John Wilson left this country on January 20, 1931, that he stayed in London for a few weeks in early March of that year, and that he applied for a German visa that same month. According to British immigration records, a US citizen called John Wilson left

England by a boat sailing for Bremen, Germany, on April 5, 1931. There's no other record of his movements.'

'You mean, you think he's still there, in Germany.'

'Yes.'

'Have you checked with the German authorities?'

'They deny all knowledge of him.'

'But you think they're lying.'

'Yes. I think he's still there – and if he is, and if he's working on rocket research, we should be concerned.'

They stopped by the edge of the river and looked across to the other side. The fields that stretched out on all sides were flat, densely forested, and sun-splattered. There were birds flying overhead.

'You're my best man for intelligence gathering,' General Taylor reminded him, 'so perhaps you can track him down.'

'I'm not so sure,' Bradley said, feeling the itch of frustration. 'We're talking about Hitler's Third Reich. One man on his own can't do much with this kind of problem. That's why we need a central intelligence-gathering organization,' he continued, warming to his favorite theme. 'The goddamned Brits have an intelligence system that puts us to shame. The last thing we had that remotely resembled an intelligence agency was Herbert Yardley's Black Chamber – which was only a codebreaking unit – and since *that* was closed down in 1929, we haven't had a damned thing to replace it. Which is doubtless why Yardley wrote his best-selling book exposing our so-called secrets – and why New York federal marshals, the goddamned idiots, have just raided the offices of a perfectly respectable publisher to impound Yardley's second book.'

The general laughed heartily at that one, then said, 'The way you pronounce the word "idiots", Mike, reminds me that you're an Irish-American.'

'Ha ha,' Bradley responded, but warmly, without malice. He was proud of his background and not ashamed of what he had become, which is not what he should have been. Although his uneducated grandparents had emigrated from Ireland and he had been raised as a Roman Catholic, Bradley had gone against convention by becoming a staunch member of the Republican party, instead of a Democrat, which most of the Irish were. He had also, after winning numerous awards for distinguished service in the battlefields of France in the Great War become a very successful lawyer, with his own law firm on Wall Street. So, yes, he was proud of his background and achievements – and knew that General Taylor, his close friend, had great respect for him.

'Anyway,' the general said, wincing when the hammering on the distant buildings started again, 'you were starting to talk a blue streak, so don't let me stop you.'

'This guy, Wilson,' Bradley continued, 'who is *possibly* an aeronautical genius, has gone off to sell his talents to a country whose whole interest in science is geared to its aggressive potential – in other words, Hitler's Third Reich.'

'So?' Taylor asked.

'So, since the Third Reich *is* devoted to war, we should be keeping tabs on Wilson – but we can't do it because we don't have the necessary intelligence-gathering organization.'

'But we *do* have that.'

'No,' Bradley insisted, 'we don't. What we have is an uncoordinated collection of different intelligence agencies – Army Intelligence, or G2; the Office of Naval Intelligence; the FBI; the Secret Service; the State Department; the Customs and Immigration services; the Federal Communications System Service; and the Treasury's Foreign Funds Control Unit – not one of which deals with the others, let alone recognizing them.'

'So?'

'So what we need is a centralized, coordinated intelligence, like the British Secret Intelligence Service.'

'A sort of Central Intelligence Agency,' Taylor said.

'Right, General. You got it!'

'Ah!' the general exclaimed softly. 'So *that's* why you came all the way from New York to see me, instead of using the phone. You want to ride your favorite hobbyhorse again and persuade me to include you in the formation of a proper, coordinated intelligence-gathering agency. Have I got it right, Mike?'

'Yeah, General, you have. I'm a highly successful, thirty-eight-year-old lawyer with a plush office in Manhattan, but the best time I ever had in my life was during the war.'

'So I gathered,' the general said. 'The Distinguished Service Cross, the Distinguished Service Medal, and the Medal of Honor . . .'

'Right,' Bradley interjected. 'Which proves that I'm a survivor – and that I'm willing to hang in when the chips are down.'

'No argument there,' the general murmured. 'Come on, let's head back.'

They started walking away from the river, back to where the men with the saws and hammers and nails were swarming like flies over the frames of buildings that would soon house a branch of army air force intelligence and the new National Advisory Committee on Aeronautics.

When Bradley thought of aeronautics, he thought of John Wilson; and when he thought of that mysterious genius, he also thought, with guilty, helpless longing, of Wilson's mistress – the middle-age, laconic, and undeniably attractive Gladys Kinder.

He just couldn't help himself.

'Anyway,' he said, 'my kids are growing up, they're both now away at college, and although I still have Joan, I'm bored with my legal work. I'm also, as you know, deeply convinced that America will, sooner or later, have to become involved with the outside world. I accepted your offer of unofficial intelligence gathering in Europe because I hoped that it would lead to stronger ties with the intelligence services already existing over there. And having been there, I'm more convinced than ever that we need a central intelligence-gathering agency – and I happen to know that you believe that also and have even discussed it.'

'You know more than you should,' General Taylor said,

'which is, of course, why we *should* take you on on a more permanent basis.'

They skirted around the building site and stopped by Bradley's car, which was parked just outside General Taylor's office, gleaming in sunlight.

'*Are* you in the process of forming such an agency?' Bradley asked as he slipped into his car.

'Very early stages,' the general replied, 'but the short answer is yes.'

'And can I be part of it?'

'Yes – when the time comes. In the meantime, you better get on the trail of this John Wilson. If we can't yet find out what he's doing in Germany, you might at least find out where he came from and just who he is.'

'I will,' Bradley said.

He watched the general walk back into his office, then drove away, feeling a lot better, disturbed only when he thought of Gladys Kinder and her relationship with Wilson.

'Goddammit!' he whispered.

CHAPTER FOUR

The two men came for Wilson at the Zeppelin Works at Friedrichshafen at eight in the morning and escorted him out of the factory without a word. Both men were wearing the black uniforms of the SS, and not those of the Gestapo, which Wilson took for a good sign. He felt no fear and asked no questions when, outside the factory, they ordered him up into the back of a canvas-topped truck that already contained a collection of men and women, none of whom looked too happy and some of whom were actually in handcuffs. Wilson sat between a Frenchman who tugged nervously at his peaked cap and a Jewish woman whose dark eyes glowed with dread, then the truck growled into life and began its journey to Berlin.

Two armed soldiers sat at the end of the truck, to ensure that no one tried to escape.

Wilson, who did not wish to escape, merely smiled at the sight of them.

The journey began in the gray mist of morning and ended in the evening, with the streetlights illuminating the monolithic architecture of Berlin. In that long eight hours they had been driven a great distance, from Friedrichshafen on the north shore of Lake Constance to steely-gray Munich, from there to Nuremberg, still somber in the noonday sun, then across the majestic, forested hills of Thuringia, with the shadows of the trees lengthening in the deepening light of afternoon, then through Dessau as darkness was falling and eventually into Berlin.

Wilson had taken it all in from the back of the truck, every glimpse he could get through the canvas flapping near the two soldiers, and had noticed, especially, the many troop trucks on the roads, the armed soldiers in even the smallest towns. He was reminded, beyond any shadow of doubt, that this country was set for war.

It was just what he needed.

Throughout the journey, the two guards had said little to the prisoners, other than ushering them in and out of the truck two or three times to enable them to eat or go to the toilet. They had done this in a distant but reasonably civilized manner, but now, as they kept their charges covered while escorting them from the truck into a large, official-looking building, they both became noticeably more tense and officious, barking their orders and even hitting some of the prisoners with the butts of their rifles when they failed to move quickly enough.

Once inside the building, which was gloomily lit and drearily institutional, the predominance of immaculate black uniforms, gleaming boots, and blond hair made it obvious that this was SS headquarters.

One of the female prisoners started weeping and a man crossed himself, but Wilson, as he had done that morning, took it as a good sign that he was in the hands of the SS, which he had wanted, and not the Gestapo.

The prisoners in handcuffs were led away. Wilson and the others were told to sit on the wooden benches lining the walls of a gloomy corridor. A golden-haired SS sergeant took their identity papers, disappeared through a door, and returned shortly after to lead Wilson away from where he had been sitting, between the dark-eyed Jewish woman and the unshaven Frenchman who had constantly murmured to God for deliverance. Glad to be rid of them, Wilson was even more pleased when he was escorted into an office and made to stop before the desk of a man he recognized from his many photographs in the newspapers – the head of the SS, Heinrich Himmler.

He did not raise his head when Wilson was escorted in, but

continued to study the papers on his desk. Wilson recognized his own handwriting and the technical sketches he had included with his lengthy letter, and smiled, feeling pleased with himself, until Himmler looked up at him.

Wilson immediately removed the smile from his face and looked deeply respectful.

Himmler sighed, as if weary. He had bland, decent features, a neatly trimmed mustache, and gray-blue eyes whose mildness was emphasized by his glistening pince-nez spectacles. He was a man without vanity or cruelty or lust – but Wilson knew, the minute he saw those eyes, that he was also quite mad.

It was what Wilson needed.

'So,' Himmler said, 'you are Wilson – John Wilson – an American citizen.'

'Yes, Herr Himmler,' Wilson replied in perfect German.

'Reichsführer,' Himmler corrected him mildly.

'Sorry, Reichsführer.'

'And you've been living in Germany, under an assumed name and with forged German identification papers, for the past three years. This is correct?'

'Yes, Reichsführer.'

'And as this fictitious German citizen, you've been doing important research work on advanced gyroscopic controls with the subsonic windtunnel at the Zeppelin Works in Friedrichshafen.'

'Yes, sir.'

Himmler offered a slight, chilling smile. 'You realize, Herr Wilson, that these are criminal offenses – that you could even be labeled as a spy and executed accordingly.'

'My purpose isn't spying, Reichsführer, as the notes and drawings I sent you clearly prove.'

'Ah, yes . . . the notes and drawings.' Himmler adjusted the spectacles on his nose and glanced down at Wilson's papers. When he raised his eyes again, he was still smiling in that slight, chilling manner. 'What these notes prove, Mr Wilson, according to my aeronautical advisers, is that you are an extraordinarily brilliant physicist and engineer. What they fail to prove is that you are not here on behalf of your government – in other words, as a spy.'

'I have no reason to love the American government – and my only interest in life is my work. That's why I'm here.'

Himmler stared steadily at him, with a cold curiosity, then smiled bleakly and indicated the chair in front of his desk. 'Please,' he said. 'Take a seat. Can I fetch you some tea?'

'No, thanks,' Wilson said as he sat down and studied the powerful, soft-faced lunatic across the desk. 'I drink as little as possible.'

'And hardly eat, so I've been told. Does that explain your remarkably youthful appearance?'

'It helps,' Wilson said, not forgetting for a moment that Himmler, former fertilizer salesman and chicken farmer, was quietly obsessed with all kinds of esoteric theories, including astrology and runes, the secret of the pyramids, the spirit of the eternal *Wandervogel,* Hörbiger's world of ice and fire, and, of course, the magical properties of certain diets. 'I eat and drink only the bare minimum,' he clarified, 'though I find that the odd glass of white wine can be beneficial.'

'You speak flawless German,' Himmler said. 'When and where did you learn it?'

'I learned it here, in Germany, Reichsführer.'

Himmler raised his eyebrows to display his scepticism. *'Here,* Mr Wilson? In the Fatherland? In a mere three years? I would think that even an adolescent, let alone a man your age, would have trouble in being so fluent in our difficult tongue after such a short period.'

'I have a retentive memory,' Wilson explained, 'and I learned it in three years. We didn't even learn French in Iowa, let alone German. I've learned it since coming here.'

He was impatient with the question, since languages came easily to him. He had never experienced difficulty in learning *anything,* so could not abide ignorance. And languages, compared to mathematics or science, were merely child's play.

'Ah, yes,' Himmler said, forgetting the vexing question of

language. 'Iowa! The heartland of America. Which is where you came from.'

'Yes,' Wilson confirmed, remembering the rolling plains, the cold winters and long hot summers, his parents working in fields of corn between sunrise and sunset while he, who could never stand the place, searched the distant horizon.

He looked back with no emotion, simply recalling it from his mind, and retained no more feeling for that landscape than he did for his parents. He remembered them treating him kindly, but that didn't mean much to him.

The past was a dead place.

Himmler nodded judiciously, glanced down at Wilson's papers, picked some up and let them fall to the desk again, then spread the fingers of his delicate, almost feminine hands over them. 'Naturally we've checked the details you gave us about your background and found them to be exactly as you stated. You're a remarkable man, Mr Wilson, perhaps even extraordinary – which would only make you all the more dangerous, should you not be what you say you are.'

'I'm a scientist, Reichsführer. I want to get on with my work. I can't do what I want to do in America, so I came here, to Germany, where I know that my particular kind of talent is much in demand. It's as simple as that.'

'*Nothing* is as simple as that, Mr Wilson, as you and I both know. You're an American citizen, and no matter your grievances, you must still love the country you came from.'

'I do not, Reichsführer. To me, it's just another country and one that can't help me.'

Himmler actually looked shocked, as if blasphemy had been spoken. 'Patriotism!' he exclaimed. 'You have no sense of that?'

'No.'

'I find that hard to believe.'

'Believe it.'

'If you were a German citizen, I'd have you shot for that attitude.'

'I'm not German, Reichsführer.'

Himmler picked up a pencil, drummed it on the desk,

tapped it lightly against his teeth, then put it down again. He sighed, almost sadly. 'Even though our country is not at war with yours, what you've done, in coming here to work for us, is virtually treason. Are you a traitor? Is that what you want to be?'

Wilson had to admire him for saying that. The chicken farmer was no fool. He looked like a schoolteacher, perhaps even a monk, but mixed in with his lunatic ideas was a steely intelligence. Not a *vast* intelligence, but a sharp one, which meant that he had to be handled carefully and never taken for granted.

'A traitor?' Wilson said. 'I don't think in such terms. I was exploited by my government, then betrayed and cast aside, and now I wish to lend my talents to those who will use them.'

'*Lend* your talents?'

The question actually amused Wilson. 'How wise you are, Reichsführer, to understand that a man of my ambition would not willingly do anything for free. Naturally, I came here for the most selfish reasons – because I live for my work and only someone like you would have the vision and courage to finance it. I'll work for you as long as you finance my research – which is why I wrote to you.'

'And you do not care to what ends your research is finally put?'

'A true scientist can't be concerned with such matters. My only concern is the pursuit of ultimate knowledge – and I know you agree with that. I'm just as much a soldier as you are – but what I fight for is science.'

'Are you as *ruthless* as a soldier, Herr Wilson?'

'Yes, Reichsführer, I am.'

Himmler smiled, obviously pleased with this response, though his smile held no warmth.

'Why me?' he asked softly. 'Of all the people in the Third Reich, why did you write to me, rather than to some influential scientist or politician? You must have known you were taking a great chance – exposing yourself as an alien who used false identification papers in order to obtain a position in one of our most important research establishments – and that I could

46

have decided to have you shot as a spy. So why me, Herr Wilson?'

'Because you're a man of vision,' Wilson said, combining a lie with a certain amount of truth. He felt that Himmler was, indeed, a man of great dreams, if not vision, who would support any kind of research, no matter how esoteric or even mad. For that, if for very little else, he would certainly be useful. 'Because you believe in the limitless possibilities of the future, will back your beliefs with actions, and will not let petty human emotions stand in your way. You and I, Herr Himmler, if I may say so, are similar that way.'

'What you say may be true,' Himmler replied, unmoved by flattery, 'but it still doesn't explain why I should give you, a foreigner, my support, particularly since you wish to take part in our most vital, and therefore confidential, research.'

'You should give me your support, Reichsführer, because my papers have shown you what I can do – and what I can do is much more than anyone you have could do.'

'Some of my scientists would take offense at that remark.'

'That wouldn't change its accuracy. My work is proof of my genius. More important, I'm engaged in a project similar to one you've already started: the creation of a revolutionary form of transport and extraordinary weapon.'

'You mean Projekt Saucer.'

'Yes, Reichsführer.'

'And how did you know about that, Herr Wilson, since the project is under SS supervision?'

'There are always whispers, Reichsführer, particularly among scientists, and naturally I picked them up in Friedrichshafen. I was also puzzled to see certain, odd machine parts in the Zeppelin Works – but when combined with some of the experiments taking place in the wind tunnel, I realized they could only relate to the development of an aircraft shaped like a saucer – the kind of machine being researched with Projekt Saucer at Kummersdorf West.'

'What kind of experiments were you doing in the Zeppelin wind tunnel?'

'Tests relating to Prandtl's boundary layer.'

'The importance of which is?'

'If we can't solve the problem of the boundary layer, the speed and maneuverability of our aircraft will always be limited.'

'Please explain.'

'The perfect flying machine will be one that requires no runway, since it will take off vertically, will be able to hover in midair, and will not be limited in flight by Prandtl's boundary layer.'

'I am not an engineer,' Himmler reminded him impatiently.

'According to Prandtl's theory of the boundary layer, the air sweeping in on an object in flight increases its resistance in direct proportion to the increasing speed of the flying object. Because of this, the speed of any flying object is finite. However, if some method can be found of removing the boundary layer, virtually limitless speed and maneuverability will be achieved.'

'And a disc shape is the best shape for this?'

'Potentially, yes. The buildup of the boundary layer is dramatically increased by the many surface protuberances of a normal aircraft – wings, tails, rudders, rotors, and so forth. If we could get rid of those – by somehow wrapping them together as part and parcel of the one, circular, smooth-surfaced flying wing – we would at least be on the road to the perfect flying machine.'

'And you think that we can accomplish this here in Germany?'

'I think you're the country with most interest in such developments and certainly the most advanced so far. Regarding vertical-rising aircraft, the Focke-Wulf Company has already announced that it has almost completed its FW 61 helicopter, which will be the first fully operational helicopter in existence. Regarding experimental tailless aircraft, or flying wings, devoid of vertical stabilizing or control surfaces, the Horten brothers of Bonn have already produced some successful prototypes. As for other problems standing in the way of limitless speed and maneuverability, it was a German, Professor Ludwig Prandtl, who, at Göttingen in 1904, defined the nature of the boundary layer. Since then, many other German scientists have been experimenting with revolutionary new types of aircraft in the hope of finding a way of defeating that layer. A disc or saucer-shaped aircraft, without any surface protuberances, is the logical outcome of that research.'

Himmler's smile was as chilling as the gaze behind his small pince-nez. 'There are those who would say that such an aircraft cannot be built.'

'The foolish always speak loudest.'

'And you think that you can help with such a project?'

'I can *complete* it, Reichsführer. I have been working toward this goal all my life and have now almost reached it.'

Himmler glanced at Wilson's technical drawings, which had been done in black ink, then raised his eyes again as he spread his slim hands in a questioning manner.

'But *are* you close to reaching it?' he asked. 'My scientists often say the same thing – but so far they have failed.'

'Just look at my drawings, Reichsführer.'

'I am not a scientist, Herr Wilson. Your drawings *look* impressive, but to me they are meaningless – though initial reports have certainly confirmed that your written work is extraordinary. These drawings will have to be studied further by people more knowledgeable than I. In the meantime, I have to consider what it is you want from me.'

'I've told you that, Reichsführer. I wrote to you not only for the reasons we've just discussed, but also because I know that the SS is gradually taking over the security and management of the Third Reich's major scientific and research establishments, that soon it will be the most powerful organization in Germany, and that you, its Reichsführer, are the only man in power with the vision to see what can be done in this particular field. Already you've implemented a disc-shaped aircraft project; only I can take that project to its completion – but I need your support.'

There was silence for a moment and Wilson waited patiently, neither excited nor frightened. He was fully in control as Himmler stared steadily at him. He did not flinch from the mild monster, but neither did he try to challenge him. Instead he let his gaze go slightly out of focus, as if gazing inward.

Which he did in a sense, thinking back upon America, remembering Goddard and how the Americans had mocked him while these clever Germans revered him. Well, Goddard was back in Roswell, struggling along on a mere pittance, while he, Wilson, if Himmler went as he thought he would, would soon have all the money and equipment he could possibly want.

Pleased, he focused again upon Himmler, whose mild gaze concealed madness.

'You do realize, Herr Wilson, that once I gave that support, you would be committed to working for the Third Reich for the rest of your days?'

'Yes, Reichsführer.'

'And that if you betrayed us, or even tried to leave the country, I would personally have you executed?'

'Yes, Reichsführer, I realize that, also.'

'You are therefore willing to commit yourself totally to the Third Reich and all it stands for?'

'Yes, Reichsführer,' Wilson said. He lied easily, as he was beyond morality, thinking only of his own plans for the future and ignoring all else. 'I'm willing to do that.'

Himmler stared steadily at him, his gaze searching, then he nodded, as if coming to a decision, though not without doubts.

'You must really despise your government,' he said, 'for what they did to you.'

'No, I don't,' Wilson said. 'Such emotions are redundant. I'm here not because I want revenge, but because my government won't support me and I think you will. It's as simple as that.'

'You are more than committed to your work,' Himmler observed. 'You are clearly fanatical.'

'I live only for my work – as you do – and that makes us superior men.'

'I think you really believe that, Herr Wilson.'

'I do, Reichsführer. I do.'

Himmler smiled at the subtle flattery but was otherwise unmoved by it. He then glanced down at Wilson's drawings, scratched his nose while studying them, shook his head from side to side in wonder, and looked up again.

'I am going to have you placed in the custody of the Gestapo,' he said, 'in their headquarters in the Prinz Albrechtstrasse. You needn't worry. I do this merely for convenience. I wish to have these drawings examined in more detail – and to have you interrogated at length, regarding your past and present attitudes as well as your work. Naturally, you will be interrogated by one of my intelligence officers – but hopefully one with an engineering background. Should the results of our investigations prove positive, you will, as you request, be given work at the rocket research establishment at Kummersdorf West. On the other hand, if our findings are negative, you will be shot and buried as the German citizen whom these false identification papers say you are. Is that acceptable, Herr Wilson?'

'Yes, Reichsführer – and thank you.'

Himmler nodded at the armed guard in the corner of the room, and Wilson was led out to begin his journey to Gestapo headquarters.

CHAPTER FIVE

Bradley met Robert H. Goddard on the porch of the latter's large frame house on a street shaded by horse chestnut trees in Worcester, Massachusetts, in the winter of 1933. The snow had not yet come, but the air was gray and cold, and the leaves were blowing around Bradley's feet when Goddard shook his hand and ushered him inside.

It was a pleasant, old-fashioned house, with its original furniture covered in relatively new slipcovers, its windows draped with chintz, and a wood fire burning in the large, open fireplace. Bradley knew that Goddard had lived here all his life, and it certainly suited him, being an unpretentious, comfortable place.

'Please take a seat,' Goddard said, his voice as formal as his appearance when he indicated the sofa by the fire. 'I'm sorry I can't offer you much – my wife's not home at the moment – but I can at least make a cup of coffee.'

'That'd be fine,' Bradley said. 'I'll have it black, with no sugar.'

Goddard nodded solemnly and disappeared into the kitchen; he returned a couple of minutes later, carrying two cups of coffee. Bradley noticed his stooped walk, which, like his bald head, had been caused by tuberculosis in his youth. Goddard handed Bradley the black coffee, sipped at his own, then took the armchair facing the settee. His eyes were brown over a small mustache, his gaze slightly suspicious, and Bradley remembered that he wasn't keen on representatives of a government that had ignored his remarkable talents for too long.

'So,' Goddard said, 'you insisted on seeing me, even after I put you off on the phone when you called me at Clark. Have you come to make me an offer?'

Bradley grinned. 'No,' he said. 'I'm in neither science nor finance. I *have* heard that you've had trouble getting financed, but that's not what I'm here for.'

'If you're not part of the government's scientific community, why come to see me? The US government has never shown much interest in my work, so I'm naturally surprised that one of their representatives should turn up on my doorstep – more so since he hasn't come to offer me help.'

'The National Advisory Committee for Aeronautics was recently formed to advise the government on every aspect of aeronautical development, political and scientific, both here and abroad. For that reason it was composed of those most respected in the aeronautical community. You were invited to join – and you rejected the offer.'

'With all due respect to Orville Wright and my good friend Charles Lindbergh, I don't consider such an offer to be of help. In making me such an offer, you were seeking *my* help – and what I need is government backing for my expensive research. That has never been offered.'

'I'm sorry.'

'I'm sure you are.'

Realizing that this was not going to be easy, Bradley decided to skip the formalities. 'In fact, perhaps to make matters worse, I'm asking for help again.'

'Obviously not scientific help.'

'No. I'm an intelligence officer for the US Army Air Force and I need information.'

'Information about my work?' Goddard asked suspiciously.

'No,' Bradley replied. 'I need to know about someone who worked with you – a man named John Wilson.'

Goddard straightened up, looking surprised, then collected himself by sipping some more coffee. When he lowered the cup and saucer to his lap, his eyes were masked.

'Ah, yes,' he said, 'Wilson. An odd bird. So why do you want to know about him?'

'Because I have to find him,' Bradley told him, 'and he hasn't left many tracks. Do you mind if I smoke?'

Goddard shook his head to say he didn't mind and Bradley, who smoked only when he didn't know what to do with his hands, lit a cigarette.

'Why do you have to find him? Has he committed an offense?'

'No,' Bradley said, exhaling a stream of smoke. 'And that's all I can say for now. But please accept that this man must be found – and you're our first lead.'

Goddard shrugged. 'I can't help you much, Mr Bradley. I doubt that I know any more about him than you do – I only *worked* with him.'

'*With* him? I thought he worked *for* you.'

'You mean as my assistant?'

'Yes.'

Goddard smiled for the first time – a slight, laconic smile. 'Well, he certainly was that – or was *supposed* to be that – but a man like Wilson doesn't work *for* anybody. He was too bright for that. '

'How bright?'

'Brilliant. He was clearly a genius.'

As Goddard wasn't known for his generosity to fellow scientists, Bradley was surprised by this description.

'*You're* supposed to be a genius,' he said. 'Are you saying that—'

'The word genius is used far too casually for my liking,' Goddard interjected, 'and so isn't one I'd normally use lightly. Yet I'd apply it without doubt to Wilson. The man was a genius.'

'How much did you learn about him?'

'Not much, Mr Bradley. He was guarded about his past, almost paranoid about remaining anonymous, and seemed to have few interests, other than space flight. Like me, he thought it possible to fly to the moon – and that's why he came to me.'

'When was that?'

'In 1930.'

Bradley saw a glass ashtray on a low table near the bookcase, so leaned sideways, picked it up, balanced it on one leg, and nicked some ash into it. 'And how did he come to work with you? Did he initially write to you?'

'No. He simply turned up out of the blue, told me he was an aeronautical engineer who had designed airships—'

'*Airships?*'

'Correct.'

'Did he say he did that work in Europe or America?'

'He certainly didn't mention Europe. In fact, I got the impression that he had never been there in his life.'

'Yet that's where most of the airships have been constructed and flown.'

'That's where the *first* airships were constructed and flown,' Goddard corrected him. 'The first was built by Henri Giffard of France in 1852; powered by a 350-pound engine, it was successfully flown over the Paris Hippodrome at a speed of six miles an hour. An internal combustion engine fueled by hydrogen from the airship's bag was then used by the German, Paul Haenlein, for his even more successful flight in 1872. Albert and Gaston Tissandier of France successfully powered an airship with an electric motor in 1883, and the first rigid airship, with an aluminum-sheeting hull, was built in Germany in 1897. And I don't have to tell you that the Germans used a number of large Zeppelin airships to bomb Paris and London throughout the Great War.'

'All European airships,' Bradley reminded him.

'Yes, of course – they were the best known. But a few airships *were* constructed here in the 1920s, and more are being constructed right this minute – so there appears to be nothing remarkable in Wilson's assertion that he worked on airship designs.'

'Which must have been just before he came to work for you.'

'Probably,' Goddard said.

'What else did he tell you?' Bradley asked.

'He was obsessed with the possibilities of space flight – and therefore with my rocket research. He said he had been inspired by the fact that I had managed to launch liquid-fueled, instrument-carrying rockets, and informed me that he wanted to work with me and learn from me.'

'I'm surprised you let him.'

Goddard didn't smile at all. 'As he was older than I,' he said, 'I was certainly initially uncomfortable with his suggestion, suspecting him to be someone simply desperate for work. However, he showed me his papers, which proved beyond doubt that he had attended MIT between 1888 and 1893 – before my time there – then Sibley College at Cornell University, in Ithaca, New York, where by 1895 he'd obtained his Bachelor of Science in aeronautics. He also proved, both verbally and with various papers he'd written and let me read, that he had an extraordinary – and I don't use the word lightly – an extraordinary grasp of aeronautics and physics. Naturally, Mr Bradley, after that, I couldn't turn him away.'

'He started working for you immediately?'

'Yes.'

'This was at your Guggenheim-financed experimental station in Roswell, New Mexico?'

'Yes.'

'For how long?'

'Approximately six months.'

'That doesn't seem too long.'

'No, but it was all he needed. During that period he helped me enormously – but he also learned everything I'd discovered so far about steering systems, gyroscopic controls, and various kinds of self-cooling combustion chambers. Those were the things he wanted to know about – and when he'd found what he needed, he left, with not even a good-bye note.'

'Not exactly showing gratitude,' Bradley said.

Goddard smiled for the second time. 'Wilson wasn't a man for gratitude – and I learned as much from him as he did from me, so I can't really complain.'

Whether or not Goddard felt the need to complain, Bradley certainly thought that Wilson's abrupt departure could only be the act of an extraordinarily cold, thoughtless, self-centered man. When he also thought of how casually Wilson had dismissed and left his former mistress, the intriguing Gladys Kinder, he was even more convinced that the man he was trying to picture clearly was not the warmest, most sensitive soul on earth. Certainly he was a man who used people and casually cast them off – a man who didn't need love or friends.

A man completely alone.

'So what did you think about him as a person?' Bradley asked Goddard, desperately hoping to fit a human face to his shadowy quarry.

'I don't know what you mean,' Goddard said with scientific detachment.

Bradley blew a smoke ring and watched it grow larger and thinner before disappearing. Then, realizing what he was doing, he felt a little embarrassed. 'Did you become friends in any sense?' he asked.

Goddard shrugged, at least displaying his confusion, which made him more likable. 'I got on well with him,' he said, 'but in an academic way. We both lived for our work, we'd both had bad times with the government, and we agreed that the mind should rule the heart – not vice versa, as is commonly believed. Oddly enough, then, though there was little warmth between us, we had much in common.'

Bradley hardly heard the last remark, for his lawyer's instincts, always turned to the unusual, had honed in on something else.

'Did you say he'd had trouble with our government?' he asked, leaning forward, forgetting the ashtray, but managing to grab it before it fell off his leg.

'Yes,' Goddard said. 'Just like me.'

'You mean the trouble was related to his work?' Bradley asked as he rearranged the position of the ashtray.

'Yes,' Goddard confirmed. 'He didn't tell me much about himself, but he *did* say that he'd come from Iowa, worked on some airship projects, and come to me when those projects were first taken over by, then dropped by, the US government.

Is that why you're interested, Mr Bradley? Were *you* involved in his problems?'

Feeling distinctly uneasy, Bradley was nevertheless able to answer honestly. 'No. I know nothing about them. It's interesting, though, that he should have said that. What do *you* think?'

'I don't think I have to tell you, Mr Bradley, that for years I've felt neglected by the US government – and if Wilson *was* working on airships, or similar projects, and was then either dropped or blocked by the government, he would feel as bitter as I do – which is very bitter indeed.'

Bradley almost *felt* Goddard's bitterness. He was deeply embarrassed by it, but disguised it by drinking more coffee and then clearing his throat.

'Did he say or do anything to substantiate such bitterness?'

'Yes,' Goddard said without hesitation. 'Just before our rocket test flight of December 31, 1930, which Wilson *should* have attended, he told me that our government didn't appreciate its brightest minds, that it would eventually make things difficult for me, and that I should consider leaving the country for good and taking my talents where they'd be more appreciated.'

'And where did he suggest, Mr Goddard?'

'Germany,' Goddard said innocently. 'He reminded me that the German rocket scientists revered my work and that because of that I'd certainly get the financing there that I couldn't get here. Two days later, while we were testing our latest rocket, he packed up and disappeared.'

'Was your rocket test a success?' Bradley asked, thinking it wise to lighten the conversation.

'It was pleasing,' Goddard replied. 'The gyroscopic controls didn't work properly and the descent parachute didn't open, but the rocket reached a speed of 350 miles per hour and a height of nearly two miles.'

'That's impressive.'

'Yes, it's impressive – but not to your superiors.'

Feeling that he'd just been slapped on the face, and also

oddly haunted by the ghostly man he was pursuing, Bradley finished his coffee, stubbed his cigarette out, placed the ashtray on the table, and prepared to leave.

'Is there anything else you can give me that might help me?' he asked.

'No,' Goddard replied, standing up to show him to the door. 'What I've told you is all I *can* tell you. Apart from that, he's a mystery.'

Bradley sighed. 'Thanks anyway,' he said. 'I'd like to apologize for how the government's treated you, but—'

'It's not your place to do so.'

'Yeah,' Bradley said, grateful for the unexpected sensitivity. 'Right. It's not my place. Thanks again, anyway, Dr Goddard – and the best of luck for the future.'

Goddard just smiled and nodded, led him to the door, remained on the porch till he drove away, then disappeared back into his attractive, old-fashioned house.

Bradley drove straight to MIT, flirted with the middle-age lady who worked in the records department, and soon learned that John Wilson had indeed attended the university before going on to Cornell in Ithaca. He was also able to ascertain from Wilson's old registration card that at the time of his enrollment, he had been living in Massachusetts with only his father, that before that he had lived with both his parents in Montezuma, Iowa, and that he had been born there on July 6, 1870.

Growing ever more intrigued by the fragmented trail of his brilliant, mysterious quarry, Bradley took the next train out of Massachusetts.

'Airships,' he muttered to himself as he sat in his reserved seat in a first-class car and lit a cigar. 'What next? I wonder.'

The train moved into darkness.

CHAPTER SIX

Ernst awakened at dawn, after a night of bad dreams, thinking he was in a cell in Stadelheim Prison, his heart pounding with fear. Then he saw his own bedroom, felt Ingrid beside him, and so heaved a sigh of relief and reached out to touch her.

She was naked beneath the sheets, her skin smooth and warm, and aroused, he rolled in against her, hoping to waken her.

She did not awaken immediately, which disappointed him again, and still caught in the web of his frightening dreams, he gazed through the windows. The curtains had not been drawn and he saw the dawn's dark-gray light, gradually illuminating the houses opposite, in the modest-priced Berlin suburb of Helensee. They had moved here a year ago, two weeks after they were married and had honeymooned in Paris – which, compared to Berlin, had been like heaven on earth. It seemed longer than a year ago (so much had happened in the turbulent period) and Ernst, now the father of a daughter, Ula, wondered where all the joy had gone.

Germany had changed dramatically in the fifteen months and he had changed with it.

Not wishing to think about it, feeling the need for escape, he pressed himself against Ingrid's spine and ran his hands over her. He heard her breathing change, felt her stiffen and then relax, so he whispered her name into her ear and she sighed and turned into him. She gazed at him with sleepy, catlike green eyes, then kissed him sensually.

It was the dawn's sole reward, and he made love with

feeling, aware that it was not like it had been, but grateful to have her. Ingrid's body was still sublime, a soft retreat from harsh reality, and he slid along her belly, sucked and licked her breasts and neck, and moved inside her with the desperate need to obliterate what had recently been haunting him – the knowledge that he was losing her love as his pride was destroyed.

When he had finished and was hoping to rest on top of her, she slid out from under him.

'I'll get breakfast,' she said.

'Please, Ingrid, stay in bed a little longer.'

'No,' she said. 'You'll be late.'

Reminded by that remark of what the day might yet bring, Ernst felt a cold chill of dread slipping through him. He had forgotten that he had been ordered to report back to barracks unusually early in preparation for possible action against the SA, or Brownshirts, who were reported to be planning an armed rebellion under the leadership of Captain Ernst Roehm.

Another police duty, Ernst thought bitterly as Ingrid, in a dressing gown, padded from the room and he slid his legs out of the bed and went into the bathroom.

As he attended to his ablutions, he pondered the fact that even he was becoming confused by the sheer number of conflicting groups within the Third Reich's increasingly nightmarish police structure. Top of the list were the Gestapo, or Secret State Police. Originally under the command of the debauched Hermann Göring, recently it had been taken under the wing of Himmler, who was also head of the SS. The SS had been formed as Hitler's personal Guard Detachment but was fast becoming the most feared police force of all. Next came the SD, which acted as the long-range Intelligence and Security Service of the SS, under the control of the dreaded Reinhard Heydrich. Last of the major groups was the SA, originally formed as part of the SD and consisting of Ernst Roehm's brown-shirted Storm Troops, who represented the military arm of the Nazi Party and were used mainly to intimidate, beat up, or murder those openly opposed to it. Now that degenerate madman, Roehm, was rumored to be planning a *putsch,* or armed revolt, against the Reichswehr . . . And today's police duty, Ernst suspected, had something to do with that situation.

He resented being involved in such duties – more so because Ingrid had frequently expressed her contempt for the SS, which she viewed as fascistic and brutal. He also resented them because what he had been promised, eighteen months ago, would be aeronautical intelligence gathering for the SS technical branch had in fact turned out to be secret service intelligence gathering against, and the arresting of, all those who opposed Hitler's National Socialist Party.

Ernst had escorted more unfortunate souls into Stadelheim Prison and Gestapo headquarters than he cared to remember – and there were stories about both of those places that he preferred to forget.

Suddenly filled with the dry-throated nervousness that always gripped him when he thought of his SS duties, he had a quick bath, dressed even more urgently in his gleaming black SS uniform, looked fondly in on his nine-month-old daughter, where she was sleeping in her cot in her own brightly painted room, then went into the kitchen to have coffee with Ingrid.

She was sitting at the table, a steaming mug in her hands, her short-cropped blond hair attractively disheveled around her delicate features. Having Ula had not made her lose her figure, which remained slim and sensual; and Ernst, as he took the chair facing her, was grateful for that.

'I'd forgotten I had to be there so early,' he said, sipping his coffee. 'I also forgot to tell you that I may not be coming home tonight. It could be a long duty.'

'What is it this time?' Ingrid asked him, her green gaze steady over her steaming mug.

'I don't know,' he lied, because he had been ordered to do so and did not dare do otherwise. 'They only said that it was some kind of police action that could take a long time.'

In fact, he had been told in confidence the previous day by Gruppenführer Josef Dietrich, commander of Hitler's elite SS bodyguard, the *Leibstandarte – SS Adolf Hitler,* that for months the SA, under the command of the notorious homosexual, Captain Roehm, had been in growing, increasingly open revolt against Hitler in particular and Himmler's SS in general, and now that conflict was coming to a head. According to Dietrich, Göring, SS chief Heinrich Himmler, and the dreaded SD chief Reinhard Heydrich had formed a secret alliance to get rid of Roehm and were going to act soon.

Ernst dreaded the form such an action might take, but tried to look unconcerned.

'Another police action,' Ingrid said, putting his previous thoughts into words and imbuing them with soft sarcasm. 'Before we married I said you'd become a policeman – and that's what you are.'

'I'm *not* a policeman,' he insisted too loudly, aware that he had had to do this too often. 'I'm not a member of the Gestapo, so stop suggesting I am.'

'You do the Gestapo's work,' Ingrid replied, not perturbed by his outrage, 'and that's just as bad.'

'I obey orders,' he said, 'and that's *all* I do. It's not the kind of work I wanted, it's certainly not what I expected, and although I don't always like what I'm told to do, I *must* obey orders.'

'You could *try* refusing.'

'That's nonsense, and you know it. I'm an SS officer, a *German* officer, and you know what that means.'

'It means you work as a policeman.'

'It means that if I don't do what I'm told, I'll be imprisoned myself – or possibly shot. Is that what you want?'

Ingrid placed her cup on the table and gazed down at her coffee, perhaps trying to hide the blush he could see on her cheeks.

'I'm sorry,' she said. 'I know you're not really a policeman. I also know you don't like what you're doing and my attacks make it worse. I hate saying these things, but I can't help myself. I hate the SS – and I can't bear the thought that you, who should have been an engineer, are doing their dirty work. It just makes me sick.'

'It sometimes makes me sick as well,' he said, 'but what else can I do? I am an officer in Heinrich Himmler's SS – and it's too late to get out.'

Ingrid raised her head again. 'Are you sorry you joined?'

He shrugged. 'I'm not sure. Sometimes I feel betrayed – they said I would be in *technical* intelligence – but at other times, and I certainly can't deny it, I want to surrender my own feelings to the general good.'

'And you think that what's happening at present is for the general good?'

Ernst heard his own sigh like a soft wail of defeat. 'We can only hope,' he said. 'At the moment, things certainly look ugly, even shameful, but one hopes that the end will justify the means – and that's all one can hope for.'

Ingrid had just been about to take his hand, but she stopped, glanced at him, sat back, and glanced vaguely around her as if looking for exits.

'Everything's changed so quickly,' she said, shaking her head in bewilderment. 'Nothing's been the same since that night outside the Chancellery. It's only been fifteen months, yet now we live in a city filled with brown-shirted brutes, secret police, intimidation and fear. It's been like a bad dream.'

Ernst knew what she meant and rarely stopped thinking about it. He, too, remembered that wonderful moment in Wilhelmstrasse, when Hitler had appeared at the window of the Chancellery to smile down on his cheering men. It had been a great moment, a transcendental experience, one that had seemed to offer the promise of a magical future. A mere fifteen months ago . . .

And since then?

Ernst could not forget that he had been one of the truckloads of SS men, hastily sworn in as auxiliaries to the SA, who had, in March 1933, just a few days before he'd married Ingrid, swarmed through the city to round up known Reds and Social Democrats and take them into 'protective custody' – a term that, even then, was rumored to mean imprisonment, torture, or execution.

Nor could he forget that he had been one of the many proud SS guards who sang the 'Horst Wessel' song in the Kroll Opera House, temporary site of the new Reichstag, the tumultuous night that Hitler, wearing his brown SA uniform and standing on a stage decorated with a huge swastika flag, made the speech that expunged democracy from the German parliament.

Nor could he forget that while the midnight calls and arrests increased, along with the whispers about torture and murder in SA and SS prison cells, he had been one of the many loyal 'policemen' who had seized union offices throughout the nation, arrested labor leaders, confiscated union files and bank accounts, shut down their newspapers, and in one awful day obliterated organized labor in the whole country.

Now the Führer, Adolf Hitler, was ruling a totalitarian state known as the Third Reich – and he, Ernst Stoll, once a mere technical student, had aided his ruthless climb to power.

Naturally, Ingrid was right: He had a lot to be ashamed of. But though he sometimes acknowledged this to himself, the shame and despair in which he writhed made him loathe her for saying it.

'I have to go now,' he said.

Feeling like someone being sucked into quicksand, and filled with the feeling that today would be a nightmare, he walked around the table, kissed Ingrid's cheek, and started out of the house.

'Don't do anything you'll be ashamed of,' Ingrid joked, trying to lighten the depression he was clearly showing.

'I'll try not to,' he replied with a smile and a wave, before stepping outside and closing the door behind him.

Waiting on the pavement in the morning's brightening light for the jeep that would transport him to Stadelheim Prison, he could not shake off his recollections of the past fifteen months and realized why he was losing Ingrid's love as his pride was destroyed. He *had* become a policeman, the emissary of butchers, and as his resistance was eroded and his pride subtly destroyed, Ingrid's respect for him, the basis of her love, was also being eroded.

The Third Reich was driving a wedge between them, just as Ingrid had said it would.

The jeep that Ernst had been waiting for turned the corner at the bottom of the street, drove toward him, and pulled to the curb. As his fellow officers, Willi Brandt and Franck Ritter, both lieutenants, were taking up the rear seats, Ernst sat up front with the driver – not without noticing that the normally ebullient Brandt was looking gloomy while Franck was clearly excited.

'So,' Ernst said, as the jeep moved out into the almost deserted road and headed for the Prinz Albrechtstrasse, 'another early-morning call for the elite. It is so nice to be wanted.'

'It depends what they want us for,' the gloomy Brandt said, 'since that may *not* be nice.'

'I always like the early-morning calls,' Franck said, sounding excited. 'It usually means action.'

'I like action in the movies,' Brandt replied. 'I don't like to be part of it. Not when it involves arresting people and throwing them into that prison.'

'They deserve what they get,' Franck said. 'If they didn't, we wouldn't arrest them. They are the dregs of society – drunks, illiterates, gypsies, communist traitors, and Jews – and what we do is for the good of the country, which is why I enjoy it.'

'You'd enjoy torturing or shooting them even more,' Brandt said in a remarkably careless outburst, 'but that doesn't make it right.'

'Those are the words of a traitor!' Franck snapped. 'I could report you for that!'

'If it gets me off this duty,' Brandt responded, 'please be my guest.'

Unnerved by the conversation, Ernst told them both to shut up, then glanced at the awakening city through which they were moving. It was a warm Saturday morning and already the news vendors were out, selling the propaganda to be found in the *Illustrierte Beobachter* and *Frankfurter Zeitung* while the Brownshirts took up their positions on the sidewalks, preparing for another day of insults, beard-tugging, and other carefully planned humiliations.

An average weekend in Berlin, 1934.

Ernst felt even worse when the jeep pulled up at the main entrance to the grim Gestapo headquarters in the Prinz Albrechtstrasse. He was startled by the number of SS jeeps and troop trucks lined up along the pavement, and even more startled when, inside the dreary, gloomy building, he found that it was packed with heavily armed SS troops.

'This is no ordinary working day,' Brandt whispered, looking even more upset. 'What the hell's going on, Ernst?'

'Something big!' Ritter exclaimed, his eyes gleaming with excitement. 'I knew it! *I knew!*'

Even as he spoke, the door behind them opened again and more SS troops hurried in.

'They've arrested Roehm!' someone whispered.

'Hitler himself did it!' someone added.

'It's us or the SA,' another voice said. 'And today will decide it.'

Hardly able to believe what he was hearing, Ernst led his two comrades up the stairs and along some packed corridors, until he came to the office of his superior, Gruppenführer Josef Dietrich. As Ernst stopped in the doorway, Dietrich barked orders to a group of SS officers. When the officers left, all looking anxious, Dietrich waved Ernst inside.

'Heil Hitler!' he snapped, then added more reasonably: 'Prepare yourselves, gentlemen. Operation Calibra has begun. You are in for a busy day.'

'I'm sorry, sir,' Ernst replied, 'but I'm not familiar with that code name.'

'No, Lieutenant, of course not. Only the most senior officers were informed. It had come to our attention that Roehm was planning a *putsch* and the ultimate destruction of the authority of the army and SS. However, early this morning, our courageous Führer, in the company of Goebbels, flew to Bad Wiessee and personally arrested that disgusting pervert and the nest of homosexual traitors he calls his stormtroopers, at the Pension Hanselbauer, near the Tegernsee. According to my reports, most of the pig's men were still in bed when the raid took place – many of them caught *in flagrante delicto* with fellow SA troops or local youths. One's stomach churns just to think of it.' Here the gruppenführer shook his head in disgust. 'However,' he continued, 'they were all rounded up and are this very moment being transported back to Berlin to be incarcerated, with Roehm himself, in the Brown House, prior to being quickly tried and judged. Today, gentlemen, we will wield our long knives – so prepare to shed blood.'

Ernst's soul plunged into despair – but he found no escape.

At ten o'clock that warm Saturday morning, he was informed that the cells of Stadelheim Prison were already packed with SA leaders. Those still in the Brown House, including Roehm, had demanded to see the Führer, but were refused and, instead, transported to Stadelheim in an armored car. There Roehm was put in a solitary cell, not far from the one he had occupied after the Beer Hall *putsch.*

Shortly after learning of Roehm's incarceration, Ernst was called to the office of Gruppenführer Dietrich, who told him that the purge was beginning.

'I personally,' Dietrich informed him proudly, 'have been put in charge of the executions of the SA men being held in Stadelheim Prison. Meanwhile, you are to go with Lieutenant Ritter to the home of General von Schleicher and once there, put him to death. You understand?'

'Yes, sir,' Ernst replied, burning hot and cold with shock and disbelief. He was being ordered to kill the former chancellor of Germany. 'I just think—'

'Don't think, Lieutenant, just obey. And when you've done that, drive straight to Stadelheim to receive further orders. Now good luck and – Heil Hitler!'

Unable to believe his ears, but forced to accept that this was real, Ernst soon found himself seated beside the hated Franck Ritter in one of the many police cars that were careening through the streets of Berlin in the great roundup of enemies of the regime. As if in a dream that was becoming a nightmare, he saw one unit, the men all wearing steel helmets and armed with rifles and submachine guns, surrounding von Papen's office. There was the sound of gunshots, sudden and frightening as they passed. Ernst felt sick to his stomach, too hot, completely unreal; and closed and opened his eyes when they passed a similar unit as it surrounded Roehm's opulent residence on the Tiergartenstrasse.

Sirens wailed in the distance.

Too soon for Ernst's liking, he and Lieutenant Ritter were being ushered by an unsuspecting cook into the study of a comfortable house in a suburb of Berlin. While Ernst licked his dry lips and fought to stop himself from shaking, Ritter asked the distinguished-looking gentleman sitting at the desk if he was indeed General von Schleicher.

'Yes, of course,' the former chancellor replied, looking up in surprise, even as Ritter pulled his pistol from his holster, cocked the safety catch, and opened fire.

The noise was appalling in that confined space.

Fumbling in a state of nerves, having not killed before, Ernst fired in a daze even as Schleicher was falling – and, worse, just as Frau von Schleicher appeared out of nowhere, rushed toward her stricken husband, and was cut down by the bullets that Ernst and Ritter were still firing.

Two bodies lay on the floor in dark pools of spreading blood.

While Ernst stood there, too shocked to move, Ritter hurried over to the bloody bodies on the floor, examined them dispassionately, then looked up and said, 'This bastard's dead, but his wife's still alive. An ambulance is coming for them, dead or alive, so let's go. There's more work to do.'

Which was certainly true.

In the courtyard of Stadelheim Prison the slaughter was well under way, but Ernst, when he reported to Gruppenführer

Dietrich, was told to make his way back to the Gestapo headquarters in the Prinz Albrechtstrasse where there was plenty of worthy work still to do.

After driving there in traffic jammed up by the police roadblocks and SS trucks being used to raid other SA groups, he was ordered down to the cells. It was a hell of smoke and ricocheting gunfire, of aggressive bawling and piteous screaming, and Ernst didn't know what to do, didn't want to do anything, turned away to rush out again, but was pushed back by an officer.

'That bastard in there!' the officer bawled. 'That rat in his hole!'

Pushed forward by the officer, Ernst found himself beside the weeping Willi Brandt in a crowd of jostling SS troops, firing his pistol, as the others fired, into Cell 16. There Gregor Strasser, winner of the Iron Cross, first class, devoted National Socialist and once the Führer's friend, dodged back and forth, his eyes astonishingly bright, trying to avoid the hail of bullets. Finally, jerking spasmodically, he collapsed in his own blood and was given the coup de grace.

The cells stank of cordite and piss and the rank sweat of terror.

There were no names after that – only bodies spurting blood. Ernst went with the others, losing control of himself, firing his pistol in dark prison cells, in the hot, sunlit court-yards, then driving across the city to execute others in their homes, then on to the Lichterfeld Barracks – here, there and everywhere, through the day, into the night – murdering SA troops and government ministers and policemen and politicians.

He fell asleep in darkness, awakened to the new day, took part in more executions at Lichterfeld Barracks and Columbia House, an SS torture chamber, until, at approximately four o'clock the following morning, he was finally allowed to holster his pistol and wash the blood from his hands.

Like his good friend Willi Brandt, he wept and then dried his stinging eyes.

He remembered returning home and telling Ingrid what had happened. He remembered, also, that she did not show any sympathy for his exhaustion, any understanding of his feelings of shame and horror, but only reviled him for what he had done, said she would never forgive him, and told him never to touch her again, because he would simply revolt her.

That morning, as he lay on the sofa, he drew his strength from contempt for her.

He became a good Nazi.

CHAPTER SEVEN

Wearing a gray suit, plain white shirt, and tie, Bradley was feeling more like a full-time lawyer and less like a disappointed, part-time intelligence agent when he picked up the telephone in his office high above Wall Street.

'Miss Kinder?' he checked tentatively. '*The* Miss Kinder, from Roswell, New Mexico?'

'That's right,' Gladys Kinder replied. 'You sound surprised, Mr Bradley.'

'Well, I certainly wasn't expecting to hear from you, so, you know, I was—'

She chuckled in a familiar, sensual manner. 'Well, here I am.'

'Where, exactly?'

'In the Algonquin Hotel. It's famous for its famous resident writers, so I wanted to stay here.'

'What are you doing in New York?' he asked, feeling guilty at how glad he was to hear her voice. 'It's a long way from Roswell.'

'I'm on my way to Europe,' she replied, 'and I'm sailing from this fair city, so I thought I'd give you a call. I remembered that you'd taken a shine to me when we talked in your hotel, so I figured you'd at least buy me a drink.'

'I really don't think—' he began, taken aback by her insolence, embarrassed by her accuracy, and horrified that his secretary might be listening. 'I mean, I—'

She chuckled with throaty amusement. 'Oh, stop worrying, Mr Bradley. I know you're not the playboy kind. I really called because I've got some information that I think might intrigue you.'

'What information?' he asked carefully.

'Wilson. You remember John Wilson?'

'Yes,' he replied, sitting up straight in his chair, even as the mention of Wilson's name revived his feelings of bitter disappointment. 'Of course I do. He's the reason you and I met in the first place, so . . .'

'Still interested in him?'

'Well, not exactly. I mean . . .' He didn't quite know how to phrase it. He didn't even want to think about it, since it made him mad and frustrated. 'That project's sort of cooled down,' he tried. 'It kinda got put on ice.'

'Ah-ha!'

'Right,' Bradley responded, already feeling too emotional just hearing her voice.

'So explain, Bradley. I thought you were hot for Wilson.'

'I was, Gladys, but various things got in the way. Basically, it was decided from above that what we had on Wilson wasn't enough to establish him as someone worth wasting good government money on. In short, I was taken off Wilson's case and given some others, so I haven't done anything about him for some time. I asked them to give me a few more days, but they cut me dead on the spot.'

'And when was that?'

'A couple of days after I'd visited MIT to check Wilson's background and education. Since he'd gone from there to Cornell, I was going to go there next, but when Taylor put a stop to the project . . . well, I was really disappointed and I kinda lost interest.'

'*I've* been to Cornell,' Gladys said. 'I went there to visit a friend before leaving for Europe; and since Wilson had once told me that that's where he'd been educated, I decided to check his records while I was there. I come cheap, so buy me lunch and I'll give it all to you.'

At once embarrassed and charmed by her unusual boldness, Bradley practically stuttered, 'Well, I don't know,

Gladys, I'm pretty busy here . . . and what with the project being put on ice and all . . . Well, I don't . . .'

'You don't want to see me before I leave for Europe?'

'Well, yeah, I do, but . . .'

'Then don't make excuses. And believe me, Bradley, when you have this information on Wilson, I don't think you'll have any problem at all in reviving the project – so you win on both counts. Now, do you want it or not?'

'I want it,' Bradley said, already excited. 'Where and when can we meet?'

'My ship leaves tomorrow, so can you meet me today? I've a prior engagement for tonight,' she said, sounding teasing, 'so how about lunch right here?'

'You can't make it any other time?'

'No.'

'Then lunch it is.'

'I'll be at a table in the restaurant. One o'clock?'

'Right,' he said. 'Thanks for calling.'

'My pleasure, Bradley.'

Feeling remarkably flustered, Bradley put the phone down just as Mark, his eighteen-year-old son, entered the office.

'Hi, Dad,' he said.

The young man was blessed with his mother's warm brown eyes and sensitive features, which no doubt helped, Bradley thought, with the many young ladies he dated in Manhattan during the weekends. In fact, Mark, though oddly shy, was a considerable ladies' man who kept one set of girlfriends in Manhattan, where he went to college, and another in Connecticut, where he lived with the family on weekends.

Bradley had always liked people who could surprise him and Mark could certainly do that.

'Hi, kid,' Bradley said, as his son took the chair at the other side of his desk. 'Is it lunchtime already?'

'Yep, it sure is. Don't tell me you were working too hard to notice. I don't fall for those tricks.'

Feeling guilty, Bradley grinned. 'Did I promise you lunch today?'

'Yeah,' Mark replied, 'but I'm letting you off the hook. Since my lecture's been canceled and I've got the afternoon free, I'm going to have lunch with Gail Mitchell, who looks sweeter than you.'

'Gail Mitchell? Do I know her?'

'I don't think so. She lives in Brooklyn Heights. I met her through a friend at college and she's rich and impossibly attractive and too tall for you.'

'I may be only five-foot-seven,' Bradley said, unburdened of his guilt, 'but what there is, is all man. Anyway, never mind. I was going to disappoint *you*. I'm having an unexpected business lunch today, so I'm glad you're fixed up.'

'Who are you lunching with?'

'Dave Marsh,' Bradley lied instinctively, impelled by the return of the guilt caused by the thought of Gladys Kinder and using the name of a friend he met often for lunch.

'You mean that other lawyer?'

'Right.'

'I think I met him at home a few years ago.'

'You did. We once invited him for Thanksgiving. He got drunk and made a pass at your mother, which gave her a thrill. Anyway, since it's urgent, I had to cancel you and arrange to meet him instead.'

'Charming,' Mark retorted.

'Well, I knew you'd have a tall lady at hand, so I wasn't too worried. Come on, let's go.'

They left the office, took the elevator down to Wall Street, and stood outside on the busy, sunlit pavement.

'Are you having a long afternoon or just lunch with your Amazon?' Bradley asked.

'Just lunch.'

'Okay. Since it's Friday afternoon, why not meet on the platform of the station at three o'clock sharp and we'll go back together?'

'Sounds good,' Mark said.

'Okay, son, I'll see you.'

While Mark sauntered off along the crowded sidewalk,

Bradley grabbed a taxi to the Algonquin Hotel on 44th Street. He found Gladys Kinder already seated in a booth in the Rose Room, drinking bourbon and smoking a cigarette.

She certainly looked her age, which she had said was thirty-eight, but even in her old-fashioned clothes, which were doubtless the rage in Roswell, she had an undeniable attractiveness and, at least to him, an oddly opaque, provocative sensuality.

She made him feel slightly out of breath.

As he sat beside her in the banquette, wondering why she had chosen it instead of an open table, she held up her glass, grinned laconically, and said, 'I've been on the wagon since last night, but I couldn't resist this. We working journalists are all the same.'

'It looks almost empty,' Bradley observed. 'Shall I order another one?'

'Why not?' she responded.

'Shall we also order the food?'

'Sure,' she said. 'Why not?'

Instantly recalling her ability to hold her liquor, and also remembering that when drinking she could be impish, Bradley ordered two more bourbons. He went through the menu with her, ordered the food for both of them, then, when the aperitifs had arrived, raised his glass to her.

'Cheers,' he said.

'Cheers, Mr Bradley,' she replied, also raising her glass and smiling.

'Mike – just call me Mike.'

'That sounds really intimate, Mike – but what the hell, call me Gladys. Not the most *romantic* name in the world, but I have to live with it.'

He had to grin at that one. 'You said you were on your way to Europe. Did you really mean that?'

'Yep. Sure did, partner. I never quite recovered from the way Wilson left me, I didn't particularly like being a middle-age spinster in New Mexico, and so I wangled myself a job as foreign correspondent to the Roswell *Daily Record*, which I've served so well so far. Those good ol' boys in Roswell always treated me fine, and when I told them I needed to get away, this is what they came up with. It doesn't pay much, but I'll see Europe, and I've dreamed of that all my life.'

'Based anywhere in particular?'

'London. But I'm hoping to go to Spain. I think things are happening there.'

'Bad things.'

'I guess so.'

Over the meal, Bradley told her what he knew about Europe, which was considerable, and all the time he felt himself falling into her, as if in a dream. She wasn't like the women he knew – she was rough-edged and laconic – but that very difference, which seemed more pronounced here, in these sophisticated surroundings, made her even more attractive to him.

Talking about their first meeting in the Roswell hotel's gloomy lobby, she said, 'You had the East Coast written all over you and I thought that was cute.'

She also joked about how shocked he had seemed when, after informing her that he was in Roswell to interview the members of Goddard's rocket team, she responded by not only telling him she had been Wilson's mistress, but by elaborating in drunkenly mischievous, intimate detail just what she and her remarkably youthful sixty-year-old lover had done together in bed.

'You looked as shocked as a cheerleader trapped in a baseball team's shower room after a winning game. God, that was something!'

Finally she reminded him that he had found her attractive, that she had seen it in his face, and that his blushing response to her teasing had simply confirmed it.

'Yes,' he murmured, 'I guess it did.'

He had never had an affair before and certainly didn't plan to start one now, but when he thought of her going off to Europe, probably never to be seen again, he was filled with an unutterable sense of loss. It was an unexpected, inexplicable feeling, and it left him bewildered.

So bewildered, in fact, that he almost forgot to ask her about Wilson – though eventually, over the coffee and brandy, he *did* get down to business.

'You said you'd been to Cornell,' he reminded her. 'Is that true or not?'

She became more serious then. 'Yeah,' she said, 'it's true.' Opening her handbag, she withdrew two sheets of typed notes, unfolded them, and spread them out on the table. She was briefly distracted by her brandy, but eventually, after imbibing and inhaling, she blew smoke and started reading from her neatly typed notes.

'Name: John Wilson. Born July 6, 1870, in Montezuma, Iowa, to Cass and Ira Wilson, both listed as farmers. Attended elementary school in Montezuma then high school in Des Moines. Stunning reports from both schools for his academic achievements – though all agreed that he seemed to have few friends and cared only for studying. In the fall of 1888, when he was eighteen years old, he signed on at MIT – apparently, shortly after his mother died and his father sold their farm in the Corn Belt and moved back to Worcester, Massachusetts, his hometown. At MIT, Wilson studied aerodynamics, with particular emphasis on the wind-tunnel experiments that took place in the Engineering A Department. In 1893 – the same year his father died – Wilson's reports, in which every subject is listed as 'exemplary,' thus setting a college record, gained him entry to Sibley College, Cornell University, where he studied experimental engineering. By 1895 he'd obtained his bachelor of science degree in aeronautics and left Cornell. The university records don't say where he planned on going when he left – but they *do* reveal that between 1896 and 1897 he returned frequently to the university to attend the lectures of Octave Chanute.'

She stopped reading and raised her eyes from the notes.

'Anything else?' Bradley asked.

'No,' she replied. 'At least not until he turned up, in the fall of 1930, to work for six months with Robert H. Goddard, whom we all know and love as the controversial rocket scientist and a later, if more renowned, MIT graduate.'

Bradley wrinkled his brow. 'Did you say 19*30*?'

'Yep.'

'You mean there's nothing on this guy from 1895 to 1930 – a period of approximately thirty-five years?'

'Not so far. He appears to have wiped his own tracks clean. We don't know what he did for a living following graduation, but we do know that he frequently returned informally to Cornell to attended Chanute's lectures, given throughout 1896 and 1897. Then, when Wilson was twenty-seven years old, he dropped out of sight completely – and he didn't reappear until 1930, when he worked for six months with Robert Goddard, before disappearing again, as completely as he'd done the first time.'

'That's incredible,' Bradley said, blowing another cloud of smoke. 'A guy can't disappear *that* completely for thirty-five years, then suddenly turn up again at sixty years old!'

Gladys sighed. 'So far that appears to be the case. Wilson seems to be some kind of authentic genius. He obtained his BA in aeronautics when they were very rare indeed, he claimed to Goddard that he had designed airships – and yet we can't find a thing on what should have been the most productive thirty-five years of his life.'

Bradley gave a low whistle.

'*Would* that be possible in this day and age?' Gladys asked, but before Bradley could open his mouth to reply, she raised her index finger and asked, more emphatically: 'One: Would a man with that track record be *capable* of designing airships? And, two: If he *was* capable of doing so, could he have done it in total secrecy for so long?'

She glanced across the crowded restaurant at the group of people arguing noisily in a cloud of cigarette smoke at a table in the middle of the room. They included William Shawn, the associate editor of the *New Yorker,* an increasingly blind and visibly drunken cartoonist named James Thurber, a matinee-idol theater reviewer, Robert Benchley, and the deceptively sweet-faced satirical writer, Dorothy Parker. Grinning slightly and shaking her head, as if she didn't believe it, Gladys turned back to Bradley.

'I'd already checked out that possibility,' Bradley said, 'and in answer to your first question – yes, Wilson *could* have gone into airship design with that kind of background. Although there were no formal aeronautical courses at MIT when Wilson was there, there were plenty of *informal* courses on propulsion and the behavior of fluids – two subjects that Goddard later made his own. And certainly, by 1896, instructors and students at MIT had built a wind tunnel and were experimenting with it to get practical knowledge of aerodynamics. As for Sibley College, the experimental engineering courses that Wilson attended would have been conducted by professors Rolla Clinton Carpenter, George Burton Preston, Aldred Henry Eldredge, Charles Edwin Houghton, and Oliver Shantz – some of the greatest aeronautical thinkers of their day. Finally, Octave Chanute was the world-famous engineer who, in 1896, emulated the successful manned hang-glider experiments of the German, Otto Lilienthal, at an aerial experiment station on the Lake Michigan sand dunes near Miller, Indiana – so, again, Wilson learned from the very best.'

'But what was the state of knowledge at the time?' Gladys asked, still skeptical about what he was telling her.

'Well,' Bradley replied, 'according to what I learned at MIT, it was certainly more advanced than is generally known. For instance, Cornell's courses at the time included mechanical and electrical engineering and machine design and construction. As for specific aeronautical texts of the time, they were surprisingly advanced and would have included the Smithsonian Institution's *Experiments in Aerodynamics*, published in 1891; the Lawrence Hargraves experiment reports of 1890 to 1894; the 1893 reports on Sir Hiram Maxim's experiments on engines, propellers, airplanes, and flying machines; and the *Aeronautical Annual* of 1895, 1896, and 1897, which contained original contributions from most of the leading aeronautical scientists . . . So assuming that Wilson was some kind of genius, he certainly could have attained the knowledge necessary to design airships.'

'Oh, boy!' Gladys exclaimed softly, obviously intrigued. 'And question two?'

'Could a man of such talents have worked in America for thirty-five years, possibly designing airships, without leaving any tracks behind?' Bradley nodded emphatically. 'Yes, Gladys, it's certainly *odd*, but I think it's possible. The period we're talking about was the greatest so far in the history of aviation – the first successful flight of S. P. Langley's flying machines; Santos-Dumont's flight in an airship from Saint Cloud to the Eiffel Tower; the Wright brothers' first successful heavier-than-air manned flight at Kitty Hawk, North Carolina; Goddard's first experiments in rocketry; Wilbur Wright's seventy-seven-mile flight in two hours and thirty minutes; then, only seven months later, in 1909, Louis Blériot's flight across the English Channel; the dogfights and airship raids of the Great War of 1914, and the continuing advances made since then – so yes, Wilson could certainly have designed airships . . . or even more advanced forms of aircraft.'

'But could he have done so in *secret*?'

'Yes, it's possible. In fact, it was a time when financiers were in fierce competition with one another to sink money into experimental aeronautical projects – so *most* of those projects were wrapped in the strictest secrecy. Wilson *could,* therefore, have worked in almost total anonymity with the full support, even encouragement, of his financial backers. And the US government,' he continued, practically talking to himself, 'quietly backed more than one aeronautical project – particularly during the late 1930s – and usually insisted that such projects be kept secret. They also occasionally took over civilian aeronautical projects and either ran them in strict secrecy or, for one reason or other, quietly aborted them.' He scratched his nose, coughed into his clenched fist, and spread his hands on the table. 'So,' he said, 'there it is.'

There was a moment's silence which seemed to last forever,

then Gladys said: 'Tell you what . . . I'll run a check on all the companies that were known to be working on such projects and see if Wilson's name pops up magically. It depends, I suppose, on whether or not he used his own name – but I'll certainly give it a try for you before I catch the boat – since the guy who obtained these notes for me, who works in the registrar's office at Cornell, is my date for this evening.'

Bradley, very much to his surprise, was upset to hear that, though he managed to hide the fact.

'Shall I call you at home tonight?' Gladys asked him.

'Sure,' he said, giving her his number, but feeling as guilty as a man arranging an assignation, 'that would be great. Now I have to go, Gladys. I'm meeting my son at Penn Station at three o'clock, to take the train home.'

He felt embarrassed saying it, but Gladys just smiled wickedly. 'Ah, yes,' she said, 'I remember. You told me all about your family. A lovely wife and a boy and girl, as I remember.'

'That's right,' Bradley said. 'Though the boy and girl are older than you might think. In fact, Mark is eighteen.'

'A good age,' Gladys said.

Yet she seemed sad at that moment, or at least a little regretful, and when they left the hotel and faced each another on 44th Street, Bradley, not normally a romantic man, hardly knew what to say.

She had somehow sneaked up on him.

'Well,' she said, offering her sunburned hand and a lopsided grin, 'it was nice to see you again, Mike Bradley. I'll give you that final call tonight, then it's au revoir, baby.'

'Thanks,' he said. 'Au revoir.'

She just stood there as he climbed into a taxi and let it drive him away.

He was almost choked up.

CHAPTER EIGHT

Bradley met Mark at three o'clock at Penn Station and they took the train back to Bridgeport, Connecticut, unencumbered with the usual rush-hour crowd of fellow commuters. As Bradley had already phoned to say they would be early, his wife, Joan, was waiting for them in her car and drove them back to their relatively modest, ranch-style home, just ten minutes from the station and surrounded by expansive gardens and protective trees. There Bradley refreshed himself with a shower, dressed in casual slacks, shirt, and pullover, relaxed for an hour with the radio and another whiskey, then joined Joan and his two children for dinner in the oak-paneled dining room.

Modestly drunk from his lunch with Gladys Kinder and the additional whiskey, and still an Irish sentimentalist at heart, Bradley, after sharing a bottle of red wine with his family, found himself glancing from his wife to his daughter, quietly startled at how similar they looked in all but their age. Joan was thirty-eight, five days older than Bradley, and although their daughter, Miriam, was still only seventeen, she and her mother were almost like twins – sharing the same delicate features, dark hair, enchanting café-au-lait eyes, and a quietly mischievous sense of humor.

Bradley, usually sentimental but now guilty because of his guiltless passion for Gladys Kinder, was even more in love with both of them tonight than he was normally.

'How did school go today?' he asked Miriam.

'The same as always,' she replied. 'Clark Gable was teaching math, Bette Davis taught history, and Errol Flynn discussed the things he knows best, then gave out his phone number. That's why I love school, Dad.'

Bradley grinned. 'Well, school's certainly improved since my day – and the results are so wonderful.'

Miriam lowered her head and blushed.

'Gee,' Mark said, 'what a sweet kid! She makes me feel so mature, so *protective,* when she blushes like that.'

'Shut up, Mark,' Joan warned him.

'Sorry, Mom,' he replied.

'Who's taking you to the prom?' Bradley asked. 'Have you decided that yet?'

'Whoever asks her,' Mark informed him.

'Shut up, Mark,' Joan warned him.

'I told you,' Miriam replied, smiling sweetly. 'Errol Flynn gave me his number and a welcoming smile.'

'He's too old for you,' Joan said.

'A nice guy,' Mark said, 'but too old.'

'What about that kid who walks you home from school? At least he looks like Errol Flynn.'

'Looks aren't everything, Dad.'

'His father's rich,' Joan reminded her.

'Money's not everything, Mom.'

'It's *nearly* everything, Miriam.'

'Will he be taking you?' Bradley asked.

Miriam sighed. 'He hasn't asked me.'

'When he asks, are you going to say yes?'

Miriam sighed. 'I suppose so.'

'A real lucky guy,' Mark said.

'Yes, isn't he?' Miriam responded.

'Please finish your desserts,' Joan said to all of them, 'so I can clear this table and put up my feet.'

'Yes, ma'am!' they all exclaimed at once.

Joan did in fact put her feet up after dinner, stretching out on the sofa, while Bradley sat on the floor beside her, having a brandy and feeling deeply grateful for the good life he had. The kids had retired to their own rooms and he was about to put on the radio, but Joan stopped him by taking hold of his wrist and pulling his hand onto her stomach, which still was as flat as an adolescent's, and seductively warm.

'No,' she said, 'I don't want to hear the radio. Let's just talk for a while.'

'Okay, dear. Sure. Anything special?'

'Nope,' she said with a lazy smile. 'Nothing special at all. How did your day go?'

'The same as always,' he replied. 'Clark Gable came by for a drink, Bette Davis dropped in for a smoke, and Errol Flynn called to discuss his marriage. That's why I love it at work.'

Joan chuckled softly, squeezed his hand, then lightly stroked his wrist. 'So what did you *really* do?' she asked. 'Was it something exciting?'

'Mostly routine,' he replied. 'The best part of the day was lunch with Dave Marsh, who sends love and kisses.'

Joan's smile was quietly radiant. 'Ah, my boyfriend!' she said softly, oblivious to Bradley's shame. 'Was this just your usual monthly get-together or something special?'

'He's going to check someone out for me,' Bradley told her. 'A guy called John Wilson. A guy who's starting to intrigue me. A real mystery man . . .'

He told her all about Wilson, taking longer than he had expected, and then added that he was expecting a late-night call from one of Dave Marsh's friends: a lady named Gladys Kinder.

When he stopped talking, Joan rolled onto her hip, to stare directly, steadily at him with her lovely brown eyes.

'Be careful, Mike,' she told him. 'Don't let this become another obsession. You're easily bored, always searching for new adventures, and I know that you're looking at intelligence work to get you out of the office. But I repeat, please be careful. Don't become obsessed with this mystery man. We have a good marriage, but it's been through its troubles, and most of those troubles occurred when you became obsessed with your work. So *please,* Mike, no matter how intriguing this man is, don't let him threaten our marriage.'

'I promise I won't.'

She went to bed shortly after and he promised to follow immediately, but instead sat on, thinking about what she had said and accepting the truth in it. They *did* have a good marriage, but it *had* had its troubles, and in nearly every instance the problem had been caused by his obsession with some job or other and his subsequent neglect of home and hearth. He loved Joan and the children, appreciated what he had, and didn't want ever again to let work, or anything else, take him away from them.

And he was silently vowing not to let this happen when the telephone rang.

'I think I've found our man,' Gladys Kinder said. 'Our mysterious Mr Wilson. In 1895, the year Wilson left Cornell, a now-defunct New York financial company, Cohn and Goldman Incorporated, financed an aeronautical company, reportedly to research and, if possible, construct passenger-carrying airships. While Cohn and Goldman denied repeatedly that they were attempting to build commercial airships – as most speculators routinely did in those days – I have confirmation that they constructed their factories in Mount Pleasant, near the border of Iowa and Illinois . . . And according to the company records, the man put in charge of the whole project was a relatively unknown aeronautical scientist named John Wilson.'

Bradley was surprised to find himself releasing the breath he had been unwittingly holding in.

'Anything else?' he asked.

'No, Mike. Those are the only clippings I could find on either Wilson or the company Cohn and Goldman.'

'It's more than enough to go on,' Bradley said. 'Thanks a hell of a lot, Gladys.'

Excited and confused at once, he was just about to hang up, but Gladys spoke urgently enough to stop him. 'One more thing, Bradley . . . In checking the clippings, I was also reminded that the following two years – 1896 and 1897 – were notable for one phenomenon in particular: the great wave of mystery airships. They called them UFOs – unidentified flying objects.'

'Why?'

'Because most of the reports indicated that the airships were more advanced than any known to have been constructed at the time. Also, they were reported to be carrying passengers, or crewmen. They landed frequently, usually to collect water for their engines, and at such times the crewmen talked freely to anyone who approached them . . . And the crewman who features most frequently in the reports is a man who called himself—'

'Wilson?'

'Right.' She chuckled and then went serious. 'I'm gonna arrange to have a friend send you the newspaper clippings about those sightings – and that's about it, Mike. After this, I'll be on my way to Europe. No more lunches. No phone calls . . .'

Her voice trailed off into a silence that spoke volumes and left Bradley grieving.

'Gladys, I don't know how . . .'

'What's domestic life like out there in Connecticut?'

'It's very nice.'

'Yeah, I thought so. Good-bye, Mike.'

'Good-bye, Gladys.'

The phone went dead. Bradley felt very emotional. He forgot to join Joan in bed, but instead went into his study and sat at his desk. He pulled out the notes he had collected on Wilson and started to ponder them.

The next morning, having not slept a wink, he rang General Taylor.

CHAPTER NINE

'I'm Lieutenant Ernst Stoll,' Wilson's new interrogator said when the cell door had closed behind the man and he took the hard wooden chair facing the bed upon which Wilson was seated. 'I am, as you can see, a member of the SS, not the Gestapo, and I work for the technical intelligence branch. Naturally,' he added, waving the papers in his right hand and offering what seemed like a shy smile, 'I know who *you* are, so shall we begin?'

'What if I say no?' Wilson asked.

'I would ignore you, of course.'

Wilson smiled. 'Let's begin, then. I take it, as you're from *technical* intelligence, that we've made a little progress – or at least finished with relatively unimportant matters.'

'That's true,' Lieutenant Stoll said, mildly amused by Wilson's impertinence. 'Your background and motivation have been ascertained, so I'm here to talk about the work you have shown us and wish to do for us.'

'Good,' Wilson said, deliberately keeping his gaze steady, searching the lieutenant's face for what it was hiding, because all faces were masks. Lieutenant Ernst Stoll was young, perhaps in his middle twenties, and while he looked diabolically handsome in his gleaming black uniform, his face did not display a confidence to match. Indeed, he seemed a little haunted, a man divided within himself, and was obviously trying to cover his doubts with his dryly polite, distant manner.

'You have a technical background?' Wilson asked him.

'Yes,' Stoll replied with a flicker of pride. 'I studied

aeronautical engineering at the Institute of Technology in Munich, then rocket technology under Professor Becker at the Institute of Technology, Berlin University.'

'Ah!' Wilson exclaimed softly, with admiration. 'Becker! So were you a member of the German Amateur Rocket Society?'

'No,' Stoll said, briefly displaying hurt and resentment, then hiding it by changing the subject. 'I trust you found the previous interrogations civilized,' he asked, looking up from his papers.

'Yes,' Wilson said. 'Perfectly civilized. Surprisingly so.'

Lieutenant Stoll raised his eyebrows as if puzzled. 'Why surprisingly so? Is it not what you would have expected from German officers?'

'Given the sounds that have emanated from some of the other cells, I take it that not all German officers are so civilized when interrogating their prisoners.'

Ernst looked embarrassed, then smiled bleakly. 'Ah,' he said, *'that.* Well, some prisoners are more troublesome than others, as I'm sure you agree. A little persuasion often goes a long way – though I hope that the noise from the other cells didn't make you lose too much sleep.'

Because he had been forced to listen, day and night, to the screaming of those being abused in the other cells or torture chambers of this Gestapo headquarters and prison, Wilson would certainly have lost a good deal of sleep had he been the kind to need a lot of it. As he was not, and as the fate of others did not concern him, he'd had a relatively comfortable time.

Nevertheless, hoping to find out more about the situation outside the prison, he said, 'Yes, I lost some sleep – particularly during that day and night two weeks ago, when this whole place turned into a madhouse of bawling and shooting.'

'You mean June 30?'

'Correct.'

The lieutenant's façade nearly crumbled, revealing revulsion mixed with shame, but he quickly regained his composure and smiled again, bleakly. 'Ah, yes, the Night of the Long Knives. That's what they call it now.'

'Is it true that the SS murdered over a hundred, maybe two hundred, SA officers and others in that one bloody purge?'

'No, it's not true,' the lieutenant replied with self-defensive anger. 'Those men weren't murdered, but executed, because they were traitors.'

'Executed without trial,' Wilson corrected him.

'You're impertinent, Herr Wilson. Count your blessings that you're American. Count them also because that purge, about which you are so sarcastic, has ensured that the SS, and not the SA, are now virtually ruling the Third Reich. The SS will therefore be in control of any research establishment in which you're likely to find yourself.'

'My request, then, is being seriously considered.'

'That's why I am here.'

Realizing that after weeks of interrogation in this prison cell, he was close to getting what he wanted, Wilson allowed himself the luxury of a feeling of triumph. When Lieutenant Ernst Stoll of SS Technical Intelligence lowered his head to study the papers on his knee, Wilson recognized his original drawings and notes, cunningly unfinished, for the kind of aircraft the Nazi's Projekt Saucer was trying, unsuccessfully, to create. It was also what *he* was trying to create, and with their help he would do it.

Lieutenant Stoll looked up from his notes and said, 'While I'm very impressed, I find it hard to believe that during the period you worked in secret – between 1895 and 1930 – you could have made the extraordinary technical advances indicated in these notes and drawings.'

'You've already tested my intellect and knowledge and know that both are remarkable – so why doubt my achievements?'

'We cannot check your actual engineering or scientific achievements until we get you into a research center; however, according to what we can gauge from these remarkable notes and drawings, your achievements were completely divorced from the general scientific achievements of the time. Those were very early days, and your achievements seem *too* advanced even to have sprung from that period.'

'It's a widely held misconception that those were early days,' Wilson replied, 'but they were in fact the most productive days in the history of science. As you've studied aeronautical engineering and rocketry, I needn't tell you about the extraordinary advances made in those fields during that period. However, I should remind you that by 1895 Röntgen had discovered X rays, Marconi had invented wireless telegraphy, Auguste and Louis Lumière had invented the Cinématographe, the first main railway was electrified, and Ramsay had detected, by spectroscope, helium from a terrestrial source. By 1896 we had Rutherford's magnetic detection of electrical waves, the construction of an electrical submarine in France, and the first successful flights of S. P. Langley's flying machines. By 1897 numerous patents for flying machines had been registered, and J. J. Thomson's work on cathode rays had led to the evaluation of the electron. The rest I'm sure I don't have to tell you: From the successful test flights of Langley's flying machines in 1897 to the first cross-channel flight took only one decade – and in that decade Robert H. Goddard had already begun his experiments in rocketry. So, Lieutenant, I was *not* too advanced for my own time – and indeed my work *did* spring from it and was nurtured by its achievements.'

Stoll smiled frostily, glanced down at Wilson's notes, then looked up again. 'Your work has been studied by our Projekt Saucer scientists and engineers at the German Rocket Research Institute at Kummersdorf, just outside Berlin. While it is agreed that your designs are remarkable, they remain incomplete and would not lead to a workable saucer-shaped aircraft. You claim that with our help you'd be able to complete this project, but why, since our own scientists have failed repeatedly to do so, should we place our faith in your undoubted talents?'

'You know I can't answer that,' Wilson said carefully, 'but can only show you what I can do when I'm actually working.'

'I understand that, Herr Wilson, but perhaps you can at least give me some indication of the direction you'd be heading in.

For instance, what would separate your work from that which is already being done by our scientists at Kummersdorf? We agree that an aircraft shaped like a saucer would fly better than any other, but that shape also has its own problems, which so far we can't solve. How, then, would you approach this problem that has so far foiled us?'

Wilson had no intentions of telling them everything he had discovered, but he knew that he had to give them enough to whet their appetites and encourage them to let him work for them. He therefore leaned forward on the bed and chose his words carefully.

'Your scientists have been researching along conventional lines,' he said, 'but a saucer-shaped aircraft wouldn't respond to conventional laws of aerodynamics, so we have to look elsewhere.'

'I'm not sure I understand,' Stoll replied, though his gaze was steady and thoughtful.

'When I was working with the wind tunnel at Zeppelin in Friedrichshafen,' Wilson said, 'I helped test many of the experimental products coming from Kummersdorf – and it soon became clear to me that the Kummersdorf scientists were trying to construct some kind of saucer-shaped aircraft.'

'You've already told us you knew that,' Stoll said impatiently.

'I remind you of it,' Wilson replied, unperturbed, 'because I also ascertained that most of the Kummersdorf designs were based on the tailless, or "all-wing," aircraft, the Horten 1, which was designed and constructed by the Horten brothers, Walter and Riemer, for the German Air Ministry, at their factory in Bonn, from 1931 to 1932. That so-called all-wing aircraft, which in prototype was a glider, had a span of forty point seven feet, a wing area of two hundred and twenty-six square feet, and a wing-loading of two pounds per square foot. It had a flying weight of four hundred and forty pounds, a gliding angle of twenty-one degrees, and a flying life of approximately seven hours.'

'Your intelligence gathering is commendable,' Stoll said sarcastically, 'but what is the point of this?'

'The Horten brothers were convinced that the most important form of aircraft would be the all-wing type, which is why there were no vertical stabilizing or control surfaces on their flying wing, the Horton 1, why it was virtually flat and crescent-shaped, like a boomerang, and why the pilot was placed in a prone position – to reduce cockpit size.'

'Yes, Herr Wilson, I know this, but—'

'That so-called *flying wing* certainly flew for seven hours – but it could never have been the basis of a flying saucer for one very good reason.'

'Yes?'

'It was still faced with the problem that's repeatedly foiled your scientists: the limitations imposed by the boundary layer.'

He could see that he had Stoll's interest, though the German was trying to disguise it by showing little emotion. Amused, Wilson said, 'Have you heard of the boundary layer, Oberleutnant?'

Stoll just smiled at the sarcasm. 'Why don't you remind me, Herr Wilson? You talk so well about these things.'

'While being four or five thousand times less viscous than oil, air *is* still viscous,' Wilson said, enjoying himself. 'Because of this, the air sweeping in on the solid body of an aircraft forms imperceptible stratifications of resistance and consequently decreases the speed of the body in flight. These layers of air are therefore known as the boundary layer – and the boundary layer increases its resistance in direct proportion to the increasing speed of the flying object, thus imposing severe limitations on its speed and maneuverability.'

'And in layman's terms?' Stoll asked, clearly amused by Wilson's enthusiasm for lecturing.

'In layman's terms,' Wilson continued, drawing Stoll into his web, 'the major problem regarding supersonic flight is to somehow move this negative air as far to the rear of the aircraft as possible, thus minimizing the expenditure of energy required to propel it through the sky. Moreover, it's possible that a revolutionary type of aircraft could – by not only *completely* removing the boundary layer, but by somehow *rerouting* it and utilizing it as an added propulsive force – fly through the skies using little other than the expelled air itself. Should this be accomplished, we would have an aircraft capable of remarkable speeds while using only the bare minimum of conventional fuel.'

'So you plan to devote all your energies to solving the problem of the boundary layer.'

'Yes,' Wilson said, playing his trump card, 'and Germany is the place for doing that.'

'I am flattered – but why Germany?'

'As I explained to your Reichsführer, the boundary layer was introduced to the world of aerodynamics by the German professor, Ludwig Prandtl, at Göttingen in 1904. Throughout the following years, many other German scientists, including professors Betz, Flettner, and Junkers, experimented with specially equipped aircraft in attempts to reduce the boundary layer. Most of the experiments were based on the 'suction' method, in which the negative air is sucked into the wing itself, through tiny holes or slots, then expelled by means of a pump located in the fuselage. While this was a step in the right direction, the resulting aircraft still required heavy, obstructive engines – also the main problem with the flying wing jet fighter the Horten brothers envisaged – but it's my belief that in order to get rid of the boundary layer completely – and in order to make use of the "dead" air not only for acceleration, but for maneuvering as well – what we need is an aircraft devoid of *all* obstructing protuberances, such as wings, rudders, and even normal air intakes, and one not requiring a large, heavy engine. In other words, this revolutionary new aircraft should be the perfect 'flying wing' that offers the least possible resistance, sucks in the "dead" air of the boundary layer, and then uses that same air, expelling it at great force, to increase its own momentum.'

'And how do you propose creating such a machine?'

'By building the perfect flying wing – a circular wing that is, in a sense, wrapped around its suction pump, with the pump being part and parcel of the engine – a machine shaped like a saucer – and by constructing it from a porous metal that will act like a sponge and remove the need for air intakes altogether. This would result in frictionless air flow during flight – an aircraft that slips through the air in the same way as a piece of wet soap slips through the fingers. Its speed and maneuvering capabilities would be literally limitless.'

Wilson felt excited merely thinking about it, and could see, in the sheltered gleam of Stoll's dark gaze, that he was feeling the same way. Nevertheless, the young oberleutnant was being careful about showing his feelings.

'This sounds wonderful in theory,' he said, 'but practise is something else. I'm not sure that your so-called porous metal is a realistic proposal.'

'In fact, it's being worked on right now,' Wilson said, 'and right here in Germany. Among the many other experiments I helped run in the Zeppelin wind tunnel were those concerning different porous metals being created by the scientists of Göttingen and Volkenroda – a compound of magnesium and aluminum. The scientists are calling it *Luftschwamm,* or aerosponge . . . and I think it will work.'

He knew that he had won the instant he saw Lieutenant Stoll fold up his papers and slip them back into his briefcase. 'It's interesting,' the lieutenant said, pushing his chair back and standing up, 'that even the great Russian, Tsiolokovsky, evinced a strong interest in circular, hyperbolic, and spherical airframes.'

'I can see that you know more about this subject than you pretend, Oberleutnant,' Wilson replied, thus making the somber SS officer smile. 'And knowing that, you clearly also know that the extensive research into all-wing aircraft and rocketry that's been carried out in Germany during the past decade is directly due to German admiration for Tsiolokovsky's theories.'

'*And* due to admiration for the American, Robert H. Goddard, for whom you worked for six months.'

'I have to admit that although he's my junior, I learned a lot from Goddard about the problems of stabilization and gyroscopic controls. That's why I wanted to work with him – it was my only weak area.'

The lieutenant smiled genuinely for the first time and said, 'Come, Herr Wilson, we are leaving. We are going to put you to work. We do not have much time, so don't bother with your possessions. This cell will be cleaned out as soon as we leave, and your possessions here, as well as those being kept by the Gestapo, will be forwarded to you this afternoon. So please, follow me now.'

Quietly exultant, Wilson was led out of the cell and up the stairs to the lobby near the front door of the building. There, while he adjusted to his sudden sense of space and movement (after weeks in his tiny cell, this lobby appeared to be immense and far too crowded), he was given an army greatcoat. Then he was led out into the Prinz Albrechtstrasse and into a waiting police car.

Seated in the rear beside the notably more relaxed Oberleutnant Ernst Stoll, Wilson gazed out the window as the car pulled away from the curb and proceeded through Berlin. In the early afternoon's gray light, the city looked solid, busy, and perfectly normal, except for a notable increase in military personnel and vehicles, which seemed to be everywhere.

'This is a city preparing for war,' Wilson said.

'Yes,' the lieutenant replied. 'You are very observant.'

Intrigued by the handsome young lieutenant's oddly haunted look and reticence, Wilson said, taking a chance, 'Am I allowed to ask if you are involved with scientific work as distinct from intelligence?'

Lieutenant Stoll sighed. 'You may ask,' he said, 'and the answer is no. I am no longer involved in scientific research per se, but instead am forced to use my scientific knowledge for the gathering and analyzing of technical intelligence material.'

'Which is why you were sent to interview me, right?'

The oberleutnant sighed again, as if deeply depressed. 'Yes, Herr Wilson, that is the case. And now I will take you to Kummersdorf West, where you will work with men less talented than I was. Such is life, I suppose.'

'You can't protest?'

'To be a member of the SS is to obey. I obey and take pride from that.'

Wilson doubted that Ernst Stoll was taking pride from his work and filed the knowledge away in his head for future reference.

The journey to Kummersdorf did not take long – it was only fifteen miles from Berlin – and the car soon slowed down at barbed-wire fences and a guarded gate. It was inspected by a particularly careful SS officer and eventually waved through, then stopped in front of an enormous hangar in a broad stretch of bare ground that ran out to more barbed wire and signs announcing that an army firing range lay beyond.

Puzzled to find only this enormous hangar and bare ground where he had expected to find a hive of activity, Wilson glanced questioningly at Stoll. The oberleutnant, as if reading his mind, smiled understandingly and said, 'Projekt Saucer has been separated from the Rocket Research Institute proper by that army firing range. Beyond the firing range are Wernher von Braun's more impressive research works, which is what you were, I assume, hoping to find.'

'Frankly, yes,' Wilson said, hearing the moaning of the wind and seeing only swaying, untended grass around that single, enormous hangar, under the leaden gray sky.

'Try not to be too disappointed,' Ernst said, as he led Wilson across the windblown grass, toward the already rusted, corrugated-iron hangar. 'You will be visiting the Research Institute on a regular basis, contributing your knowledge to their rocket projects, but most of your time will be spent here, in conditions of strict secrecy, where you will work more specifically on Projekt Saucer. Even those who work at the other side of the firing range do not know what we're doing here.'

The main hangar doors were closed and the small side door was guarded by armed SS troops who gave the Nazi salute when Stoll approached. After returning the salute in a desultory manner, Stoll motioned Wilson into the hangar. Stepping inside, Wilson was temporarily blinded by the bright light. He adjusted to it as Stoll came in behind him and stood beside him, then saw an enormous open floor, surrounded by glassed-in offices and filled with machines and a few men in oily coveralls.

Raised about six feet off the concrete floor on a hydraulic platform was the skeletal prototype of a saucer-shaped craft, about forty feet in diameter and rising up to a central dome.

Its discus-shaped ribcage of steel covered what looked like two Hirth 80 hp engines.

'It'll never fly,' Wilson said.

Stoll smiled. 'No, it won't.'

Obviously pleased by Wilson's perception, he led him across the hangar floor to one of the larger offices. Stepping inside, he suddenly stiffened, gave the Nazi salute and said, 'Heil Hitler!' then stepped aside to introduce Wilson to a man who, even wearing his Reichsführer's uniform, did not look like a soldier.

'So, Herr Wilson,' Heinrich Himmler said, 'we meet again, yes?'

'Yes, Reichsführer – I'm glad to say.'

'I'm sure you are, Herr Wilson – since if we hadn't met again here, you would now be a dead man.'

Reminded by that remark that his assessment of Himmler was not amiss, Wilson glanced over the lunatic's shoulder at the men grouped behind him. As they were all wearing oily coveralls, they were either scientists or engineers.

'Would you care to inspect our flying saucer, Herr Wilson?'

'I do not have to inspect it, Reichsführer,' Wilson replied, 'to know that it won't fly.'

Himmler simply smiled. 'How arrogant you are, Herr Wilson! But come,' he added, crooking a delicate index finger and indicating the men standing nervously behind him, 'please let me introduce you to the rest of our team. This,' he said, indicating with a nod a young man with a lean and hungry look, 'is Flugkapitän Rudolph Schriever, who originally designed this flying saucer, which you insist will not fly. And this,' he continued, when Wilson had shaken the hand of the solemn young designer, 'is the physicist Klaus Habermohl, and his associate, Otto Miethe. And this,' he ended, when Wilson had shaken the hands of Habermohl and Miethe, both of whom were middle age, 'is Dr Giuseppe Belluzzo who, though Italian, has become an invaluable member of our team. Gentlemen, I give you Herr Wilson, an American genius!'

Ignoring Himmler's quiet sarcasm and the resultant nervous chuckles, Wilson shook the hand of the small, plump, balding Belluzzo and expressed his gratitude that he would soon be working with him. When the rest of the team had crowded around him to congratulate him on his work, which they had assessed for Ernst Stoll, Wilson said to Schriever, 'Few experiments work out the first time, and the fact that this particular saucer will not fly is of no great importance. What *is* important, Flugkapitän, is that you've already made such progress and that now, if we all work together, we can build successfully upon it. I therefore congratulate you, Flugkapitän, for building the first flying saucer.'

'Thank you, Herr Wilson.'

Schriever bowed stiffly, acknowledging Wilson's praise. Before anything else could be said, Himmler walked away from them and Oberleutnant Stoll urgently waved his hand, indicating that he and Wilson should follow.

Falling in beside Stoll, Wilson left the office and found himself standing in the great hangar, beside Himmler, who was facing Rudolph Schriever's skeletal flying saucer prototype and smiling in his mild, chilling way.

'You do not think it will work?' he asked.

'No, Reichsführer,' Wilson replied.

'Then you are very diplomatic, Herr Wilson, which means you are cunning.' He then turned to Wilson, looked up through his glittering pince-nez, and said, 'Flugkapitän Schriever, for obvious reasons, is still in charge of this project, but you are the one from whom we expect results. Once a week you will visit Wernher von Braun at the Rocket Research Institute at the other side of the firing range, and anything you have discovered that is of no use to this project but may be of use to von Braun, you will pass on to him, to be used as he sees fit.'

'I understand, Reichsführer.'

'You understand also, I hope, that I will be kept informed of your progress, or lack thereof, by Oberleutnant Stoll here' – he indicated the nervous Ernst Stoll with a nod of his head— 'and that anything you wish to discuss, you must discuss with him – not with Flugkapitän Schriever.'

'Yes, Reichsführer, I understand.'

'Good,' Himmler said. 'Now is there anything you want to know before I leave?'

Wilson glanced across the hangar, saw that mostly empty, valuable space, then returned his gaze to Himmler and said, 'My task is a large one, and apart from scientists and engineers, I am going to need hundreds of unskilled laborers. Where will I find them?'

Himmler adjusted the pince-nez on his nose, gazed across the vast hangar at the glittering skeleton of Schriever's saucer, then looked up at Wilson with a thin, icily controlled, deadly smile.

'The camps,' he said, almost whispering.

CHAPTER TEN

The administration buildings at Langley Field, Virginia, had been completed when Bradley made his next visit – officially as an advisor on aeronautical law, unofficially as one of General Dwight Taylor's intelligence agents – to attend a meeting of the recently formed National Advisory Committee for Aeronautics. Seated with him around the table in the main building were his old friend General Taylor, of the still too informal army air force intelligence branch, and the twelve members of the committee. Though most were Pentagon officers with technical backgrounds, also included were the aging yet still dapper Orville Wright who, in 1903, at Kitty Hawk, North Carolina, with his brother Wilbur, had made the first airplane flight in history; and Charles A. Lindbergh, the handsome, aristocratic flyer who had won the nation's heart when, in 1927, he had made the first nonstop airplane flight between two continents in his now-legendary monoplane, *The Spirit of St Louis,* then won the sympathy of that same nation when, four years ago, his two-year-old son had been kidnapped and murdered.

Since its formation, the committee had been meeting once a month to discuss national and international aeronautical developments. This day should have been no different from any other . . . but most of those present were looking shocked.

'Eighteen years ago,' a radio announcer was saying, 'dejected German soldiers retreated from France across the Hohenzollern Bridge spanning the Rhine. Twenty-two days ago, at eleven-thirty a.m. on March 7, 1936, three of Adolf Hitler's battalions crossed that bridge again, this time marching back into the Rhineland.

Within hours twenty-five thousand German troops had occupied the Rhineland, with no retaliation from the French. Today, March 29, 1936, again without benefit of guns, ninety-eight point eight percent of the electorate voted for Adolf Hitler, thus making him the Führer of all Germany. War in Europe is now virtually guaranteed . . .'

General Taylor turned the radio off, stared thoughtfully at it for a moment, then returned to take his seat at the head of the long committee table.

'Well, gentlemen,' he said, 'there it is. Adolf Hitler's now the absolute dictator of the Third Reich – and he's not going to be satisfied with the Rhineland. As the man said, this clearly means war in Europe.'

'War in Europe is not our concern,' said a silvery-haired gentleman from a cloud of cigar smoke at the end of the table.

'I think it is,' Taylor replied, 'to the degree that it affects Germany's interest in aeronautical research, which already is alarmingly advanced. Mike,' he added, turning to Bradley, 'what do you think?'

'I'm seriously worried,' Bradley said. 'The Nazis *are*, as you say, already dangerously advanced in aeronautical research – and I think it's safe to say that most of that research will now be turned toward its potential for warfare.'

'It still doesn't affect us,' the dapper Orville Wright said, 'since America is taking an isolationist stance – and Europe's a long way away.'

'I don't believe we can cling to isolationism for too long,' Bradley said, 'and as long as there's even the faintest possibility that we'll be involved in war, sooner or later, we should be seriously concerned about technological advances anywhere in the world – but particularly in Nazi Germany.'

'Your concern seems extreme,' a technical advisor said, puffing on his pipe and pursing his lips to blow the smoke out. 'Have you reasons for this?'

'For the past couple of years,' General Taylor said, 'Bradley, in an unofficial intelligence capacity, has been trying to track down someone for us – a mysterious physicist and aeronautical engineer called John Wilson, who once worked with Robert Goddard' – here the general glanced at Goddard's friend, Charles Lindbergh – 'before reportedly traveling to Germany to work for the Nazis, possibly under a false passport.'

'Bradley's already asked me about this John Wilson,' Lindbergh pointed out, 'and I had to tell him, honestly, that I'd never heard of him in connection with Goddard until Bradley himself mentioned him. Obviously, as Bradley had already done, I then checked with Goddard and received confirmation that Wilson had indeed worked with him in 1930 for approximately six months.'

'So what's so worrying about this fellow?' Orville Wright asked impatiently.

'What worries *me*,' Bradley said, 'is that according to even Goddard, this Wilson was a scientific genius with a particular interest in rocketry and space flight. He also appears to have been a completely unemotional, ruthless son of a bitch who didn't give a damn about anything other than his own work.'

'Sounds like your average scientist or politician,' someone said, thus encouraging a spasm of cynical laughter around the smoke-wreathed table.

When the laughter had died down, Bradley said patiently, 'What I'm trying to get across is that this mysterious Wilson, who's possibly a scientific genius and utterly ruthless, had reason enough, and is certainly fanatical enough, to contribute his genius to a foreign power, irrespective of its nature or motives. And it seems clear from the evidence that the country he's chosen is Nazi Germany.'

There was a long, uncomfortable pause until Charles Lindbergh said thoughtfully, 'Are you suggesting that this Wilson was actually more advanced in his thinking than Goddard?'

'Yes,' Bradley said without pause.

'I find that hard to credit,' Lindbergh said.

'So did I,' Bradley replied, 'but not any longer.' He pushed his chair back, stood up, and walked around the table, distributing to all the members of the committee typed copies of Wilson's *curriculum vitae.* While they were reading it, he lit a cigarette, smoked it, and gazed out the window, thinking of how far aeronautics had advanced since Samuel Pierpont Langley, American astronomer, secretary of the Smithsonian Institution, and aeronautical theorist (ironically also born, like Goddard and Wilson's father, in Massachusetts, where Wilson himself had attended MIT), had sent his quarter-scale, steam-powered 'aerodrome' into a flight over the Potomac River and these very fields, which had since been named in his honor. From those innocent beginnings, nearly forty years ago, a dark new age was dawning . . .

'Has everyone finished reading?' General Taylor asked, obviously impatient to continue.

Most of the heads, hazed in smoke, nodded affirmatively.

'It's certainly impressive,' Orville Wright said, 'but it doesn't prove that this man created anything out of the ordinary, in secret or otherwise.'

Aware of Wright's illustrious position in the history of aviation, that Charles Lindbergh had been forthright in his support of Robert H. Goddard, and that both men might therefore be more skeptical than most, Bradley said, 'While I can't confirm that Wilson worked on airships more advanced than those built officially, I think it's worth pointing out that during the period 1896 to 1897 – when Wilson had left Cornell University and disappeared completely to work, as we now know, on airship design and construction – America suffered what is now known as the Great Airship Scare.'

'I remember it well,' Orville Wright said. 'It lasted for months. There was a great wave of sightings of mysterious airships that were actually carrying passengers, or crew members, who reportedly spoke to the locals when they landed. At the time I put it down to mass hysteria.'

'Well,' Bradley said, 'maybe it was and maybe it wasn't – but certainly most of the reports of contact between the airship crews and the witnesses mentioned a crew member who called himself Wilson. Please, gentlemen, bear with me.'

Bradley withdrew from his briefcase the press clippings that Gladys Kinder had sent him, spread them out on the table before him, and talked while reading from them, one by one.

'As you all probably know,' he began, 'the first major UFO flap was indeed in 1896 – beginning about November of that year and continuing until May 1897. That was five years *before* the first experiments of Orville, here, and his brother, Wilbur; but there were, by that time, various airship designs on the drawing boards or in the Patent Office. For instance, according to my clippings here, on August 11, 1896, patent number 565805 was given to Charles Abbot Smith of San Francisco for an airship he intended having ready by the following year. And another patent, number 580941, was issued to Henry Heintz of Elkton, South Dakota, on April 20, 1897.'

'In all fairness,' Lindbergh said, 'you should point out that while many of the UFOs sighted were shaped roughly like the patented designs, there is no record of those airships having been built.'

'Okay,' Bradley said, 'I concede that – but the fact that there's no record of them doesn't necessarily mean they weren't built.'

'But the reported UFOs resembled the airships on the patented designs?' a disembodied voice asked from farther along the table.

'Yes,' Orville Wright said. 'At that time the general belief was that aerial navigation would be solved through an airship, rather than a heavier-than-air flying machine – so most of the earlier designs looked like dirigibles with a passenger car on the bottom.'

'Cigar-shaped.'

'Right.'

'Okay, Bradley,' General Taylor said. 'Please continue.'

'What stands out in the 1896–97 sightings,' Bradley continued, 'is that the unidentified flying objects were mostly cigar-shaped, that they frequently landed, and that their occupants often talked to the witnesses, usually asking for water for their machines.'

'I remember that,' Orville Wright said, still proud of his memory.

'Now, the most intriguing of the numerous contactee stories,' Bradley went on doggedly, 'involved a man who called himself Wilson – he never gave his first name.'

Bradley's throat felt dry, so he swallowed, coughed into his fist, then started reading again from his notes and clippings.

'The first incident occurred in Beaumont, Texas, on April 19, 1897, when one J. B. Ligon, the local agent for Magnolia Brewery, and his son, Charles, noticed lights in a pasture a few hundred yards away and went to investigate. They came upon four men standing beside a large, dark object that neither of the witnesses could see clearly. One of those men asked Ligon for a bucket of water, Ligon let him have it, and then the man introduced himself as Mr Wilson. He then told Ligon that he and his friends were traveling in a flying machine, that they had taken a trip out to the gulf – presumably the Gulf of Galveston, though no name was given – and that they were returning to the quiet Iowa town where the airship and four others like it had been constructed. When asked, Wilson explained that electricity powered the propellers and wings of his airship. Then he and his buddies got back into the airship and Ligon watched it ascending.'

'I get your drift,' Orville Wright said. 'That particular Wilson said he was returning to the quiet Iowa town where the airship and *four* others like it had been constructed – and *your* Wilson, the one in these notes, originally came from Iowa.'

Bradley just raised his hands in a questioning manner, then started reading again.

'The next day, April 20, Sheriff H. W. Bayer of Uvalde, also in Texas, went to investigate a strange light and voices in back of his house. He encountered an airship and three men – and one of the men introduced himself as Wilson, from Goshen, New York. Wilson then inquired about one C. C. Akers, former sheriff of Zavalia County, saying he had met him in Fort Worth in 1877 and now wanted to see him again. Sheriff Baylor, surprised, replied that Captain Akers was now at Eagle Pass, and Wilson, apparently disappointed, asked to be remembered to him the next time Sheriff Baylor visited him. Baylor reported that the men from the airship wanted water and that Wilson requested that their visit be kept secret from the townspeople; then he and the other men climbed back into the airship and, quote, its great wings and fans were set in motion and it sped away northward in the direction of San Angelo, unquote. Incidentally, the county clerk also saw the airship as it left the area.'

He glanced up from his notes to see what effect he was having on the learned gentlemen; thirteen faces stared attentively at him through a haze of cigarette and cigar smoke, so he lowered his gaze and started reading again.

'Two days later, in Josserand, Texas, a whirring sound awoke farmer Frank Nichols, who looked out from his window and saw brilliant lights streaming from what he described as a ponderous vessel of strange proportions, floating over his cornfield. Nichols went outside to investigate, but before he reached the large vessel, two men walked up to him and asked if they could have water from his well. Nichols agreed to this request – as farmers in those days mostly did – and the men then invited him to visit their airship, where he noticed that there were six or seven crew members. One of those men told him that the ship's motive power was highly condensed electricity and that it was one of five that had been constructed in a small town in Iowa with the backing of a large New York stock company.'

'So what we're talking about,' Lindbergh said, 'are five or six airships, originating in a small town in Iowa.'

'Right,' a granite-faced Pentagon general confirmed from a haze of smoke.

'The next day,' Bradley continued, 'on April 23, witnesses described in this *Houston Post* clipping as two responsible men, reported that an airship had descended where they lived in Kountze, Texas, and that two of the occupants had given their names as Jackson and . . .'

'Wilson,' General Taylor said with a sly grin.

'Right,' Bradley said, not returning the grin, but instead concentrating on his reading, which was making him feel oddly self-conscious. 'Four days after that incident, on April 27, the *Galveston Daily News* printed a letter from the aforementioned C. C. Akers, in which Akers claimed that he had indeed known a man in Forth Worth, Texas, named Wilson; that Wilson was from New York; that he was in his middle twenties; and that he was of a mechanical turn of mind and was then working on aerial navigation and something that would astonish the world.'

'That letter could have come from a hoaxer,' Orville Wright

pointed out with a jab of his finger, 'after he'd read the original story mentioning the unknown Akers.'

'Finally,' Bradley read, deliberately ignoring the famous, and famously testy, old man, 'early in the evening of April 30, in Deadwood, Texas, a farmer named H. C. Lagrone heard his horses bucking as if in stampede. Going outside, he saw a bright white light circling around the fields nearby and illuminating the entire area before descending and landing in one of the fields. Walking to the landing spot, Lagrone found a crew of five men, three of whom engaged him in conversation while the others collected water in rubber bags. The men informed Lagrone that their airship was one of five that had been flying around the country recently; that theirs was in fact the same one that had landed in Beaumont a few days before; that all the airships had been constructed in an interior town in Illinois – which, please note, borders Iowa – and that they were reluctant to say anything else because they hadn't yet taken out any patents. By May that same year, the wave of sightings ended – and the mysterious Mr Wilson wasn't heard from again.'

As Bradley gathered his notes and clippings together, there was a bewildered, or disbelieving, silence from those sitting around the table and either smoking or drinking water or beer. Eventually, when the silence became too obvious, Lindbergh propped his elbows up on the table, rested his chin on his clasped hands, and said, 'So what's being suggested here is that the mysterious Wilson of the so-called Great Airship Scare of 1896–97, who made frequent remarks about having constructed the airships – either five or six – in a small town in Iowa, is the same Wilson who worked for Robert Goddard and now works for the Nazis.'

Bradley shrugged and again raised his hands in a questioning manner.

'We're talking about a sixty-six-year-old man!' Lindbergh pointed out in softly spoken disbelief.

Unable to refute that point, Bradley said, 'I'm not saying it's definite, but it's certainly worth investigating. We *do* have proof that a John Wilson was born and raised in Montezuma, Iowa, and that when he left Cornell University, he was placed on the payroll of the New York financiers Cohn and Goldman, who owned an aeronautical research factory located in Mount Pleasant, Iowa. I should therefore remind you, gentlemen, that Mount Pleasant, while in Iowa, is practically on the border of Illinois – the other location given by Wilson for the construction of his airships – and that it's close to the town of Montezuma, where Wilson was born and raised. These could be coincidences, of course, but I seriously doubt it.'

There was another uncomfortable silence until Orville Wright, who did not smoke or drink, broke it with a fit of coughing, waved his neighbors' cigar smoke away from him, and said, 'So assuming that both Wilsons are one and the same, do we know what he's up to in Nazi Germany?'

'Yes,' General Taylor said, looking relieved to be on home ground. 'According to British intelligence, there are reports that an American scientist – identity unknown, but believed to be John Wilson, who disappeared in Germany in 1931 – is presently working in a secret research establishment at Kummersdorf West, about fifteen miles from Berlin.'

There was silence around the table for a moment, while they all took this in.

'Are there any known results of this collusion?' Orville Wright asked.

'We have an unverified report,' General Taylor replied, 'from a source who worked in the Rocket Research Institute at the other side of the army firing range that divided it from the more secret hangar in Kummersdorf West, that although even Wernher von Braun didn't know what was going on in that hangar, the American scientist, presumably Wilson, would visit him once a week to pass on to him any technical innovations he had discovered that might help in the development of what we believe to be the A-2 rocket program.'

'*Rockets?*' Orville Wright asked.

'Yes, Orville, rockets.'

Wright wrinkled his brow and looked almost shocked, then asked plaintively, 'But do we have to be *concerned* with such developments? Are they not simply pipe dreams, like those of Goddard?'

'Goddard's rockets are no longer pipe dreams,' Lindbergh said angrily.

'Well,' Taylor said in his quietly remorseless manner, 'we can't be too sure just how much Wilson's innovations have contributed to this, but we do know from British intelligence that as early as December 1934 – about a year after Wilson is believed to have started working at Kummersdorf – two highly advanced A-2 rockets, constructed at Kummersdorf, gyroscopically controlled, and powered by oxygen-and-alcohol-fueled motors, were launched from the island of Borkum in the North Sea and reached an altitude of one and a half miles. And I should make it clear, unpalatable as it may seem, that those stabilized, liquid-fueled rockets are the only known, serious challengers to the rockets of Wilson's old work mate, Robert H. Goddard.'

'I find this unbelievable,' Orville Wright said, looking unusually flushed.

'Believe it,' General Taylor replied shortly. 'In fact, just a few weeks ago, shortly after Hitler's infamous advance across the Hohenzollern Bridge, Captain Walter Dornberger, the head of the Rocket Research Institute, his assistant, Wernher von Braun, and their team of one hundred and fifty technicians demonstrated some more motors at Kummersdorf, including one with an unprecedented three thousand five hundred pounds of thrust. And while it was widely believed that the brilliant von Braun was responsible for this great achievement, he resolutely refused to take credit for it, insisting that others, whom he claimed he could not name, deserved most of the credit.'

'And you think von Braun was referring to those on the other side of the firing range?' Lindbergh asked.

'Yes,' Taylor replied. 'To those on the other side of the firing range in general – but maybe to Wilson in particular, since the most revolutionary advances have been made since his arrival at Kummersdorf.'

There was another awkward silence, which was certainly not the norm, and Bradley glanced at Lindbergh, who was gazing distractedly at the table, remembered the widely publicized kidnapping and disappearance of his child, and felt stricken with sympathy and shame.

He knew what the shame was and could certainly not disown it: He had promised Joan that he would never again let work come between him and her, let alone him and the children; but he knew that in the past year, even against his better judgment, he had let Wilson become an obsession that was keeping him away from his family more than he had planned. It was causing problems at home, as his obsession with legal work had done before – deeply wounding Joan and thus angering Mark and Miriam – and so, when he looked at Lindbergh, at that courageous and haunted face, he was filled with shame because he knew he was ignoring what Lindbergh had lost – the precious gift of a family.

As if reading his mind, Lindbergh looked up, stared directly at him, then, breathing deeply, almost wearily, returned Bradley's thoughts to the matter at hand by asking 'Can we take it that this Wilson is still at Kummersdorf?'

'Yes,' General Taylor said. 'According to British intelligence—'

'What would we do without them?' a muted voice asked sarcastically.

'According to British intelligence,' Taylor repeated, smiling knowingly at Bradley, 'the recent demonstration at Kummersdorf so impressed the German commander-in-chief, General Fritsch, that permission has since been given for Dornberger and von Braun to build an independent rocket establishment in a suitably remote part of Germany, where research and test firings can be carried out in the strictest secrecy. It's believed that the chosen site is near the village of Peenemünde, on the island of Usedom, off the Baltic Coast. It's also believed that the unknown American, whom we believe to be John Wilson, will *not* be going with the rocket team but will be left where he is, with the other members of his team – doing only God knows what, in Kummersdorf West.'

The final silence was far too long, filled with too much tension, and forced even Bradley, schooled in law and psychology, to try escaping it by gazing out the window at the cloud-streaked, iridescent blue sky over the green fields of Langley.

'So,' Lindbergh said, offering him a reprieve, 'we can take it that John Wilson exists and is working in Germany. However, we're not at war with Germany and Germany isn't at war with Europe – at least not yet – so what's the point of this meeting?'

He was staring directly at Bradley, his gaze concerned, not accusing; but Bradley, who could think only of Joan and his children – of the blessings he was abusing as he faced this tragic figure – was incapable of making a coherent answer. He thought of Lindbergh's murdered child, of all he had owned and lost, and realized that even understanding that, he, Mike Bradley, blessed with a loving wife and children, was letting his obsession with John Wilson threaten all he loved most.

He felt shame and a terrible helplessness, for he knew damned well that he wouldn't stop until this mystery was solved.

He would risk all for that.

'Let me put it another way, Mr Bradley,' Lindbergh said. 'Since you've investigated this case and called this meeting to discuss it, what is it that you're trying to tell us?'

'If we get into a war,' Bradley said, 'we might have to stop that man.'

'Stop him?' Orville Wright asked hoarsely.

'Yes,' Bradley said without thinking. 'Stop him dead in his tracks.'

Chapter Eleven

Ernst was unhappy as he hurried through the jostling shoppers in the Friedrichstrasse, late for his lunch appointment with Ingrid. In fact, he was slightly hung over, as he was so often these days, and was reminded, by the stout, red-cheeked housewives all around him, that the Berlin he now knew so well by night was very different from the more respectable city that the sun shone upon.

When the sun set on Berlin in this troubled year of 1937, powdered and rouged young men solicited in the yellow lamplight of the Kurfürstendamm, government officials and men of commerce rubbed cheeks with sailors and soldiers in dimly lit bars on the Motzstrasse, hundreds of men dressed as women and women dressed as men danced in the riotous ballrooms of the West End, the novel, the bizarre, and the perverse were nightly paraded before the noisy crowds in the Scala or the amusement palaces of the Wintergarten, the nightclubs, cabarets, revues, vaudeville shows, and erotic Tanzbars were packed with male and female prostitutes, pimps, transvestites, fetishists, homosexuals, and drug addicts. In general, while the National Socialists called for a new moral order, the spirit of decadent pleasure prevailed to a background cacophony of jazz, dancing feet, exploding champagne corks, screams, laughter, and tears.

A very different world, indeed – and one that Ernst had, in the company of his fellow SS officers, become increasingly familiar with in recent months.

He thought of this with a certain amount of shame when

he saw Ingrid sitting, in a fur-collared winter coat and broad-brimmed hat, at a table by the window of the Kranzler Café.

Haunted by vague snatches of memory from the previous evening's debauch ... Hot dogs and beer at the Scala with Willi Brandt and Franck Ritter, then naked girls at the Schauspielhaus, then Ritter embracing a drunken sailor by the toilet in a Tanzbar, then an opium dream of sensual perversity with the endlessly inventive, amoral Brigette ... Yes, haunted and guilty, he uneasily composed himself as he entered the café and joined Ingrid at her favorite table by the window.

'My dear,' he murmured, brushing her rouged cheek with his lips and then sitting facing her. 'Sorry I'm late.'

'You're always late,' she accused.

'I can't always guarantee getting away on time. My superior officers don't think that way. What are you drinking?'

'White wine.'

'Already? At lunchtime?'

Ingrid shrugged in an indifferent manner. 'It helps pass the time,' she said.

Not wanting her to drink alone, and feeling thirsty anyway, Ernst ordered a beer for himself.

'Shall I order lunch now?'

'I'm not really hungry,' Ingrid replied. 'Just get yourself something.'

Ernst shook his head. 'I'm not hungry either,' he said, still feeling ill from the previous evening and yearning only to slake his thirst with the beer. 'Still, I think *you* should eat. You don't eat enough these days.'

'I'm just dieting, Ernst.'

'For me?'

'For you.'

'That's nice,' he said.

Knowing she didn't mean it, he was also discomfited by her steady gaze. Though still green as jade, it was not as bright as it had been. Sitting in this particular café reminded him of the day he had proposed to her, the day Hitler became chancellor, and filled him with remorse and incomprehension at how they had both changed. They had been young and in love then, but now, four years on, they were saddened adults who seemed to have lost each other along the way. Ingrid was still pretty, but in a less sensual, more matronly way, and the darkness in her eyes came from disillusionment, caused mainly by him. He knew it and was wounded by it, but could do little about it, since he too had changed beyond repair, if not for the better.

Best not to dwell on that . . .

'So,' he said instead, 'how are the children?'

'They're fine,' she replied. 'They haven't changed much since last week. Ula complains that you only come home at weekends, but Alfred is still too young to miss you, so you needn't feel *too* bad.'

'You're being mean to me.'

'I'm not.'

'It's not my fault that I can only come home weekends. We're compelled to live in the barracks during the week, and that's all there is to it. I know it's not particularly nice for the children, but we just have to live with it.'

'You *like* being away from home. You can't wait to get back to your SS friends. When you're home, you have little patience with me or with the children. You're not nice at all, Ernst.'

'That's not true,' he replied.

Yet as he took his first sip of the beer the waitress had brought, he had to acknowledge that Ingrid was right. His daughter, Ula, was now three years old and beautiful, his son, Alfred, was a mere two months old and lively, but he saw them so rarely these days, he hardly knew them at all. He felt guilty over that but could not ignore Ingrid's charge that deep down he preferred not being home.

In truth, he now felt suffocated by Ingrid's presence – something that had begun after that dreadful weekend now remembered as the Night of the Long Knives. Ashamed of himself at the time, he now accepted the necessity of that bloody purge and could not tolerate the fact that Ingrid despised him for taking part in it.

For weeks after the purge, she had not let him touch her, meanwhile pouring scorn upon him; but later, after reluctantly surrendering to him and becoming pregnant with Alfred, she had rejected him with more finality than before.

'You have blood on your hands,' she had told him, 'so keep them off me. I don't want to be contaminated by you or what you represent. You've arrested and killed innocent people, once reluctantly, now willingly, and I can't bear the thought that my children will learn about what you do. Don't touch me. Don't ever touch me again. Take your pleasures elsewhere.'

Which is exactly what he had done. Which in turn was why he spent so much time with his comrades – not just in the barracks, as he insisted on pretending with Ingrid, but in the drunken, decadent pleasures of a Berlin unrestrained by moral values, in the nightclubs and cafés and erotic Tanzbars of the night; and, most irresistible of all, in Brigette's snakelike embrace . . .

Just thinking about Brigette made him feel sick with lust and shame, though he tried not to show that to Ingrid. After drinking some more beer, he placed the mug back on the table, wiped his lips, and smiled more casually than he felt.

'So, who have you arrested this week?' Ingrid asked him.

The remark wiped the smile from his face and filled him with anger.

'No one,' he said. 'As you know, I'm now based at Kummersdorf West, in charge of technical intelligence. My duties involve the gathering of information relating to foreign and domestic scientific research. I don't arrest anyone.'

'But you spy on the scientists you deal with. You keep your eyes and ears open.'

'Yes,' he said. 'Naturally.'

'You think it's natural to spy on people?'

'Not natural,' he said with a weary sigh. 'A necessity, Ingrid. Someone has to do it – and I take pride in doing it well.'

'But why do you have to keep your eye on our own scientists and engineers? Can *no one* be trusted these days?'

'It's not that bad, Ingrid,' he lied, knowing that in these

troubled times *no one* could be trusted, that the enemy within was always a danger, and that the importance of the work being done at Kummersdorf West called for even more vigilance. It would be more than his life was worth to tell Ingrid about Projekt Saucer and the strange American, Wilson, working there under a German alias, but when he thought about it, he did so with a mixture of awe and resentment.

He was in awe of Wilson's genius, about which he had no doubts, and resented the fact that those who worked with him – Schriever, Habermohl, and Miethe – were doing the work that he, Ernst Stoll, was better equipped to do.

'You wanted so much to be a rocket engineer,' Ingrid said, as if reading his mind, 'and instead you've become someone who reports on the achievements of others. That must really hurt, Ernst.'

The mockery, which rolled off her tongue with relish, was even more hurtful.

'I only hurt to give you pleasure,' he replied. 'I hope you're suitably grateful.'

'Don't be bitter, Ernst.'

'I can't help it,' he replied. 'You complain because I don't come home much and that I've little patience when I do come home – yet you do nothing but pour your scorn upon me. What makes *you* so superior?'

'I don't feel superior. I just despise you for the way you've accepted what the Nazis are doing.'

'If I didn't, I'd be imprisoned – or even shot.'

'That may be true, Ernst. But you don't accept it just because of that. Now you actually believe in it.'

'I believe in the Führer. He may not always be right, but he knows the end justifies the means – and I also believe that.'

'That's despicable,' Ingrid said.

Ernst simply shrugged. This argument could lead them nowhere. Each time they met it was the same, always ending in an argument, and already he yearned to be back at Kummersdorf, keeping his eye on John Wilson.

The American fascinated him – even frightened him a little. He was sixty-six years old, yet looked fifteen years younger, and his eyes, which were still bright with intelligence, were also as cold as ice. Ernst thought him slightly inhuman, a man divorced from normal emotions, but one whose genius, allied to obsession, was producing remarkable results in the hangars of Kummersdorf. In fact, the dream of a saucer-shaped aircraft was coming closer each day . . .

'What are you thinking?' Ingrid asked him.

'Nothing,' he replied, unable to discuss the American or Projekt Saucer.

'You're certainly not thinking of me or the children – that much I can tell.'

'Please, Ingrid, stop this.'

'Why? I'm enjoying it! I can tell by the dreamy look in your eyes that we're not in your thoughts.'

'You're trying to pick a fight.'

'It keeps me awake, darling. I need something to keep me awake while you sit there in front of me, hardly looking at me, probably yearning to be with your virtuous comrades and the whores you all play with.'

'Ingrid!'

'I know, Ernst! I know everything! Do you think I'm a fool? Did you really think I didn't know that when you were supposed to be sleeping in the barracks, you were getting drunk with your SS friends and probably picking up the whores in the Motzstrasse? Do you think I'm dumb, Ernst?'

'That isn't true at all!' he lied, shocked and angry that she had guessed what he was up to.

'Of course it's true, Ernst!' Her green eyes were bright with rage. 'That's why you're away from home so often. That's why you stay out half the night and come home exhausted. Those whores are in your clothes. They're in the pores of your skin. You can't wash the smell of them away, so don't try anymore. I don't want your damned denials, Ernst. I just want the truth.'

Why didn't he tell her? Get this marriage over and done with . . .

Because SS men didn't get divorced and have successful careers.

'Do we have to discuss this now, Ingrid? Can't it wait for a better time?'

'What better time? There *is* no better time. I wanted to get this off my chest, which is why I asked you to meet me here.'

'All right. So you've got it off your chest. Can we now change the subject?'

'No. That's not all I wanted to say. I also wanted to tell you that your work appalls me, your promiscuity humiliates me, and that if we must live together like this, let's quietly live separate lives.'

'We already do, Ingrid. You haven't let me touch you for months. I think that's separate enough – and it certainly explains why the whores you mention seem so attractive.'

And he couldn't help smiling when he said it, taking pleasure from vengeance.

Surprisingly, she returned his smile with one of her own.

'Good,' she said. 'I'm glad you find them attractive. That means you won't be too upset when I confess that I've been seeing another man for a while now – a nice man, ten years older than you, but so much kinder and decent. I just thought you should know.'

Ernst burned hot and cold, felt his whole body stiffening, then had to control the racing of his heart and a suffocating mixture of rage and humiliation. He wanted to kill her.

'*Why* did you want me to know?' he managed to ask.

'Because I've lived for too long with the knowledge of your philandering and now I want it out in the open.'

'You want revenge.'

'I've already had that, Ernst. That's how my affair started – though it isn't why it continued. I just came to care deeply for my lover and I won't keep it hidden.'

Ernst had to resist the urge to slap her face.

'You want a separation?' he asked.

'Yes,' she replied.

'You can't have one,' he told her. 'The SS doesn't approve

of divorce, so I won't even consider it. And if you try to go ahead with it, the SS will ensure that the children are handed over to me. Are you willing to pay that price?'

She looked at him with hatred. 'No, Ernst, I'm not. You know I'd never give up the children.'

'Then the marriage continues.'

'I won't give up my lover.'

'And I won't give up my whores. Let's just live our separate lives together and keep our mouths shut.'

The gleam of hatred receded, but her gaze remained antagonistic. 'I don't think we can do that,' she said.

'Perhaps not normally,' he replied, 'but I also had something to tell you – and clearly, in the light of this conversation, it's come at the right time.'

'Oh? What?'

He could not resist swelling slightly with pride. 'Reichsführer Himmler has plans for a special expeditionary force to travel by boat to the Antarctic early next year – and has personally suggested that I go with it.'

'The . . . *Antarctic?*'

'Yes.'

'For what purpose?'

'He didn't say,' Ernst replied honestly, though he knew that the expedition was in some way related to Projekt Saucer. 'He only suggested that he'd be pleased if I volunteered – which of course I did instantly. Now, Ingrid, you and I can live separate lives without too much pain – at least for a few months.'

He sat back in his chair and gazed steadily at her, finding it easier to hide his rage and humiliation behind a display of pride. Ingrid studied him at length, not sure if she should be pleased or not, then nodded in a thoughtful, accepting manner and said, 'Yes. I think that will be good for both of us. It's come at the right time.'

Ernst sighed and sipped some beer, thinking of how the blood from wounded emotions could be so easily mopped up . . . Yet even as that cynicism gripped him, he saw Ingrid's tears.

She sniffed, but failed to hold the tears back, so wiped them away with her hand and shook her head sadly. 'What happened, Ernst?'

The question drove a stake through his heart, and he writhed with the pain of it. He knew what had happened – Adolf Hitler – but he couldn't admit that now. The love they had shared had been destroyed by his devotion to duty . . . or, more accurately, by his fear of the consequences of disobedience. Now, when he saw Ingrid's tearful eyes, he understood that he was giving away what he valued the most: her love and his pride.

'Nothing in particular,' he lied, debasing himself even more. 'We just drifted apart. Let's say we both grew up.'

She quivered as if whipped, but then managed to control herself. 'I have to leave now,' she said in a distracted, conversational manner, 'and collect the children from my mother's. Can I take it you'll be home tonight for dinner?'

'No,' Ernst said, watching her dry her eyes and stifling his pain, 'I don't think I will be. Now that we're leading separate lives, I see no point in lying.'

Ingrid smiled bitterly and nodded, then wiped her eyes with a handkerchief. 'Are you leaving now as well?' she asked, standing up and glancing out at the wintry sunshine over the busy corner of the Friedrichstrasse and Unter den Linden.

'I have five minutes to spare,' he said, 'so I'll just finish my beer.'

'Just one, I hope,' she said without thinking.

'Yes, Ingrid,' he replied automatically. 'Just one, then I'm leaving.'

She leaned down to kiss him frigidly on the cheek, then waved good-bye and walked out.

How pretty she still is, Ernst thought helplessly, as he watched her departing through the dense crowds, looking elegant in her fur-collared, belted coat and broad-brimmed hat. How very attractive!

Then, with a grief that lacerated him, he ordered another beer.

* * *

The day became confused after that. Feeling cold after his
second beer, he decided to have a cognac and drank it while
brooding about Ingrid and life's disappointments. Ingrid was
disappointed with him and he felt the same about life in
general, and when he thought about that, after having another
brandy, he could only think of the American, Wilson, in the
hangar at Kummersdorf, creating the kind of aircraft that he,
Ernst, had once dreamed about . . . as a student at the Institute
of Technology, when he and Ingrid were still in love.

He thought a lot about John Wilson. The American
fascinated him. He was an old man, a *very* old man, kept alive
by his faith.

Yes: faith – what Ernst had once possessed, but lost – and
because of that, the American was working miracles while
Ernst simply observed him.

He felt sick just to think of it.

He not only feared the odd American, but also what he was
building.

A miraculous, saucer-shaped aircraft.

A terrible weapon.

Filled with an awe and resentment exaggerated by
drunkenness, Ernst, who had been given the afternoon off, had
too many brandies, then went to meet his SS comrades in a
Tanzbar recommended by Franck Ritter. Colored lights bled
through smoke, a tacky band was playing, and two practically
naked girls were performing an erotic dance with umbrellas.
Sitting at a table near the wall at the back of the room, Willi
Brandt was drinking a stein of beer and gloomily watching the
dancing girls while Franck Ritter, resplendent in his SS
uniform, was fondling the gaudily dressed transvestite sitting
beside him. Ernst joined them at the table, had another few
drinks, compared notes with Brandt on the various erotic acts
on the stage, then left in disgust when the insatiable Ritter led
the giggling transvestite by the elbow into the toilets.

'The elite of the New Order!' Ernst exclaimed. 'Is this what
we've come to?'

He and Brandt did a tour of familiar haunts, but ended up, as usual, in the White Mouse in the Französischestrasse in time for Brigette's evening performance. The revue bar was filled with uniformed officers of the Reichswehr and SS, plus fat-bellied businessmen and their whores, and they roared their approval and gave the Nazi salute when Brigette came on stage, almost naked except for a steel-studded, black-leather halter and gleaming jackboots, with a peaked military cap slanted rakishly over red hair and her tongue licking brightly painted, pouting lips.

She was grinding her hips lasciviously and cracking a bullwhip over the naked spine of the man who was crawling across the stage on his hands and knees. Brigette sat on his back, riding him like a horse, and she kept cracking the bullwhip and gyrating upon him until, when he was prostrate beneath her, she slowly, seductively removed her steel-studded, leather halter and let him reach up to her . . .

It was a crude, erotic performance, arousing the audience to fever-pitch, and though Ernst was disgusted and drank far too much brandy, he too was aroused by what he saw and could not wait to have her.

He had her soon enough – an hour later, in her apartment when she teased and tormented him, whispering 'My pretty boy! My sweet lieutenant!' and sent him into spasms of relief and bottomless shame. With her diabolical artistry, her finely controlled sense of debauchery, she helped him forget Ingrid, the loss of his career, the frustration and fear that he always felt at Kummersdorf when he saw Wilson working. He took Brigette like a savage, was in turn devoured by her, felt exultation and grief as he shuddered and spent himself, then rolled off her and thought of the Antarctic with unbridled longing.

He could hide from himself there.

Chapter Twelve

'Good afternoon, Herr Wilson,' Himmler said in his frostily polite manner. 'I am sorry to have had to bring you all this way, but I have good reason for doing so.'

'Naturally, Reichsführer,' Wilson said, taking the wooden chair at the other side of Himmler's desk in his room in the Pension Moritz and glancing out at the soaring, snow-covered Austrian Alps. He had been dragged out of bed that morning, flown from Berlin to Munich, put on a train to Salzburg, then brought here, to the picturesque village of Berchtesgaden, in a jeep driven by a blond SS moron. Himmler enjoyed pulling such surprises, but Wilson was not amused.

'Can I order you some herbal tea, Herr Wilson?'

'Thank you for considering my tastes, Reichsführer, but I've already had my morning tea and I don't drink after breakfast.'

Himmler seemed mildly amused. 'I know that you're careful about what you eat and drink,' he said, 'which may explain why, for a sixty-six-year-old man, you look remarkably youthful. In fact, you still only look about fifty, which is truly amazing.'

'Coming from you, Reichsführer, I take that as a compliment. It *is* true that I'm careful about what I eat and drink. I also believe that most people do too much of both, so I'm frugal even with what I permit myself.'

'Do you take vitamins?' Himmler asked with somber interest.

'Yes. I've done so all my life. I eat and drink the minimum, take vitamins every day, and meditate whenever I get the chance. In this way, I've managed to hold off the aging process, though it must come eventually.'

'And then?'

'With your continued backing of the SS medical experiments, I'm sure we will soon find surgical remedies for the aging process -- and when we do, I'll be one of the first to make use of them.'

'That would be a great gamble, Herr Wilson.'

'Not at my age,' Wilson replied.

Himmler smiled, then clasped his hands under his chin and said, 'You believe in the Superman, Herr Wilson?'

Wilson knew just whom he was dealing with -- an insane visionary -- but he also knew what he, personally, wanted -- and when he saw the priestly madness in Himmler's eyes, he was convinced he could have it.

'I believe that man's destiny is to evolve into the Superman,' he said truthfully, though not without regard for Himmler's ego, 'but that we humans, if not constrained by wasteful emotions, can hasten that process.'

Himmler nodded approvingly. 'Good,' he said. 'I believe in this also. We cannot let sentiment stand in the way of progress. We must eradicate man's imperfections -- if necessary, creating the New Man from the bones of the old. We must cleanse the earth by purifying the blood. We must exterminate the Jews and the infirm and maladjusted, use the lesser races as slaves to the Reich, create a race of pure Nordics. History will exonerate us. What we do, we do for progress. We are changing the course of history and aiding evolution -- and when we die, as surely we must, our achievements will live on. You and I understand this.'

'Yes, Reichsführer,' Wilson said, not interested in the Aryan race, but willing to use Himmler and his ilk to create his world of pure science, which is all he now lived for.

Perverse? Most certainly -- though he could live with that truth. All across Berlin, in the Reich's most august offices, were the other high priests of the demonic New Order: Hermann Göring, Joseph Goebbels, Rudolph Hess, Martin

Bormann – alcoholics, drug addicts, occultists, and degenerates – the very epitome of that gross irrationalism which Wilson so much abhorred. There too the Gestapo butchers, the drilled ranks of the SS, and all the torture and murder that went on every day in the basements. Wilson had to accept it. Science could not moralize. Those irrational brutes were no more than the means to achieving his ends. Progress needs its trampled bones. Death gives way to more life. Evolution knows neither right nor wrong and transcends ephemeral matters. So, he would work with them. In doing that, he could use them. And glancing out at the snowy slopes, then returning his gaze to Himmler, he felt nothing but hope for the future, the glow of fulfillment.

'Why did you wish to see me, Reichsführer?'

'I wish to take you on a little walk that I think will be instructive to you. But first, I would like to be informed about the progress of Projekt Saucer.'

'Now that the rocket teams have left for Peenemünde and we can use their facilities, we're making quicker, more definite progress. As you know, I decided to stop work on the larger flying saucer prototype and instead concentrate all our efforts on making a miniature version of it, which can be used as an antiaircraft weapon. The final drawings for that smaller saucer will soon be completed – in the next week or two.'

'Good,' Himmler said. 'And you think this smaller version will actually fly?'

'I know it will,' Wilson said firmly.

'What kind of antiaircraft weapon will it be?'

'As a miniature version of the larger prototype, it will be a small, flat, circular flying machine, powered by a turbojet engine. It can be used as an antiradar device that, by flying in the vicinity of an aircraft in flight, will overionize the atmosphere surrounding it and, by so doing, subject its radar to the adverse action of powerful electrostatic fields and electromagnetic impulses.'

'And if it works—'

'It will, Reichsführer.'

'– you can then construct a larger version without fear of it failing.'

'Exactly, Reichsführer.'

'And who contributed most to this final design? You, or the officer nominally in charge of Projekt Saucer – Flugkapitän Schriever?'

Wilson thought carefully before answering.

He was aware that his greatest innovations were likely to be stolen from him and passed on to the rocket scientists now at Peenemünde and other, even more secret SS research establishments. He understood, also, that Rudolph Schriever, who had more arrogance than scientific talent, was spying on him for Himmler and would, while doing so, also try to take credit for his achievements. For this reason, while pretending to be open with Schriever and his fellow engineers, Wilson had actually showed them only selected parts of his great work – just enough to convince them, and thus Himmler, that he was worth keeping on. Also, by letting them steal relatively minor aspects of his work to utilize in their own, otherwise largely worthless designs – and by then praising them individually, secretly, for those designs – he was subtly setting them against one another, which kept him in control.

Naturally, because Himmler trusted his young flugkapitän, Wilson could not inform him of this fact and instead said, 'I must confess that Flugkapitän Schriever was surprisingly innovative and contributed greatly to the final designs. He is an excellent physicist.'

Clearly pleased that he had chosen correctly, Himmler asked: 'And the others? How are they faring?'

'No problems,' Wilson replied, not wishing to show his contempt for his fellow scientists, but being careful not to praise them too highly either. 'Of course Habermohl and Miethe are only engineers, but their designs for various parts of the saucer have been quite helpful. Miethe designed the outer shell for the latest model and deserves a commendation for that alone.'

'I will see to it,' Himmler said, then gave a light sigh,

unclasped his hands, and pushed his chair back. 'So,' he said, standing upright, 'let us go for our short walk.'

He led Wilson out of the room and into the heavily guarded and crowded lobby of the rustic pension. Glancing across the room, Wilson saw the handsome, uniformed architect, Albert Speer, sitting on a settee and discussing the architectural plans spread out before him and his assistants. Himmler nodded coolly at him, then, when four uniformed SS guards had closed in around him, he led Wilson across the crowded lobby and out of the pension.

'Is the Führer here?' Wilson asked, having noted the strong contingent of armed guards inside and now noting the many more outside.

Himmler nodded in the direction of nearby hills where Wilson saw a figure in *lederhosen* walking through the snow, accompanied by a woman, whom he assumed was Eva Braun, and guarded by half a dozen armed SS troops.

'He's staying in the pension,' Himmler explained, 'while renovations are made to the Berghof. Come! This way, Wilson.'

Followed by the four SS guards, he led Wilson to a jeep that was parked right in front of the pension. When they were both sitting in the rear, one of the armed guards climbed into the front and drove toward the majestic, snow-covered slopes of the Kehlstein Mountains.

When they had left the village behind and were passing through the guarded gates of an area closed off by barbed-wire fences, Himmler waved to indicate the ugly dormitory barracks clinging to nearby slopes and said, 'Those barracks house hundreds of construction workers. This was once a solitary, very beautiful mountain valley, but it's now the auxiliary headquarters of our beloved Führer. In order to make this conversion, Bormann tore down centuries-old farms and numerous votive churches, despite the protests of the parishes. Also, despite further protestations, he confiscated state forests and made this a private area that extends from the floor of the valley to the top of the mountain and covers approximately two and a half square miles. Finally, with no regard to the exceptional beauty of the area, he turned forest paths into paved promenades, laid a network of tarmac roads through the formerly lovely landscape, and erected barracks, garage buildings, a hotel, a manor house, a complex for the growing number of our workers, then, finally, those ugly barracks desecrating the once-virgin slopes.' He glanced around him with satisfaction, adjusting the pince-nez on his nose and squinting into the sun. 'As a lover of beauty, do I disapprove of this?' he asked rhetorically. 'No, of course not! It's the German genius to do what's necessary, no matter the cost. Do you understand, Wilson?'

'Yes, Reichsführer, I do.'

Himmler nodded. 'Good!'

The sound of explosions reverbated around the valley as the jeep took a corkscrew bend, away from the Scharitzkehlalm ravine, then took the steep, winding road up the side of the Hoher Göll.

'They're dynamiting,' Himmler explained when Wilson glanced in the direction of the explosions. 'When war breaks out, as it must, Bormann intends having underground quarters for the Führer and those most important to him.'

'Very wise,' Wilson murmured.

The five-mile road that ran up to Hitler's *Teehaus* had been hacked out of the side of the mountain by the sweat of slave labor. It stopped at an underground passage blasted out of the mountainside, just below the summit. Following the armed guard, Himmler climbed down from the jeep and led Wilson along the underground passage, until they arrived at a copper-lined elevator, its shaft, about four hundred feet deep, hacked out of the solid rock. That elevator took them down to an immense, high-walled gallery, supported by baroque Roman pillars. At the end of the gallery, also hacked out of the mountain, was a dazzling, glassed-in, circular hall.

Standing in that great hall, looking out through an exceptionally tall, wide window, Wilson saw only the other snowcapped mountains and a vast, azure sky – an over-whelming experience.

'The impossible made actual,' Himmler whispered proudly, indicating with a gentle nod of his head that extraordinary view. 'If our dreams are grandiose, our actual achievements are more so – the achievements of men who can make the impossible commonplace. Come! Follow me!'

He led Wilson across to the panoramic window, from where they could look down on the snow-covered earth, with Berchtesgaden and Salzburg clearly visible in a mosaic of brown and white.

Pointing at a distant mountain peak, Himmler asked Wilson if he knew what it was. When Wilson shook his head, he said, 'That mountain is the Untersberg. According to legend, the Emperor Charlemagne still sleeps there and will one day rise again to restore the past glory of the German Empire. I believe that day has come – that our Führer is the reincarnation of Charlemagne and will return us to glory.'

He removed his gaze from the distant mountain and looked at Wilson through his glittering pince-nez. Wilson, who knew that he was mad, also knew not to smile.

'Now look down there,' Himmler said, pointing with his index finger, then sweeping his hand from east to west, to indicate the vast, snow-covered valley. 'Other than the villages and towns, what do you see?'

'Just the snow-covered earth,' Wilson said.

'Exactly,' Himmler said. 'And when war comes and we move underground, that is all you will still see – just the snow-covered earth.'

Wilson grasped instantly what the lunatic was driving at. ... The dream of the Thousand Year Reich had been born out of mysticism: the Cosmic Circle of Munich; the Anthroposophy of Rudolph Steiner; the Theosophy and Rosicrucianism of Vienna and Prague; a belief in Lemuria and Atlantis, ice and fire, Man as Superman ... Yes, he grasped what Himmler was thinking and now knew he could use him.

'You despise the weaknesses of mankind, don't you?'

Himmler said, staring steadily at him.

'Yes,' Wilson confessed.

'And like me, you believe in the evolution of the human race from Man into Superman.'

'Yes,' Wilson agreed, though he conceived of a superior race based on science, rather than a race of so-called Supermen based on the mystic strength of the *Volk* and other romantic, idiotic German theories.

'Do you know of the theories of the great Austrian cosmologist, Hans Hörbiger?' Himmler asked, his gaze unnaturally steady behind the glittering pince-nez.

'I don't believe so,' Wilson lied. Actually he was fully cognizant of the fact that Himmler revered the so-called unorthodox, obviously mad, Austrian cosmologist's theories on the birth of the universe and the destiny of Nordic man, but he didn't want Himmler to realize that he had checked him out and now knew so much about him.

'A great man,' Himmler said reverently. 'A man despised by the scientific fraternity of his day for speaking the truth.'

'I'm sorry,' Wilson said hesitantly, carefully. 'I just don't know—'

'No,' Himmler said abruptly. 'Naturally not. They would not have taught you his theories in the United States of America where, as even you know, the truth is rarely respected.'

'He was a cosmologist?' Wilson asked, as if confused.

'Yes,' Himmler replied. 'Hörbiger's theory is that the mass of free matter in the universe is in the form of frozen ice, that chunks of this ice periodically fall into stars and cause immense explosions, which in turn form planetary systems, and that since the world is formed from ice and the fiery explosions they cause – ice and fire, you understand? – it is the natural heritage of Nordic men.'

He glanced sideways, as if expecting a reply, and receiving none, continued melodramatically: 'Yes, Nordic men! *German* men! And Hörbiger believed that a return to such a world would eventually lead to men who were gods . . .' Mercifully, at that moment Himmler turned away to survey the snow-covered valley. 'A world of eternal ice,' he whispered portentously. 'A world under the earth!'

Quietly exalted by his vision, he turned away from the window, walked to the center of the vast room, then faced Wilson again.

'You are a man obsessed,' he said, 'so I know you will understand me. I do not envisage my SS as a commonplace police force, but as a religious order devoted to the creation of the Superman. Indeed, right from the start it's been my intention eventually to isolate the elite of the SS from the world of ordinary men for the rest of their lives. It is also my intention to create special colonies of this elite all over the world, answerable only to the administration and authority of this new order. My first step in the creation of this new elite was to create my special schools in the mountains of Bavaria, where the finest of the SS are indoctrinated in my ideals and convinced that they are men far finer and more valuable than the world has yet seen. My second step was the creation of the *Ahnenerbe* – the Institute for Research into Heredity –whose function is to finance and publish Germanic researches and to supervise the anthropological medical experiments on the inmates of the concentration camps. And my third and most important step is the *Lebensborn* – Spring of Life – which will, through the controlled mating of elite SS men and pure, Aryan women, breed out all imperfect traits from the German character and physique within one hundred years.'

He walked across the vast room, his footsteps echoing eerily, then stopped directly in front of Wilson, to stare calmly at him.

'And while all of this is happening,' he asked, 'where will I isolate the elite of my SS?'

Wilson turned to the side, to nod in the direction of the snow-covered valley below. 'In a world of eternal ice,' he said. 'A world under the earth.'

'Yes!' Himmler whispered. 'Correct! But not here. Not in Germany.' He walked to the window, pressed the palm of his hand against the glass, then turned back to Wilson. 'Our beloved Führer is anxious for a foothold in the Antarctic,' he said. 'For this reason, he is sending an expedition, commanded by Captain Alfred Richter, to the coast due south of South America. From there, seaplanes will be catapulted from the deck of our aircraft carrier *Schwabenland* with orders to fly back and forth across the territory that Norwegian explorers had arrogantly named Queen Maud Land. It is our intention to make a far more thorough study of the area than the Norwegians had done, to photograph as much of the area as possible, and to then claim the land for the Third Reich. When that is done, Herr Wilson, we will do there what we are about to do here and all over Germany – build underground quarters for the elite of my secret order and the slave labor necessary for our purposes.'

Wilson saw the insane grandeur of the concept – even though he knew it would not work. Then, even as he was formulating his own secret plans, Himmler approached him, took hold of his shoulders, and shook him with a rare display of passion.

'Do you now understand, Herr Wilson, why I am so interested in you? I will create the perfect man, you will create the perfect machine, and between us we can create a perfect society under the ice. Hörbiger's world of ice and fire turned into a reality! My perfect men, your pitiless science, and all the slave labor we require. *This is what you are here for!*'

He turned away to wave his right hand, indicating the snow-white earth, the hazy horizon, and the unseen Antarctic . . . 'Your flying saucer will take us there and protect us and finally give us dominion. Now let us go back down.'

Wilson, seeing his dream forged by a madman, followed Himmler out of the Berghof and back down the mountainside.

Chapter Thirteen

After eight weeks at sea, with another seven to go, Ernst had a craving for dry land that made a mockery of reason. Anchored in the South Atlantic Ocean, near the South Sandwich Islands, the *Schwabenland,* the command ship of the expeditionary fleet, had become his prison and home, always swaying and creaking. For most of the three weeks they were at anchor, Ernst's sole view of Antartica was of distant white peaks in a constant, sunstreaked haze beneath an azure sky as, on behalf of Himmler, he supervised the ruthless takeover of Norway's Queen Maud Land.

Daily for three weeks, two seaplanes had been catapulted from the deck of the fleet's aircraft carrier, to fly back and forth across those frozen wastelands, photograph the area, and, as ordered, drops thousands of sharp-tipped steel poles, all weighted at the tip to make them dig into the ice, with small swastikas attached to the other end. The thought of covering a vast expanse of the Antarctic with swastikas attached to steel poles seemed slightly idiotic, even comical, to Ernst, but he had his duty to perform and did it commendably, keeping his face straight, keeping his eye on his men, and receiving the film they brought back after taking aerial photographs of that same vast, icy, largely uncharted wilderness.

Surprisingly, they had found many areas free of ice, which is what Himmler had told Ernst he was particularly interested in.

He'll be pleased, Ernst thought sourly.

Divorced from dry land and the world he had known so well,

with little to do other than keep his eye on the men, Ernst spent too much time thinking about what he had lost – his engineering career, then Ingrid's love and respect – and brooding bitterly about how he was being used as a disciplinarian when he should have been working on Projekt Saucer with that oddly unfeeling American genius, Wilson.

God, yes! The American and Projekt Saucer . . . Already, it all seemed so far away, beyond the ever-distant, always-changing horizon, first shrouded in mist, then azure blue and silver striations, then blood that boiled out of the sun and poured over the ocean.

Ernst recalled it with disbelief and undeniable pride, since it had been, after all, his first journey away from home: the eerily gray Baltic Sea and the sickening swells of the English Channel, then the grim coastline of France and white-walled houses on the cliffs of Portugal, giving way to the volcanic peaks of the Canary Islands and the yellow, sun-hazed ribbon of Morocco . . . He had never been there, had not walked on foreign soil, and felt the loss more acutely, with a pain that surprised him, when the South Atlantic Ocean surrounded him, blue and green, its waves whitecapped, and offered a different light, more subtle colors, alien creatures, as the boat plowed through darkening waters into shadows cast by towers of gleaming ice.

He had seen all that and more, was disturbed and exalted by it, yet used it as his route of escape from the shame of his recent past . . . great blocks of rock and ice, flashing chasms of snow, a shroud made of dark, drifting cloud, a sudden, upthrusting glacier. Time passing and stopping. His gloved hands on the ship's railing. Then ice-encased mountains, seals and whales and pelagic birds, the air dazzlingly clear then the anchor being dropped in blue water where the sky was a mirror . . .

He had certainly left home far behind him.

Yet he wasn't made happy by it, because he was still unable to forget what he had lost in his private and public lives: the career he had wanted since childhood and the woman he still loved.

He had wanted to be a rocket engineer and gain Ingrid's respect.

And had failed on both counts.

Instead, he had become a military policeman and jaded degenerate, living only for instant thrills with willing ladies . . . or whores like Brigette.

Ah, yes, Brigette and Ingrid, his whore and his wife.

He thought about them night and day, but mostly at night, when he would toss and turn in his tiny cabin, on his uncomfortable bunk bed, listening to the splashing sea, the moaning wind outside the porthole, and drifting in and out of uneasy sleep punctuated by recollections and dreams of sensual experience. He thought of Ingrid with romantic longing, of Brigette with helpless lust, and spent himself shamefully in the darkness, with an adolescent's despair, hot-cheeked guilt, and irresistible self-pity.

The days were less tormenting, but certainly more boring, because all he could really do was patrol the creaking ship and check that his men were not up to mischief – which, given this particular location, was highly unlikely. He would never be a seaman and was easily confused and annoyed by the ship's bewildering array of hatches and bulkhead doors, steep steps and low-slung pipes, with its constant rumbling and groaning and creaking, its claustrophobic confines.

For this reason he could hardly endure even the common cabin, where he sometimes tried to read, and instead spent as much time as possible in the open air, watching the seaplanes being catapulted off the end of the nearest aircraft carrier, or coming in to land on that same, dangerously swaying deck, silhouetted in the sun's silvery striations or against the rippling, glassy sea.

If not the planes, a wandering albatross, flocks of prions, Cape pigeons . . . or the volcanic rock of the distant South Sandwich Islands, which, rising jaggedly on the horizon, looked like portals at the entrance to some awful world. The purgatory to which he would be condemned for his recent debauchery.

'God help me,' he whispered more than once to the night's starlit darkness.

Luckily, he was often joined in his lonely vigils by Captain Alfred Richter, the commander of the expeditionary fleet, a grizzled, disheveled, gray-haired, pink-faced veteran who enjoyed conversation, did not mince his words, and was volubly contemptuous of the people Ernst had come to revere.

'Remarkable!' he had said with a sneer during their first conversation, over dinner, in his cramped, smoky cabin. 'The Bavarian window cleaner has finally returned home – driving back into Vienna in his Storm Trooper uniform, giving the fascist salute, and welcomed by pealing church bells and hysterically cheering crowds who appear to be delighted that he's made their country a mere province of Germany . . . But since, four days later, their beloved Führer announced the so-called spring cleaning of Austrian Jews, I think we can assume that their cheering has tailed off into silence.'

Though shocked at such disrespect for the Führer he so admired, Ernst offered no protest, instead letting Richter break the monotony by rambling on about the madness of the Third Reich and those who controlled it.

'Drug addicts, sexual degenerates, occultists and mystics – the lunatics have taken over the asylum and called it the Third Reich. And who's in charge of the lunatics? Another two lunatics! Hitler and Himmler – two mild souls possessed by demons – one wanting to be God of a pure Aryan earth, the other hoping to create the Super Race with a bunch of blond morons. These are leaders of men?'

If Richter despised the Third Reich and all it aspired to, he was particularly venomous about the man who had dreamed up this Antarctic expedition – namely, the Reichsführer, Heinrich Himmler.

'A madman!' Richter rasped. 'He belongs in an insane asylum! Unlike you, I don't know him personally, but I know what I've heard. He's a bureaucrat of demonology, an administrator of inane dreams, a superficially cool customer who thrives on demented enthusiasms – mesmerism, reincarnation, clairvoyance, runes, the Thousand Year Reich, the possibility of turning mortal men into immortals, the search for Hörbiger's world of ice and fire – and this lunatic shares his dreams with Hitler, who is equally mad!'

At first Ernst was outraged, as if hearing blasphemy, and he turned away, hiding his flushed cheeks, and looked out to sea. An immature albatross had been circling out there for hours, always close to the surface, supported by the updrafts of air produced by the whitecapped swells. It made Ernst remember the wonders of aerodynamics and the work going on in the hangars of Kummersdorf – with the American genius, Wilson, the German egomaniac, Schriever, the ailing Italian physicist, Belluzzo, and their engineering assistants, Habermohl and Miethe – and filled him with a healthy flush of resentment at what Himmler had done to him.

Instead of working as an engineer with Projekt Saucer at Kummersdorf, he was supervising the dropping of flagged poles into the Antarctic wilderness.

It wasn't even a joke.

'A world of ice and fire?' he asked Richter to distract himself. 'Is that why we're here?'

Richter laughed sardonically. 'What do you think?' he said. 'Has he not told you what he believes in? His mad dream of the Super Race?'

'No,' Ernst replied honestly, 'he hasn't. He only gives me his orders.'

So Richter told him about Himmler, about his bizarre faiths and dreams, pointing out that his SS was essentially a religious order, that his men were bound by blood and oath, and that he wanted to isolate them, to brainwash them and remold them, to mate them with the purest German women and produce blond perfection, then forge those already perfect men in the strengthening flames of eternal war.

'He used to process chickens,' Richter said with a sneer, 'and now he wants to process people. He has a dream of a disciplined order of masters and slaves – the masters like human gods, the slaves to do their bidding – and he wants them in a world of ice and fire, which is where we are right now. The fire is the endless war that Himmler hopes to wage – he believes, after all, that war keeps a nation strong – and the ice is right here in the Antarctic, which he views as the natural home for Nordic man.'

They were now on the open deck, looking across the ice-filled sea, and Richter waved his hand to take in the distant peaks and glaciers, obscured in a white haze.

'That's why he wants this place – as the secret base for his new order. He wants to finish here what he began in the Wewelsburg Castle – his secret society, a Black Jesuit order, with its Death's Head insignia, reversed swastika, and occult rites, dedicated to the re-creation of the Germanen Order, which he views as the Super Race. The man is mad – and unstoppable.'

Ernst cast his gaze southward, looking beyond the Antarctic Convergence, where dark clouds hovered over an oasis of light and frozen mountain peaks and ice falls, which, being dimly perceived, looked like part of a mirage. He tried to visualize that vast wasteland, the brown earth between ice and snow; then he pondered the possibility of the finest of his SS comrades being imprisoned and trained there and set free only when called upon by their leader, the Reichsführer Heinrich Himmler, to set a torch to the world of normal men and turn history to ashes.

Himmler . . . and Wilson . . . and Projekt Saucer . . . in a world of Eternal Ice.

'Areas free of ice,' he whispered to Richter, though really addressing himself. 'He specifically asked us to find areas free of ice. Places where we could land.'

'Of course!' Richter exclaimed. 'Why do you think he's claiming that land for the Third Reich? Photographing it? Having it mapped out?'

'I'm not sure. I—'

'*Lebensraum* – space! – German conquest and

expansionism. That madman wants to come here, to bring his Death's Head SS here. He wants to isolate them from the world as completely as possible – well beyond the reach of normal men – and what could be more removed and isolated than that hellhole of snow and ice? He'll create his new order there, beyond the influence of the human world, and those who're raised there will know nothing but what they're taught. They'll be raised and trained for war, and nothing *but* war – the eternal conflict that Himmler thinks is necessary to an order of Supermen.'

Richter rubbed his frozen nose. 'Do you understand, Stoll? It's Hörbiger's so-called cosmic world of ice and fire – and Himmler hopes to create it out there, in that frozen world, underground. That's why we're stealing Queen Maud Land.'

Ernst finally understood and was struck dumb with the knowledge – simultaneously overwhelmed by the grandeur of the concept and deeply shocked that he had learned about it only through this old naval captain, whose contempt was appalling.

Avoiding Richter after that, he stayed alone as much as possible, thinking of Wilson's flying saucer, potentially the world's most powerful aircraft, and relating it to this Antarctic expedition and the search for ice-free land.

Himmler's world of fire and ice – the flying saucer and the Antarctic . . . The flying saucer was the machine of the future . . . and that future was here.

Ernst was awed by the concept.

On the final day of the expedition, just before the fleet turned back, Ernst, as instructed by Himmler, took the rear seat in a seaplane and had the pilot fly him to the Antarctic and land on an ice-free area in Queen Maud Land.

It was not a long flight, but it seemed almost magical, transporting him abruptly from sunlit space to snow-filled wilderness, black shadow, blinding light, a great silence, the gleaming Nothing, and when the skis of his aircraft slid along the ice cap, he felt that he was on another planet – vast and desolate . . . dead.

The Antarctic, spread out all around him, looked boundless and unreal.

Another world for the taking.

He made the pilot stay in the aircraft while he climbed down alone, glanced around that alien landscape of icefalls and glaciers and snowbanks and polar plateaus – all frighteningly empty and hauntingly silent – and then solemnly unraveled a larger swastika from its frozen steel pole. He hammered it into the ice-free soil, working awkwardly with his gloved hands; then, breathing steam, he stepped back to give the Nazi salute.

'I now claim this land for the Third Reich and name it Neuschwabenland.'

His embarrassed, whispered words were still echoing eerily around him when he climbed back up into the seaplane and let the pilot fly him away from what could be his future home.

That thought chilled his soul.

Chapter Fourteen

Bradley was relieved to step out of the sweltering June weather of the town of Des Moines, Iowa, and into the air-conditioned coolness of the immaculately clean, modern nursing home. When he told the white-uniformed receptionist behind the desk that he had an appointment with a resident, Abe Goldman, she smiled pleasantly, checked her register, said, 'Yep!' and hit the button of the bell on the desk with the palm of her hand. 'I'm calling someone to take you in there,' she explained. Then, when she saw him fingering his sweaty collar, she asked, 'Are you from out of state, Mr Bradley?'

'Yep,' he replied, amused by her air of amusement.

'Can't stand the humidity, eh?'

'No, not really. It can get pretty hot in Connecticut, but it's never this humid.'

'You know New York?'

'Yep.'

'I've only seen it in the movies.'

'It looks just like it does in the movies.'

'Gee, I'd just love to go there.' She was middle aged and attractive and reminded him of Gladys Kinder, so he was glad when a male attendant arrived and said, 'Someone for Abe?'

'This nice gentleman from New York,' the receptionist said. 'The one sweating too much.'

'Can't stand the humidity, eh?' the male attendant said with a broad grin.

Bradley just shook his head.

'You'll soon cool down in here,' the attendant said. 'Okay, sir, follow me.'

Bradley was in fact already cooling down in the air-conditioning when the attendant led him away from the lobby, along a well-carpeted corridor, through an expansive community room filled with old people, many wearing dressing gowns, and out onto a patio overlooking a smooth green lawn.

'You a relative of Abe's?' the attendant asked, leading Bradley along the patio.

'No,' Bradley replied.

'He's one of our favorite residents,' the attendant said. 'A real old-time character – though not originally from here-abouts.'

'No, he was originally from New York.'

'That's right,' the attendant said, stopping when they reached the shaded end of the patio, where an old man was sitting in a wheelchair. He had lively, pugnacious, Jewish features and a mop of surprisingly thick gray hair. He was dressed in a vivid, sky-blue dressing gown and smoking a cigar. 'Abe,' the attendant said, 'here's your visitor. Mr—'

'Bradley. Mike Bradley.'

Abe Goldman removed the cigar from his pursed lips and squinted up through a cloud of smoke. 'The guy from Wall Street, eh?' he asked rhetorically, raising his hand.

'That's right,' Bradley said, shaking the old man's hand and surprised by the strength of his grip. 'It's good of you to see me.'

'Not at all,' Goldman replied, waving Bradley into the chair facing him. 'It's not often you meet a stranger in this asylum, so I'm happy to see you.'

'It's not an asylum,' the attendant corrected him.

'No,' Abe said, 'it's a *nursing* home. Only the people who run it are crazy; *we're* just old and decrepit.'

He quivered with soundless mirth as the attendant grinned at Bradley, shook his head in a rueful manner, then said, 'Enjoy!' and walked away. Bradley settled into his chair facing the grinning old man, whose thick-lashed brown eyes were still bright.

'So,' Goldman said, 'you said on the phone you wanted to talk about my old company.'

'That's right. Goldman and Cohn. Based and registered in New York, back in the nineties. A finance company, I gather.'

'Yep.' Goldman shook his head emphatically. 'Old Jack and me, we made a goddamned fortune and retired at an early age. Of course, Jack,' he said, blowing a cloud of smoke, 'kicked off a few years back. He didn't smoke or drink, that was his problem – living clean isn't good for you.'

'I'll try to remember that,' Bradley said.

'You do that, son. Pearls of wisdom from the ancients. Now what did you want to know?'

'Is it true that your company was involved in the financing of airship designs?'

'It sure is, son. And it's what made us rich. There was a lot of loot in airship designs if you knew which hands to shake.'

'You built a secret research center here, in Iowa, didn't you?'

'Yep. That's why I'm retired here. Jack Cohn and I, we both came out here in the nineties, to supervise the research center – then, when we had to close it down, we decided to stay on. Our wives and kids loved it here.'

'I want to ask you about that – about why you closed the plant down – but first I want to know if your chief aeronautical engineer was a guy named John Wilson.'

'I do believe it was. I'm not good at remembering names, but I'm good at the faces and I'd never forget that engineer – he was a weird one, I tell you.'

'Weird?'

'He surely was – though he was also the most brilliant designer we'd ever used. Miles ahead of the others.'

'What do you mean by weird?'

Goldman inhaled and puffed, looking thoughtful. 'Not too sure,' he said. 'Such a long time ago. At my age, memory plays some awful tricks. Not reliable, son.'

'I don't mind,' Bradley said.

Goldman puffed out his cheeks and blew more smoke; he had a lot of it in there. 'Brilliant,' he reiterated. 'But cold. Cold as ice. Something almost inhuman about him there. Always well mannered and pleasant, but not really concerned. He *saw* people – he watched them like a hawk – but he never seemed to *feel* anything.'

'Obsessed with his work?'

'Christ, yes. It was bread and water to him. He had nothing *except* his work. I remember once asking him about his childhood – you know, I thought he might have been mistreated as a child or something – and he said no, that his parents had been fine, he just hadn't been interested, that's all. Life, he said, was too precious to waste on small things, or the *ordinary*, and his parents, while decent, had been ordinary, so he lost interest in them. He thought that people wasted their lives, that most of them were too emotional, and that the mind and what it could achieve were all that really mattered in life. Any human activity that didn't have a specific, evolutionary purpose was to him a complete waste of time, maybe even degenerate. You know – sports, games, romantic love, kids, reading for fun – you name it – if it wasn't somehow advancing science or evolution, it was pretty despicable.'

'Yet he was well mannered and polite.'

'Right. You couldn't even prod him to anger. I *do* remember him telling me that any emotion that blurred objective thought was an unhealthy emotion. He didn't involve himself with people – he worked with them or studied them – and although he had some women in his life, I think they were just there for the sex – a way of scratching at the one distracting itch he couldn't get rid of.'

'He wasn't married?'

'No – and never had been.'

'A real loner.'

'More like a recluse. I don't think we socialized once – we only met to discuss work – and even then, it was always at the research center.'

'How did you find him?'

'Me and my partner – Jack Cohn, God rest his soul – were looking for someone, preferably young, bright, and willing to work cheap, to design passenger-carrying airships, which we were convinced would revolutionize transport. So, we placed an ad in various newspapers, asking for aeronautical engineers, and Wilson called and we fixed up a meeting. He'd just graduated from Cornell University, in Ithaca, New York, which was convenient, since that's where we were based. Anyway, we met him and he impressed the hell out of us – he was so obviously brilliant – and we had no hesitation in putting him in charge of our airship development project.'

'Why did you move it all the way from the East Coast to here?'

'Wilson's idea. In those days, you know, there was an awful lot of experimentation going on – patents flying all over the place – and so all of us were obsessive about protecting what we were doing. Lots of secrecy, right? So we wanted our project to be kept under wraps and preferably located well away from the prying eyes of our competitors. Jack, I think, suggested California, but then Wilson said he knew of this great place near where he'd come from – in the wilds of Iowa, near the Illinois border – and when he also informed us that land and property there were cheap, we bought the idea. We sent Wilson out here to find us what we needed, and he came up with the plant in Mount Pleasant. We not only built the plant there, but took all our workers from the area – which meant there was no gossip back in New York.'

'When was that?'

'About 1896. Thereabouts. My memory's not all that good, you know. It's as flimsy as I am.'

Bradley grinned. 'And did you actually design some workable airships?'

The man inhaled more smoke, nearly choked and coughed it out, stubbed the butt of the cigar out in an ashtray, then wiped his watery eyes with his fingers.

'He sure did,' he confirmed, nodding emphatically. 'Five in all, with one uncompleted by the time the project closed.'

That figured, Bradley thought. All the reports about Wilson during the Great Airship Scare had reported him as saying that five or six airships had been constructed in Iowa, near the Illinois border. So five had been completed, one left unfinished, in Mount Pleasant, Iowa.

'What were they like?' he asked.

'Dirigibles,' Goldman replied. 'The most advanced of their time. The hot-air balloon was contained inside a cigar-shaped aluminum structure and powered by Wilson's internal combustion engine and propellers, all of which were fixed ingeniously to the gondola. The five completed models were secretly test-flown throughout the second year of the project – I think, 1897 – but of course we couldn't keep 'em invisible, so they caused quite a stir.'

'The Great Airship Scare of 1897.'

The old man shook again with silent mirth. 'Right,' he said, when he had managed to control himself. 'Those test flights were made about three years before Zeppelin flew his first model and over six years before the first heavier-than-air flight of the Wright brothers – but they were undertaken in as much secrecy as was possible under the circumstances. Wilson nearly always took the airships up at night, but he often had to land to ask for water for his airship's engine – and in doing that he scared a helluva lot of people. Of course, some of his crewmen really enjoyed the whole thing – you know, reading about themselves as possible invaders from Mars and so on. It was all a bit of a joke to them.'

'Not a joke to the nation,' Bradley observed, remembering what he had read about the great scare.

'Right,' Goldman replied. 'Someone even managed to get some photographs when one of Wilson's airships flew over Rogers Park in Illinois. Those photographs were reproduced in a couple of newspapers – the *Chicago Times-Herald* and *The New York Times,* as I remember – and that really turned the airships into a sensation.'

'Yet they weren't seen after 1897. Why?'

'Wilson destroyed them.'

'Pardon?'

'You heard me. That mad bastard destroyed his own creations. He was utterly ruthless.'

Bradley was just starting to wonder if Goldman was insane when the old man glanced furtively left and right, then leaned forward with a sly grin on his face.

'You don't believe me, uh?'

'I'm beginning to believe this Wilson was capable of anything . . . but that seems a bit too much.'

'You want me to show you something really special, Mr Bradley?'

'*Show* me?'

'Yeah, show you. I could do with a day out of here – and it's still only morning. If you're willing to drive eighty miles and back I'll show you what he was up to.'

'Where would we be going?'

'Toward Mount Pleasant, of course, where my construction plant was located.'

'I've already checked it out,' Bradley said, 'and didn't find a damned thing. Your plant's long gone, Mr Goldman. Every last sign of it.'

Goldman grinned again and winked, then shook his head from side to side. 'No,' he said. 'Not there. You looked in the wrong place. Wilson had this other hangar, his secret place, that even I didn't know about until he was long gone. You want to see what Wilson was doing behind our backs? Then let's head for Mount Pleasant. I could do with a day out.'

'It's a deal,' Bradley said.

They had a pleasant drive, out of Des Moines and along a seemingly endless straight road, past the rambling farmsteads that dotted the green and brown hills, toward where an azure, white-clouded sky met a silvery horizon. Abe Goldman loved it, beamed with pleasure beside Bradley, and kept leaning sideways, to put his weathered face near the rolled-down window, all the better to receive the rushing wind, fresh air, and hot, burning sun.

'This is what I left New York for,' he explained, breathing deeply and gratefully.

Though Bradley was burning with impatience, he didn't press the old man to talk anymore about Wilson and his airship project, but instead let him engage in routine conversation about the weather, the changes in the country in general and New York in particular, and anything else that took the voluble Abe Goldman's fancy. They were on the highway to Iowa City, which made an easy drive, but turned off an hour later and took a road that ran as straight as an arrow between golden fields of wheat and corn, to Montezuma, where Wilson had been born.

As Abe Goldman now wanted lunch, Bradley stopped at a diner on the edge of town.

Helping Abe out of the car, Bradley recalled his visit to this town a few years back, when he had gone to the farm that had once belonged to Wilson's parents and found it still operating, its clapboard house recently repainted and gleaming white in the sunlight.

'The man now running the Wilson farm,' he explained to Abe as they entered the diner, 'is the son of the people who bought it from Wilson's father shortly after his wife, Wilson's mother, died and he decided to move to Worcester, Massachusetts, where *he* had been born.'

'A lot of people need their roots,' Goldman replied.

'Not Wilson,' Bradley said.

'Even Wilson,' Goldman insisted. 'He may not have returned to his hometown, but he came back to the state. That's close enough, partner.'

Faced with the possibility that Wilson might, after all, have had some sentimental leanings, Bradley felt more confused when he entered the diner and sat down to lunch with Abe Goldman. They both had hamburgers and french fries, with lots of relish and salad on the side. For such a fragile old man, Abe had a surprisingly healthy appetite, enjoying his food.

'So are you going to tell me why Wilson destroyed his own airships?' Bradley finally asked him.

'Sure,' Abe said. 'Seems unbelievable, right? But that son of a bitch was the most ruthless guy I ever met.' Abe munched on his burger, washed it down with Coca-Cola. 'The reason the airships spotted in 1897 weren't seen again is that the designs Wilson gave me and Jack Cohn to patent were for unworkable airships. He patented the *real* designs under a couple of pseudonyms. Of course, we didn't know about this – nor did we know that the son of a bitch was selling his genuine designs to some industrialist in Germany, almost certainly with an agreement to ensure that our airships were destroyed. We only figured this out later. First, the engines of our airships were blown up by an unknown demolition expert, obviously Wilson. Second, Wilson disappeared, leaving only his ingeniously faked drawings, from which we couldn't reconstruct his particular internal combustion engines and structural designs. Third: A couple of years later the first German airships took to the sky and were clearly based on Wilson's designs.' Abe grinned and shook his head in helpless admiration. 'By that time,' he continued, 'since we'd nothing to sell, Jack and me had gone bust and were too busy making our money back in other fields to pursue the son of a bitch through the courts.'

'But you knew what he was up to during that time?'

'Sure. He used the money from the sale of his patents to open his own research establishment across the state line, in Illinois. We could never verify what he was up to there, but there were certainly some odd rumors over the next few years, most notably that by 1903, just before the Wright brothers made their first successful flight at Kitty Hawk, Wilson had secretly produced even more advanced aircraft, reportedly turboprop biplanes, that had actually managed to cross the Atlantic Ocean.'

'He couldn't have done that without US government help.'

'Well,' Abe said, obviously enjoying his startling revelations, 'everything was wide open then – it was early days for aviation, with not too much legislation – so he could have done it with *clandestine* government aid. Then, of course, he went that little bit too far and that led to his downfall.'

'A little bit too far?' Bradley was amused by the triumphant glint in old Abe's eyes, but he was also intrigued. He had never heard anything like this in his life, and it made Wilson seem almost diabolically ruthless and even, in a chilling way, awesome.

Having finished his large lunch, Goldman sat back, lit a cigar, and puffed a cloud of foul smoke.

'There were rumors,' he said, 'about highly advanced experiments with the problem of the boundary layer – and even dangerous experiments with atomic propulsion. Regarding this, there's one year I haven't forgotten and won't *ever* forget.'

'Yes?' Bradley inquired, his amusement tinged with growing impatience at the old man's teasing.

'In 1908,' Goldman said, 'shortly after the world celebrated Louis Blériot's widely publicized flight across the English Channel, from Calais to Dover, there was a great explosion in the Tunguska region of Siberia – an explosion so big that some believed it had been caused by a crashing meteor or alien spacecraft. The reason for that mysterious explosion has never been found – but I can confirm that there were whispers in aeronautical and related circles that it'd been caused by the failure of one of Wilson's more dangerous experiments: when his mostly highly advanced experimental aircraft, reportedly powered by some primitive, faulty form of atomic propulsion, malfunctioned – possibly in conjunction with damage caused by the uncontrollable vibrations of the boundary layer – in an otherwise astonishingly successful flight from these here United States to goddamned Russia.'

Feeling chilled to the bone while hot sunlight poured through the window, Bradley was just about to express his disbelief when Goldman, finishing off his Coca-Cola, wiped his lips with the back of his hand and said: 'While that could either be the true explanation for the Tunguska explosion or pure science fiction, what *is* for sure is that shortly after the so-called most frightening, inexplicable phenomenon of the twentieth century, Wilson's plant in Illinois was closed down by the US government, all of his designs – or at least those they found – were either classified as top secret or destroyed, and Wilson was offered work with the US government.'

'Which he didn't take.'

'No,' Goldman confirmed without hesitation. 'Apparently deeply embittered – can you imagine how *we* felt? – and with the Great War underway, he left Illinois for good and, according to occasional reports, spent the next decade drifting from one small aeronautical company to another, keeping his light under a bushel, but making a good living by selling his smaller, less important innovations to commercial airline companies and construction plants, and finally going to work for six months with another pioneering genius, Robert H. Goddard.'

'Which is where I came in.'

'Pardon?'

'Nothing,' Bradley said. He was beginning to feel a bit unreal. He glanced at his wristwatch, noted that time was running out. 'Are you finished, Abe? I think we'll have to get going.'

'No sweat,' Goldman said.

Once back in the car, they drove for another hour, arrived at Sigourney, which seemed sleepy in the afternoon light, then passed the road signs for Washington and Wapeelo and eventually headed along an empty road that cut through a quiltwork of green and gold, lawns of finely mowed grass, more fields of corn and wheat beyond which, Bradley knew from his previous visits, lay the rolling green fields of Mount Pleasant.

Thinking of that place, and of the airships constructed and destroyed there, Bradley suddenly realized that he might be on a wild goose chase, led by a senile old man.

'If Wilson destroyed his airships,' he said, expressing his despairing thoughts, 'what can you possibly show me now, Abe?'

Goldman was unfazed. 'Remember me telling you about the rumors that Wilson had constructed a highly developed aircraft that had actually managed to fly as far as Russia?'

'Yes,' Bradley said. 'The one with some primitive form of atomic propulsion.'

'Right,' Goldman said, pleased. 'Well, that aircraft certainly wasn't any kind of goddamned *airship*.'

'Naturally not,' Bradley said. 'Probably some kind of advanced airplane.'

'Exactly,' Goldman replied. 'When that son of a bitch was making airships for us, he had already superceded them and was secretly experimenting on his *own* project in another hangar, well away from our establishment at Mount Pleasant. It's my belief that that project was for the construction of an aircraft designed solely to conquer the boundary layer and be powered by some form of atomic propulsion. I think that a miniature version of such a craft, remote-controlled, was tried out in 1908, flew as far as Siberia, then malfunctioned and blew up over the Tunguska forest.'

'Jesus Christ,' Bradley whispered without thinking.

'You're impressed?' Goldman asked.

'Yeah.'

'Then stop being impatient and keep driving. You *want* proof? I'll *give* you proof!'

Shortly after they passed the sign indicating Mount Pleasant, Goldman coughed more cigar smoke from his lungs, hammered his chest with his fist, then jabbed a finger at a narrow side road and said, 'Turn up there, son.'

'We're not going to Montezuma?' Bradley asked, confused.

'You've already been there,' Goldman reminded him, 'and found nothing worth seeing. Now do as I tell you.'

Bradley kept driving until Goldman told him to stop, halfway along a narrow track that ran between two fenced-in fields of tall, untended grass. That was unusual. Untended fields were rare here. Then he looked across the field to the east and saw, in the distance, an enormous barn, probably once used for grain.

Goldman reached into his pocket, pulled out a bunch of keys, and held them up to him.

'Here,' he said. 'One of these is the key. Go take a look at what that son of a bitch was building when we thought he was only constructing airships. Have a *good* look, son.'

Bradley felt foolish and disbelieving, but he took the bunch of keys from the old man and started across the road. He parted the barbed wire, clambered awkwardly through the fence, then started the long walk across the field, through the waist-high, untended grass. The grass was like an endless sea, undulating in the breeze, whispering all around him, brushing at him, as if trying to suck him down. He felt nervous and unreal, adrift from himself, and was dazzled by the silvery-streaked azure sky, in which white clouds drifted.

Ahead of him, the immense barn loomed larger, isolated between land and sky, breaking up the horizon.

Beyond it was Illinois.

Bradley was breathing heavily and sweating by the time he reached the barn, and he stood there for a moment, getting his breath back. He glanced over his shoulder and saw his rented car sitting in the road beyond the fence, minute in that vast, undulating sea of grass. Shaking his head in wonderment, he turned back and studied the barn.

It was certainly huge, obviously once used for storing grain, and the single, steel lock on the door had turned red with rust.

Not quite so breathless, but still sweating too much, Bradley tried one key after the other until he found the correct one. He turned the key once, slipped the lock off the chain, pulled the chain through its steel rings, and let it fall to the ground. Then he took hold of the edge of the large door and pulled it toward him, walking backward as he did so, until it was more than halfway open, letting sunlight pour into the barn's darkness.

That sunlight shone on something metallic, making Bradley's heart leap.

Feeling as nervous as someone entering a haunted house, he walked into the barn.

He didn't get very far.

Chapter Fifteen

The flying saucer prototype looked bigger than it really was where it rested, on a raised hydraulic platform, in the middle of the immense, cluttered hangar. Essentially a large ring plate with adjustable wing discs that rotated around its fixed, cupola-shaped cockpit, it had a diameter of forty-two meters and a height from base to canopy of thirty-two meters. Made of silvery-gray metal that reflected the overhead lights, it looked like a giant spinning top, and it made Wilson smile.

It would soon fly – but not much.

The only saucer that would fly in any real sense was the one Wilson was secretly designing in miniature and would use when he needed it.

As long as he lived, he would not forget the awful devastation caused by the failure of the crude atomic propulsion system used in the otherwise surprisingly successful test flight of his first disc-shaped aircraft, which had actually managed to fly as far as Russia. However, since the catastrophe over the Tunguska region of Siberia in 1908, caused by the explosion of his pilotless aircraft, he had accepted that atomic propulsion was out of the question. Instead, he had concentrated all his efforts on conquering the boundary layer and trying to find less air-resistant material for his flying saucer's structure, so far using highly advanced but orthodox aircraft engines. He had not succeeded in America, though he was on the way to succeeding here – but he was carefully keeping his most important discoveries for his own use.

He fed Schriever only a little at a time ... never quite enough for his needs, but enough to make Schriever think he was making progress and to keep Himmler happy.

It was a delicate maneuver, which Wilson had practiced before – with the US government, before they had withdrawn their support and made him quietly drop out of sight, to eventually end up here in Nazi Germany.

He would always do what he had to do.

He placed his suitcase on the floor, tired from his week of relentless traveling all over Germany. Nevertheless he did not sit down but looked through the glass walls of his office at the men, some in coveralls, some in uniform, who were gathered by the hydraulic platform under the large flying saucer prototype. He recognized the lean and hungry Flugkapitän Rudolph Schriever, who was dangerous, and his engineers, Habermohl and Miethe, who were not, as well as that fat Italian fool, Belluzzo, who would soon have to go.

The four of them were obviously discussing some aspect of the construction while Schriever, who still thought he ran Projekt Saucer, studied the technical drawings in his hands and barked like a dog.

What an ass! Wilson thought.

Not that he had much time for any of them ...

The two engineers, Klaus Habermohl and Otto Miethe, were uninspiringly efficient when merely turning nuts and bolts but embarrassingly inept when aspiring to the greater heights of design. So far, contrary to what Wilson had told Heinrich Himmler in Berchtesgaden, their so-called contributions for various parts of the flying saucer, including the outer steel casing, were relatively useless.

As for the ambitious flugkapitän, he was brighter than the others but remained, nevertheless, a mediocre engineer with pretensions to being a great aeronautical innovator. That was his machine out there, a crude saucer-shaped aircraft, and although he had based much of his design on Wilson's innovations – and then insinuated to Himmler that they were his own – Wilson had given him only those innovations that already were obsolete. Schriever's saucer would fly in a crude manner eventually – when Wilson wanted it to do so – and until then, as Schriever was Himmler's spy, Wilson would give him just enough to keep him happy and full of himself.

Which just left that fat fool, Belluzzo, who, by his very lack of courage, was the most dangerous of all.

Wilson had to get rid of him.

Surprisingly, the aging Italian physicist, who had actually completed the first drawings for the saucer Schriever was now claiming as his own, had turned out to be the biggest thorn in Wilson's side. A basically timid man, he had been cowed by the aggressive, manipulating Schriever and, as a consequence, had tried to curry favor with him by repeatedly implying that Wilson could not be trusted. Ever since then, according to Habermohl, who revered Wilson and kept him informed of such intrigues, Belluzzo had become Schriever's spy and was supporting him in his attempts to take the credit for Wilson's ideas when talking to Himmler.

A nest of vipers, Wilson thought. Nevertheless, since he wanted to be rid of them all eventually, he would start by getting rid of Belluzzo, while simultaneously making Schriever less suspicious of him.

He would do it today.

Knowing that Schriever would be coming to see him at any moment, Wilson opened his briefcase, removed a selection of the technical papers he had collected during his week of traveling, and, as they were of no great significance, spread them out on his desk.

He knew that when Schriever entered the office, he would try, in his idiotically surreptitious manner, to see what they contained.

So he would actually give the fool these technical papers for innovations that were relatively useless.

No sooner had this thought made Wilson smile than Schriever walked in.

'Ah, Wilson, you're back!' he exclaimed in his friendly, false manner.

'Yes,' Wilson replied.

'You had a profitable trip?' Schriever asked, looking dashing in his flugkapitän's uniform, his forced smile slightly illuminating his lean, darkly handsome features.

'*Very* profitable,' Wilson said.

Schriever took the chair at the other side of Wilson's desk and gave his fullest attention.

'What did you find?' he asked breathlessly. 'Anything exciting or useful to us?'

Wilson had traveled far, talked to many, and learned a great deal. In factories hidden in the densely forested areas of the Schwarzwald he had been shown an experiment with a liquid gas that would, when blown with considerable force over an aircraft, catch fire from the exhaust and cause the aircraft to explode. In the R-Laboratory in Volkenrode he had been involved in heated discussions about electrostatic fields and gyroscopic controls and also discovered that by mixing a certain percentage of myrol with air, internal combustion engines would immediately begin to detonate irregularly or, depending on the mixture, stop completely. In the Henschel aircraft company he had examined a television component that would enable pilots to control bombs and rocket bombs *after* they had been launched, as well as a microtelevision camera that would be installed in the nose of an antiaircraft rocket and guide it precisely to its target. In the Luftwaffe experimental center at Oberammergau, in Bavaria, he had been given a demonstration of an apparatus capable of short-circuiting the ignition system of another aircraft engine from a great distance by producing an intense electrical field . . . and he had also learned about the development of radio-controlled interceptor weapons and planes, electromagnetic, electroacoustical, and photoelectric fuses, and even more advanced warheads that were sensitive to the natural electrostatic fields that surround aircraft in flight. In the experimental center at Göttingen, he had been privileged to observe the test flight of a light-winged aircraft that had a slot running along the entire length of its wing span and an extra propellor in the fuselage to suck in the boundary layer and increase the lift of the original airfoil by eight times. And finally, most important, at Berlin-Britz he had been shown a Kreiselgerät, the prototype of a new mechanism that had so far managed to reduce the oscillations of a violently shaking body to under one-tenth of a degree, thus paving the way for the conquest of the boundary layer.

He did not tell Schriever any of this.

Nor did he tell him that upon seeing the results of the oscillation tests in Göttengen, which had proved beyond doubt that the boundary layer could be conquered, he had suggested to Professors Ackeret and Betz that they concentrate on a revolutionary new structural design that would be devoid of all obstructing protuberances, such as wings and rudders, devoid even of the normal air intakes, and powered by a more advanced turbine engine – in other words, a more advanced version of the Horten brothers' tailless aircraft, or 'flying wing,' that would offer the least possible air resistance, suck in the dead air of the boundary layer, and then use that same air, expelling it at great force, to increase its momentum.

The eminent professors had agreed to do just this . . . though Wilson didn't tell Schriever that.

'Naturally,' he said instead, 'the first thing I did was examine the Horten II, D-11-167, prior to its test flight in Rangsdorf, which turned out to be highly unsatisfactory. This so-called tailless aircraft possesses great static-longitudinal stability and complete safety in relation to the spin, but its control surfaces are so heavy that measurements of maneuvering stability couldn't be carried out. The unsatisfactory arrangement of its undercarriage necessitates too long a takeoff, the relation between its longitudinal, lateral, and directional controls is unsatisfactory, its turning flight and maneuverability are both fraught with difficulty, and side-slipping cannot be carried out. With regard, then, to what we are doing, the Horten brothers are valueless.'

Wilson threw the drawings and technical summaries of the Horten brothers' flying wing across the desk as if they were dirt. Schriever picked them up as if he agreed . . . but then, as

Wilson noted, let them rest on his lap and placed his hands protectively on top of them, no doubt to use later in his saucer designs.

'Anything else?' he asked.

Wilson nodded and tried to feign excitement. 'Yes,' he said. 'Some exciting innovations. The kind that could make your flying saucer even more powerful.'

'What?' Schriever asked. *'What?'*

Knowing that Himmler's sole interest in a flying saucer was its potential as a weapon of war, Wilson told his devoted disciple, Rudolph Schriever, about such oddities as the proposed *Windkanone* – a cannon that shot gas instead of shells – and the *Wirbelringkanone*, or whirlwind annular vortex cannon, which was designed to shoot and then ignite a gas ring that would spin rapidly on its own axis and form a fierce ball of fire. Whether such weapons would work in practice was an issue of great doubt, but because Schriever wanted only news of weapons that would sound magical to his beloved Himmler, he lapped up what Wilson was telling him and snapped the relevant research papers from Wilson's hand as if wanting to eat them. Then, when Wilson offered him no more, he stood up to leave.

'One moment, Flugkapitän,' Wilson said.

'Yes?' Schriever responded impatiently, now wanting to leave. 'What is it *now*?'

'I feel I should warn you,' Wilson said as Schriever turned back to face him, 'that certain people are plotting against you.'

As most people in the Third Reich were already frightened of being plotted against or being reported for some damning misdemeanor, Schriever looked suitably shaken and sat down again.

'Plotting against *me*?' he said. 'Who would do that?'

'Belluzzo,' Wilson said without hesitation.

Schriever looked stunned. *'Belluzzo?'* he repeated. 'But he's my most trusted colleague, Herr Wilson!' he blurted out, thus inadvertently confirming what Wilson had suspected.

Wilson sighed, as if saddened. 'I'm afraid your trust has been misplaced,' he said, leaning his elbows on his desk, resting his chin in his hands, and staring with concerned intensity at the clearly shocked Schriever. 'I have it on good authority – one of Himmler's aides, in fact – that Dr Belluzzo has been trying surreptitiously to steal credit for the great contributions you've so far made to Projekt Saucer and has even, in some of the reports, credited certain innovations to himself. He's doing this, I know, because he's so clearly jealous of your authority over the project, but I'm afraid he's being taken seriously by those around Himmler, which means that if he isn't stopped soon, those lies will soon reach Himmler himself and you'll have to defend yourself.'

Looking flushed, Schriever gazed through the glass wall at the flying saucer in the middle of the vast hangar, stared disbelieving at Dr Belluzzo, who was plump and gray-haired and wearing an oil-smeared white smock, then returned his stricken gaze to the front.

'What will I do?' he asked, sounding frightened.

'You have to stop him,' Wilson said dryly.

'And how do I do that?'

'Get rid of him, Schriever.'

'And how do I do *that*?' Schriever asked.

Because Schriever did not know that Wilson was sixty-six years old, and because Wilson looked about fifteen years younger, he did not think he was in any way endangering himself when he said, 'Belluzzo is nearly seventy and beginning to show it, so why not put in an official report about his physical and mental condition, describing him as senile and progressively distracted and therefore an increasing threat to Projekt Saucer? Recommend that he be removed from the project and treated for his own good.'

'*Treated?*'

Wilson shrugged and sat back in his chair. 'Let's be honest,' he said. 'If you put in such a report, Belluzzo will be classified as mentally ill and incarcerated in a concentration camp as an undesirable. If there was another course of action I would certainly recommend it, but there isn't, and under the circumstances . . .'

He didn't finish his sentence, but merely raised and lowered his hands as if it were in the lap of the gods. Schriever, released from moral responsibility in the matter, nodded his gratitude and stood up.

'Yes,' he said. 'Of course. It's the only thing to do. And thank you, Herr Wilson.'

'My pleasure,' Wilson said.

When Schriever had left, Wilson gathered the remaining technical notes together, placed them back in his already stuffed briefcase, then phoned through for his driver to come and collect him. When the uniformed SS driver arrived, he picked up Wilson's suitcase and walked ahead of him, merely glancing at the large flying saucer on the raised ramp, and led him out to the waiting car.

Wilson looked toward the firing range. He was on the proper side of it now. Wernher von Braun and his rocket teams had moved to Peenemünde on the island of Usedom, off the Baltic Coast, and Projekt Saucer had been moved to this side of the firing range, into the bigger, better-equipped hangars. As Wilson had felt increasing resentment at having regularly to pass on certain of his innovations to von Braun's A-2 and A-3 rocket projects, he had been relieved in more ways than one when they finally left.

He slipped into the car, sank into the rear seat, and relaxed during the fifteen-mile journey, through the cloudy, gray afternoon, to his new apartment in the Kürhessen district of Berlin. His former nurse, Greta, who'd been warned of his arrival, had prepared dinner for him.

Assigned to look after only him when he had been recuperating from the second of what he knew would be many operations designed to aid his longevity, Greta had also been instrumental in satisfying his old man's odd sexual whims, mostly of an oral and masturbatory nature. Then, when he had been awarded this spacious apartment by a satisfied Heinrich Himmler, Greta, obviously attracted by his authority and good position in the Nazi hierarchy, had agreed to move in with him as his nurse, housekeeper, and mistress, with her duties in the latter category few and far between, as Wilson now noted without rancor.

Sexually abused as a child by her father, twice married, now widowed and a professional nurse, she was well-proportioned and auburn-haired with an attractive, worldly face, cold gray eyes, and a great deal of knowledge about the sexual needs of men, which was all Wilson needed. Greta had few illusions, was not blinded by emotionalism, and was probably even relieved to be receiving so much for doing so little. She kept a clean apartment, cooked only for herself since he never ate cooked foods, helped him produce the semen he needed for his continuing experiments, and had her occasional affairs on the side, about which he did not complain.

Sometimes she even gave him advice, as she now did over dinner.

'Did you visit the factory before you came home?' she asked him as she tucked into her Wiener schnitzel and he nibbled his dried vegetables and biscuits.

'Yes,' he replied. 'Everything was in order.'

'Did you see Rudolph Schriever?'

'Yes, of course. Why?'

'He came here yesterday,' Greta said, 'and feigned surprise when he didn't find you here. When I said you weren't returning until today, he made a great play of smacking his forehead with his hand and telling me what an idiot he was, that he'd simply forgotten.'

'You thought his visit was deliberate?'

'Yes,' Greta said, wise in the ways of men. 'In fact, I'm convinced of it. I think he just wanted an excuse to see how we lived – perhaps even look around.'

'Which you didn't let him do.'

'Of course not!'

Wilson smiled. 'I hope you invited him in for some tea, at least.'

'Yes, I did – and his eyes wandered all over the place. I could see he wanted to check out the other rooms, but I kept him pinned to his chair.'

'Not physically, I hope.'

'No, he's not my type. I merely pinned him to the chair with my gaze and eventually let him go.'

'I hope the poor man at least enjoyed his tea.'

Greta didn't return his smile. 'Don't trust him,' she said.

'I don't.'

'Good. You can't trust *anyone* these days. But that kind, they're the worst.'

'What kind?'

'The kind who are weak but have ambitions. They're always the worst.'

'I'll remember that,' Wilson said.

A few hours later, when he'd had a bath and was preparing for bed, he asked her to masturbate him and ensure that his semen wasn't lost. She did it with practiced ease, making him come into a small dish, and when he saw it, he was reminded of his adolescence in Iowa, when he would hold his fresh semen in his hand and try to sniff out its properties.

He had been a scientist even then, always detached, investigating, and now, these many years later, nothing had changed. He was experimenting with himself, trying to find the secret of life, so this form of masturbation, while offering relief from his waning sexual agitation, was also serving a scientific purpose.

Greta transferred his semen from the small dish to a glass vial and put the latter into the refrigerator, to keep it cool until tomorrow, when she would deliver it to the experimental laboratory of the hospital where she worked. There the technicians, following Wilson's written instructions, would experiment with it. He was searching for a way to extend his life before his time ran out.

He slept soundly that night.

Three days later, two Gestapo agents wearing black greatcoats arrived at Kummersdorf to take Dr Belluzzo away. The old man was shattered, not knowing why it was happening, and he protested in vain and collapsed into panic, and was staring entreatingly at Schriever and Wilson even as he was dragged away.

He was not seen again. He disappeared into the camps. A few months later Wilson heard that he had died of a heart attack, reportedly induced by increasing ill health, though more likely caused by maltreatment.

His original, unworkable designs for a flying saucer were locked up in Schriever's safe.

Clearly, Schriever thought he might find some use for them.

The thought of this amused Wilson who, no longer bothered by the old Italian physicist, was able to get on with his secret work with no spy looking over his shoulder and his conscience as clear as it always had been.

His *Feuerball* was taking shape.

Chapter Sixteen

Ingrid's mother answered the door, stared at Ernst in surprise, then looked embarrassed and tried to hide it by crying out, 'Ernst! You're back at last!' She took him into her arms to give him a hug, then stepped back and waved him inside. 'Come,' she said. 'The children will be so pleased to see you. They've missed you so much.'

Noting that she hadn't mentioned Ingrid's name and still looked embarrassed, Ernst picked up his suitcase and stepped into the apartment he had not seen for three months. It was late in the morning and both his children were in the living room, four-year-old Ula setting up blocks for baby Alfred, now fourteen months old. Alfred knocked the blocks down and giggled delightedly while Ula glanced sideways and saw Ernst, studied him with slowly dawning recognition, then shyly stood up to greet him.

'It's your father!' Ingrid's mother exclaimed, as if Ernst had been gone for three years instead of four months.

Realizing that he must seem like a stranger to his own daughter, and filling up with love for both children, Ernst set his suitcase down, fell to his knees, and swept the children into his arms, hugging them passionately.

'Don't be embarrassed,' he said, stroking Ula's flushed cheek and golden locks. 'I know I've been gone a long time and must seem like a stranger to you. But you'll get used to me again, my darling, before very long. And how pretty and grown-up you look. And Alfred!' He grasped the gurgling baby under the arms and held him up in the air.

'What a fine boy he is! Do you look after him, Ula?'

'Yes,' Ula replied, smiling.

'Good,' Ernst said. '*Very* good!' He stood up and glanced around the room. 'Ingrid isn't here?' he asked, wondering why his mother-in-law was looking after the children.

'No,' his mother-in-law said too quickly, blushing again. 'She went to visit some friends.'

'Who?'

'I don't know,' she replied, avoiding his gaze. 'She told me, but I can't remember the name. I mean, she didn't know you were coming back today, so . . .'

'When did she leave?' Ernst asked, feeling more disturbed.

'This morning.'

'Then you must have been here all night, Maria.'

'Yes – yes, I was!' And she nodded her head vigorously. 'I didn't want to have to get out of bed too early, so I decided to sleep here. But please, Ernst,' she added, changing the subject and waving toward the couch, 'sit down and take your boots off and let me fix you some tea. You must be exhausted.'

'I'm fine,' he replied, then knelt on the floor by his suitcase and proceeded to open it, determined to distract himself from his dark thoughts. 'I arrived in Berlin last night but had to report straight to barracks – and yes, I *would* like a tea. Here, Ula,' he said, opening the suitcase, 'I have some presents for you and Alfred. All wrapped up, just like Christmas!'

Already getting over her shyness, Ula unwrapped the doll that Ernst had, in fact, bought only this morning, right here in Berlin, along with Alfred's box of rattling toys. Nevertheless, she was delighted with it, and for the next half hour or so, Ernst enjoyed his tea, enjoyed watching his son and daughter playing with their presents, made desultory conversation with his normally pleasant but now clearly uneasy mother-in-law, and determined not to show the anger and suspicion he was feeling over Ingrid's unexpected absence.

After all, they had agreed to live separate lives, so he could not complain . . .

The practice, however, was more difficult than the theory.

As he sat there, sipping tea, appreciating the feminine coziness of the apartment after the rigors of his sea voyage, he had to choke back his feelings of disappointment and loss. He had just returned from an epic journey, an historically important endeavor, and was not even being welcomed back by his wife . . . He filled up with self-pity, despised himself for it, and had managed to accept what he had wrought by the time Ingrid returned.

When she walked in and saw him, her face turned bright red. She was wearing a long gray coat and a broad black hat, but removed them first and composed herself. By the time she had crossed the room to kiss his cheek, her face had turned pale again and her vivid green eyes were cautious.

'Ernst!' she exclaimed, whispering into his ear. 'I didn't realize . . .'

Not having known the touch of a woman's body for a long time, he instantly filled up with longing when, for the brief duration of her chaste kiss, Ingrid could not prevent her body from touching his.

'I know,' he said as she stepped away from him, leaving only the intoxicating smell of her scent, the seductive warmth of her lips, and the bitter knowledge that she no longer desired him. 'They didn't tell us when we would be returning, so I couldn't tell you. Still, here I am.'

'Yes, Ernst.' Her once-radiant smile was hesitant. 'Here you are!' Her gaze slipped away from him, fell on her mother, roamed the room, then finally, reluctantly, returned to him. 'So,' she said with forced gaiety, waving her hand to indicate the children. 'Have you noticed the change in them?'

The banality of the question almost amused him, and he did indeed smile. 'Remarkable,' he said. 'And Ula looks as lovely as her mother.'

At least Ula liked that remark, blushing and giggling.

'Tea!' Ingrid said, trying to be gay. 'At least mother's looked after you. Would you like something stronger?'

'A little schnapps would be nice.'

'You didn't ask me for that,' Ingrid's mother said too shrilly, then, looking confused, added, 'Anyway, I have to be going now – and I'm sure you two have lots to talk about. My bag's packed already.'

'Mother, you don't have to—'

'No!' Ingrid's mother protested. 'I can't stay another minute! I promised to have chocolate with Fraulein Vogt at the Konditerei before I go home – and if I stay here any longer, I'll be late. I've already called for a taxi and packed my overnight bag.'

The repetition was a product of her embarrassment. Clearly she was as relieved as Ernst was when the taxi came for her. When she had gone, after more oddly melodramatic hugging and kissing (which merely confirmed for Ernst that his suspicions about Ingrid were well founded), he felt the oppressive weight of the silence that filled up the cozy room.

Having poured two glasses of schnapps, Ingrid handed one to him and sat facing him. As he drank, feeling better with each sip, he studied his playing children, the golden girl and the giggling baby, glanced repeatedly around the room with its heavy, darkly varnished cupboards, lace tablecloths, doilies and curtains, Germanic bricabrac and paintings, and realized that no matter how homey it was, it was no longer his home.

He was a German soldier, an SS officer – the elite of Himmler's elite – and that made him different.

He no longer needed this.

'How was the trip?' Ingrid asked him.

'It wasn't a *holiday*, Ingrid.'

'I'm sorry. I didn't mean it to sound like that. I just thought it might have been exciting or glamorous. Was it?'

'No,' he said, offended at the very notion, 'but it was certainly worth doing.'

'Why?'

'I can't tell you that,' he said, though he wished that he could, now remembering with increasing pride how he had hammered the swastika into the snow-covered earth of Antarctica in that vast, haunting silence.

'Another vitally important secret of the Third Reich?'

'Your sarcasm is not required.'

He felt a touch of anger, but his sexual desire softened it. Ingrid had always been attractive – a prize catch, in fact – and right now, even trying to keep her distance, she glowed with an inner light, probably caused, as he bitterly realized, by the man she had come from. He tried to be objective about it, to keep their agreement in mind, but after four months at sea, faced with her sensual gratification, he surrendered to the very emotions he had been trained to despise.

'Where were you, Ingrid?'

She glanced at the children, then back at him. 'Do we have to discuss this now?'

'I've been away for four months,' he said, though he hadn't intended doing so, 'and you were gone when I came back.'

'I didn't know you were coming back,' she reminded him.

'You know what I'm talking about, Ingrid. Why was your mother here?'

'I was visiting a friend.'

'All night?'

'Yes,' she said. 'All night.' Before he could say anything else, perhaps frightened of his reaction, she told Ula to pick up their toys and take them into the bedroom. 'Your father and I have to talk,' she said, 'so you can play in there for a while.' When Ula had picked up the toys and started toward the bedroom, Ingrid, carrying Alfred, followed her daughter through the door; returning, she sat down, crossed her legs, and sipped some more schnapps.

'So,' she said, 'let's discuss it.'

'All night,' Ernst said, echoing her words with soft, deliberate malice.

'You knew before you left that I had a lover.'

'And you've just been with the same man?'

'Yes.'

'It's nice to know that it's lasting.'

'Yes, Ernst, it is.'

'Is he better than me in bed?'

'I don't think that question's relevant.'

'What is?'

'A lot of other things, Ernst. Sex isn't everything.'

'We both enjoyed it once.'

'I've never denied it.'

'But now you enjoy it more with him.'

'It's more than that, Ernst.'

'Yes,' he said, 'lots of other things. Such as?'

'Love and affection.'

'You and I are *married*, Ingrid. Please remember that. Marriage isn't that easy.'

'No,' she said, 'it isn't that easy. Maybe that's why we failed.'

'I don't see how I failed you.'

'You gave me up for Adolf Hitler.'

'Be careful about what you say, Ingrid.'

'I want a divorce.'

He sighed, shook his head in disbelief, then finished his schnapps. 'We've discussed this before,' he reminded her, placing his glass on the table that separated them, 'and you know it's out of the question. I won't risk my career with a divorce. Who *is* this man anyway?'

'You don't need to know that.'

'Not Jewish, I hope.'

'No.'

'Do I know him?'

'No.'

'If I discover that he's Jewish, I'll turn you in – for the good of the children.'

'How noble you are, Ernst.' Ingrid lit a cigarette, blew the smoke toward the ceiling, then gazed obliquely at him through a blue haze. 'All right,' she said, 'for the good of the children, let's remain man and wife. I'll continue seeing my lover, you'll continue seeing your whores, and we'll both live happily ever after, while supporting the Third Reich.'

'Some day your tongue will get you into trouble.'

'At least it's still *my* tongue.'

The schnapps had helped to calm him down and now kept him in control. He stood up and straightened his jacket, feeling very calm indeed, then walked around the low table and leaned down and slapped her face. Once. No more. A single, stinging blow. Then he straightened up and saw her look of shock and smiled thinly at her.

'Be a whore,' he said, 'but do it discreetly or you'll get worse than that.' She didn't reply. She was rubbing her red cheek. He could hear the children playing in the bedroom and his heart went out to them. They were the new generation, the future, and he had to protect them. 'I'm going out,' he told Ingrid. 'I won't bother you with my attentions. Anything I want, I'll get from my favorite whore, who knows me better than you do. I anticipate being back for my supper, so please have it ready. When I'm on duty or at the barracks, you can do as you please; but when I'm here you will treat me as your husband. Is that understood?'

'Yes,' she said.

'Good.'

When he left, he closed the door without slamming it – like a dutiful husband.

With most of the day to kill before he had to report directly to Himmler, he took a packed, clattering tramcar to the city center, noted with grim pleasure that his newly laundered SS uniform encouraged people to lower their gaze nervously in his presence, disembarked in the Kurfürstendamm, and planned what to do while having his next glass of schnapps in a busy café. Realizing that his relationship with Ingrid was definitely finished and surprised at his lack of emotion about it, he thought of Brigette in the luxurious apartment on Tiergartenstrasse and knew instantly how he wanted to spend his afternoon.

'Darling!' Brigette exclaimed in that inimitably sensual, breathless manner when he phoned from the café. 'You're back at last from the high seas! Did you bring me a present?'

'Yes,' he lied, amused and excited by her husky-voiced, challenging mockery.

'Was it *expensive*, dear Ernst?'

'Yes, Brigette, it was.'

'Then come straight over, darling! I *can't wait* to see you!'

He bought her a diamond brooch in an expensive shop on Tauentzienstrasse, then walked to her apartment, still trying to adjust to the contrast between the isolation of sea and the energetic bustle of Berlin with its tramcars, buses, taxis, horsedrawn cabs, and growing number of army vehicles. An occasional mounted Storm Trooper made his way through the noisy traffic on his horse, the Nazi swastika and anti-Jewish signs were visible everywhere, and the green-uniformed, respected members of the Reichswehr mingled on the pavements with the feared Brownshirts, black-uniformed SS, and elegantly dressed shoppers and businessmen. All in all, on the surface, where the fear was not visible, the Third Reich seemed purposeful, energetic, and surprisingly prosperous.

Brigette also looked prosperous, even more so than usual. She came to the door wearing a shimmering lime-green bathrobe of pure silk, artfully opened at the top to expose her voluptuous, bare breasts, and her red hair, immaculately combed, fell around her calculating blue eyes and full, sensual lips. Her cigarette was in an ebony holder and her fingernails, Ernst noticed, were painted the same color as her hair.

'Ah!' she exclaimed with a throaty purr. 'My handsome lieutenant! I've missed you *so* much, *cheri*!'

She used the French endearment deliberately, making it sound deliciously decadent, and Ernst stepped quickly into the room and kicked the door closed behind him. He took her into his arms, pulling her to him, feeling her heat, and she just smiled, rubbing her belly lightly against him, then blew a cloud of smoke.

'Mmmm,' she murmured, letting her body sink against him. 'You greedy boy! You poor, famished hero. Did you miss me terribly, darling?'

'Yes,' he said, already breathless.

'And dream about me?'

'Yes, yes!'

'And remembered the things we had done together?'

'Yes, damn you! Yes!'

She chuckled, let him feel her heavy breasts, licked the side of his neck. 'And did pretty boy bring his expensive gift?'

'Yes', he said, almost bursting.

'You're so kind,' Brigette whispered, breathing into his ear, then chuckled throatily, jerked his hands off her and stepped away from him. The dressing gown had been tugged off one shoulder, exposing her breast. Ernst could feel his heart racing. Brigette held out her hand.

'I'm just a child at heart,' she explained. 'I can't wait to see it.'

She was smiling, but meant it, so he gave her the brooch, thinking of the many men who gave her presents, financial and otherwise. While she unwrapped his particular gift, he gazed into the bedroom behind her and noted that the bed was badly rumpled, as if used for more than sleep. Nothing had changed, which was fine by him. No more emotional entanglements: just gratification. Sensual pleasure and duty.

'Has my precious lieutenant been home yet?' Brigette asked as she unwrapped his gift.

'Yes,' he said.

'And how were your lovely wife and children?'

'Fine,' he said. 'In good health.'

'And you've come straight from there?' she asked with sly, exciting mockery as she pulled the wrapping paper off the box and let it fall carelessly to the carpet.

'Yes,' he said, unable to take his eyes off her bare skin, his senses in disarray.

She removed the lid from the gift box, studied the brooch with widening eyes, removed it and pinned it to her silk nightgown where it fell in shining folds and shadows over a perfect breast. She glanced down at it, her lips pouting greedily, then looked directly at him.

'Ravishing,' she said. 'Welcome back. Now what would you like to do?'

'Everything,' Ernst said, then stepped up to her, slid the dressing gown off her shoulders, and lowered his head.

'Nice,' Brigette said. 'Nice.'

When she was ready, she led him into the bedroom and let him share her unmade bed, where he finally felt at home.

Three days later, satiated by his loveless sexual exertions with the diabolically sensual Brigette, Ernst was walking with his beloved Reischsführer, Himmler, through a long dark tunnel that had been carved out of the Kohnstein Mountain, near the town of Nordhausen in the southern Harz mountain range in Thuringia.

'I have a dream,' Himmler was saying quietly, academically, 'of an Atlantis reborn from the ashes of the forthcoming war: a society of masters and slaves, ruled by the elite of my SS. The new temples will be the factories, the laboratories and universities; the new religion will be knowledge and conquest: the return of the Superman. And where will this new order be created? In the *Antarctic*, Lieutenant!'

The tunnel had only recently been hacked out of the interior of the mountain and was gloomily illuminated by the electric lights strung along its whole length. There were many people still working in it, mostly prisoners from the camps, few looking healthy, most covered in mud. All took great pains to keep their eyes lowered as Himmler and his entourage of assistants and bodyguards walked past them, watching them laying steel tracks and fortifying the walls that formed the great tunnel, as wide as a highway, at the end of which, as Ernst noticed with relief, there was a circle of light.

'You understand now, do you not, Lieutenant,' Himmler continued rhetorically as they tramped through the long tunnel, his normally soft voice even more difficult to hear because of the constant banging and clanging of the heavy work going on all around them, 'just how important your mission to the Antarctic was? The elite of my SS, the best of the best, will find a new home under the ice of the Antarctic, and there, uninterrupted and isolated from the imperfect world of normal men, will be forged into the first of the Supermen.

You have found the location for us, Lieutenant Stoll, and should be proud of yourself.'

As they walked deeper into the cold, dimly lit darkness of the tunnel, Ernst noticed that the slaving prisoners, most of whom looked underfed, were being guarded by immaculately uniformed SS officers, most armed with pistols or submachine guns, some carrying bullwhips. The clothes of many of the prisoners were in ribbons; some had skin that was freshly scarred.

A society of masters and slaves, he thought, and it all begins right here . . .

'I am not so sure, Reichsführer,' he said, emboldened by the favor he had recently found with Himmler, 'that such an ambitious project, no matter how admirable, would actually be feasible.'

'I respect you for expressing your doubts,' Himmler said, feeling kindly disposed toward Stoll for his achievement in the Anatarctic, 'but what are they based on?'

'To create hidden colonies under the ice,' Ernst began, 'may not be that easy. The undertaking would have to be immense, and I do not think—'

'Look around you!' Himmler interjected with a rare display of excitement, waving his gloved hand to indicate those slaving along the length of the great tunnel. 'This is but one of two tunnels, eighteen thousand meters long. Leading off these tunnels will be fifty side chambers, a work area of one hundred and twenty-five thousand square meters, and twelve ventilation shafts, which already have been bored down to here from the peak of the mountain. As for these workers,' he continued, indicating with a careless wave of his hand the hundreds of unfortunates already working in the dimly lit gloom under the threat of bullwhip and bullet, 'they are merely the tip of the iceberg. Where they come from, there are thousands more – and thousands more after them – and we can obtain them whenever we need them and do what we will with them. Our supply of labor is endless.'

He stopped to study some prisoners who were laying down

the steel rails for the trains that would soon run through the tunnels, bringing in more workers, equipment, and, possibly, food. Ernst noticed, once more, that these particular workers were half starved, and understood that they would be worked to death and then casually replaced. A society of masters and slaves hidden under the earth . . . He was moved by the grandeur of the concept and suddenly saw its potential.

When a bullwhip cracked behind them and someone screamed, Himmler twitched and walked on.

'The slaves destined to work here,' he explained as they continued walking toward that expanding circle of light from the outside world, 'will come from a separate camp located in a hidden mountain valley, less than a kilometer from the entrance to this tunnel. And a new underground complex, to be linked to this one by another network of tunnels, is already being constructed sixteen kilometers under the ground around the town of Bleicherode, only twenty kilometers from Nordhausen. Between them, Nordhausen and Bleicherode will constitute the first of my SS underground factories – virtually living towns. And what we are doing here, Lieutenant, under the earth, we can also do under the ice of the Antarctic.'

At that moment, they stepped into the sunlight that was pouring into the end of the vast tunnel. Glancing down, Ernst saw a strip of ragged, bloodsoaked cloth in the mud, but he put it out of his mind as, walking beside Himmler, whose respect he had gained, he raised his face to let the sunlight warm it, then left the tunnel behind him.

The peaks and valleys of the densely forested mountains of Thuringia were spread out all around and below him in the sunlight of spring.

He breathed deeply of fresh air.

Himmler, also breathing the fresh air, again waved his hand – this time to take in the peaks and valleys spread out below and around them, under a radiant blue sky streaked with fat, snow-white clouds.

'This whole area,' he said in his quietly grandiose manner,

'from the Harz Mountains to Thuringia, south of Prague and across to Mähren, is already littered with other tunnels and underground factories similar to this one – and soon they will be totally insular colonies, worked by masters and slaves, and unrestricted by commonplace, so-called moral thinking. And since the masters are the elite of my most trusted SS troops, the existence of these places is unknown to those who are not my most valued initiates. Unknown,' he added, lowering his voice even more and staring steadily at Ernst through his glittering pince-nez, 'even to those closest to our beloved Führer. Do you understand what I'm saying?'

'Yes, Reichsführer,' Ernst said.

Himmler nodded solemnly. 'And what we can do here,' he then repeated in his softly insistent manner, 'we can also do in the land you have claimed for us in the Antarctic. Yes, Lieutenant,' he said, nodding again, 'you have found the place for us.' Ernst swelled up with the pride he had almost lost through Ingrid.

'The German genius,' Himmler said, 'has rendered the impossible the commonplace – and there, though invisible to the naked eye, my first colonies are taking shape underground.' He nodded, as if bowing to that sacred earth, then glanced sideways at Ernst. 'It is my belief, Lieutenant, that these underground colonies, if created in the Antarctic, can, with the aid of the American's flying saucer, ensure the success of our forthcoming conquest of the whole Western world. By the time that has been completed – as surely it must – we will have moved the first of our men to the Antarctic to begin the Hörbiger Projekt: the creation of a society under the ice and the first steps toward the supremacy of Nordic man, who will, given time and Wilson's technology, evolve into the Superman.'

Aware that he had been selected and shaken by the honor, Ernst wanted Himmler to take hold of his shoulders and gently shake him like a beloved son; but he understood that his Reichsführer, a true soldier, even a genius, could not stoop to the display of such emotions in front of his men. Understanding this, he tried to control his own emotions and instead simply nodded.

'Now that we have laid claim to Neuschwabenland in the Antarctic,' Himmler said, his pince-nez magnifying his mild eyes, 'it is my intention to ship specially trained SS troops, scientists, slave workers, and equipment there to first construct, then live in, an underground research establishment and its attendant accommodations, which will in time become a self-contained, living colony under the ice. And from there, with the aid of the products of Projekt Saucer, we will spread the rule of the Third Reich across the whole world. *We will do this, Lieutenant!*'

Ernst was taken aback by the sudden intensity of Himmler's words, then swept away on a wave of exultation by his Reichsführer's unprecedented display of emotion. He had to look away from him to find the freedom of sky and light, but was drawn back when Himmler actually touched him, tugging the sleeve of his uniform.

Ernst looked down and saw the eyes behind the pince-nez as prisms reflecting light.

'You have done a wonderful thing,' Himmler said. 'You have planted our swastikas in the ice. I am now placing you in charge of this great operation: to create Hörbiger's world of ice and fire under the Antarctic ice and, at the same time, keep a check on the vital progress of Projekt Saucer. This, Lieutenant Stoll, is your great mission on behalf of the Fatherland. Do not disappoint me.'

'No, Reichsführer,' Ernst replied, realizing in a flood of exhilarating emotion that he would be going back to Kummersdorf West and the world he belonged to. 'I will not disappoint you.'

Then he looked over the forested hills and valleys with the pride he had almost lost.

Chapter Seventeen

'I didn't get very far,' Bradley said, describing what he had seen in the immense barn in that desolate field near Mount Pleasant, Iowa. 'In fact, I'd barely walked past the door when the rim of that goddamned thing was in front of me.'

Recalling that eerie experience with vivid clarity, he wasn't comforted by the fact that the man to whom he was talking – retired US Army Air Force Wing Commander Dwight Nicholson – had insisted that they hold this conversation in a darkened room and was breathing like a man at death's door.

'It was shaped like a great steel saucer with a Perspex dome on top, taking up half the floor space of the barn and starting to rust. At first, I couldn't grasp what I was seeing, but it gradually dawned on me. It was the superstructure for some kind of flying machine – one shaped like a saucer.'

'A piloted machine,' Nicholson said, his voice sounding ghostlike.

'Yes. The Perspex dome turned out to be a circular cockpit, located at the center of the disc. The cockpit was fixed and the disc, in two parts, like one saucer placed upside-down on another, would have revolved around it.'

'And of course it was only a shell – there was no engine inside.'

'Right,' Bradley said. 'Even the goddamned control panel had been smashed to hell. He left nothing to chance.'

'Wrong. He left the prototype. He could have blown it up. Why didn't he?'

'He didn't want to draw the attention of the neighboring farmers.'

'Or he wanted *something* to be found . . . to leave his mark.'

Nicholson smiled, inhaled on his cigarette, and blew a couple of smoke rings toward the window overlooking the garden of his home in McLean, Virginia. The sun, shining brightly outside, was filtering through the drawn blinds and forming webs of light in the darkness around him, illuminating his dreadful face.

'Just what we found,' he said, his twisted smile displaying admiration. 'The superstructure for a saucer-shaped aircraft – but with nothing inside. Either that bastard had gutted his own machine, taking everything of value, or there'd been nothing inside it in the first place.'

'Which means?'

'We all believed then, and I believe now, that the craft that exploded over Tunguska, Siberia, wasn't piloted – it was some kind of missile – and that the superstructure we found later was a prototype for the first of his piloted craft. That's what we found – and what *you* found. Some smart cookie, that Wilson.' Nicholson shook his head from side to side, as if he couldn't believe it. 'We didn't know he'd left another one, that's for sure. In a barn in *Iowa?*'

'Right. Up near the border of Illinois. Not far from Mount Pleasant, where Cohn and Goldman had their research establishment. Apparently Wilson had been working in secret on the flying saucer in that barn while ostensibly producing airships for Cohn and Goldman.'

'In other words, he took them to the cleaners. They were financing his saucer project without knowing it.'

'Right,' Bradley said. 'It was Goldman's belief that Wilson had secretly been trying to solve the problem of the boundary layer and also working on a crude atomic propulsion system. This suggests that the propulsion system managed at a later date to fly *some* kind of object – as you say, some kind of missile – as far as Russia before it malfunctioned, blew up, devastated the forests of Tunguska, and led to the US government closing down Wilson's research establishment in Illinois and either classifying or destroying what they could find of his work.'

'Which is why you came to me?'

'Yes. After finding the remains of that saucer, I checked out what Abe had told me and learned that it was essentially correct – that after Cohn and Goldman had gone bust, the US Army Air Force had opened a file on a similar company located just across the state line, in Illinois. Unfortunately, in those records, the names of those involved had been erased. But then I saw, in other records in Washington, that you'd been in charge of that operation just before you retired. And since you're an old friend and all . . .'

Nicholson smiled. 'Yeah, Mike, I understand. Can I take it that this is all off the record?'

'You *are* retired, Dwight.'

'I still want it to be off the record. I don't want my name mentioned.'

'You have my word on it.'

Nicholson nodded and grinned laconically. You could actually see the twisted grin in the semidarkness, but it didn't look real.

'Okay,' he said. 'This is all based purely on recollection; I don't have any backup.'

'I'll take what I can get, Dwight.'

'Are you sure you don't want a drink?'

'It's only ten in the morning.'

Nicholson simply shrugged, sipped some whiskey, inhaled and blew more smoke, which made Bradley feel bad.

In 1918, when Bradley had just about turned twenty, he'd been a naval aviator under Nicholson's command, flying the old wood, wire, and canvas biplanes from their primitive carriers out at sea to the bloody battlefields of the western front. After the war, when Bradley had gone into law, Nicholson had returned to the intelligence work he'd been doing previously for the army air force. Then his wife, at fifty-eight, had died from a brain hemorrhage, and after that the spirit had gone right out of him. Still with the army air force's technical intelligence branch, he'd developed a drinking problem, then ulcers, and had then been retired prematurely, looking like an old man. About a year ago, he had bought himself an old de Havilland two-seat *Tiger Moth* biplane and started to give flying lessons. Under the influence of alcohol, he'd crashed the plane, killing his passenger and seriously burning himself. Now his face was hideous, his skin livid and scarred, his lips practically burned off, along with his hair and eyelids, and he lived here alone, in this too-large house in McLean, Virginia, smoking and drinking most of the day and going out only rarely.

It was frightening to visit him.

'What Goldman told you was substantially correct,' he said in an unnatural tone of voice. 'I don't think I have to tell you that after the Great Airship Scare of 1896 to 1897, the army air force began taking a particular interest in anything new or novel in the aeronautical field.'

'That figures,' Bradley said.

'Well, since most of the major reports mentioned a man named Wilson – and since most of them also named either Iowa or Illinois as the origin of the mystery airships and their equally mysterious crew members – it wasn't too difficult to discover that a certain John Wilson, exceptional graduate of MIT and Cornell, was designing and constructing airships for the Cohn and Goldman Company in Mount Pleasant, Iowa. Since this was a perfectly legal occupation, we did nothing but surreptitiously keep our eye on his progress. We only became concerned when shortly after the end of the scare, we received a pretty startling report, stating that Cohn and Goldman's five airships had been destroyed by an unknown demolition expert, thus breaking the company, and that while no evidence could be found to prove that the deed had been done by Wilson, it had been ascertained that he'd mysteriously made a small fortune at approximately the same time and, shortly after, opened his own research establishment in Illinois. It was believed, but could not be proven, that he had made that money by illegally selling his airship designs to a German aircraft company, possibly Zeppelin – and according to Cohn and Goldman, the designs he had let them patent were actually worthless. So, while Cohn and Goldman went bust, Wilson was opening his own research plant in Illinois . . .'

'And?'

'We paid him a visit in Illinois. We informed him of our suspicions, which he naturally denied, and when we asked him what his intentions were, he said he was moving on from airships to heavier-than-air manned flight but was being hampered by his limited financial resources. Clearly the money paid by the Germans would not last forever.'

'What did you think of him personally?' Bradley asked, still trying to fit a face to his mysterious quarry.

'I'll never forget him,' Nicholson replied without hesitation. 'He wasn't even thirty, but he seemed a lot older – though what burned itself into my memory was his coldness. A really *strange* kind of coldness. He wasn't arrogant, rude, unfriendly, or antagonistic – no, none of those things. He was just remarkably detached, inhumanly pragmatic, almost machinelike in the way he listened and responded . . . He lacked normal emotions . . .'

Nicholson shivered, as if brushed by a cold breeze, then stubbed his cigarette out and slumped back in his soft chair.

'Did the air force get involved with him?' Bradley asked.

'Yes,' Nicholson said. 'Nervous about what he might do, but with no legal right to stop him, we decided to get some jurisdiction over him by offering the money he would need for his more ambitious projects. He accepted on the grounds that we didn't attempt to supervise him and content ourselves with monthly reports and regular inspection visits to his plant. We agreed, thinking that would be enough for us – but naturally, given Wilson's nature, it wasn't.'

'So you were involved with the saucer-shaped aircraft?'

'No. We didn't know a damned thing about them. Wilson conned us, just like he'd conned his previous financiers. What we got in our reports, and what we viewed in our many inspection visits to his plant in Illinois, was the prototype for a highly advanced turboprop biplane – and frankly, we were more than impressed. Clearly, we were dealing here with a genius – and by 1903, even before the Wright brothers had made their first, widely publicized flight at Kitty Hawk, I was privileged to witness the secret test flight of Wilson's completed aircraft. That flight was more than successful – it was absolutely astonishing . . . and that's when we got scared.'

'Why?'

Nicholson reached for the bottle of whiskey, filled his glass up to the brim, drank almost half of it, topped the glass up again. 'After the notorious Cohn and Goldman affair,' he said, his voice emanating from the semidarkness in a quavering, ghostlike manner, 'we knew that Wilson couldn't be trusted. For that reason, I'd planted one of my own engineers in his team with orders to keep his eyes and ears open for anything not mentioned in Wilson's reports or viewed by us during our visits. While this man never got too close to Wilson, he did pick up enough whispers to convince him that Wilson – just as he had done with Cohn and Goldman – was showing us only the tip of his particular iceberg; that even though his turboprop biplane was more advanced than anything else we knew about, he was reportedly working on some other project, involving the boundary layer and some unknown form of propulsion, in another hangar, located a mile or two from his main plant.

'Knowing how advanced the biplane was, we were naturally scared shitless at the very thought of boundary-layer experiments and an *unknown* propulsion system – then, when in 1908 our man reported whispers about the flight of a small, pilotless object that had actually managed to reach Russia, we naturally became very concerned indeed . . . And we were preparing to take over Wilson's plant and demand the location of his secret hangar when that dreadful explosion occurred over Tunguska, in Russia. It occurred *over* Tunguska, you understand, and we knew what that meant.'

'Something exploded in the air.'

'Right.'

'And whatever it was, you don't think it was piloted.'

'No, we didn't then and I still don't. Bear in mind that Wilson's secret work was being conducted in what was no more than a converted barn near the main plant. Given this, I think it's safe to assume that he wasn't designing something nearly as big as an airship or aircraft. In fact, our spy had heard from other engineers stories about a small, disc-shaped object – no more than a foot in diameter – which when test-flown looked like a fiery ball. It's my belief that that small, probably remote-controlled object was what exploded over Tunguska – and that the large, saucer-shaped superstructures since found were just that: empty superstructures for the larger, piloted craft that Wilson intended to construct along the same lines as the smaller object. Then, of course, when the smaller object exploded over Russia, we had to put a stop to it.'

'How did Wilson respond to that?'

'He blandly denied our charges as well as the existence of his secret hangar, or barn, so we closed down his plant in Illinois, confiscated everything we could find – which naturally didn't include anything we hadn't already known about – and told Wilson that if he wanted to continue working on research projects, he would have to do it under our supervision, in our own research establishments. Wilson said he would think about it . . . A few weeks later, we found that empty super-structure in a hangar a few miles from his plant in Illinois. We never found anything else . . . and then, before we could interrogate Wilson about it, he fled Illinois and went underground. I never saw him again.'

He lit a cigarette, blew another cloud of smoke, then raised the glass to his twisted lips and drank it. Bradley stood.

'Thanks,' he said. 'And look after yourself, Dwight.'

'There's nothing left to look after,' his friend replied. 'It's just a matter of time now. A real glamorous business, being a pilot – right? We don't believe this can happen.'

'Right,' Bradley said.

He placed his hand on his friend's shoulder, squeezed it affectionately, then turned away and walked from that dark place without glancing back.

The sunshine was wonderful.

* * *

In the train back to Connecticut, he opened the latest letter from Gladys Kinder, this one dated October 5, 1938.

Dear Mike,

This morning the Germans marched into Czechoslovakia to ecstatic cheers, the pealing of bells, and the pronouncement by Adolf Hitler that this was the latest step in his glorious march into the great German future. God help Europe, I say.

Did you miss my letters, Mike? I hope so. Apart from my telegrammed communiques to the Roswell Daily Record, *my letters to you, to your office high above Manhattan, are my only real contact with America. That reason for writing is important – it's my hold on where I came from – but I have to confess that I also write them out of girlish compulsion.*

You were so charming, Mike.

Ah, ha! you're thinking. She's making fun of me again! Well, maybe so . . . But I hope you missed my letter, missed the letters, missed me. Not that you'd admit it if you did – you lamentably decent married man, who found me too bold by far. I think that's what I loved in you.

I also love the odd formality of your letters – written secretly, doubtless – God, yes, I enjoy that thought! Bradley scribbling in secret, his cheeks flushed, above the towers of Manhattan.

Your letters, which are filled with a lawyer's reticence, somehow manage to make me feel like a scarlet woman. That's quite an achievement, bud. You make me feel that I'm wallowing in iniquity without its actual pleasures – and that's another achievement!

Enough! Let's be serious . . .

I haven't written for the past eighteen months because I've been traveling. Spain, of course, with the International Brigade, meeting Orwell and Hemingway and all the other, less celebrated intellectuals who idealistically swopped their pens for rifles and often died for the privilege. I didn't carry a rifle – my pen and notebook were too heavy – but I was in the market of Guernica, buying some groceries, when the German air force bombed it with high explosives, set it alight with incendiary bombs, then strafed the men, women, and children with machine-gun fire. What I saw there is best not described, but it left its mark on me. It was all I could take.

I returned to London in time to describe, for the loyal readers of the Roswell Daily Record, how King George VI and Queen Elizabeth were crowned, with magnificent pomp and splendor, in Westminster Abbey. I loved it all, I do confess – it was like a Hollywood musical: the golden coach drawn by eight grays, with four postilions and six footmen, plus eight grooms and four yeomen of the Guard walking beside it. What with that and the royal outfits of deep red and snow-white ermine, not to mention the thousands thronging the Mall and Trafalgar Square, I doubt that Cecil B. De Mille could have done it better – and certainly, after Spain and some weeks in Nazi Germany, it all seemed so civilized.

I was reminded of you when, a week before the Coronation, the great German airship, the Hindenburg, exploded in New Jersey, after crossing the Atlantic from Frankfurt. Then Jean Harlow died and was followed by George Gershwin and I started to think of passing time and my age – and the fact that the last time I saw you, which was only the second time, was almost five years ago. I was going to write you, but I was packed off to Germany by my good friends in Roswell.

The first thing I reported from Germany was the reorganization of the concentration camps, most notably the new establishment opened at Buchenwald, in Thuringia, to house more enemies of the state, and the changes of administration in the camps at Dachau, Sachenshausen, and Lichtenburg, all of which are democratic enough to take women prisoners as well as other automatic enemies of the glorious Third Reich, including Jews and Communists, though gypsies, the mentally ill, and other so-called undesirables are certainly in line for consideration.

God help Europe, indeed!

Here in London, they're already building air raid shelters and providing local authorities with millions of sandbags. What can this mean, we ask? 'Peace for our time,' says Neville

Chamberlain. Pull the other one, Neville . . .

*And so I think of you. I think of you when I think of America,
which I did when Harlow and Gershwin died and my age
started telling. And I thought of you and my age when the*
Hindenburg *exploded and I was reminded of airships and
aeronautics in general and my former lover, John Wilson, in
particular because through him I met you.*

*Can you believe that we first met nearly eight years ago?
Can you believe, also, that we've actually only met twice and
that the last time was nearly five years ago? We met through
John Wilson, are haunted by him, and are helplessly tied to
one another by his ghost.*

Three up for John Wilson.

*You keep writing and asking me questions about Wilson
and it makes me feel worthless. I've been married and divorced
and I've known lots of men, but you, Mike Bradley, solid citizen
and moral man, are only interested in what I knew about
Wilson. I feel as if I'm invisible.*

Okay, down to business . . .

*I asked a pragmatic friend in the British Defence
Department to check their report on the Tunguska explosion
in Siberia and tell me what their assessment of it was. Frankly,
given normal British skepticism, their assessment was almost
weird in its conviction that something* odd *had occurred and
that it had not been caused by a meteor or other extraterrestrial
source. In fact, according to British intelligence: (1) nothing
crashed* into *the Tunguska forest; (2) the angle of the trees
bent by the blast proved that the explosion had occurred above
them, not within them; (3) pieces of an unknown metallic
compound were found at the scene of the devastation; and (4)
just before the explosion, a lot of those living in the area
reported seeing what appeared to be a small, fiery ball
sweeping across the sky above the forest. Then it went down
and – whammo!*

A small fiery ball with a dark core, possibly metallic . . .

*The public stance in Britain was that the explosion had
been caused by a meteorite – but the private stance, at least*

*that of the Department of Defence and British intelligence, was
that it had been caused by some kind of man-made object that
did not – repeat: did not – come from Russia, but from outside
its borders. Also, the reported sightings seemed to suggest that
the object, whatever it was, had not come down from the
stratosphere, but had been completing a descending trajectory
at the end of a flight from west to east. In other words, it could
have come from Europe, the Atlantic Ocean, North America,
Canada, Alaska, or even farther . . . Unless it originally left
Russia, circled the globe and returned to its source, which
seems too ridiculous. The Brits, then, decided that if a
terrestrial object had been involved – and they certainly
weren't too sure of that – then it probably emanated from
Europe, possibly Germany.*

So what do you think, bub?

*I know what you think. You think it came from Wilson,
from Iowa or Illinois, and that it flew from North America,
across the Atlantic Ocean, across Europe, then on to Russia
. . . And having known Wilson, I think you might be right.*

*Is Wilson still in Germany? Yes, I think so – but I still can't
confirm it. Asking questions there, I quickly found out, can
be pretty dangerous. Nevertheless, I'm going back there, for
the humble Roswell* Daily Record, *and if I find out anything
at all, I'll certainly let you know.*

*I really enjoy writing these letters. It's like having a drink
with you. I never loved John Wilson – he was too cold and
remote for that – and when I met you, though you've never
laid a hand on me, I understood why. I can write about Wilson
now because he's everything you're not: a man whose lack of
feeling reminds me of all the feelings you hide.*

*You wanted me so much, Bradley – you couldn't hide it and
I couldn't resist it. But what I loved you for (yes, I did and
still do) was the knowledge that no matter how much you
wanted me, you also loved your wife and kids too much to let
me be a threat to them.*

Which just made me love you more.

I can say that now – can't I, Mr Bradley? Because being

at the other side of the Atlantic Ocean, I'm no longer a threat to you.

That's why I'm bold with you.

I'll write again when I get back from Germany. Adios, mi amigo.

Yours from too great a distance,
Gladys

Hiding his emotions, as Gladys had known that he would, Bradley folded the letter neatly, placed it back in his billfold, and gratefully climbed off the train when it arrived in Bridgeport. Given the guilt he was feeling over what he had not done, though had certainly briefly contemplated, he was glad that Joan didn't know when he was coming back and so wasn't at the station to meet him. Instead, he caught a bus, which he had not done for years, and simply by doing that for a change, felt that he had stepped back in time and was returning from high school.

That journey home, through the greenery of Connecticut, certainly made him feel young again, if only for a short time. And feeling young, he thought of Gladys, who also made him feel young, and recalled all the letters she had sent him over the years, ever since leaving the United States to work in England and Europe. The letters were like the woman, at once laconic and suggestive, and as they had only met twice and hadn't seen one another for almost five years, Bradley couldn't quite work out just how sincere they were, let alone what his reaction to them was or should be.

He had certainly found her very attractive and, in truth, still did, but he found the addiction more disturbing because he could not believe in it. He thought of her too much, even dreamed erotically about her – and could only explain this lasting attraction as part and parcel of his growing obsession with the mysterious John Wilson.

If not for Wilson, whom ironically he had never seen, he would not have met Gladys Kinder in the first place.

Two obsessions in one.

Stepping down from the bus as the sun sank beyond the trees, he walked up the garden path of his ranch-style house, thinking guiltily of Gladys Kinder, whom he had loved only in dreams, and of her former lover, now his quarry, John Wilson, whose genius, being ruthless and amoral, was increasingly frightening.

God knows what Wilson was creating in Hitler's Third Reich.

Maybe *only* God knew.

The first thing Bradley saw when he entered the house was the partially eaten birthday cake on the table. He briefly froze where he stood, on the threshhold of the living room, burning up with guilt when he saw Joan, standing by the table in the brightly lit room, turning to face him, her lovely smile absent.

'Welcome home,' she said quietly, venomously. 'You missed the party, unfortunately.'

'I'm sorry,' Bradley said. 'Dammit, I forgot. I got involved with—'

'A man called Wilson. Yes, Mike, I guessed. You promised you wouldn't let it become an obsession. Dammit, *you promised*!'

'I'm sorry. Where's Miriam?'

'Here, Dad.' He glanced to the left and saw her sitting on the couch beside her fiancée, Ralph Beaker. 'Don't worry about being so late. I'm not bothered, honest.'

'*I'm* bothered,' her mother retorted, sipping sherry and looking pretty with her angrily flushed cheeks. 'He never remembers anything anymore. He hardly remembers he lives here.'

'He's not that bad,' Miriam said with an encouraging smile that made Bradley feel worse. 'And he's still my one and only dad – the best in the house.'

She was twenty-two today, taller than Bradley, slim and darkly attractive like her mother, and he could hardly believe she was that age and engaged to be married. No more than he could believe that his son, Mark, was now twenty-three, married, with a pleasant, pregnant wife, and living in New

Jersey, from where he commuted to Manhattan to help in the law office now that Bradley was otherwise engaged with his informal intelligence gathering.

'Dammit,' he said, shocked that time was passing so quickly and therefore feeling more guilty, 'I really *am* sorry, Miriam. It's just this job. I just—'

'Come and give me a kiss, Dad, and then have some cake. It's only my *birthday*, for God's sake!'

'Now if you forget to turn up on our *wedding day*,' Ralph said with a laconic grin, 'she just might—'

'Believe me, I won't forget.' Grinning brighter than he felt and ignoring Joan's angry glance, he walked across the room, shook Ralph's hand, then leaned down to kiss his daughter on the cheek. 'Can I join you all in a drink at least?' he asked.

'Sure,' Miriam said. 'Why not?'

The evening progressed smoothly enough after that, with the liquor easing the tension for everyone, apparently, except Joan. Though she tried hard to be pleasant, she let him know with every glance that his increasing neglect of his family, caused by his obsession with John Wilson, would not be quickly forgiven. Bradley anesthetized himself with liquor, getting drunk without showing it, and when he spoke to his daughter's fiancée later that evening, he knew that at least the younger folk were unconcerned.

Not that it helped him much.

In bed, Joan lay as stiff as a plank and stared at the ceiling. When he reached out to her, she rolled onto her side and whispered, 'No! Not tonight! Don't think that being drunk will make it better. I'm not that easily swayed.'

'Dammit, Joan, I just forgot!'

'You forget too much too often these days. Our marriage nearly broke up before when you became obsessed with your legal work; now that you're becoming obsessed with intelligence gathering, we're going through the same thing. You're just a boy at heart, Mike, easily bored, wanting adventure; and when that particular itch gets a hold of you, God help us all. You even forgot your daughter's goddamned birthday! Go to hell, Mike. Just let me sleep.'

He felt cut to the quick, flayed by the brutal truth, yet as he lay there beside her, his eyes closed, trying to sleep, his guilt gave way to fantasy, to visions based on speculations, some of which involved Gladys Kinder, whose face he knew so well, and others involving a man called Wilson, whose face was a blank wall.

His twin obsessions formed the roots of a tree whose branches spread through his sleep, drooping over a dark abyss.

A ball of fire with a spherical, silvery core arched through that vast, disturbing darkness and drew him into oblivion.

He slept the sleep of the haunted.

Chapter Eighteen

'It will work,' Wilson said emphatically, buttoning up his greatcoat and glancing at the relatively small, disc-shaped metal object that was resting on the raised platform in the work bay of the second most secret area of Kummersdorf. 'We still have a lot of work to complete, but I believe it will work.'

The dark, lean-faced Rudolph Schriever, wearing oil-smeared coveralls, smiled with scarcely concealed excitement. The *Feuerball* was about three feet in diameter, had the general shape of two plates placed one upon the other, and had no visible air intakes or other obstructing protuberances, such as wings and rudders. Thus it had a smooth, seamless appearance. It was, in fact, the first flying wing that Wilson had attempted to construct since his disaster over Tunguska, and he was using it as a prototype for the larger, piloted craft being constructed laboriously in the main hangar.

'What we have here, gentlemen,' he continued as Habermohl and Miethe began draping a protective canvas sheet over the saucer-shaped, metallic object, 'is a circular flying wing that will offer the least possible air resistance, suck in the dead air of the boundary layer, and then use that same air, expelling it at great force, to increase its momentum even more. *However*,' he added deliberately, looking directly at the excited Schriever, 'even with this design, the boundary layer, though dramatically reduced, will still be present – and until we find a means of defeating it, the capabilities of our *Feuerball* and larger saucer will be severely limited. This, gentlemen, is the problem we still face. Good night to you all.'

He turned away and walked out as the canvas sheet fell over the *Feuerball* and Schriever's look turned to one of frustration. Leaving the workshop and stepping into the freezing November winds that howled across the nearby firing range into the lamplit parking lot, Wilson glanced at the main hangar, its walls being swept by searchlights, then smiled to think of Schriever's frustration. He climbed into his car, given his own car at last, drove out through gates guarded by SS troops, and headed back to Berlin.

He was amused by Schriever's frustration. Knowing that the ambitious young flugkapitän was nominally in charge of Projekt Saucer and reporting directly to Himmler, usually with exaggerated declarations of his own contributions to the work in progress, Wilson had continued to massage his ego by helping him to believe in his own importance. But occasionally, as he had just done, he could not resist slapping him down with another, seemingly insurmountable problem.

What he had not told Schriever, and was not about to, was that he knew how to solve the problem of the boundary layer: by using a kind of porous metal similar to that which he had created so many years ago. Undeterred by the previous disaster and now with vast technical and human resources he had not had, he knew that he would soon meet with success.

Tentatively named *Luftschwamm,* or aero-sponge, and essentially a combination of magnesium and aluminum, his unique metal was being created under his personal guidance in the research plants of distant Göttingen and Volkenrode. When completed, it would be used only for the flying saucer that he intended to construct without Schriever's knowledge. As for Schriever's *Feuerball* and flying saucer, they would fly well enough to keep him and Himmler happy – but that's all they would do.

Approaching the outskirts of Berlin, he looked into the evening darkness and was surprised to see a red glow in the sky above the rooftops of different areas of the city. The glowing pulsated and shifted, here and there obscured by smoke, became a deepening, eerie crimson as he came closer to it. The city's in flames, he thought, rolling his window down, smelling smoke. As he drove on toward home, he realized that it was the Kürhessen district, where he now lived, that was aflame.

Then he heard the breaking of glass, screams and shouts, then more glass breaking and raining upon stone, obviously the pavements.

Shop windows were being smashed.

Instantly alert, he drove into the Kürhessen district and was surprised, at this late hour, to see the streets packed with people. A nearby synagogue was on fire, and the crimson and yellow light of the flames illuminated a nightmare. Fashionable, middle-class people were clapping and cheering as roaming gangs of youths beat Jews senseless with lead piping, smashed the windows of their shops, and strewed their possessions along the gutters while Storm Troopers looked on smiling, when not actually joining in. Broken glass was everywhere, glittering in moonlight and crimson glare, splashed with the deeper crimson of human blood, spreading over the road. Another Jew screamed and was beaten down by swinging lead pipes as more women applauded.

Wilson kept driving.

It was a hellish, dangerous business, with violence and destruction all around him. He drove past more burning synagogues, more gangs of youths in pursuit of Jews, was waved on by exultant Storm Troopers. The air was filled with thickening black smoke, illuminated by flames, and rang with desperate cries. He heard gunshots, more smashing glass, screams and oaths. As he turned off the main road, away from a blazing shopfront, he passed a gang of youths who were beating a bearded old man with wooden poles. Women were wailing as their husbands and children were kicked and battered. Then eventually he found himself outside the apartment building where he lived quietly with Greta.

He climbed out, locked the door of the car, and noticed that a black SS car was parked a few doors farther along. He also noticed that a lot of neighbors were talking excitedly to one another. He hurried inside as another gang of youths came running along the street, filled with blood lust and bawling excitedly.

Animals, Wilson thought. Civilization is a sham. We are still protecting our caves. Thank God, in whom I do not believe, that science will change all that.

When he let himself into his apartment, Greta was gazing down through the window.

Beside her was the recently promoted SS Captain Ernst Stoll, also gazing down at the street below, his face handsome and solemn.

They both turned to look at Wilson, then Greta hurried forward, kissed him on the cheek, and stepped back again.

'Thank God you weren't hurt,' she said. 'We were worried about you.'

'No,' he replied. 'I'm fine ... but what's going on?'

'I believe it was—'

'The recent murder of Counselor Ernst von Rath,' Stoll explained, 'has led to anti-Jewish riots here and in the Magdeburg-Anhalt district.'

Wilson was surprised to find Stoll there, as he hadn't seen the captain for many months. Obviously the recent assassination of the German Foreign Office official in Paris by a demented young Jew, Herschel Grynszpan, had been used as yet another excuse to arouse more anti-Semitic feelings. Wilson said, 'I suspected that Rath's death would lead to trouble, but these riots seem ...'

'Yes,' Stoll said with a thin smile, 'organized. With the assistance of the Storm Troopers and SA – since our beloved Führer has declared that the riots, now spreading throughout the country, should not be discouraged. Taking the Führer at his word, Goebbels has ordered a pogrom, and right now, with the aid of the SD, SA, and SS, hundreds of Jewish shops, homes, and synagogues throughout Germany are being set to the torch and the Jews themselves, after public humiliation and abuse, are being rounded up and sent to concentration camps – a night to remember, yes?'

Ignoring Stoll's dry mockery, Wilson went to the window and looked down on the street where, in the lamplight, an unfortunate Jew was being tugged by his beard along the street by a laughing Storm Trooper while a gang of youths spat upon him, kicked him, and took punches at him.

Wilson, though feeling nothing for the Jew, had no respect for the youths.

'Animals,' he said, putting his thoughts into words. 'We're still as mindless as savages.'

'You see cruelty down there, Herr Wilson?'

'I just see wasted energy.'

When he turned away from the window, Ernst was smiling sardonically. 'Ah, yes,' he said, 'you have no time for human emotions. You prefer the intellect, the calmly reasoning mind, the cold light of pure thought.'

'That's correct,' Wilson said, ignoring Stoll's soft sarcasm. 'Most human emotions are primitive impulses. I prefer science, unimpeded by human weakness.'

'You love science – and love is an emotion.'

'No, Captain Stoll, I *don't* love science. In fact, I *respect* it. Only science can lead us away from the caves and into our destiny.'

'Which is?'

'Knowledge for the sake of knowledge. The evolution of reason.'

'Naturally,' Ernst said. 'You're the most ruthless man I ever met – and I've met a few. You are made of ice, Wilson.'

So Stoll, though no longer shocked by the gross behavior of his military friends, nevertheless could still be shocked by his unyielding single-mindedness. Wilson recognized that far from being the cynic he pretended, Stoll was in fact a disillusioned romantic of the most impressionable kind.

This one I can use, he thought.

'I haven't seen you for a long time,' he said. 'Not since you were shipped to the Antarctic. What are you doing here?'

'Because of my services in the Antarctic, I have just been placed in charge of your research institute at Kummersdorf.

In future, then, you will report directly to me, since I, and not Flugkapitän Schriever, will act as your channel to Himmler.'

Secretly pleased to hear this, Wilson took care not to show it, and simply said, 'You didn't come here to tell me that, so why did you come?'

'I want to show you the state of Germany,' Ernst said. 'The country you work for. I want to know what you think of it. Are you willing to come with me?'

'Now?'

'Yes.'

'Is that an order?'

'This is the night of breaking glass, Mr Wilson, and I want you to see it. No, it's not an order – it's a suggestion. This is a night to remember.'

Wilson grinned, knowing he was being tested, then nodded his head. 'All right, I'll come.'

'I want to come as well,' Greta said. 'I don't want to be left here.'

There were screams and shouts from outside, then the sounds of more breaking glass. Wilson glanced at the window, then at Greta, and saw the excitement in her hard eyes.

'Of course,' he said. 'Why miss such an experience? Let's all go right now.'

The gang of violent youths had disappeared from the street, leaving the bloody man groaning in the gutter. Many stolid citizens stared on from their doorways without coming forward to assist him. As Ernst stepped out of the doorway, the black SS car that Wilson had noticed earlier pulled up to them and stopped to let them get inside. When they were seated, with Ernst up front beside the driver, the car moved off smoothly.

It was a journey through hell.

Ernst made the driver take them through the riot-torn city, first through their own district, which was burning and wreathed in smoke, then to the Magdeburg-Anhalt district where the broken glass glittered in the moonlight around a great many broken, bloody bodies and the debris from looted shops. The assaults were continuing. People ran to and fro, some laughing, others screaming. Applause drowned out cries of terror, and the synagogues they passed were on fire and collapsing in showers of sparks. From there they drove to the train station and went inside. Ernst led them to the platforms where hundreds of frightened Jews were being herded onto the trains that would take them away.

'To where?' he asked rhetorically.

'The concentration camps,' Wilson said.

'Correct,' Ernst said. 'The concentration camps. Now let's see something else.'

He was like a man obsessed, wanting to plumb the depths of horror, but Wilson saw where the real horror lay – not outside, but within. He saw it in Greta's excitement when she watched the beatings and humiliations, in the revulsion that Stoll could not hide when he saw the same sights, in the dread that started filling Stoll's gaze when he saw Wilson's indifference.

Finally, in the SS hospital on the outskirts of Berlin, in the laboratories and operating theaters where the human experiments were conducted, Wilson saw Stoll looking at him, trying to search for a weakness. He merely nodded, quite deliberately, in his most thoughtful manner, and said, while casting his gaze over the tortured people on the tables, 'It's good that there are many more where these came from. The experiments on longevity and other matters will take lots of time.'

Ernst practically stepped away from him, as if touched by scorching heat. 'And that's all you see here, Wilson? This is nothing but meat?'

'We are merely the creatures of evolution,' Wilson said, 'and as such, we each have our part to play. Life is nature's experiment. The whole world is nature's laboratory. Those who will be used, will he used – and those, such as myself, who must use them, can do so without guilt. This human flesh is the material of evolution – like burnished steel and gunpowder. It is here to be *used.*'

Ernst didn't reply. He simply glanced at the silent Greta and saw the excited gleam in her whore's eyes. Then he drove them back to Berlin, through the now eerily deserted and smoke-filled streets of Kürhessen, with its broken windows and looted shops and burned synagogues and crumpled, dead Jews. Only then, just before Wilson entered his apartment, did Ernst blurt out, 'You're a monster!'

'No,' Wilson replied, knowing that he had won and that he would be able to manipulate Stoll in the future. 'I'm just a man with a purpose.'

Then he closed the door and turned into Greta.

'More semen,' he whispered.

Chapter Nineteen

The three troop trucks rumbled through the streets of Cracow, Poland, just before midnight. Sitting up front in the second truck, watching its headlights illuminating the falling snow and the helmeted heads of the soldiers in the truck ahead, Ernst was suffering from his familiar mingling of excitement and *angst*. The white streets were deserted, like those in a troubling dream, and the headlights of the trucks were beaming off the closed doors and shuttered windows of the houses in this old part of the city. Ernst thought of the residents cowering inside, praying that the roaring trucks would not stop outside their own homes. The thought made him smile grimly.

'If this keeps up,' he said, 'Cracow will soon be like a ghost town.'

'I doubt it,' Lieutenant Franck Ritter replied, moving the automatic weapon propped up between his knees and adjusting his black SS jacket. 'The damned Jews breed like lice and replace themselves as fast as we can get rid of them. We could be doing this forever, Captain, and there'd still be too many left.'

'But we're not after the Jews tonight,' the more concerned Lieutenant Willi Brandt said behind them. 'This area we're cleaning out is inhabited by ordinary Poles.'

'They're all vermin to me,' Ritter replied with a humorless, wolfish grin, 'so I'll enjoy what I'm doing.'

'You always do,' Ernst said dryly.

Ritter was about to make a retort, but was distracted when

211

the trucks ground to a halt with a squealing of brakes. Familiar with the routine, Ernst's troops jumped out of the back without waiting for his command and were already spreading out along the lamplit street and hammering noisily on the doors of the houses with the butts of their rifles when Ernst jumped down to the road, followed immediately by the enthusiastic Ritter.

Ernst, shocked by the sudden cold, cursed softly to himself, then hurried along the road, barking orders at his men and reminding them that no violence was to be used unless resistance was offered. His men were bawling at those inside and still drumming on the doors with their rifle butts, then someone remembered to turn on the trucks' sirens. That ghastly noise, added to the rest of it, made the bedlam more frightening.

Lights came on behind many windows, the wooden doors creaked open, then wails of protest merged with the bawling of the troops as they entered the buildings.

When the door of his chosen apartment block had been opened, Ernst, with a reluctant Willi Brandt and grinning Franck Ritter, followed his troops into the building.

This raid was on a street located near the university and containing select residential buildings, so Ernst was not surprised to find himself in an elegant hallway, with deep carpeting on the floor and what looked like antique paintings on the walls. The door had been opened by the residents of the nearest ground-floor apartment – an elderly couple, both wearing expensive dressing gowns and looking frightened. When the soldiers had parted to let Ernst walk through, he stopped in front of the couple, gave the Nazi salute and 'Heil Hitler!' then said, 'We are requisitioning this building in the name of the Third Reich. Please pack whatever belongings you can fit into one suitcase each and then enter one of the trucks parked outside. The soldiers at the door will assign you to a truck and you'll come to no harm if you don't resist. Now please do as you're told.'

The old woman burst into tears. Her husband looked

stunned. 'You cannot—' he began, trying to rally his senses. 'I will not permit—'

Ritter stepped forward and smartly slapped the man across the face. 'You'll do as you're damned well told,' he said grimly, raising his submachine gun, 'or pay the price, you old goat. Now go and fetch your suitcases.'

The woman sobbed even louder, but tugged her husband back into the room while the soldiers, at a nod from Ernst, hurried up the stairs to get the other residents out. Hearing the drumming of rifle butts on doors, the soldiers bawling, women shrieking and sobbing, Ernst stepped up to Ritter, stared grimly at him, and said, 'Don't you ever dare do anything like that again without my permission!'

Ritter flushed with anger. About to make an angry retort, he glanced blindly at the embarrassed Willi Brandt, but then changed his mind and grinned crookedly instead..

'Yes, *sir*,' he said, clicking his boot heels in mock obedience.

Ernst turned away from him, went back outside, and saw that residents of the other two buildings were already being led out into the road. Most were carrying suitcases. The men looked shocked and confused, some women sobbed, the children seemed dazed, as all were urged up into the back of the trucks. Satisfied that the operation was proceeding in an orderly fashion, he went back inside just as Willi Brandt, who would never make a good soldier, walked into the first ground-floor apartment, looking pale and distraught. Ernst went to the doorway, looked in, and saw that Willi had stopped in front of the two old people. Instead of packing, they were holding one another on the sofa, the man trying to comfort his wife as she sobbed into his shoulder.

'You're not in danger,' Willi was saying. 'You won't be harmed, I promise you. You've committed no offense and are simply being rehoused. Wherever you go, you will not be harmed. It's unfortunate, but at least you're in no danger – I can promise you that. Now, please, before you make someone angry, pack your suitcases.'

Ernst wanted to laugh at Willi's naïve assertion that the old people would not be harmed, for he knew that they were merely another two of the estimated one million Poles who had so far been expelled from their homes to make way for the Germans from the Baltic and outlying regions of Poland. True enough, they would not necessarily be killed outright; but it was from such unfortunates that Ernst would be selecting the men, women, and children who would be used as slave labor in the underground weapons research factories of the Third Reich, as guinea pigs in the so-called anthropological medical experiments that Himmler and the icy American, Wilson, were hoping would lead to the secrets of longevity, or as prisoners branded fit enough to be shipped secretly to Neuschwabenland in the Antarctic where, under the most appalling conditions, they would help construct Himmler's SS base under the ice and snow.

However, as this particular couple were too old to be of much use in any way, they would almost certainly end up in a concentration camp, which they would be unlikely to survive.

Still, Brandt's well-intentioned remarks did the trick. Upon hearing them, the old woman actually managed to stop sobbing long enough to whisper, 'Thank you, Lieutenant,' and then lead her husband into the bedroom to start packing their suitcases.

'You're too kind for your own good, Lieutenant Brandt,' Ernst said laconically, thus making an embarrassed Brandt turn around to face him. 'Some day that kindness will be misconstrued as weakness – and you might pay the price for that.'

'I was merely—' Willi began.

'Yes, Willi, I know.' Ernst grinned and walked past him to glance into the bedroom. The old couple were indeed packing their two suitcases, both with tears on their pale cheeks. 'Hey, old man!' Ernst said. 'Does the owner of this building actually live in it?'

'Yes, sir,' the old man said, his voice trembling. 'Mrs Kosilewski, who lives in the attic.'

'Thank you. *Auf Wiedersehen.*' Ernst grinned and turned away. 'Keep your eye on them,' he said to Brandt, 'and make

214

sure they get into one of the trucks. It's either them or you, Willi.'

'Yes, sir,' Brandt replied.

Reminded, as he left the room, of the striking difference between Brandt's kindness and Ritter's growing cruelty, and convinced that the latter would profit more than the former in the Third Reich, Ernst started up the stairs, to ensure that everything was proceeding properly on the floors above. When he heard the bawling of his soldiers and saw those respectable, middle-class Polish citizens shuffling sobbing from their apartments, each carrying a single suitcase and otherwise leaving behind not only their possessions but their homes, he realized just how far from home he was . . . far from Germany, far from Projekt Saucer, far from what he had been. Now, once more, he was a policeman instead of an engineer.

He was a party to genocide.

Someone on the second floor was slow to leave his apartment and Ernst saw a submachine gun, speedily reversed, its butt swinging, as Ritter struck the unfortunate man between his shoulder blades and made him lurch forward. The man cried out as he started falling, his wife quickly jerked him upright, then both of them hurried down the stairs, even as Ernst went up the next flight. When on the third floor he saw more adults and children leaving their homes forever in the belief that they would at least be rehoused somewhere decent, he thought again of the spread of Himmler's underground research factories, of the medical experiments that Wilson wanted, of their ultimate destination, Neuschwabenland, and felt bitter at the recollection of just how brief his return to Kummersdorf had been. He had no sooner settled back into the supervision of Projekt Saucer than the blitzkreig against Poland had commenced, the Polish air force had been destroyed, and Poland's ground forces routed. Then Himmler, having deprived him of his rightful place in that historic event, had sent him here to organize the rounding up of the human labor force required for the underground factories and the colonization of the Antarctic.

He tried to think of it as a great honor, his guarantee of a place in history; but sometimes, as right now, surrounded by sobbing women and shocked children and beaten men, he could not resist yearning to be back in Berlin, overseeing Wilson and the German engineers.

Sometimes, it had to be admitted, this work made him feel dirty.

Pushing his way through the harassed Poles milling about on the third-floor landing, he glanced through the window and saw his armed troops forming a pathway from the front door of the building to the trucks, their shadows elongated in the yellow lighting of the streetlamps and falling over the bowed heads and shoulders of the Poles who shuffled dispiritedly between them. Now viewing the Poles as mere numbers, his allotment for this evening, he climbed the last flight of stairs to the closed door of the attic. Because he knew that the cow of a landlady would be hiding inside, he hammered his clenched fist repeatedly on the wooden door.

'I know you're in there, Frau Kosilewski!' he shouted. 'So please open the door!'

'The door's not locked,' a surprisingly sensual voice replied. 'You have only to enter.'

Feeling foolish but also amused, Ernst opened the door and looked in. The attic was enormous and beautifully furnished, and when he stepped in, he saw the landlady sitting in an armchair, calmly smoking a cigarette. She was wearing a black silk dress, which clung closely to her luscious body, and her feet were in high-heeled shoes that emphasized the curves of her legs, one of which was crossed over the other, exposed from the knee down.

No cow at all, Ernst thought.

'I have packed, as you can see,' the woman said, indicating the suitcase nearby with a lazy wave of the hand holding the cigarette, 'but thought I would wait until I was called.'

Ernst walked farther into the attic and stopped close enough to the woman to observe that she had pitch-black hair that fell to her shoulders, as well as eyes as dark and deep as the ocean.

'You thought we'd forget you?' Ernst asked her, aware that he was becoming aroused by the sight of those elegantly crossed legs, the artfully arched foot, the high, full breasts under the tight black silk, that steady, measuring gaze.

Mrs Kosilewski smiled and shook her head. 'No, Kapitän,' she said. 'I didn't think that for a moment. We all know how efficient the Germans are. I merely decided to wait until the last moment – to avoid the crush and chaos.'

She pursed her brightly painted lips, sucked on her cigarette, pursed her lips again to blow some smoke rings. She knew just what she was doing.

'You live here alone?' Ernst asked, feeling hot and somnolent with desire, his thoughts slipping and sliding.

'Yes, Kapitän. I'm not married. I *was* married, but my husband died four years ago, which is why I now run this place.'

'*Ran* it,' Ernst corrected her. 'You run it no longer.'

She nodded, her gaze steady upon him. 'Yes, Kapitän, I know. May I ask whom you intend moving in here instead?'

'Germans from the Baltic and outlying regions of the country. No Jews. No Poles.'

'I am not a Jew, Kapitän.'

'But you *are* a Pole,' he reminded her.

She just smiled more knowingly. 'And will you be in charge of those Germans, Kapitän?'

'In a nominal sense, yes. I'll be visiting the building occasionally, if that's what you mean.'

Mrs Kosilewski uncrossed her long legs, crossed them the other way, rubbed her hand along her thigh to wipe ash off the tight dress, then pouted her painted lips to exhale more smoke rings. Ernst, now feeling dizzy with desire, could hardly take his eyes off her.

'Then why send me away?' she asked, her voice shivering through him. 'Surely I would be of better use to you here – to attend to the house, which I've done so well so far, and look after the Germans when they arrive.'

'And why should I be concerned with that, Frau Kosilewski?'

'Because if I was here to look after the house, my dear Kapitän, then I could also look after you.'

Her dark gaze was steady, if obscured by the cigarette smoke, and he saw the painted pout of her lips turning into a broader smile. He hadn't possessed a woman for months and was reminded of that bitter fact as she leaned across her raised knee, drawing his gaze to her firm breasts. He felt breathless, almost choked by his rising lust, and knew he could not resist her.

'Your soldiers have cleared out the top floor,' she said, almost whispering. 'They'll soon be leaving, mein Kapitän.'

'We have at least five minutes,' Ernst replied. 'I think that should suffice for now.'

He walked across the attic, closed and bolted the door, and by the time he had turned back to Frau Kosilewski, she was already undressing.

The spoils of war, Ernst thought grimly.

He went back there a lot. When not on duty, he practically lived there. He had married Ingrid for love, then cheated on her and been cheated by her. Since then, having also betrayed the values he held most dear, he found that he could temporarily regain his lost pride in the bodies of hardened women. He assumed that Kryzystina was one of those, a woman seasoned by bad experiences, and he was thrilled by the knowledge that she was buying her freedom with her body, selling herself for salvation. She certainly knew how to do it well – she had the sexual repertoire of a whore – and it helped him pass the darkness of those nights that his frustrations made restless.

'No,' she told him, 'I'm not a whore, but I want to survive, and for a woman living alone in a city ruled by a conquering army, that isn't easy. I was born on a farm near Dabrova, to barbarously ignorant peasants, and my father treated me like a beast of burden for all of my days there. I was beaten regularly, often starved as punishment, and eventually abused sexually by him, roughly and often. One day I stabbed him with a bread knife – not fatally, but in the stomach – then I fled for good. I was sixteen years old and was soon taken in by a gang of gypsies. The man who picked me, who naturally took his pleasure with me, soon started selling me to other men – he was as primitive as my father. So, a year later, when we were camped in a village near Cracow, I fled to the city, obtained work in a garment factory, attracted the eye of my boss, a decent man, and became his wife when I was twenty. We had a good life for eight years, but he died four years ago. His family inherited all his wealth and I got this house. As I couldn't afford its upkeep, I moved into the attic, let out the rest of the rooms, and was just getting back on my feet when Germany invaded Poland and you, my handsome Kapitän, came to requisition it for your fellow countrymen. Don't call me a whore because I offered myself to you. You know what the alternative was.'

They were naked in bed, which was still in the grand attic, both sweat-slicked from the ardors of a love that had little love in it. Ernst was stirred by the sight of her heavy breasts, bruised lips, and disheveled hair, and so slid his hand back between her thighs to find her still wet. 'Not all women would sell themselves for a house,' he said. 'Some have more sturdy principles.'

She glanced skeptically at him, then shook her head on the soaked pillow and chuckled deeply, sardonically. 'Just for my *house*?' she said. 'I think you know better than that, Ernst. I didn't just want to remain in this house: I also wanted to stay alive. And I think we both know, my pretty, that most of the people moved out of here were not destined for a very lengthy future.'

'I don't know what you mean.'

'I think you do, Ernst. You know as well as I do that Hitler is already transforming Poland into a massive killing ground and that the planned extermination of the Jews is an open secret among your high-ranking officers.'

Ernst grinned and slipped his fingers inside her, making her sigh. 'What a bright girl you are, Kryzystina,' he said. 'And how did you know all that?'

'I know because some of the high-ranking officers who shared my bed before you came here told me so. I also know because it's hard to keep secret the fact that at least once a week the Central Station is packed with Jews being moved out to an unknown destination, but one widely believed to be unpleasant.'

Ernst was arousing himself by playing with her. 'Very clever, my Polish pet.'

Kryzystina sighed and turned into him, to throw one long, smooth leg over him and let him have more of her. 'And don't we all live in terror,' she whispered into his ear, 'of the so-called house-cleaning, or murder, of hundreds, perhaps thousands, of Polish intellectuals and those of a similar class? Could I risk that, my pretty one?' Her tongue slipped into his ear, her teeth nibbled his earlobe, and her hand slid down his sweating body to take hold of him and guide him into her. 'So why did you clear out this house?' she whispered. 'And all the other Polish houses? Not just to rehouse us, my savior, as you slyly suggest, but to move us to Majdanek or Auschwitz, from where we would not return. Can you call me a whore because I choose you instead of a camp? I think not, my sweet one.'

They made love like two animals – that day and many others – and Ernst dwelt on what she had said, thought of Himmler and Wilson, and realized that what they were doing had the grandeur of evil. In accepting that, he lost his shame and replaced it with pride, plunging himself into his work for Projekt Saucer with renewed vigor. He planned the roundups of Poles and Jews, led the raids on their streets and ghettoes, and divided them into groups on the platforms of Central Station, right or left, life or death. Those chosen for death would not die easily – they would first be experimental fodder – and those blessed with the gift of life would work as slaves for the Third Reich in the multiplying underground factories where Himmler, with the aid of the icy American, Wilson, was creating the weapons that would ensure that the New Order would eventually conquer the world.

Projekt Saucer was at the heart of this great endeavor – and he, the once-rejected Ernst Stoll, was an important part of it.

Yet he still felt frustrated.

'I missed the blitzkreig,' he explained to Kryzystina. 'It was my life's great disappointment. When our army smashed through this damned country, when we destroyed your air force, when the Battle for the Corridor ended and your whole army was routed, I was still an administrator at Kummersdorf, south of Berlin. Now our troops are preparing to follow the Panzer divisions into Belgium, Holland, and Luxembourg, then on to France and Paris itself – and instead of going with them, I'm stuck here, in this Polish cesspit, a shepherd of Jews and other subhumans, a man cleaning out vermin.'

'You're still a soldier,' Kryzystina reminded him.

'No, I'm not. I'm a policeman.'

'You take it all too seriously,' she told him. 'Come and take me instead!'

Ernst needed little encouragement.

Because he did not like his work and detested Cracow and its inhabitants, he performed his duties mechanically, efficiently, not thinking too deeply about it, and otherwise vented his frustrations by confiding in Kryzystina. As there were few places to go in Cracow, he never saw her outside the attic, but he fed her hunger for expensive presents, brought her unauthorized food, wine and cigarettes, and when not trading sardonic putdowns with her, unburdened himself of his *angst*.

'I'm not a soldier,' he insisted, repeating his most common complaint. 'I should be on the road to Paris with the fighting troops, but instead I am here, in this miserable Polish city, arresting people by the hundreds and moving them on to the camps. It's my duty to do this and I do it well, but I was cut out for other things.'

'Engineering?'

'Rocket engineering. That's what I was going to do. Instead, I became a supervisor at the research center at Kummersdorf, spying on my fellow Germans, an old Italian and an illegal

American, whose genius put me to shame, though his ruthlessness shocked me. My God, what a monster!'

'An American?' Kryzystina asked him, surprised, as her nimble fingers played in his pubic hair. 'An *American* is working for the Third Reich?'

'Yes,' Ernst replied. 'In secret. He has a false passport. He cares for nothing but his work – the construction of a saucer-shaped aircraft – and since that project is also close to Himmler's heart, he was allowed to work for us. It's an unusual, maybe dangerous, situation, but Wilson is worth the risk. He's the coldest man I know, obsessed, slightly inhuman, but the advances he's made are extraordinary and fill me with envy. If not allowed to join the great advance on Paris, I should at least be back there, working with Wilson. But I'm not. I'm stuck here. Still taking part in Projekt Saucer, but not in the way I want.'

'And what way is that?'

'To take part in the actual design, as an engineer, which I should have been, and not just collecting Jews and Poles for our labor force.'

Kryzystina stretched out beside him, now knowing him, fitting to him, and asked, breathing warmly in his ear: 'A labor force only for Projekt Saucer? Is that why you're rounding up those people? To work for Projekt Saucer in the camps?'

Ernst felt impatient, his thoughts scattered by his erection. 'No,' he said. 'Don't be ridiculous. There are no research plants in the camps. Those I select don't go to the camps; they're sent to our growing number of advanced weapons factories, scattered over Germany and Bavaria and hidden underground or inside mountains. There they'll perform the heavy labor required. They'll certainly be worked very hard, but at least they might live.'

He said it with confidence as he rolled between her spreading thighs and inserted himself into the velvet glove that could make his thoughts reel; but he knew, when he had finished, when his thoughts had scattered and returned intact, that he had not told the truth, as even those being used by

Projekt Saucer would not necessarily live very long. Recalling the tour that Himmler had given him through the immense tunnel being hacked out of the densely forested hills of Thuringia to contain the planned underground factories at Nordhausen and nearby Bleicherode, he remembered the armed SS guards and the cracking of their bullwhips, which then, as now, were an indication that the welfare of the labor force would not be considered. And that labor force was being sent out by train from most of the major cities of Poland, to the increasing number of factories hidden underground, from the Harz Mountains to Thuringia, south of Prague and across to Mähren . . . a vast network of secret factories devoted to the design and construction of advanced weaponry and aircraft, including the rockets of Wernher von Braun and the flying saucer of the obsessed American, Wilson . . . factories in which the work force would, if necessary, be worked to death.

A brutal truth that appeared to have given Wilson no qualms at all.

'He *has* one other obsession,' Ernst confided to Kryzystina as they rested after their sexual exertions. 'An obsession with longevity – though that also is treated as part of his work. Wilson is old – in his mid-sixties, I think – but he looks and acts fifteen years younger than that, which he insists is due to a lifelong strict diet – no cigarettes or alcohol, no fatty foods; only fruit juice, cereals, fruit, and nuts – and, oddly, no exercise other than lots of walking. He also ascribed it to a lack of emotional entanglements, which he said were, apart from their well-known psychological effects, an inducement to quicker physical deterioration.'

'What about sex?' Kryzystina asked.

'I gather that it's fine,' Ernst replied, amused, 'as long as it's performed unemotionally – for the reasons I've already stated. Sex as pure *exercise* is healthy, but romantic love or sex used for emotional release are both damaging to physical as well as mental health.'

'You poor man,' Kryzystina crooned in his ear, reaching down for his penis. 'Let me arouse you sexually, therefore emotionally, and thus ruin your health.'

Ernst slapped her hand away. He was grinning, but felt uneasy. There were times when you couldn't help wondering just how right or wrong Wilson was.

'What's so strange,' he said, hoping to talk out his troubled thoughts, 'is that that particular obsession has also been dragged into his work – as everything is with him, sooner or later. It's as if he's treating even his own life as material for research – and so the state of his health and the possibilities of longevity, while important to him on a personal level, are more important for what they can add to his envisaged Super Race. Which is why some of those sent to the camps will have a fate *worse* than death.'

'What fate?'

Realizing that he had already said more than he should, Ernst shook his head and said, 'Nothing. Forget it.'

He lit a cigarette – he had started smoking only recently – and realized that *he* could not forget it. Indeed, who *could* forget the hideous, 'anthropological' experiments already being conducted, with Wilson's sly encouragement and at Himmler's command, in the surgeries and operating theaters of certain concentration camps as well as in secret SS laboratories located all over Germany?

Even now Ernst was haunted by the memory of the infamous Crystal Night thirteen months ago, when, in a fit of perversity or perhaps overwhelming frustration, he had driven Wilson through Berlin's violent, blazing streets to a Nazi hospital on the outskirts of the city. There, in the laboratory, he'd shown him the contorted limbs, frozen anguish, and, in some cases, dismembered heads of those who had died on the operating table in some of his requested experiments. Wilson had remained unmoved, insisting that science was all that mattered. He wanted the secret of immortality, or at least longevity, and would do anything, no matter how cruel, to uncover it.

And he had insisted that he was not a monster, but just a man with a mission.

What kind of man?

Already depressed, Ernst suddenly felt crushed by fear, so he stubbed his cigarette out, rolled onto Kryzystina, and tried to lose himself in her body, where nothing could reach him.

Ernst snapped to attention in the office of his superior officer, Major Riedel, gave the Nazi salute, and said, 'Heil Hitler!' Riedel returned the salute with a weary wave of his hand, told Ernst to stand at ease, and gazed up from his desk in a thoughtful, searching manner.

Ernst's former friend, the sadistic Lieutenant Franck Ritter, was standing at the other end of the desk, wearing his black SS uniform and trying hard not to smile. Major Riedel waved his hand again, this time indicating the many photographs pinned up on the wall behind him.

'You've seen these photographs before, Captain?'

'Yes, sir,' Ernst replied.

'Then you know what they are, do you not?'

'Yes, sir,' Ernst said, getting the distinct feeling that he was in trouble, but unable to guess why. 'They're photographs of Polish resistance fighters being hunted by the Gestapo. The SS also have orders to keep a watch out for them or anyone suspected of knowing or harboring them.'

'Correct.' Major Riedel glanced at Ritter, then stood up and planted his finger on one of the photographs. 'Do you know this man, Captain Stoll?'

'No, sir.'

'Can you see him properly from where you're standing?'

'No, sir, but I don't know anyone on that list.'

'Please step forward and check the photograph properly.'

Ernst did as he was told, walking around the far side of the desk and glaring at Ritter. He then stood beside Riedel to study the photograph up close. He saw a handsome young Pole with sensitive features and unusually bright, fearless eyes. When he had studied it, he shook his head and said, 'No, sir, I don't know him.' Then he marched back around the desk and stood stiffly in front of it.

He noticed Ritter's thin smile. Major Riedel nodded and glanced at Ritter, then sat in the chair behind his desk, where he clasped his hands under his chin and pursed his lips thoughtfully.

'The man is Andrzej Pialowicz,' he said. 'Does the name mean anything to you?'

'Yes, sir,' Ernst said, growing more confused and nervous. 'It's the name of a leading Polish resistance fighter, presently on a Gestapo and SS death list.'

'Correct again, Captain. I'm glad to note that you are, at least, reading the directives being sent out from here.'

Ernst did not reply, as there was no reply to give. He simply glanced at Ritter and noticed his smirk.

'Andrzej Pialowicz is indeed the most wanted man in Cracow. In compiling a dossier on his activities prior to the fall of Poland, we discovered that among his many other female conquests was a Jewish woman living right here in Cracow. Rather than arrest this woman, we placed her under surveillance in the hope that she would eventually lead us to Pialowicz – which she did. She was observed leading him out of the Wawel Cathedral – apparently where he had been hiding – and then driving him away in her car. Since it was our belief that Pialowicz was being taken to rejoin the other members of his resistance group, and since the overzealous oberleutnant in charge of the squad of SS troops took this as his opportunity to catch the whole gang, he did not arrest Pialowicz or his mistress, but instead followed them at a discreet distance – with two other SS men, in an ordinary Polish car with Cracow number plates. The journey ended at a warehouse in an industrial area south of the city. Pialowicz entered the warehouse alone and his girlfriend turned her car around and headed back to the city. Deliberately letting the woman go, since he knew where she lived, the overzealous young oberleutnant called up for support, then led an inept assault on the warehouse. In the ensuing fracas, some resistance men and SS troops were killed – but Pialowicz managed to elude us again and has not been seen since.'

'I'm sorry, sir,' Ernst began, 'but I'm not sure—'

'Why we called you here?'

'Yes, sir.'

Major Riedel smiled bleakly, then sighed as if in despair. 'Naturally, Captain Stoll, as we were keeping a watch on Pialowicz's girlfriend, we saw everyone entering or leaving the building in which she resided – and to our surprise, Captain, one of the most frequent visitors was you. Pialowicz's girlfriend, as you will have gathered by now, was also your mistress, Kryzystina Kosilewski.'

Ernst turned cold with shock, then felt himself burning. He glanced at the floor, felt nauseated, so looked up again.

'Do you wish to deny it, Captain Stoll?'

'No, sir.'

'Good,' Major Riedel said, 'since although we were aware that you are in charge of that building and therefore have good reason for going there, we were intrigued by both the frequency and lateness of your visits, so took the liberty of checking with the other, now mostly German, residents. Lieutenant Ritter, here, was in charge of that particular task and can confirm that according to her neighbors, Frau Kosilewski was opening her door to you on a regular basis and that when you visited, you stayed there for a long time, indeed often all night. You were also observed taking her parcels of groceries and other contraband items. Do you wish to deny *this*?'

'No, sir,' Ernst said, wanting to die, but rescued by a hot wave of hatred when he saw Ritter's thin smile.

'I'm glad to hear it,' Major Riedel said, unclasping his hands and sitting back in his chair, looking more weary than outraged. 'You *do* know, of course, that it's an offense for a German soldier, much less an SS officer, to knowingly fraternize with a Jew.'

'I didn't know she was Jewish, sir. In fact, she categorically denied it the first time I met her.'

'But you knew she was Polish.'

'Yes, sir, I did.'

'Lucky for you, Captain, you're an exceptional officer with particularly close ties to our beloved Reichsführer – otherwise I would have you shot for this.'

'Yes, sir. Thank you, sir.'

'Lucky for you, also, that stripping you of rank would necessitate a lengthy and potentially embarrassing report to our beloved Reichsführer, which could rebound unpleasantly on me personally.'

Unable to break the ensuing silence, Ernst heard his own heartbeat, resounding like a gong in his head, tolling his doom. He glanced sideways at Ritter and caught his triumphant smirk.

'As you will have guessed,' Riedel said wearily, 'we will now be arresting your mistress, the Jew bitch Kosilewski.'

'Yes, sir,' Ernst said, feeling as if his face had been slapped, his stomach kicked by a heavy boot.

'I would like to punish you by having you personally make the arrest, Captain, but since that could make matters more complicated than they are, I will instead insist that you accompany Lieutenant Ritter to your whore's house and stay by the van while the lieutenant and his men drag her out. If nothing else, I want you to see that, Captain Stoll. Do you understand why?'

'Yes, sir,' Ernst said, already feeling the awful humiliation that the major wanted him to suffer.

'Good. Now get out.'

Shocked and shaking, feeling alternatively hot and cold, Ernst followed the gloating Ritter out of the office, then along the gloomy corridor of the building, down a flight of stairs, then out into the freezing, windblown courtyard, where a small, black, windowless van, used for collecting suspects, was waiting. While two armed SS soldiers climbed into the rear, Ernst sat up front beside Ritter and the driver, shaking even more with humiliation and dread as the van started off and headed through the narrow streets of Cracow in the afternoon's darkening light.

'What will happen to her?' he asked Ritter.

'She's all mine,' Ritter replied with a leer. 'I've been given twenty-four hours to make her talk, but I won't need that long.' His leer widened lasciviously over blackened teeth. 'She'll give me everything soon enough.'

Ernst closed his eyes, knowing exactly what Ritter meant. He shivered with revulsion and the shame he had thought was long dead in him, then protected himself from it with a rage at what Kryzystina had done to him. The whore. The *Jewish* whore. He opened his eyes again, saw the charcoal light of late afternoon, and sat up straight when the van braked to a halt in front of her house.

'Can't I just wait in here?' he asked.

'No,' Ritter said, grinning again. 'You have to come out and identify her.'

'You already know who she is.'

'That's not the point,' Ritter said. 'The point is that *you* identify her. That's your punishment, *sir*.' Ernst nodded and climbed out, determined to hide any weakness from Ritter, and let his rage against Kryzystina protect him from sentiment as the lieutenant and the two soldiers entered the building with theatrical urgency. They came back out soon enough, this time with Kryzystina, who was sobbing and protesting in vain as the two soldiers dragged her across the pavement and Ritter, bawling something that included 'Jew bitch whore!' slapped repeatedly at the back of her head. Then he grabbed her by the hair and jerked her head back to let Ernst get a look at her.

Already her face was bruised and her dark eyes tearful. She saw Ernst and gasped.

'Yes,' Ernst said. 'This is the woman Kosilewski ... The woman I know.'

'Oh, my God!' Kryzystina exclaimed in disbelief.

The soldiers dragged her away from Ernst and threw her into the van, then climbed in behind her and slammed the doors shut. Ernst followed Ritter into the front and turned away from his gloating grin, but was forced to listen to Kryzystina sobbing in the back. The journey seemed interminable, all the way back to the grim, guarded entrance to the SS headquarters and basement cellars where, he knew, Kryzystina would be tortured and interrogated by Ritter.

He tried to walk away then, but Ritter called him back. 'Excuse me, *sir*,' he said, forcing Ernst to turn around and see Kryzystina, no longer sobbing, but with pale, tear-streaked cheeks, staring at him with fierce hatred and condemnation from between the two soldiers. 'Don't you want to say goodbye to your Jewish whore?'

Ernst could not reply, but he didn't turn away. The soldiers dragged Kryzystina toward the entrance. She suddenly howled like a wild animal, and only when Ritter had kicked her into the building did Ernst make his escape.

Kryzystina did not talk in twenty-four hours – nor in twenty-four days. Three weeks later, she was, according to a frustrated Ritter, still in her basement cell, a bloody mess but unbroken, and waiting for the train that would take her to the living hell of Auschwitz.

During that time, Ernst managed to recover from his humiliation and shame by remembering Kryzystina only with hatred. He accepted that he had made a fool of himself, shed a tear when he learned that the German army had entered Paris, and threw himself more devotedly into his task of finding suitable candidates for forced labor in the underground factories or a worse fate in the concentration camps.

In doing this, he paid penance for his sins and regained his lost pride.

Because Kryzystina was one of those earmarked for the camps, there was no way of avoiding her at the station – nor, by this time, would he have attempted to do so if he could. Indeed, when he saw her bruised and scarred face in that hopeless queue of the damned, a cloud of steam blowing across brown eyes darkened even more by weeks of torture, he felt neither surprised nor shocked, only a quiver of suppressed rage. Then, on a perverse whim, he had an SS guard with a snarling dog drag her out of the queue, to be placed before him.

When she recognized him, her eyes brightened with the enduring strength of contempt, and her lips, which had been shivering with despair, formed a line of defiance.

'You're a terrible mess, Frau Kosilewski,' Ernst said sardonically, 'and where you're going, the treatment will be even worse than what you've already had. Would you like me to help you?'

'What's the price?' she replied.

Ernst pointed at the queue forming at the far side of the platform and said, 'The people in that queue have been selected to live, while these poor wretches' – he indicated the queue she had just left – 'have been selected for death. Tell me where your boyfriend, Andrzej Pialowicz, is hiding and I'll let you leave this queue and join that one over there.'

She stared at him with disbelieving eyes, too shocked to speak.

'This queue or that one,' Ernst said. 'Life or death, Kryzystina. Now, where's Andrzej Pialowicz?'

She spat in his face.

Ernst didn't have time to react before the SS guard stepped forward, struck Kryzystina with his bullwhip, then hurled her back through the snarling dogs, into the queue leading to certain death.

Kryzystina didn't look back at Ernst to see him wiping her spittle from his forehead. Instead, she stared straight ahead, as if he had never existed, and didn't even look back when she was herded into the carriage, dissolved behind a cloud of steam, and then became just another nameless face in a mosaic of the damned.

Then Ernst crossed the platform and boarded the other train – the one taking those destined to work in the underground factories in support of his Reichsführer's Projekt Saucer.

That train, when it moved out of Cracow, took him back to Berlin.

Chapter Twenty

'Nostradamus,' Himmler said, sipping effetely at his tea, 'foretold the conquest of France by Germany. Did you know that, Herr Wilson?'

'No,' Wilson said. He had not known and did not wish to know, any more than he wanted to be reminded that Adolf Hitler based many of his most vital decisions on the advice of his Swiss astrologer, Karl Ernst Krafft; or that Hitler's deputy, Hermann Göring, ran *his* war with the aid of rainmakers and teams of clairvoyants; or that *his* deputy, Rudolf Hess, who had recently flown to England without permission in an insane attempt to establish peace with Britain, kept a pet lion, believed in astrology, and was known to have dabbled seriously in the occult; or that Himmler himself, now sipping his tea so sedately, was as mad as a hatter.

The world is being conquered by a gang of lunatics, dope addicts, sadists, occultists, and degenerates, Wilson thought, and I'm forced to use the scum.

'I believe that Nostradamus,' Himmler droned on, 'also prophesied the conquest of the West by a race of Aryans at approximately this time. Did you know *that*, Herr Wilson?'

'No,' Wilson said, though he knew what Himmler was driving at. Since he and the Reichsführer had last met, the German forces had overrun Norway, Denmark, Holland, Belgium, France, Yugoslavia, and Greece. They indeed seemed unstoppable, and the fall of the West had seemed guaranteed. However, Hitler had then become obsessed with his mystical notion of *Lebesraum* – German expansionism and

233

space – and was now preparing to invade Russia, even against the protests of his own generals. It was a two-front war that had defeated Germany in 1918 and would, Wilson reasoned, do so again – which is exactly why so many of Hitler's finest officers had protested the planned invasion in the first place. Yet even now, as he and Himmler were having their chat over tea, fighter planes, bombers, Panzer tanks, and three million foot soldiers were massing along a 930-mile front, from the Baltic to the Black Sea, prepared to advance into Russia and certain doom.

The beginning of the end is in sight, Wilson thought, which means that my time is running short, my situation becoming more tricky. I must be more careful now.

'You are an admirably concise conversationalist, Herr Wilson,' Himmler said, his eyes, magnified by the pince-nez, as dead as his smile. ' "Yes" and "no." A curt nod of the head. A distinct lack of verbal elaboration. No more said than is absolutely necessary. A man of few words.'

'I'm sorry, Reichsführer.'

'You have no need to be. Clearly it is in your nature. I think you're a man who trusts in his own nature and devoutly follows his chosen path.'

'That's true,' Wilson said.

They were having their tea in Wilson's glass-paneled office in the main hangar at Kummersdorf. After glancing at Himmler's immobile bodyguards, both granite-faced and wearing menacing black-leather overcoats, Wilson studied Captain Ernst Stoll who, in his SS uniform, was sitting silently beside his beloved Reichsführer.

After returning about a year ago from Poland, where reportedly he had laid the groundwork for the regular move-ment of Jews and Poles to either the concentration camps or the secret underground and research establishments of the rapidly growing Third Reich, Stoll had been a changed man: a more fanatical Nazi, now devoted to Himmler, and untiring in his dedication to Projekt Saucer and its ultimate goal, which was to protect an underground colony of SS masters and their slaves in Neuschwabenland.

Yet as Wilson knew, Stoll remained a frustrated romantic ... and Wilson could use him.

Indeed, he already had.

By the time Stoll had returned from Poland with his renewed dedication to Himmler's planned world of ice and fire, Wilson had come to understand something important: While it was true that German scientists as a whole were producing extraordinary innovations in weaponry and aeronautics, it was equally true that their separate projects were not being coordinated. So great were the rewards for success in Nazi Germany, but so terrible the penalties for failure, that even formerly cooperative scientists had been reduced to currying favor by competing ferociously with one another.

In this sense, the Peenemünde situation was typical.

While Himmler had the cream of his rocket engineers working on the V-1 and V-2 rockets at Peenemünde, on the Baltic, the V-1 was a Luftwaffe project, the V-2 was an army project, and both sides were competing instead of putting their heads together. Similarly, while various research establishments scattered throughout Germany and Austria were working separately on gas turbines and jet propulsion, heat-resistant and 'porous' metals, and gyroscopic mechanisms and boundary layer-defeating airfoils, only Wilson had had the sense to link their often startling innovations together, into the one, revolutionary aircraft.

That aircraft was not Schriever's flying saucer, about to be test-flown. It was the small, disc-shaped *Feuerball*, which Wilson was ostensibly creating as a flying antiradar device, but which in fact he was secretly using as an experimental prototype for a full-scale, vastly more advanced flying saucer, to be constructed and used only when he saw fit.

As Stoll did not know about the secret *Feuerball* experiments, he had been more than willing to arrange for Wilson to travel the length and breadth of the Third Reich on numerous visits to other research establishments.

Wilson had already used him, then, and would do so again

. . . for something much more important.

'You have that faraway look in your eyes, Herr Wilson. What are you thinking about?'

'Nothing, Reichsführer.'

'You never think of nothing, Herr Wilson. You think all the time.'

'I was just thinking about the flying saucer,' Wilson lied, 'and wondering if we'll succeed.'

'I never thought you'd doubt yourself for a moment. I am truly surprised.'

'I have doubts occasionally,' Wilson lied again. 'All human beings do.'

'You are not as human as most, Herr Wilson. You think too much and feel too little.'

Wilson nodded. 'Perhaps.'

'And yet you have doubts.'

'Yes,' Wilson lied for the third time, not wanting Himmler to know and fear his invincible arrogance.

Himmler placed his empty cup on the small table beside him, then stared steadily through his glittering pince-nez. 'In the words of our beloved Führer: "One must listen to an inner voice and believe in one's faith." Would you not agree, Herr Wilson?'

'If the inner voice is self-conviction, then, yes, I agree.'

'I do too,' Himmler said. 'Which is precisely why nothing can stop me.'

'You're a resolute man, Reichsführer.'

'And you aren't?' Stoll asked.

'Only average, Captain Stoll.'

Stoll's smile showed a degree of dry amusement. 'I think not, Wilson. In fact, you're a man so resolute, you'd stop at nothing to get what you want. Now isn't that so?'

Be careful, Wilson thought. 'No, I don't think so.'

'There are rumors,' Himmler said, ostentatiously studying his immaculate fingernails, 'that the dearly departed Dr Belluzzo did not deserve the fate he received. What do *you* think, Herr Wilson?'

'I'm afraid I haven't thought about it,' Wilson said, 'apart from assuming that when the SS decided to arrest him, they had their reasons.'

'Are you aware of what those reasons were?'

'His superior officer, Flugkapitän Schriever, believed Belluzzo to be mentally incompetent and possibly dangerous.'

'Did you share that view?'

'I can't remember if I discussed it with Schriever or not, but I have to confess that if I'd been asked, I would have been bound to agree with him.'

'But you had no direct hand in Schriever's report?'

'No. None at all.'

Himmler spread his hands in the air and smiled frostily. 'Good,' he said. 'That's all right, then. After all, no one is going to miss Belluzzo, who was not even German.' He then clasped his hands together, stopped smiling, and added softly: 'It's just that one worries if one suspects that one's staff are becoming too ruthless in their ambitions.'

'Naturally, Reichsführer.'

He stared steadily at Himmler, giving nothing away, but knew that the Reichsführer was aware of what he had done and would not forget it.

'I like a man of initiative,' Himmler said, 'so long as it doesn't make him *too* ambitious.'

'I understand perfectly.'

'Good,' Himmler said.

Realizing that he had gained Himmler's wary admiration, Wilson stared across the broad expanse of the hangar, to where the Schriever flying saucer, about to be test-flown for the first time, was being prepared. It was resting on a large steel platform that could be wheeled out of the hangar. Forty-two meters wide and thirty-two meters high, it looked immense in the enclosed space. Indeed, raised up on the steel platform, it cast its shadow over the cover-alled engineers working around it, including Habermohl and Miethe. Schriever himself was being helped into his flying suit, since he was the test pilot.

It was a completely circular aircraft, shaped like a gigantic, inverted steel bowl and supported on four thick, hollow legs that housed the gas-turbine rotors which, it was hoped, would give it its vertical-rising capability. Another four gas-turbine rotors were positioned horizontally at equal distances around the rim of the circular body, for control of horizontal flight.

It was lamentably primitive, Wilson knew. It would fly enough to satisfy Himmler and keep Schriever pleased with himself, leaving Wilson free to get on with the design of the real, vastly more advanced machine.

Wilson's deception was necessary. There was no one he could trust. The Third Reich was filled with ambitious, frightened men who wished to make an impression. Wilson did not trust Rudolph Schriever. He saw the madness in Himmler's eyes. He remembered his troubles in America, the heavily guarded hangars in Iowa and Illinois, the businessmen and politicians and generals who had ruthlessly stolen his life's work. The same thing could happen again, because the war's end was beginning: When the battle for Russia commenced, the Third Reich would start to bleed. How long would Himmler last then? And how long could Wilson then keep his secret? He wanted to make real his secret masterplan, but what guarantee did he have that he could do it? The Nazis devoured their own kind, so they might devour even Himmler – either that or the Reichsführer would turn on Wilson, destroying all he had gained.

Heinrich Himmler: the Reichsführer. Wilson was not deceived by his mild gaze. His neat fingernails were polished with blood and his smile hid hysteria. No, Wilson didn't trust him, and so he gave Himmler only a little – the prototype for a flying saucer that was merely a crude airplane – while explaining repeatedly that his problems were many and he needed more time.

It was a delicate maneuver. A great cunning was required. The flying saucer had to fool Schriever and the other engineers; it had to be a considerable achievement by their standards though still lacking something. Thus Wilson had used obsolete technologies with slightly advanced ideas, letting Schriever and his engineers take pride in what they imagined was their great achievement: a saucer-shaped aircraft. Gas turbines and liquid-fueled rockets were still the basis of their technology, but Wilson had already surpassed that. The real achievement was his other, secret *Feuerball,* and most of that was in his head . . . So he gave a little and took a great deal and listened always to Himmler.

'Your health is good?' he was asking.

'Yes,' Wilson replied.

'The recent operation was a success?'

'Completely, Reichsführer.'

'To experiment on yourself shows great courage – or, perhaps, faith. I have to admire that.'

'I am nearly seventy, Reichsführer. My time is running out. I am old and my body begins to fail me, and I have to prevent that if I'm to continue my life's work. Since the choices are otherwise nonexistent, it's certainly worth the risk; and while so far we've only managed to repair my stomach and do some minor skin grafts, given time, if we continue medical experients in the camps, I'm convinced that we'll eventually reach the stage where we can make flawless skin grafts, replace faulty hearts, develop mechanical limbs, and maybe even make great advances in human longevity . . . The possibilities are limitless.'

Himmler scratched his nose, adjusted his pince-nez, then nodded solemnly. 'I agree,' he said softly. 'We need that – and more than that. Let us sum up what we've achieved so far and see what we've got . . .'

His voice trailed off as he stared at Schriever's saucer. The doors of the hangar were being opened and sunlight was pouring in.

'We have our underground factories,' Himmler said. 'We have the location for our New Order. We have our masters, the SS, and our slave labor and your own crystal genius.'

'We have everything,' Stoll said.

Himmler smiled but shook his head. 'No, we still don't have enough. We need more than normal men. What we need is a biological mutation that will lead to true greatness. We must learn to control our work force. Not with whips and not with guns. What we need is automatic control of their bodies and minds. The human brain must be examined, the body's secrets must be explored. We must try to steal their will and their physical strength and leave them just what *we* need. The so-called democracies cannot do this – their regressive morals would forbid it – but here, at the dawn of the new era, there is nothing to hinder us.'

He smiled at the listening Ernst Stoll, as if giving approval.

'We must use the *Ahnenerbe*, hand in hand with the *Lebensborn*, in order to study racial characteristics and breed only the finest. That will solve the first problem – and only in that way, will we be able to create the Superman. Nevertheless, that leaves the problems of the work force, and we must solve those also. Control of body *and* mind. We must find a brand-new method. I think of medical and psychological experiments of the most extreme kind. The camps are ours to command. The scum there is our base material. The New Order needs a wealth of mindless muscle and your genius must find it.'

Wilson did not reply, as there was nothing for him to say. What Himmler wanted, he also wanted, but for very different reasons; what Himmler wanted was an insane dream that he totally rejected. Yet he listened, because Himmler had the power, and he still needed that.

'Do you understand?' Himmler said. 'My New Order will come to be. It will be broken into colonies, each individual, each with its work, all divided into masters and slaves, existing just to support us. There's no problem in the Antarctic. It's just another Nordhausen. You ship the subhumans in to build your underground complex, you control them with brain implants and our Death's Head SS, and then you move in your scientists and technicians and administrators, and you bind them all together with fear of their all-seeing masters. And once there, where can they go? There is no way in or out. They will live underground, seduced by power or cowed by fear, the masters bound by their blood oaths, by their religious conviction; the subhumans by torture and the threat of death and their singular lack of a way out. Yes, American, it is possible. We are halfway there already. You must work, you must complete this great project, before we settle the matter. Now let us see this test flight.'

The hangar doors had been opened fully. The flying saucer was being wheeled out on the broad platform, its steel body now silvery. Wilson followed Himmler and Stoll, out of the office, across the sunny hangar, then into the summery afternoon. The collapsible legs let the platform be lowered to the ground, where the wheels were removed, and the platform became a glittering launching pad with the saucer resting upon it.

Flugkapitän Rudolph Schriever was standing in his flying suit directly in front of the saucer, his helmet under his arm. He stepped forward and gave the Nazi salute and looked uncommonly nervous.

'Good luck' were the only words spoken by Himmler.

'Thank you, Reichsführer!' Schriever responded, visibly swelling with pride, then saluted again and turned away, to climb the stepladder that led up the gleaming, sloping body to the saucer's centralized cockpit.

The Perspex canopy had been removed. The saucer reflected the sunlight. After Schriever climbed carefully into the dome-shaped pilot's cabin, the canopy was replaced and locked in position. The engineers retreated and shielded their eyes. Himmler and Stoll hurried behind the sandbags with Wilson, then Himmler scratched nervously at his nose and adjusted his pince-nez. The saucer resembled a metallic mushroom – or, perhaps, a giant spider. Its four legs, which housed the gas turbine rotors, thrust down obliquely. There was a roar as the hollow legs spewed flames and filled the air with black, oily smoke. The saucer shuddered and shrieked. Yellow flames spat at the platform. The roaring changed and became a deafening sibilance as the machine started rising. Himmler covered his ears. His body appeared to be shrinking. The saucer shuddered and roared, lifted tentatively off the ground, hovered briefly and swayed unevenly from side to side and was obscured by the swirling smoke. Himmler turned and stared at Wilson. His mild eyes were like the sun. The saucer roared and hovered just above the ground as Himmler gripped Wilson's wrist.

'A new era!' Himmler exclaimed as the ground shook beneath them.

Chapter Twenty-One

Bradley and Joan made love that afternoon more tenderly and satisfyingly than they had done in months.

They had flown to the island of Oahu, Hawaii, for a vacation in the hope of repairing the damage done by Bradley's increasing obsession with John Wilson's unheralded, innovative work on rocket research and what he might be creating in Nazi Germany. That obsession had grown dangerously over the years, encouraging Bradley to be more distracted, keeping him away from home too much on his many investigatory trips, and making him increasingly thoughtless when it came to his family. Consequently, the gulf between him and Joan had widened. She had even threatened divorce. Bradley, though desperate to be part of a proper intelligence agency, such as the British Secret Intelligence Service, and use its greater resources to track down Wilson and put a stop to his activities, had begun to see the error of his ways.

Well, not quite . . .

While he had continued to use his powerful Wall Street law firm and influential clients as his personal link to Washington, DC, and General Taylor's army air force intelligence unit, he had become increasing frustrated by the lack of progress regarding his proposals for a centralized intelligence-gathering organization. Earlier in the year he had been informed by Taylor that the beginnings of just such an organization had been made – an Office of the Coordinator of Information, or COI, with its headquarters established in the State, War, Navy

Building next to the White House. When another unofficial agent, William Donovan, had been appointed above Taylor as coordinator of information, Bradley had been crushed by disappointment and decided to turn his back completely on his intelligence ambitions.

A few months later he had suggested this vacation in Hawaii as a sort of second honeymoon, designed to bring him and Joan closer together and let them start all over again.

It appeared to have worked. Admiral Jeffrey Paris, an old friend of Bradley's buddy, General Taylor, and captain of one of the battleships anchored off Ford Island, had found them an attractive villa on the green hills overlooking Honolulu. Bradley and Joan had settled in with pleasantly surprising ease, gradually unwound, talked through their differences, and finally come together in bed like much younger lovers.

That afternoon Bradley had woken up from the nap they had taken to prepare them for the Saturday evening dance in the Pearl Harbor Naval Officer's Club, to which they had been invited by Admiral Paris, and found himself luxuriating in Joan's warmth as well as in his newfound peace of mind.

He felt younger than he had in years. Swelling with love when he thought of how close he had come to losing Joan, he reached out to her, ran his fingers lightly over her, stroked her raised hip and waist, then rolled into her spine, slid his hand around to her soft breast, and let his passion awaken her. She turned into him, almost purring, her smile sleepily radiant, and they pressed their naked bodies together and became one again.

'God, I love you!' he whispered.

Later, bathed and dressed – Bradley in a white dinner jacket and black bow tie; Joan in an elegant, off-the-shoulder evening dress – they had an aperitif out on the walled patio overlooking Honolulu. Bradley gazed through palm trees, palmettoes, and hibiscus toward the US Pacific Fleet, anchored in the vast bay. There were destroyers and minesweepers, oilers, tenders and submarines; and off Ford Island the battleships formed two lines, not far from the airfield where dozens of planes stood side by side. The battleships looked magnificent, glinting gray in the brilliant sunlight. Beyond them, far away, where green sea met blue sky, were the flapping white sails and gleaming brass railings of private yachts and expensive motor cruisers.

'It sure as hell isn't New York,' he said, turning back to face Joan across the glass-topped wickerwork table and appreciating the warmth of her girlish smile, the sunlit sheen of her auburn hair.

'Don't even *think* about New York,' she said. 'We'll be back there soon enough. Let's enjoy what we've got while we've got it. I'm blooming just sitting here.'

'You look it. Making love must be therapy.'

'All men are disgustingly vain,' she said, 'and you're just praising yourself.'

He had to smile at that. 'Touché, my sweet. Nevertheless, it's nice to see you smile. I thought I'd lost that forever. I nearly did, didn't I?'

'I'll admit, I was worried.'

'You don't have to anymore. I've put it all firmly behind me. Not meaning to discuss New York, but I'm satisfied to be back in Manhattan, doing what I'm supposed to do.'

'You're such a good lawyer,' she told him. 'I hate to see that talent wasted. I really didn't mind you doing that unofficial snooping for General Taylor during your trips overseas, but the thought of you becoming involved in *official* intelligence gathering made me real scared.'

'You've read too many novels, Joan.'

She smiled at that. 'Yes, I suppose so . . . but I also know how involved you can become – and *were* becoming over Wilson – so I'm glad you changed your mind and went back to legal work.'

'I'll now settle into my respectable middle age and watch my married kids make mistakes with *their* kids.'

'There are worse ways of growing old.'

It was a wise remark that made him appreciate her all the more and count his lucky stars that their marriage hadn't been destroyed by that Wilson business.

Unfortunately, once he thought of Wilson, he also thought of Gladys Kinder, whose letters from London were still arriving at his Manhattan office, bringing him news of the war in Great Britain, along with plenty of teasing, oddly disconcerting sexual comments.

No longer could he doubt that he had been instantly attracted to the woman, maybe dangerously so. If that feeling normally would have faded with the passing years, her letters were resolutely keeping the memory of her alive. Now, though he certainly enjoyed reading the letters, his rapprochement with Joan made him wish that Gladys Kinder would stop writing and let him forget her. He hadn't laid a hand on her, nor even made a move toward her, but her letters, piling up over the years, made him feel that he had.

Suddenly realizing just how treacherous emotions could be, and frightened by how close he had come to hurting and losing Joan, he reached across the table to squeeze her hand.

'Right,' he said. 'There are worse ways of growing old. And we have such *good* kids to be concerned with. I want to thank you for that – it was your doing. I love you all the more for it.'

'Oh, God, Mike, shut up, you're making me blush. Finish your drink and let's go.'

He grinned. 'Yep, let's do that.'

They drove down the steep, winding road, through lush tropical greenery, past pineapple plantations and rickety, makeshift stores run by Chinese, Japanese, and Hawaiian families, to the road that ran along the seafront of Honolulu, past the Pearl Harbor naval base and adjacent Hickam Field, home of the 17th Army Air Corps. Having decided to eat alone, before meeting Admiral Paris and his wife for drinks in Waikiki, they drove into the center of Honolulu, through narrow streets filled with bars, pawnshops, Chinese grocery shops, tattoo parlors, and photo galleries, and parked near the corner of Maunakea and Hotel Street, outside a window filled with the carcasses of smoked pigs and ducks hung on meat hooks.

'If what we eat looks like what's in that window,' Joan said,

'I don't think I'll get through my meal.'

'You're going to love it,' Bradley replied. 'You'll probably *eat* like a pig!'

'It's always so *noisy* here!' Joan exclaimed good-humoredly. 'That's why I love it, dear.'

They had dinner upstairs in Wu Fat's Chinese Restaurant, surrounded by gilded decorations and walls painted a garish red, under a very high ceiling and rotating fans. The food was delicious, the atmosphere exotic, and Joan, as if to prove Bradley right, ate like a pig.

'So many *men* in here!' she whispered, wiping sweet and sour sauce from her lips.

Bradley glanced around him and realized that she was right: The place was filled with sailors, marines, and soldiers, some with Chinese, Japanese, or Hawaiian girlfriends, most on their own. Right now they were happy, eating and drinking, having a good time, but he knew that before the night was out there would be lots of fighting. Saturday night in Honolulu was never without its fair share of action, which is why he enjoyed it.

'God help them,' he said. 'They're the social pariahs of Hawaii. Serving your country doesn't exactly make you popular. Come on, luscious, let's go.'

'You just want to take me down there to sell me,' Joan said – in this area of Honolulu, close to the docks, servicemen actually queued up in the streets to get into the brothels located above the shops – 'but I don't think I'm worth that much.'

'It's a fluctuating market,' Bradley replied, 'so you might be surprised.'

Joan's laugh was surprisingly raucous, making Bradley feel terrific, and he put his arm around as they walked back down the stairs, joined the noisy throng in the street, and eventually drove to Waikiki, four miles farther on.

'We should retire here,' Joan said, as the taxi cruised along the palm-lined road and she studied the large houses in expansive gardens. 'For what we pay, you could buy a mansion here and have a really great life: lovely weather, golden beaches, beautiful people. Why *are* we in New York?'

'We're not in New York; we're in Connecticut.'

'Same difference,' Joan said.

Surrounded by the pink walls and Moorish tiles of the Royal Hawaiian Hotel, they had cocktails with Admiral Paris and his wife, Marisa, the former a silvery-haired, pink-faced, world-weary handsome man, the latter a raven-haired, good-humored woman whose features, though formed over fifty years, were those of a carefree woman ten years younger.

'I hope you like that villa we found for you,' Marisa Paris said as she stirred her exotic cocktail with a straw. 'Are you happy up there?'

'Blissful,' Joan replied. 'The villa is lovely and the view is stupendous.'

Marisa sighed melodramatically. 'Gee,' she said, 'I'm glad. I get so *nervous* finding places for friends of friends – you just never know, right?'

'Right,' Bradley said. 'But you *picked* right, so stop worrying.'

'Taylor told us to take care of you,' Admiral Paris said. 'He described you as two very rare birds – friends worth any effort. You've obviously warmed his cold heart.'

Bradley chuckled at that. 'I've never *seen* his cold heart.'

'Taylor isn't cold, but he's tough – and a good judge of people. A man like that I can trust.'

'You've known him a long time?'

'Yep. We've conducted a friendly rivalry for years: army against navy. I claim to sail the high seas, where the air is fresh and healthy, and I tell him he's just a soldier, a kind of policeman, his nose rubbed in intelligence muck.'

'It's necessary,' Bradley said with a nervous glance at Joan.

'Sure it is,' Paris replied. 'I know that. I just josh him to score the odd point. He isn't bothered at all. In fact, right now he's setting up a kind of centralized intelligence bureau. I'm not sure exactly what kind, but that's his latest obsession.'

'Marisa,' Joan said to Paris's wife, 'are you going to sit here and let them talk about their work?'

'No way,' Marisa said, placing her empty glass on the table and looking melodramatically determined. 'I'm going to insist we leave right this minute and have us some *fun*.'

'Right!' Joan said.

'Right!' Bradley added.

Yet when they left the hotel and drove back to Honolulu, he could not help but feel bitter disappointment at learning that a centralized intelligence agency was being set up and he, who had pushed so strongly for its formation, had not been called. Of course he understood why – he had told Taylor that he wanted out – but he still felt obscurely betrayed, as if, in some part of his subconscious, he had wanted Taylor to insist that he come in.

Dammit, he thought, I'm such a hypocrite. I should learn to grow up . . .

Then, as they entered the Naval Officers Club in Pearl Harbor, he looked at Joan's flushed face, saw the radiance of her smile, and realized that in every possible way he had done the right thing.

'Let's have the time of our lives,' he said.

The dance began late in the evening and went on until the early hours of the morning when the white-jacketed officers and women in flowing ballgowns, most more flushed than they had been six hours before, started drifting away, either back to their quarters on the base or, as the cacophony of revving cars indicated, to their homes in the lushly tropical hills above Waikiki and Diamond Head.

Because they had been drinking, Bradley and Joan, at the invitation of Admiral Paris, returned to their home in the officers' quarters, where they had a few hours' sleep. The next morning, after showering and changing into the less formal clothes they had brought with them, they joined Paris and Marisa for breakfast in their modest kitchen. Outside, in the base and in Honolulu, the church bells were ringing.

'I still feel drunk,' Marisa said.

'Go to church and confess,' her husband said.

'You look surprisingly fresh,' Bradley complimented her. 'It must all be in the mind.'

'It's in *my* mind,' Joan retorted. 'Or at least in my head. My head feels like it's stuffed in cotton wool. What on earth did we *drink* last night?'

Admiral Paris laughed and placed his coffee cup back on its saucer. 'Just a few little cocktails,' he said. 'The ones with flags sticking out of them.'

Then his cup rattled in its saucer and the coffee slopped out. 'What the hell . . . ?'

The table shook again as Paris stared down at his cup. The other cups and saucers also rattled, then, even as Bradley heard a distant explosion, the floor beneath him shook more violently and the telephone rang shrilly on a table that was bouncing on the tiled floor.

Paris kicked his chair back, picked the telephone up, and was listening with widening eyes when the antiaircraft batteries outside started firing. 'Goddamn!' Paris exclaimed. 'Right!' Then he slammed the phone back down and stared at the three of them. 'We're being attacked by the goddamned Japanese,' he said. 'They've already attacked Wheeler Field and Schofield Barracks! Dammit, those sons of bitches caught us napping. Their planes are bombing us right now!'

Even as he spoke, a plane roared low overhead and away again, making the house shake. Bradley glanced at Joan, saw her wide, confused gaze, then he followed Paris out of the house, to stand on the porch.

A black pall of smoke was already billowing over Pearl Harbor and a frightening number of Japanese dive bombers, fighters, and torpedo planes were flying in from the sea, their wings glinting in brilliant sunlight, to swoop down in waves and bomb and strafe Ford Island and the harbor.

Bradley saw the bombs dropping, tumbling over like black birds, and heard the awesome blast of the explosions even as fierce balls of fire were lifted up on clouds of billowing, oily black smoke over what he knew were the battleships near Ford Island and the defenseless, parked planes on the airfield nearby.

'Oh, my God!' Joan exclaimed softly behind Bradley. He felt her fingers tugging at his shirt, as if to pull him back into her.

'Dammit!' Paris exclaimed. 'I've got to get back to my ship!' He glanced at his wife. 'You better get the hell off the base, Marisa. Go with Bradley and Joan. Go back to their place up in the hills and I'll call you later. Okay?'

However, even as he spoke, some Japanese Zeros roared in low overhead, through the black puffs of smoke from the American antiaircraft batteries, to pass on and strafe downtown Honolulu and the lush hills beyond. A series of explosions tore through the greenery, blowing palm trees apart, setting fire to the foliage, filling the air with flames and smoke between the houses dotting the hills, as the planes, their machine guns still chattering viciously, ascended gracefully and circled back toward the sea.

'No,' Marisa said. 'I'm staying right here.'

'And so am I,' Joan said.

'Then stay indoors,' Admiral Paris said. 'And you better stay with them, Mike.'

'I'll drive you down to the fleet landing,' Bradley said, 'then come straight back. Marisa might need your car.'

'Right,' Paris replied. He hurried into the house and came back out with his naval jacket, still buttoning it even as he kissed his wife's cheek and slipped into the car. Bradley also kissed Joan, then got into the driver's seat, turned on the ignition, and screeched away from the house.

The Japanese planes were still attacking, whining above the explosions and gunfire. Bradley drove past men and women, sometimes even children, who were standing on their lawns or porches, wearing only pajamas, dressing gowns, or even underwear, gazing up in disbelief at the boiling, black, flame-filled smoke and diving Japanese planes.

'Christ!' Paris exclaimed. 'They even caught us with our aircraft on the ground. Ford Island must be a junkyard!'

Certainly the fleet landing was a nightmare.

Even before he had braked to a squealing halt, Bradley saw the columns of water geysering up between the boats and ships of the fleet, many of which were on fire, pouring black oily smoke, breaking apart and sinking, while the barrels of the guns of the antiaircraft batteries and surviving ships spat yellow flames. Balls of fire ballooned brilliantly over sinking ships. Sailors in flames were jumping overboard. Japanese Zeroes were bursting into flames and falling into the sea between the ships and boats, where in a haze of gray-,black-, and crimson-tinged smoke more sailors were trying to clamber into lifeboats or swimming or drowning.

Admiral Paris jumped out of the car as it shuddered to a stop, slammed the door behind him, looked, appalled, at what was happening, then leaned back down to the window and said, 'Thanks, Mike. Now get the hell back to the house and look after our ladies.'

'Will do,' Bradley said.

As the admiral hurried off to find a boat to take him to Ford Island and Bradley reversed the car, sailors with blistered faces and limbs, their scorched, blackened flesh hanging in strips from blood-smeared bone, were being helped out of whaleboats and carried away on stretchers to the waiting ambulances and hospital trucks. Bradley drove off to a concerto of wailing sirens, blasting ships' horns, whining planes, dementedly chattering machine guns, pounding antiaircraft batteries, exploding bombs, and bawling or screaming men. Japanese Zeroes were still winging in low overhead, strafing the base, as he drove through the streets of the officers' quarters.

Hardly believing what was happening, Bradley was further shocked when he stopped in the driveway of Admiral Paris's house. Bullets had smashed the concrete paving and stitched a line up the front wall, broken the windows, and peppered the roof.

Mesmerized for a moment by the sight of the broken windows, finally Bradley raced into the house. Then stopped in his tracks when, just inside the living room, he saw Marisa rocking Joan in her arms and trying to wipe the blood from her soaked clothing as she wept over her.

'Oh, God!' Marisa choked out between her sobs. 'Oh, God, please! Oh, God, *please!*'

In one hideous moment Bradley took in the bullet-stitched walls, smashed picture frames and furniture, glass-strewn floor, and Joan in Marisa's arms, both covered in blood. Bradley knelt down, saw that the blood was Joan's, heard an anguished groan, realized it was his own, then reached out to touch his wife's forehead. It was icy cold.

'Oh, Jesus!' he said.

Her breast and stomach were covered in blood and her breathing was harsh.

'*Call an ambulance!*' he heard a hysterical woman screaming – then realized it was actually his own voice and shuddered convulsively.

'I've already called for an ambulance' – Marisa sobbed – 'but they're all so damned busy. But they're coming. *They're coming!*'

'Joan!' Bradley hissed. '*Joan!*'

She opened her eyes. 'Oh, God,' she said, 'it hurts.' Her eyes were dazed, but she gradually recognized him and gave him a weak smile. 'My man,' she said. 'My ever-loving, handsome husband. What a fine face you have.'

'Thanks,' Bradley said.

'I'm all right,' Joan said. 'Aren't I?'

'Sure,' Bradley lied, 'you're okay. No problem at all. It's just a matter of—'

'The children, Mike. Look after the children. And our grandchildren too.'

'Shut up,' Bradley said. 'Don't talk that way. Jesus, Joan. Oh, my God!'

'Hey, there, don't be—'

But her final words didn't make it – only blood escaped from her lips. Then she coughed and spluttered, choking on that blood, sighed, as if too weary to be bothered, and closed her eyes for the final time.

Bradley was stupefied. He couldn't believe that she was gone. He kept glancing around him, as if time would move backward, and when it didn't, he just clung to her, holding her tightly, refusing to let go, and shedding all the tears he had held in since the days of his childhood.

The Japanese planes left and returned, then left for the final time. Bradley accompanied Joan's body to the morgue and held her hand in the silence.

The only sound was his sobbing.

Chapter Twenty-Two

Joan was flown home and buried back in Connecticut, near the house where she and Bradley had shared so much together. Mark and Miriam attended the funeral, bringing their children with them, and even though that made Bradley feel older, it also encouraged him.

Life went on and Joan still lived through her children and grandchildren, all of whom had loved her as much in life as they missed her in death.

Yet it wasn't enough.

He felt broken up inside. He had Christmas with his children and grandchildren and some friends, but the love that they showered upon him only made him hurt more. He saw the New Year in alone, in a house that now seemed too large, and shortly after, feeling lost in the house, he decided to sell it.

Mark and Miriam didn't need it. They now had their own homes and families. The house was only a morgue for his recollections of things won and lost, a graveyard for his past. Not a home any longer.

'I'm putting the house on the market,' he told Mark.

'Gee, Dad . . .'

'It's unbearable with your mother gone, Miriam.'

'Yes, Dad,' Miriam said. 'I can understand that.'

He sold it quickly enough, but the contents were a problem, because so much of what had seemed so necessary was now useless debris. He gave his children what they wanted, offered the rest to his friends, gave what was left to various charities, and took only his personal things.

On the last day, when he was sorting through the papers in his desk drawers, he came across the letters from Gladys Kinder in Europe, tied together in chronological order and looking well thumbed.

He sat down, feeling breathless, filled with love and guilt and heartbreak – his love for both women; his guilt over a betrayal that had taken place only in his thoughts; his heartbreak over the loss of both women, one living, one dead. Then, feeling confused, he decided to burn the letters. But he couldn't bring himself to do it, so he packed them away with his other things and left his home for the final time.

Needing the bright lights of Manhattan, he took an apartment near his office, started working himself to exhaustion, drank too much, and started staying in at nights, wanting only the silence.

That silence was broken by General Taylor, who called uninvited.

'You look terrible,' he said.

'I guess I do,' Bradley replied.

'What you need is a real distraction,' Taylor said, 'and that's why I'm here. Do I at least get a drink?'

Bradley poured him a bourbon. Taylor carried it across the office, taking a seat under the window, in striations of gray light.

'I'm really sorry about Joan,' he said. 'I don't know what else to say.'

'Don't say anything, General.'

'We've counted the cost,' the general said. 'Apart from Joan, it was terrible. In the first attack, the Japs capsized one battleship and completely destroyed three others. In the second attack, they sank three destroyers and badly damaged two others. Everything on Ford Island was destroyed, including our airplanes, and we had nearly three thousand casualties, most of them fatal. Luckily, they missed the entire aircraft carrier fleet – which was out to sea at the time – but no doubt about the damage they inflicted . . . and now the

United States is at war. We've lost our virginity.'

'Right,' Bradley said, feeling drugged.

'Our almost total lack of knowledge about Japanese intentions,' Taylor said, 'due to the fragmentation of our intelligence gathering and lack of cooperation between those involved in it, has compelled us to do what you've been suggesting for years: namely, form a centralized intelligence agency – the Office of Strategic Services, or OSS – which we hope to have running by the middle of next year. I want you to join the organization as an agent.'

'I don't want to,' Bradley said.

'Yes, you do,' Taylor insisted, sipping his bourbon and sounding determined. 'We've just been informed by British intelligence that according to various European resistance groups, remote-controlled bombs and flying rockets are being constructed at a Nazi research center in Peenemünde, in the Baltic. Based on that information, British intelligence conducted further research and can confirm that in 1936, work did in fact begin on the construction of a secret proving ground in the vicinity of a small fishing village called Peenemünde and that it's since become one of the Nazi's most advanced experimental stations. Analysis of aerial photography taken in the past few weeks shows that the proving ground exists, that the southern part contains workshops where, we believe, the missiles are constructed, and an extensive settlement that has since been verified as being occupied by the scientists. A little farther on, near the village of Karlshagen, are barracks for soldiers and workers, plus a prisoner-of-war camp and con-centration camp.'

'Sounds very cozy,' Bradley said, not wanting to know.

But Taylor persisted. 'Since we'd already informed the Limeys about your old friend, John Wilson, they're now working on the theory that the new weapons, while ostensibly being made at Peenemünde, may in fact be the indirect products of Wilson's genius in that field, since the rocket team was originally based in Kummersdorf, Berlin, at the other side of a former firing range where Wilson and some other German rocket scientists were working at the same time.'

'That sounds logical,' Bradley said sourly.

Taylor was unmoved. 'So the British Secret Intelligence Service,' he continued doggedly, 'recently got in touch with us and asked us if we had any opinions about their latest theory. Naturally we agreed that in all probability their theory is substantially correct and that Wilson, the traitorous bastard, is largely responsible for the Peenemünde flying bombs and rockets. This has naturally led all of us to wonder just how advanced Wilson is and what other diabolical innovations he has up his sleeve. It has, in fact, convinced us that he has to be tracked down and taken off the stage – and that's why we want you. We want you to find that son of a bitch and terminate him.'

'I'm too old,' Bradley said.

'Bullshit,' Taylor replied. 'We need you because you were once an excellent pilot, have done unofficial intelligence work both for the US army and as a civilian lawyer, know a hell of a lot about aeronautics, speak French and German, know Europe like the back of your hand, and are obsessed with John Wilson and what he's up to.'

'True, but I'm still too old,' Bradley said, feeling only the pain of his loss and the lack of enthusiasm for life that Joan's death had engendered.

'No, you're not,' Taylor said. 'You're just in a state of shock. And that's exactly why you need this kind of distraction – and why you'll be good at it. As for your general fitness, if you join OSS, you'll be put through a tough retraining program, with a special emphasis on espionage, self-defense and undercover, or guerilla, operations. So when the time comes, you *will* be fit enough. And believe me, Mike, you *need* this job to help you forget Joan. You need it – so take it!'

Deeply moved by what his friend was trying to do for him, and aware, also, that he really did need something special to distract him from his anguish, Bradley said, 'And once I finish with the training . . . What happens then?'

'You'll be posted to London, to help the British Special

Operations Executive track down Wilson and put an end to his activities. Now do you want it or not?'

Bradley leaned forward in his chair, covered his face with his hands, and knew he had to escape.

'I want it,' he said.

Chapter Twenty-Three

'They are perfect specimens,' the white-smocked hospital surgeon informed Wilson and Ernst Stoll as he removed the guillotined human heads from the laboratory's refrigerator and placed them into tin cans.

'Jewish only?' Wilson asked.

'No', the orderly said, placing the last severed head in a can, then starting to place the lids back on. 'When we received a letter from Professor Hirt, the head of the Anatomical Institute of the University of Strasbourg, telling us that the number of skulls in the university's collection was too limited, we started obtaining them from captured Russian troops, and these heads are mostly those.'

'All undamaged?'

'Of course! Once the heads of the living specimens are measured and selected, death is induced by injection, then the head is severed from the body and shipped in these cans, which will be hermetically sealed, to the Anatomical Institute.'

'Good,' Wilson said. He turned to Stoll, who was looking distinctly queasy, and said, 'There is much we can learn from these heads. There are ways we can use them: the psychological and *physical* creation of the Superman and a work force that has no free will. Himmler's Institute for Research into Human Heredity, the *Ahnenerbe*, must not be wasted on quasi-mystical research, but utilized for a more practical purpose: medical and surgical experimentation of the most fearless kind. We must look at the human brain and learn how to control it, study the human body and learn how to change it.

In doing this, we can create a new kind of man – any kind that we want. This is what we are doing here.'

'Can we leave now?' Stoll asked.

'Yes,' Wilson said. After thanking the surgeon, he led Stoll out of the laboratory and back through the corridors of the SS hospital, taking note of the fact that the young kapitän was still looking queazy and understanding that he could use his moral qualms when the occasion called for it.

Right now, however, he was intent on preparing Stoll for the world he would inherit. To that end, as they passed the guarded doors of other laboratories and operating theaters, he said, 'Our experiments are wide-ranging and in fact know no bounds, which is why we're using human beings instead of just animals. It's through our ruthless experimentation on these human beings that we're learning about brain manipulation, limb and other bodily replacements, the causes, nature, control, and use of fear, even the effects of freezing and decompression – all of which will be useful when we move to our underground colony in the Antarctic.'

Ernst nodded thoughtfully, trying to accept the unpalatable. Wilson knew, as they walked out of the hospital, that he would in time do so.

The hospital entrance was heavily guarded by armed SS troops, and more troops were placed strategically at the far side of the road. Wilson glanced along the street of this suburb of Berlin, quiet and almost empty in the gray light of August, and thought of how the whole of Germany had become a huge armed camp in which fear, torture, and death were commonplace.

It was a prototype for the kind of colony he envisaged in the Antarctic; but the world he would create would be controlled by scientists and dedicated to the advancement of knowledge – it would not be controlled, as Himmler thought, by his blond young gods of war and dedicated to his mystical notions of a world of ice and fire.

'I haven't seen you much lately,' he said to Stoll, as the chauffeur-driven SS car carried them around the outskirts of

Berlin, through the outlying villages, past columns of troop trucks, and out toward the research center at Kummersdorf, south of the city. 'What have you been up to?'

'My work with the *Lebensborn* organization,' Ernst replied, rolling the window down to let air in, then lighting a cigarette.

'Which many Germans still think are maternity homes.'

'Yes.'

'And this work keeps you busy?'

Ernst sighed. 'It's all for Projekt Saucer, Wilson. As you know, the real aim of the institutions is the controlled breeding of the perfect Aryan, a Nordic superrace, through the disciplined mating of men and women selected in accordance with the racial principles defined by the *Ahnenerbe*.'

'Yes,' Wilson said, feeling impatient, 'I already know that. But are you exploiting the *Lebensborns* for our purposes?'

'Yes,' Ernst said, sounding weary. 'For the past eighteen months, when not actually at Kummersdorf, I've been organizing the kidnapping of thousands of racially valuable children from all over Europe, as well as the Soviet Union, and shipping them to the many *Lebensborns* now spread throughout the Reich, where they undergo special training to Germanize them. The past records of such children are erased and their parents, if not exterminated, are not told where they are. Within weeks of arriving at the *Lebensborns,* the children can remember little of their past, have been given new names – which also helps them to lose their former identity – and have been taught that they have not descended from the ape, but from the SS. Given their political indoctrination and total devotion to the Reich, these children, when they become of age, will voluntarily take part in our human stock breeding and go on to create the racially perfect, totally loyal, new breed of man, to be controlled by our Nazi elite in our SS colonies under the ice. You should be proud of me, Wilson.'

It was a small attempt at levity, so Wilson smiled at him, then glanced up at the bombers that were heading for England. 'How are things going in Neuschwabenland?'

'Progress is slow and painful, but at least it is being made.

Many workers have already been shipped out from the camps and are digging out their underground accommodations in terrible circumstances. The death rate is high – from cold, exhaustion, and sometimes hunger – but the first underground area will soon be cleared, more men and materials will then be shipped in, and by the end of next year, we should be able to start shipping in the scientists as well as the first children from the *Lebensborns*. It is *your* side of the work, Herr Wilson, that is now going slowly.'

'Time is of the essence, I know, but this thing can't be hurried.'

'You must understand,' Ernst said, 'that since the defeat in Russia, our beloved Reichsführer is becoming even more concerned that we perfect your flying saucer – which he views as the ultimate weapon – and also ensure that the underground space in Neuschwabenland is completed and fully manned before the present war comes to an end.'

'The *present* war?' Wilson asked, amused.

'As you know,' Ernst replied rather stiffly, almost offended, 'this war is merely the prelude to a thousand-year war – the one that will turn the German soldier into the Superman.'

'Ah, yes,' Wilson said, amused by Stoll's passionate sincerity, '*that* war.'

'Yes,' Ernst echoed him, 'that war. And ever since Stalingrad, which marked the beginning of the end of this war, Himmler has become almost desperate to ensure that everything is prepared for our escape to Antarctica.'

'But everything *is* being prepared, as you've just so vividly demonstrated.'

'Not fast enough,' Ernst said. 'That's why he wants another test flight of the flying saucer. He views it as the most vital part of our operation – an undefeatable weapon as well as a means of flying in and out of there with impunity – and he's growing worried that it will not be completed in time.'

'I'm sure it will be,' Wilson said, 'though nothing under the sun is guaranteed.'

'It has to be,' Ernst replied, 'so let's hope that this test flight is successful. Otherwise there'll be trouble.'

'From Himmler?'

'Yes.'

Wilson had to force himself not to smile. The car had reached Kummersdorf, and as the driver slowed down on the approach road to the research center, where high barbed-wire fences surrounded flat, windblown fields, he tried to imagine the expression on Rudolph Schriever's face when the flying saucer, which he was claiming as his own, failed to fly. Wilson knew it would not fly – he had ensured that it would not, because its failure would give him what he needed to get rid of Schriever and place Stoll on his side.

He had it all worked out.

When their papers had been checked at the heavily guarded gate, they were waved through. They proceeded along the road, past the old firing range, now overgrown, to the research center's collection of ugly, corrugated-iron and concrete hangars, which also were protected by heavily armed SS troops.

On Stoll's instructions, the driver took them between two of the hangars and parked at the far end. There, in an open space between the firing range and an overgrown hillock, the latest version of the so-called Schriever saucer was sitting on its lowered steel platform, prepared for takeoff. The gas turbine rotors that had been housed in the previous model's four hollow legs had been replaced with a series of variable jet nozzles arranged all around the outer rim, just below the saucer's center of gravity. Combined with the machine's lack of rudders, ailerons, or other protruding surfaces, this gave it a more graceful, seamless appearance.

Looking eerily beautiful in the fading mist of late morning, the saucer appeared to tower over the men who were either working around it or simply observing it from behind the concrete bunkers and heat shields placed across the hangar's open doors. Even as Wilson and Stoll climbed out of the car, Himmler was being led out of the hangar, his pince-nez reflecting the sunlight. He was accompanied by his usual bodyguards. Schriever, again in his flying suit, walked proudly beside him. Himmler stopped walking when he saw Wilson and Stoll coming toward him.

'Ah!' he said softly. 'Captain Stoll, and our American genius! I thought we had lost you.'

'No, Reichsführer,' Ernst replied, stopping with Wilson in front of him. 'We were checking the progress of the medical and surgical experiments at one of the *Ahnenerbe* hospitals.'

'Impressive, are they not?'

'Yes, sir.'

'And many of them were suggested by Herr Wilson, here, who is nothing if not fecund in many fields.'

'Thank you, Reichsführer,' Wilson said, then nodded coolly at Flugkapitän Rudolph Schriever, whose darkly handsome, saturnine features were illuminated with the glow of his newly found arrogance. 'Are you looking forward to the test flight, Flugkapitän?'

'Yes, Herr Wilson, I am. I have the confidence that the saucer will fly this time.'

Wilson smiled. 'I hope so.'

'I am always a little confused,' Himmler said in his quietly probing, slightly sardonic manner, 'as to who is responsible for what regarding this saucer. According to certain sources, including yourself, Flugkapitän Schriever here is mostly responsible for the machine; according to others, the credit should go to you. Who, then, do I praise or blame should this machine fly or crash?'

'I am willing to take the blame if it crashes,' Schriever said too quickly, thus demonstrating an unexpected slyness at taking the credit for the machine. However, while Wilson had previously let him take most of the credit, in the hope that he would not attempt to bite the hand that fed him by bad-mouthing him to Himmler, he now had good reason for taking the blame for what was about to happen.

'No, Reichsführer,' he said. 'I cannot let Schriever do that. I must confess that I'm responsible for the latest innovations in this model – particularly the multidirectional jet-propulsion system – and if anything goes wrong, and I pray it won't, the blame is all mine.'

Convinced that the machine would work and that Wilson was trying to steal his credit, Schriever turned red and was just about to retort when Stoll, after giving Wilson a puzzled glance, said diplomatically, 'I think we better begin the test, gentlemen, while conditions are excellent.'

'Of course,' Himmler said.

Schriever saluted and marched off, very upright and determined. He was climbing the ladder up the side of the saucer even as Wilson retreated behind the concrete bunker with Ernst, Himmler, and the bulky SS bodyguards. Staring through the protective, reinforced glass viewing panel of the bunker's wall, Wilson watched Schriever lowering himself carefully into the raised, centrally located pilot's cockpit. When he was strapped in, Habermohl and Miethe replaced the Perspex canopy, locked it into position, then climbed back down to the ground and pulled the ladder away. When they also were safely behind a concrete bunker and a waving flag had indicated that the test could begin, Schriever switched on the saucer's electrical system. Wilson heard the bass humming sound and saw the variable jet nozzles around the rim turning down toward the ground. When the jet nozzles were facing the earth, the engines roared into life.

The noise was extraordinary, an earth-shaking clamor, and the red and yellow flames spitting out of the downturned jets formed a circle of fire that was obscured and distorted by the smoke and dust billowing up from the scorched, hammered ground. The saucer vibrated violently, sank down on its collapsible legs, then bounced back up, swayed dangerously from side to side, and eventually lifted slightly off the steel platform, borne up on a bed of spitting flames, the smoke swirling around it.

It hovered tentatively in the air, its silvery body tinged with crimson, the yellow flames and black smoke forming a river of light around it. Then it rose even higher, thirty yards, then fifty, and hovered uncertainly again, tilting slightly from left to right. Then the jet nozzles moved and the flames shot out horizontally. As they did so, half of the nozzles cut out and the saucer was thrust forward instead of upward, in a sudden, brief, horizontal flight.

Very brief, indeed – as Wilson had known it would be – for just as it shot forward, heading toward the old firing range, the side not spitting flames tilted dramatically toward the earth and the flaming nozzles, now aiming at the sky, increased its downward momentum,

'Oh, my God!' Ernst exclaimed.

Schriever turned on the other jet nozzles in time to make the saucer level out just as it was about to hit the ground. It bounced along like a spinning top, out of control, turning wildly, shrieking and sending up great curving waves of earth and debris even as the engines cut out and the smoke streamed away from it.

'Get him out!' Ernst bellowed at the engineers.

Habermohl and Miethe ran like the wind, carrying the stepladder between them, and threw it on the sloping side of the saucer and climbed up to the cockpit. They unlocked the cover, let it fall to the ground, hurriedly helped a shocked Schriever out, and ran back to the bunker, practically dragging the pilot between them. They had just hurried behind the concrete wall when the saucer exploded.

It shuddered and collapsed, its legs giving way. Then it lay there, tilted on one side, some of its metal plates blown off, the flames shooting out from inside it and licking over the cockpit.

Himmler stared at Wilson, his cheeks pale, his lips tight, then he glared at Ernst and stalked off, saying nothing at all.

'We're in trouble,' Stoll said.

Chapter Twenty-Four

'We can no longer depend on the American genius or Projekt Saucer,' Himmler said in his quiet, chilling manner from behind his desk in SS headquarters in Berlin. 'Whether or not an actual workable saucer can be achieved is beside the point, since clearly this war won't last as long as we had hoped and the time required to complete the flying saucer will not be available.'

'With all due respect, Reichsführer,' Ernst said, relieved to have found Himmler so calm after the disastrous test flight but wondering why his throat was still dry, 'we must give Schriever and the American more time. If we wish to populate Neuschwabenland, we will need something more advanced than our finest airplanes.'

Himmler held up his hand in a rather lordly gesture of rejection. 'Yes, yes,' he said, 'I know that. I am not a fool, after all. But since the American's saucer has failed again – and he *did* admit that he was responsible for it – I'm convinced that we can no longer depend on it as our final weapon, but must instead turn our attentions to Wernher von Braun's V-1 and V-2 rocket projects at Peenemünde. All the tests there have been highly successful – indeed, I witnessed two tests myself, as well as others, at my own rocket center at Grossendorf. Given the excellent results, it is anticipated that remote-controlled rockets will soon fall on London. Since our beloved Führer also believes in the rockets, that is where we should concentrate.'

'Yes, sir,' Ernst said, not wishing to contradict his

increasingly distracted Reichsführer, though he knew that Himmler's real reason for concentrating on the so-called secret weapon program was based on his desire to take control of the whole of Germany's military production.

Indeed, to this end, he had recently tried to talk Wernher von Braun into working under his command at Grossendorf. After failing to do so, he had persuaded General Fromm into letting him reinforce the *Abwehr* security net around Peenemünde with his SS, which actually was his first step in removing the hated *Abwehr* from his path. His next move, then, as Ernst well knew, would be to gain total authority over the V-1 and V-2 rocket projects, despite the protests of the *Abwehr*'s army generals and he would surely succeed.

'So, Kapitän,' he continued, 'I will leave you in charge of Projekt Saucer, for what it is worth, while I personally supervise the more successful activities of von Braun and his rocket team. I hope this makes sense to you.'

'Naturally, Reichsführer.'

In fact, Ernst was secretly delighted. Ever since the humiliating surrender at Stalingrad, followed all too closely by the reverses in Africa and catastrophe in Italy, Himmler had shown increasing signs of emotional instability – finely suppressed hysteria, a slight quavering in his voice, the constant blinking and rubbing of weary, dazed eyes. Ernst, who sensed that he was growing mad, was more wary of him.

Not that Himmler was alone. Berlin was now filled with rumors that Adolf Hitler was going mad, or was at least in bad health and frequently doped with the drugs supplied by his quack, Dr Theo Morell. If that was true, it would do Himmler little good because, as Ernst knew, when Himmler gazed upon his beloved Führer, he looked into a mirror.

Ernst still believed in the SS, in the promise of the New Order, but he could no longer trust his once-beloved Reichsführer. Therefore he was pleased that Himmler had lost interest in him and Projekt Saucer and was, instead, going to turn his attentions elsewhere.

He almost sighed with relief.

'There is this other little problem,' Himmler said, clasping his hands under his babyish chin and looking severe.

Ernst suddenly felt nervous. 'A *problem,* Reichsführer?'

'Yes, Captain, a problem. I believe you had a similar kind of problem in Poland – one concerning a woman.'

Suddenly remembering Kryzystina Kosilewski in Cracow, and shocked that Himmler should have found out about her, Ernst could only swallow with a dry throat and let his heart race.

'Poland, Reichsführer? If you mean—'

Himmler waved his hand and smiled, like a father to his son. 'A Jew bitch, I believe,' he said.

'Yes, sir, but I assure you, I—'

Himmler waved his hand again and kept smiling, as if amused by Ernst's discomfiture. 'It's all right,' he said. 'That's all in the past now. We can but hope you've learned your lesson from it and will not repeat it.'

'Definitely not, sir!'

'How is it, then, Captain Stoll, that according to a report received this day from one of your fellow officers—'

Ritter, Ernst thought bitterly.

'—your wife has been seen to fraternize with a Wehrmacht officer whose sympathies, it is known, are no longer entirely with our beloved Führer. Worse: Your wife has also been reported as drinking too much lately and, apparently, making loud, drunken pronouncements in public about what she deems to be the failings of our glorious Third Reich. Do you have an explanation for this, Captain Stoll?'

'I swear to you, Reichsführer, I didn't know,' Ernst said, caught between humiliation and outrage to learn what Ingrid was doing behind his back. Of course, she had told him that she was quietly living a separate life and he had tried to deal with it by forgetting about it. Now he had not only been reminded of her other men, but been informed that her separate life was not lived so quietly. He felt like murdering the bitch.

'You didn't know she was seeing another man?' Himmler

271

asked in his oddly pedantic manner.

'No, sir,' Ernst lied.

'Are you having marital problems, Captain?'

'To be frank, Reichsführer, yes – though I'd hoped they wouldn't interfere with my work.'

'Most admirable, Captain. Unfortunately, we cannot have the wife of one of our finest officers making a fool of herself in public, much less offering insulting remarks about our glorious Third Reich while cavorting with a potentially traitorous officer.'

'No, sir, of course not. What do you suggest, sir?'

'The officer in question is Wehrmacht Lieutenant Eberhard Tillmann. Formerly a fine officer, he took part in the blitzkreig against Poland and was also one of the first to enter Paris. Unfortunately, since the reversal of our fortunes at Stalingrad and in Africa, he has taken to making subversive comments to those who will listen. What do *you* suggest, Captain?'

Already incensed that the man was his wife's lover, Ernst was even more outraged to hear that the bastard had been given what he had been denied: a part in the blitzkreig against Poland and the subsequent, magnificent advance across Europe and right into Paris.

'With your kind permission, Reichsführer, I will have this man transferred to the Eastern Front to take charge of a penal regiment. I will also ensure that my wife keeps her peace in the future.'

'Excellent,' Himmler said. 'I respect a man who knows when to place his duty before personal feelings. You are dismissed, Captain Stoll.'

Ernst saluted and left the office, choking up with fury, and marched toward the exit, not looking at his fellow SS men. He noticed only the usual collection of pale-faced, frightened people waiting to be interrogated, standing along the corridors, huddled pitifully on the wooden benches, ignored by the SS guards with the pistols and submachine guns who, in their black uniforms and leather boots, looked decidedly ominous.

A nation living in fear, Ernst thought, is a disciplined nation.

We will need that when we move underground to forge a strong, fearless Aryan race.

In the meantime, before that happened, he was being assailed by mundane problems, the main one being the wife he had once loved so dearly.

He walked out of the building, into rain and a cold wind, and waved at one of the SS cars parked in the road. The driver moved up to him, let him in, and then drove off. Ernst, sinking into the rear seat, looked out at the ruins that had been caused by the Allied bombing and thought of the night Hitler had become the Chancellor of Germany and he and Ingrid had gone to bed in the Adlon Hotel. They had loved one another then with the innocence of idealism, but now both of them were older than their years and had become bitter enemies.

Human relationships were treacherous, ephemeral, without substance, so he was glad to be involved with the SS and what it represented: an ideal state beyond petty, individual considerations; the subordination of the self to the whole in order to create a new, better man in an orderly world.

It was something to cherish.

He slapped Ingrid's face as soon as he walked into the apartment.

'Don't look so shocked,' he said quietly. 'You know what it's for.'

She covered her flushed cheek with her hand, staring at him through her fingers. 'No,' she said, 'I don't know what it's for. And you have no right to—'

'Eberhard Tillmann. A Wehrmacht lieutenant, I believe. Presumably as good in bed as he was on the march to Paris, but now joining my wife in publicly abusing the Fatherland. *Now* do you understand?'

Ingrid removed her hand from her face and stared defiantly at him. 'Yes, Ernst, now I understand. As I also understand why we won Paris – he *is* that good in bed!'

Ernst slapped her again and she fell against the sideboard, straightening up as some decorative plates fell off and smashed on the floor. The children's bedroom door opened and two faces peered out – Ula, now nine years old, and Alfred, who was six. Ernst, who saw so little of them these days, was shocked by how mature they looked and how fast the time passed.

Ashamed that they should have heard him smacking their mother, he covered it with a display of cold anger.

'Stay in your room and close the door,' he said. 'Your mother and I are talking.'

'Yes, Papa,' Ula said, her azure eyes emphasized by the golden hair that fell on her blushing cheeks. Then she pushed the gawking Alfred back into the room and quietly closed the door.

'A nice thing for the children to see,' Ingrid said, rubbing her stinging cheek. 'Their father striking their mother.'

'Not as bad as eventually learning that their mother's been behaving like a whore.'

'I don't charge, Ernst. I do it for love.'

He wanted to strike her again, but refrained because of the children. 'Do you know how I learned about it?'

'No.'

'From Himmler! You understand, you stupid bitch? I learned about my wife's public infidelities from the Reichsführer! Can you imagine my shame?'

'The Reichsführer?' She at least had the decency to look shocked. 'How did *he* know about it?'

'Your damned boyfriend, this Lieutenant Eberhard Tillmann, is known to have made comments against the Third Reich in general and the Führer in particular, so the SS had him placed under surveillance, which means they also watched you. Reportedly you're just like him now. You drink a lot and talk in public. Your own insulting remarks about the Reich-borrowed from him, no doubt – have been overheard by the SS officers doing the surveillence, one of whom, I'm sure, was Franck Ritter, who can't stand my guts. *Do you know what you've done, you whore?*'

He had hissed his last words with explosive, pent-up fury and grabbed her by the lapel of her blouse, jerking her face close to him.

'You could have ruined me,' he whispered heatedly. 'You could have had me stripped of rank. You could have had me transferred as a guard in one of the camps. *Damn it, didn't you think of that?*'

She jerked away from him, looking at him with frightened eyes. 'No,' she said, 'of course I didn't think of that! I'm in love. I just—'

He stepped up to her again, leaned over her, wanting to crush her. 'Don't tell me you're in love. I don't want to hear those words. You said you would live your own life *quietly,* and I agreed to let you do it, then you turned it into a public performance, for the whole world to see and hear. Drunk in public with your traitor! Parroting his traitorous words! And then I'm called into the office by the Reichsführer – *by Himmler!* – and told to put my own house in order. Damn you, I could kill you!'

'*Don't hit me again!*'

He had raised his hand, but thought of the children and lowered it, then walked away from her, a safe distance, where his temper could cool. Studying her, he was startled by how little she had changed, by the realization that she looked almost as young today as she had the day he had proposed to her, ten years ago. God, how he had aged since then, yet this bitch had remained unchanged: still the same short-cropped blond hair, the same green eyes, the same pale-faced beauty. He realized then, with deep bitterness, that in some helpless, torturous manner he still loved her and wanted to have her.

She *deserved* to be punished.

'I won't hit you again,' he said. 'You won't make me stoop to that. But you must put an end to this affair and keep your mouth shut in public.'

'I promise to be more careful in public. I give you my word.'

'And your affair with Lieutenant Tillmann?'

She shook her head. 'I can't . . . I can't possibly stop seeing him. I don't think I can do that.'

'You must!'

'I'm sorry, but I can't. If I said I would, I'd be lying.'

'Then, my dear, I'll have to make it easy for you – with my Reichsführer's consent.' Her gaze turned from confusion to dread and he savored his words. 'As soon as I return to barracks, I'll arrange the transfer of your beloved Lieutenant Tillmann to a penal regiment on the Eastern Front. Do you know what that is, dear? A penal regiment is composed of soldiers who have been found guilty of some offense and given the choice between military prison or serving in a regiment used solely for the most dangerous missions. The chances of survival for the regiment's members are therefore slim – though they *do* have a chance. So Lieutenant Tillmann, your traitorous lover, will be gone within the week and is unlikely to ever return. Don't worry about trying to keep yourself away from him – you won't have a choice.'

Ingrid threw herself at him, beating at him. He grabbed her wrists and pinned them behind her back and forced her into the wall. She didn't look so pretty now, for her face was streaked with tears, and he held her until she stopped struggling and sagged in his arms. When he released her, she slid to the floor, breathed deeply, then calmed down.

'I'm leaving home,' she said, 'and I'm going to take the children with me. I'm going back to live with my parents in Wannsee, and if you want to see the children, you can visit them there – but that's *all* you can do. We'll be man and wife only in name. That should keep your superiors happy. Then as soon as this war ends, I'll apply for divorce. Believe me, I'll do it.'

'That's fine by me, Ingrid.'

He went in to see his children, embraced them passionately and kissed them, then quickly left the bedroom and walked to the front door. He passed Ingrid who remained kneeling on the floor with her head bowed, and left without looking back, not even slamming the door.

It was a dignified exit.

'My handsome kapitän!' Brigette exclaimed with throaty sensuality, tugging him into her embrace and pushing the door closed behind him. She was wearing only her dressing gown,

through which he felt her animal heat, and he was instantly
aroused by her full breasts and sly, pressing loins. Yet even
as he pressed his lips to her neck, she pushed him gently away
from her. 'Greedy little boy,' she said with a mocking smile.
'Did you bring me a present?'

'Yes,' he said, his ardor dimmed a little as he handed the
wrapped present to her. 'A diamond necklace – a very *expensive*
necklace – from that shop on Tauentzienstrasse.'

'Ah!' Brigette exclaimed with a bright, greedy smile as her
long, painted fingernails ripped open the paper. 'Then it *must*
be expensive!' She threw the paper on the white carpet, held
the diamond necklace up, letting it dangle from her fingers,
turned it around and studied it in the winter's light falling in
through the window. '*Wunderbar!*' she said softly.

'Put it on,' Ernst said.

'You sound rather hoarse, my dear Ernst.'

'Put it on!' he repeated.

She stared thoughtfully at him, eventually gave a knowing
smile, then placed the necklace between her breasts and
clipped it behind her neck.

'What now, my love?'

'Take off the dressing gown.'

Brigette did as she was told – but slowly, seductively, like
the professional stripper she was, and then stood in a lazily
sensual pose before him, curvaceous and marble pale, naked
except for the necklace glittering on her full breasts.

'Was I worth it?' she whispered.

'Yes,' he said.

'Then come and take what you paid for.'

He had her right there on the floor, on a carpet as soft as
eiderdown, not worrying about love or its loss, losing himself
in pure lust. Brigette wrapped her legs around him, writhed
under him, rolled above him, trailed her wet tongue down the
length of his heaving body and then over his lips and eyes.
He wanted that and nothing else – a loveless coupling, her
expertise – and his pleasure was increased by the knowledge
that she cost only money. She did not demand his loyalty or

arouse his emotions just to poison them; she gave him what he wanted for a price that he could easily afford. He wanted that now – his only commitment was to the Fatherland – and so he took it and reveled in his freedom and orgasmed with pleasure.

Later, when he had bathed and dressed, Brigette made him a meal that he washed down with wine and followed with half a bottle of cognac, after which, though it was still only afternoon, he felt drunk and self-pitying.

'Ingrid's leaving me,' he confessed, 'and she's taking the children with her. She had a lover and now she's leaving me! Such is feminine reasoning.'

Brigette licked at her glass of cognac. '*You* have a lover,' she mocked him. 'You have a mistress – me.'

'That's different. I'm a man. And it wasn't until Ingrid and I were growing apart that I took up with you.'

Brigette chuckled. 'Such is *male* reasoning, my pet! And as I recall, Ingrid only took on a lover when she'd found out about you.'

'She's a whore,' Ernst said.

'No, darling, *I'm* a whore. Ingrid is only a wounded woman who's now taking revenge.'

'I don't care,' Ernst said. 'I'm not interested in her motives. I only know that our marriage has been poisonous on both sides and I don't want any more emotional involvements as long as I live. I have my work and it costs me no emotion while giving me great satisfaction. That's all I want now.'

Brigette smiled and drank some cognac. 'There speaks a true man,' she said. 'In the end, all men turn to their work for the satisfaction they lack at home. Soon you won't even need me – you'll make love to the SS.'

'You're being sarcastic,' Ernst said, 'but there's a certain truth in what you say. My allegiance to the SS, to the Fatherland, is now stronger than love or blood. The Reich towers above personal concerns and is founded on discipline. That's what I want now – discipline – not wasteful emotions. Yes, thank God for a man's work.'

He left shortly after, having sobered up sufficiently to drive, and went directly to the research center at Kummersdorf, to have words with Wilson.

It was growing dark when he arrived there, the buildings swept by restless spotlights, and he parked and hurried into the main hangar, past the stone-faced SS guards. Wilson was in his glass-walled office, studying drawings of a flying saucer, but he raised his head when Ernst entered, to look at him with that unblinking, disconcerting gaze.

He had been in the hospital recently for some mysterious operations, and certainly they seemed to have been successful, for now, though he was gray-haired and lined, he looked otherwise remarkably youthful. And his eyes, even though he was smiling faintly, had the brightness of ice.

'Captain Stoll!' he exclaimed softly in his oddly glacial, polite manner. 'This *is* a surprise! I was just about to finish and go home. What brings you here so late?'

'Some news,' Ernst replied.

'Regarding the failed test flight?'

'Yes.' Ernst glanced through the windows at the hangar beyond and saw the scorched, gutted saucer on the metal platform, some metal plates hanging loose. 'Himmler was most upset—'

'I gathered,' Wilson interjected dryly.

'—and claims that he now has more faith in the V-1 and V-2 rocket project at Peenemünde. He is going to switch his attention to that and leave us to struggle on without support, with me in charge, until he decides what to do about us.'

Ernst was startled when he saw what he thought was the beginning of a smile on Wilson's lips, but the American, as if realizing that fact, retreated instantly back into a solemnity that showed not the slightest trace of concern.

'And what's going to happen to me?' he asked in a surprisingly calm, almost academic manner.

'He didn't mention you personally,' Ernst said. 'I think he's just going to forget you. You're safe for the moment, but your time here could be limited. We'll just have to wait and see.'

Wilson nodded. 'Yes, Kapitän.'

Ernst realized at that instant that Wilson was actually pleased with what he had heard.

He wanted to be left alone.

Perplexed, Ernst said, 'Good night, Wilson,' then turned away and walked out.

He had a miserable three weeks, living mostly in the SS barracks, which depressed him, and returning only occasionally to his apartment, which, having been vacated by Ingrid and the children, simply depressed him even more. However, his feeling of being in limbo regarding Projekt Saucer was resolved when, in early September, he was called back to the Reichsführer's office. Himmler, trying to sound as casual as possible, said, 'You have heard, have you not, of the recent bombing of Peenemünde by the RAF?'

'Yes, sir,' Ernst replied.

'Exactly *what* have you heard, Captain?'

'That Peenemünde was seriously damaged,' Ernst said, deliberately understating the case, for he knew full well that on the night of August 17, Wernher von Braun's rocket research center on the Baltic had been bombed by a mass of RAF Lancasters and Halifaxes, which dropped thousands of tons of explosives and incendiary bombs, reportedly almost totally destroying the complex.

'And that's *all* you know, Captain Stoll? That Peenemünde was *seriously* damaged?'

'Yes, sir.'

'Then let me give you the full facts,' Himmler said in an unusual display of frankness. 'Fifty of the important development and test buildings were destroyed, including Wernher von Braun's laboratory. Not one of the hundred-odd buildings used to house the scientists was left standing. The foreign workers' settlement was a heap of rubble. The concentration camp suffered greatly. And, finally, included among the dead were several hundred German girls from the women's auxiliary service, one hundred and seventy-eight scientific workers, Dr Walter Thiel, and senior engineer Helmut Walther. A total loss of seven hundred and thirty-five people, plus the destruction of sewage and power lines, water mains, railway tracks, and the road running down the middle of the complex. In short, Captain Stoll, it was for us an unprecedented disaster!'

'I'm sorry, Reichsführer.'

'We will recover, Captain,' Himmler insisted, sounding unusually passionate. 'We *will* recover!'

'Of course, Reichsführer. Naturally.'

As if satisfied with Ernst's confirmation of his own faith, Himmler nodded solemnly, adjusted the pince-nez on his nose, then became more relaxed.

'I'm sure I do not have to tell you,' he said, 'of my conviction that Peenemünde could not have been bombed had some disgusting traitor not betrayed us.'

'Yes, Reichsführer,' Ernst replied, despising himself for this groveling.

'So,' Himmler said, 'because of this conviction, and also because of the subsequent air raids on the Zeppelin and Henschel-Rax works, I insisted to our beloved Führer that everything connected with the rockets should be put under the care of my SS.'

'And he agreed?'

'Naturally, Captain Stoll. And I have since decided that the experiments involving firing the rockets will be moved to central Poland; the development works to caves in the mountains near the Traunsee, in Austria; and mass production to our underground factories in Nordhausen, in the southern Harz Mountains. Meanwhile, the eastern side of Peenemünde will be rebuilt and camouflaged from the air in a way that makes it look like a deserted battlefield. You agree with this, yes?'

'It is brilliant, Reichsführer. But if we move the development works to Nordhausen, we will need to expand the labor force there.'

'That has already been arranged,' Himmler replied, in the testy manner of a man whose judgment is being questioned. 'Three thousand prisoners from Buchenwald will be used as slave labor and housed in a new subcamp named Dora, which also will be underground. We will then expand Dora until it has approximately fifteen thousand prisoners, which should be enough.'

'Excellent, Reichsführer. I will be proud to take command of—'

But Himmler cut him short with an impatient wave of his hand, which was, as Ernst had long noted, rather effeminate. 'No,' he said. 'You will not be in command. Since I have already put you in charge of Projekt Saucer – which, I must confess, I now have grave doubts about – I am placing General Hans Kammler in charge of the transfer and, subsequently, the whole mass-production plant, which will now be known as the Nordhausen Central Works.'

'Yes, sir!' Ernst said, trying to hide his shock.

'Do you have any further questions, Captain?'

'No, sir.'

'Then you may leave.'

Realizing that he had just been removed from his position of authority over the SS secret weapons program and relegated to what Himmler now viewed as a relatively minor Projekt Saucer, Ernst left the SS headquarters in a state of confusion.

He took the news straight to Wilson.

Chapter Twenty-Five

Arriving in London in February 1944 as an OSS colonel, Bradley was completely unprepared for the full extent of the city's devastation. Having remembered London from his many pre-war trips to Europe, he was shocked by the scorched, blackened ruins and debris-strewn rubble, the ugliness of the barrage balloons at the end of their steel cables, the gun emplacements in the parks, the sandbagged doorways, blackout curtains, and reinforced walls of even the city's most elegant buildings.

When he impulsively mentioned this observation to British Lieutenant-Colonel Mark Wentworth-King, shortly after meeting him in the headquarters of the Special Operations Executive at 64 Baker Street, the raffishly good-humored SOE officer told him that much of the devastation was fairly recent, because London was in fact suffering its heaviest air raids since the Blitz of May 1941.

'The blighters are coming over practically every night,' the lieutenant-colonel told him, 'so keep your head down, old chap. Take a chair. Have some tea.'

Weary after his night flight from Washington but otherwise feeling unusually healthy because of his weeks of intensive OSS training in physical fitness, espionage, self-defense, and guerrilla operations, Bradley pulled up a chair at the other side of Wentworth-King's desk and appreciated the hot tea that was poured for him.

'I've never seen so many troops in my life,' he said, 'as I've seen in the streets of London today. And not only English. Also

Irish, Scottish, Welsh, French, Hungarian, Polish, Australian, Canadian, and American. They formed a regular flood out there. Just how soon do you expect the big push?'

'Fairly soon,' Wentworth-King said.

British reticence. Bradley knew it and was used to it. 'Just how soon is "fairly soon," Colonel?'

'In good time,' Wentworth-King said.

Bradley sighed. 'This is a pretty damned good cup of tea,' he said.

'Naturally,' Wentworth-King replied. 'It *is* English, after all.'

'Three cheers for the English.'

Wentworth-King smiled, lit a cigarette, then glanced down at the papers on his desk and turned some of them over. 'Mmmm ... quite a record.'

'Thanks,' Bradley said.

'The Distinguished Service Cross, the Distinguished Service Medal, and the Medal of Honor for exploits in the battlefields in France in 1918,' Wentworth-King insisted upon reading aloud, as if he hadn't read the documents before. 'Unlikely member of the Republican Party in New York—'

'Why unlikely?' Bradley interjected.

'One naturally assumes that those of Irish extraction will be Democrats.'

'I'm sorry I missed the boat.'

'On the contrary,' Wentworth-King continued with a slight, amused smile, 'you didn't miss the boat at all, but traveled far and wide on it ... A successful lawyer with offices in Wall Street. Specialist in international law and used your knowledge to assess, on behalf of the US secretary of state, the military aims and capabilities of Europe, particularly Nazi Germany, before the outbreak of war. Encouraged by boredom and the fact that you were too old to take active part in this war to perform other unofficial services for General Dwight Taylor of US Army Air Force intelligence. Eventually through him, and with the blessing of President Roosevelt, were given the job of laying the groundwork for some kind of centralized intelligence agency, rather like our own. Worked at this in a purely unofficial, civilian capacity whilst trying to establish a more formal intelligence organization to deal with the European situation. When OSS was finally established, based on the Office of the Coordinator of Information, or COI – which ironically was based on your unacknowledged recommendations – you were invited by General Taylor to join the new intelligence organization, did so, then underwent retraining, and, as a much fitter, hopefully more dangerous man, ended up at the other side of my desk. Why, Colonel Bradley?'

'Why *what*?'

'Why have you ended up at the other side of my desk? Our intelligence man in Washington requests that we bare our breasts to you, though does not tell us why. What are you *after*?'

'The benefit of your experience,' Bradley said diplomatically. 'OSS is a relatively new organization—'

'Established two years ago,' Wentworth-King interjected with the air of a man who likes to get his facts right and wants you to know it.

'—and while we're proud of our track record so far, we're willing to admit that compared to the British Secret Intelligence Service, we're pretty raw meat.'

'I beg your pardon?'

'Compared to your organization, Lieutenant-Colonel, OSS is badly lacking in real know-how. I've therefore come here for two purposes: the first is to learn all you can teach me; the next is to make use of that learning for a particular mission.'

Pleased with the compliments, Wentworth-King smiled, inhaled on his cigarette, then blew a cloud of smoke. 'Exactly what would you like us to teach you that you don't know already?'

'I've already had basic intelligence training by your fellow Brits at a COI training school on a farm in Toronto. It was tough, but not enough. I'd now like to be trained in codebreaking by one of your signals intelligence units at Bletchley Park. I'd also like to be briefed on British propaganda and psychological warfare methods, including the so-called

Doublecross or XX system in which, I'm informed, you use captured German spies as counteragents and playbacks.'

'Informed by whom, Colonel Bradley?'

'By your intelligence man in the White House.'

'I am reassured to hear that. Anything else?'

Bradley shrugged and spread his hands in the air. 'Anything you can give me. I'm hoping to parachute into Europe, so obviously I'll need extensive training in that. I also need to perfect my otherwise excellent French and German – and I need to know what to watch out for when I'm in Nazi-occupied territory. You get the picture, I'm sure.'

'Aren't you a bit old for this, Colonel?'

'I'm an exceptionally fit forty-nine, Lieutenant-Colonel, recently trained by the US Marines and some of your own boys. I think I can handle it.'

Wentworth-King nodded and offered a half smile. 'And what exactly is your mission, Colonel Bradley? Do we help you with that as well?'

'You already have,' Bradley said. 'We're after an American rocket scientist named John Wilson who is, according to *your* reports, working under a false passport at a Nazi research establishment at Kummersdorf, near Berlin.'

'Ah, yes,' Wentworth-King said. 'I remember him well. An interesting chap, your Mr Wilson. Not exactly patriotic, but bright, and well looked after by Jerry.'

'We think he may be contributing more than rocket research to the Nazis.'

'Oh?'

'Yes. In the States, as far back as the early 1900s, Wilson was already experimenting with a crude form of atomic propulsion. When, after the Tunguska explosion of 1908, the US government attempted to take over his project, he ruthlessly destroyed most of the evidence of his work, then went underground. After working anonymously in America for a good thirty years, he fled the country and went to work just as ruthlessly for the Nazis. Since it's also believed that he's contributed to the Peenemünde rocket program, we're seriously concerned about what else he's up to and think he has to be stopped. That's why I have to be parachuted in as soon as humanly possible.'

The lieutenant-colonel sighed, tapped his teeth with a pencil, and looked decidedly skeptical. 'Germany?' he queried. 'Berlin? You actually think that's possible, Colonel? And how far do you think you would get if you *didn't* get captured? Kummersdorf is an SS research establishment – top secret, well guarded. You wouldn't stand a hope in hell, old son. It's just not in the cards.'

'It *has* to be,' Bradley said.

The lieutenant-colonel sighed again, as if dealing with a child, then dropped the pencil and raised his hands in the air in mock defeat.

'I am here to serve,' he said. 'I will do all I can. In the meantime, let me take you to your lodgings and then, while you're waiting for decisions, I'll ensure that you learn all you need to know. Okay?'

'Okay,' Bradley said.

He was pleasantly surprised to find himself located nearby in a small but cozy private apartment in Shepherd Market, Mayfair. After unpacking, he lay fully clothed on the bed and tried to sleep, but instead, as he often did these days, fell in and out of troubled reveries, in which he vividly relived his happier days with Joan, then their mutual pleasures and triumphs, and finally that ghastly day at Pearl Harbor, when she had died in his arms.

He still cried at remembering that.

Bradley wept. He felt the tears roll down his cheeks. Lying there on his back, he was consumed by a dreadful anguish, a grief that was mixed up with guilt because he, who had been with Joan at the time, had actually survived. He knew to think that way was senseless, an aberration of wounded emotions, but the thought that he hadn't deserved to live while Joan had died was one that never quite left him. It also brought back the memories, waves of love, pits of guilt, making him see the good and bad in their marriage dreadfully magnified . . . Yes, the two years since her death would have been hell had it not been for OSS.

General Taylor had rescued him, inviting him into the organization, ensuring that throughout the year immediately following Joan's death, Bradley was worked to exhaustion and distracted relentlessly. He'd been reacquainted with marine training, introduced to new weapons, taught espionage, self-defense, and guerilla operations, turned into the kind of fighting machine that murders quietly in darkness. He had become someone else, someone busy, never alone, and when it was finished, when he was fit and highly skilled, Taylor had put him to work. He had spent another year in America, tying up the loose ends on Wilson, and only then had he been shipped out to London . . . to find himself in this comfortable, private apartment, weeping tears for the dead.

Thank God, he had work to do.

He slept through the afternoon and awakened in darkness, when he remembered to pull his blackout curtains across before turning the lights on. Then he had a bath, put on his army uniform, poured a drink, and took Gladys Kinder's letters out of his suitcase. There were a great many of them – she was a prolific writer – and he spread them out in separate years on the bed and then started reading them.

She was part of his guilt.

Her letters formed a vivid picture of the life she had led over the past decade: the Spanish civil war, then Czechoslovakia and Italy, then the fearsome days of the Blitz and London as a city at war, at once defiant and tragic. The letters had told him about all that, but also about her private life – the numerous men she had known, her good and bad affairs, her fear of losing her independence combined with the fear of growing old alone – and they had told him, in racy jokes with a serious subtext, that she had fallen in love with him the minute she met him, had never quite forgotten him, and even now cherished the memory of him and wrote to him to touch him.

They were extraordinary letters.

It wasn't surprising that his throat became dry when he picked up the telephone.

She answered immediately.

'In my letter I told you to call me at eight-thirty p.m.,' she said, 'and you called on the dot. It can only be Mike Bradley calling. Welcome to London, Mike.'

He was smiling already.

They agreed to meet an hour later in a famous pub in Soho, in the West End, and when Bradley left his apartment, he felt like a nervous schoolboy going on his first date.

The blackout was in force and he found himself in moonlit darkness, walking along with the aid of a flashlight beamed down at the pavement. He went along Half Moon Street, turned into Piccadilly, and walked toward the Circus, passing the Ritz Hotel and the elegant façade of Fortnum & Mason and inky black doorways surrounded by sandbags and often filled with the shadowy figures of men and women in intimate contact. He heard chuckling and ecstatic groaning, voices calling invitingly to him, and saw cigarettes glowing in that darkness where other women were waiting.

At first he was disbelieving, then shocked, then amused and touched, and soon accepted that a city at war was a place like no other.

This was more evident in Piccadilly Circus, where cars, taxis, tramcars, and buses, all with their headlights dimmed, crawled through a flood of soldiers, sailors, airmen, and their women, as they poured around Eros, mostly drunk and in good cheer, then swept along Shaftesbury Avenue, to tumble, with much shouting and laughing and giggling, between piled-up sandbags and through blackout curtains, into the countless pubs and clubs that were spread liberally, noisily, around the network of packed side streets that led into Soho.

Bradley too eventually slipped between piled-up sandbags and through blackout curtains to find himself in a smoky, old-fashioned pub jam-packed with servicemen of every nationality. Having been warned about this by Gladys, he tried to find her in the jostling mass of noisy revelers, failed to recognize her, so fought his way through to the bar and tried to order a whiskey. He failed at that also, because the barman was too busy, but then a hand fell on his shoulder and squeezed it affectionately as a woman's voice called out to the barman, 'John! Get my friend here a Scotch! And be quick about it!'

Mike turned and saw Gladys Kinder smiling at him in that vividly remembered, still laconic manner. She was ten years older and had gray in her auburn hair, but otherwise she seemed just the same and he was instantly drawn to her.

'Well, well,' he said, finding himself bereft of better words. Then, feeling ridiculously formal, he offered his hand.

Gladys looked down at his hand, grinned in amusement, then took hold of it and vigorously shook it.

'You're too much,' she said. 'You're more formal than the English. I didn't expect to find you tearing my clothes off, but to not even get a kiss on the cheek—'

'You're right,' Bradley said. 'Sorry.' He leaned forward and kissed her cheek, feeling childishly embarrassed. Then he was given his glass of whiskey by the barman and raised it to Gladys. She touched her glass to his and they both drank, then smiled at one another in a silence that was awkward only on Bradley's side.

'God,' Gladys finally said, 'it's good to see you again after all these years. You're still the most attractive man on earth, though I know you'll hate me for saying it.'

'No, I won't,' Bradley said, even though he was blushing. 'I'm embarrassed, but I can't help feeling pleased. All men are boys in the end.'

'How right you are, Mike.'

'*You're* looking good.'

'That's a pleasing white lie. I'm forty-eight this year and I don't like it, though I'm learning to live with it. In London, in this war, that's much easier to do, since there's nothing like the constant threat of death to make you appreciate life, regardless of age and a spinster's traumas.'

'I can't imagine you suffering such traumas.'

She grinned and shrugged. 'Well, not really. Reporting this war keeps me busy, as well as giving me the chance to meet a *lot* of people. As for men, since I'm always interviewing those fighting the war, I know more men than I can count, and in that sense have a pretty good time. Still, I needed to write to you, Mike. I only met you twice, but I really missed you and that's something I can't ignore. I hope you missed *me* a little bit!'

'Yes, Gladys, I did. And that took me by surprise. I didn't know how much I'd miss you until you'd left and then I couldn't believe it. I mean, after only two meetings . . .' He shrugged. 'It seemed stupid.'

'Romantic?'

Bradley blushed again. 'Yeah, I guess it was, in a way. And I really loved getting your letters, and that seemed odd as well.'

'Love at first sight, Mike.'

'I can't believe in that, Gladys. Some people, they just meet and hit it off – and I guess we were two of them. It's a rare kind of friendship.'

'Can men and women be friends that way?'

'Yes,' Mike said doubtfully, 'I think so.'

'Nothing sexual? Not even a little bit?'

'You're teasing me, Gladys.'

She roared with laughter at that, finished her drink, ordered two more. 'Anyway,' she said, 'I'm sorry about your wife. That must have been hard on you.'

'It was. I even stopped reading your letters for a while. They just made me feel guilty.'

'I teased you a lot in those letters.'

'That's right, Gladys, you did.'

'And you never knew when I was joking or not?'

'No.'

She chuckled in a throaty, sensual manner. 'I'm a regular bitch that way.'

'I used to get disturbed.'

'And now?'

'We are here as two old friends.'

'Anything you say, pal.'

Yet her broad grin got to him, drawing him into her warmth, and he knew that he was lying and was not just her friend: that he had been attracted to her from the start and felt that way right now. It was ridiculous (they were too old for such nonsense) but there it was, plain as day. There was something lasting between him and Gladys Kinder, and he couldn't deny it.

He felt he'd known her forever.

'So what are you actually in London for?' she asked him as they sipped at their fresh drinks.

He glanced around the crowded pub, saw sweaty faces through clouds of smoke, the uniforms of many different nationalities; heard a piano pounding in the far corner, voices singing a bawdy song. 'Are you asking as a friend or as a journalist?'

'Take your pick,' she replied.

Bradley grinned at that. 'It's too noisy to talk in here,' he said. 'Can we go for a walk?'

'Sure, Mike. Let's go.'

They finished their drinks and left the pub, walked through Soho, which was packed, then crossed Charing Cross Road, took some dark side streets, and ended up in Covent Garden Market. They kept their flashlights turned down, making their way through moonlit darkness, passing the empty vendors' carts, which were covered in canvas for the night, and then crossing the much busier Strand and on down to the Embankment, where the moonlight and stars shone on the river Thames and streaked the water with silver. There were whores along the Embankment as well, negotiating with the servicemen, and Bradley felt a little embarrassed when he passed them with Gladys.

'I love it,' she told him, as if sensing his embarrassment. 'The less violent, more human commerce of war – a pound of flesh for some silver. You can't keep human nature down. So,' she added, getting back to her last question, 'why *are* you in London?'

'I'm a member of OSS,' he said. 'Have you heard about it?'

'Of course, Mike. The Office of Strategic Services. A fairly new intelligence agency. Are you somehow linked up with the invasion?'

'No. I'm still after Wilson. That's what I'm here for.'

Taken by surprise, she stopped walking and stared at him, then she shook her head and gazed across the river, to where the warehouses of the docks were silhouetted against the clear, starlit sky.

'I'd forgotten all about him,' she said. 'That old man who was great in the sack. Good God, he must be over seventy by now! Is he still alive?'

'We think so,' Bradley said, standing beside her, shoulder to shoulder. 'We receive reports from European resistance groups and he still features in them. At least an American scientist does, so we assume that he's Wilson. We think he helped the rocket scientists and is working at a research establishment near Berlin. The Brits aren't concerned about him – they're willing to wait until the invasion – but our government still wants to talk to him about a few things, notably the Tunguska explosion that you told me about and, even more worrying, about what he's creating for the Nazis. We have reason to think he's making an extremely powerful weapon that could be turned against us when we attempt the invasion. That's why I want to go now.'

'*Go* now? You mean parachute into Germany?'

'Right.'

'Goddammit, Mike, that's crazy. It's plain suicidal.'

'I think I can make it.'

'You think wrong, believe me.'

'I still want to go.'

'Why not wait until the invasion and follow the troops into Germany?'

'They may not get there.'

'They will. And in the meantime you could have a good time in London, the world's finest city.'

'I can't wait that long.'

'It won't be long.'

'You don't know that.'

'I know it's going to be this year. *Everybody* knows that.'

'I don't care. I want to go as soon as possible. I'm frightened that he's going to create something unbeatable before we get there to stop him. If he can invent something more powerful than the rumored rockets, he could stop us winning the war.'

'The secret weapons *are* only rumors.'

'I'm not too sure about that.'

'And that's why you can't wait to get to Wilson?'

'Yeah, right.'

'I'm sorry, Mike, but I don't believe that. I think it's something much more than that.'

'What?'

'You tell me.'

Bradley sighed. 'I've got a bee in my bonnet about this Wilson. He's haunted me for years. I have to meet him, face to face, and find out exactly what makes him tick. He appears to have few normal feelings – you confirmed that when we first met – but he's clearly a genius, he wants anonymity, and his ruthlessness appears to know no bounds. The man's like a ghost – he exists and yet he doesn't. I dream about, or imagine, the things he's invented and they keep me awake at night. I know all about him yet know nothing. I've got to study his face.'

'You'll see nothing but the face of pure logic – a void that transcends morality. You'll see the end of the world.'

'Maybe that's what I'm after.'

Gladys was just about to reply when a distant siren wailed, then another, and another, until the very air seemed to vibrate with that terrible sound – a high, nerve-shattering wailing.

'What the hell?'

'Those are the air-raid sirens,' Gladys said. 'That means the Germans are coming. Have you ever seen an air raid, Mike?'

'No.'

'Then let's stay right here.'

'Aren't we supposed to take shelter?'

'They come over nearly every night,' Gladys said, then

reached out for his hand. 'Let's just stay here and watch.'

Glancing left and right along the Embankment, Bradley saw men and women hurrying in every direction, heading, as Gladys explained to him, for the concrete and brick air-raid shelters, the platforms of the underground train stations, or the more comforting confines of pubs, clubs, hotels, or even the rooms of prostitutes. Even as he was watching them, he heard a distant, muffled rumbling emerging out of staccato explosions, and he looked along the river to where clouds of black smoke were bursting under the stars and being crisscrossed by phosphorescent lines of tracer bullets that formed a web around the rise and fall of shadowy shapes flying in from the sea.

He was looking at an immense fleet of German bombers – too many to count.

'God almighty!' he whispered.

Gladys squeezed his hand and the wind beat at his face as more ack-ack guns opened fire. The beams of searchlights swept the sky. He heard the distant explosions, felt the ground beneath him shaking, and saw clouds of black smoke billowing up from sheets of yellow flame and spreading out to cover the rooftops in the sky turning crimson.

'They're pounding the docks,' Gladys said. 'God help the poor bastards there.'

She squeezed his hand again and he appreciated the gesture, being almost overwhelmed by the spectacle along the river, by the knowledge that the fabulous mixture of fire and smoke and light was being created by destruction and death on a terrible scale. Over there, where the bombs were falling, people were dying in flame and smoke, being crushed and suffocated and incinerated and blown apart, while the buildings were collapsing into rubble and hot ash and choking dust.

Yet from here it was beautiful.

Bradley choked up with emotion, feeling torn by awe and shame, then raised Gladys's hand to his cheek and pressed her knuckles into his skin in mute affirmation. Then the bombers were overhead, suddenly roaring like ravenous beasts, and he actually saw the bombs falling, turning lazily in the moonlight, and then the river erupted in a series of mighty explosions, the water geysering up and fanning out and raining down over the debris of the boats that had been hit and blown apart while he was blinking.

Icy water poured over him and he pulled Gladys down, held her tight behind the wall, and looked up to see the British fighter planes, the famous Spitfires, descending on the German bombers like birds of prey, their guns spitting fire as they dove and climbed and returned, until one of the bombers exploded, shuddered in midair, erupted in fire, and went down through a black pall of smoke that obscured its last seconds.

The rest of the bombers passed on, heading toward the East End, still dropping their bombs, their guns firing at the attacking Spitfires. Gladys tugged at Bradley's hand. He looked at her and saw her pointing toward the city. The dome of St Paul's Cathedral, majestic in its halo of crisscrossing searchlights, towered over the rubble that burned and smoked far below, protected, as if by a miracle, from the destruction surrounding it.

Bradley's heart was racing. He wanted to cry with joy. He felt Gladys's hand, her fingers slipping between his, then she raised his hand and kissed his fingers one by one as the ground shook and bellowed. Bradley took a deep breath, tasted smoke, heard more bombing. Then he saw Gladys's face, erratically illuminated in flickering crimson and white light, moving in toward him, her eyes wet, until her lips touched his.

They kissed there, on the Embankment, kneeling behind the protective wall, then clung to one another, exploring each other like children, and stood up only when the bombers had returned and flown back toward the sea, leaving silence and a pall of black smoke that was streaked with red flames.

'I love you,' Gladys Kinder said.

Bradley was speechless.

Of course, she laughed about it later. She had meant it, but she laughed about it. She told Bradley that the expression on his face had just made her want him more. Yet they didn't go to bed together. They talked around it, but didn't do it. Bradley wanted to do it, but felt foolish, too old, and Gladys said that to do it would probably spoil a beautiful friendship.

'Right,' Bradley said. 'I agree.'

He loved being with her, loved her flirting and teasing, and was enthralled by her conversation, her stories of politics and war, and was jealous when she mentioned the many men she had known over the years. She showed him the city, always kissed him good night chastely, and in letting him know she loved him and simply wanted to be with him, she raised him out of the grave of his grief and turned him into a new man.

Yet he still wanted to complete his mission, to find Wilson before it was too late. After five unparalleled days with Gladys, he tried to get back to work.

'I'm sorry,' Lieutenant-Colonel Wentworth-King said after pouring Bradley a cup of tea in his cramped office in the busy SOE headquarters, 'but your request to parachute into occupied Europe has been denied.'

'*What?*'

'I think you heard me.' Wentworth-King sat behind his desk and lit one of his awful British cigarettes. 'You will not be allowed into occupied Europe until after D-Day.'

'What the hell!'

But Bradley's intended protest was cut off by an airy wave of the hand and a rather chirpy, British public-school grin. 'Fear not,' he said, holding up a bulging, official envelope. 'You have not been forgotten. I have here, in this envelope, enough detailed instructions to keep you busy for the next year or so and certainly busy enough until the invasion.' Still grinning, he handed Bradley the envelope and asked, 'Did you know about this when you first came to see me?'

'No,' Bradley said, staring at the bulky envelope. 'Whatever it is, I didn't know a damned thing about it.'

'Operation Paperclip,' Wentworth-King explained. 'You were concerned with the Peenemünde scientists, I believe?'

'Yes,' Bradley said.

'Well, OSS has decided to mount an operation – code-named Paperclip – to seize the German rocket teams and prevent them from falling to the hands of the Soviets, who will also be greatly interested in them.'

'And what about Wilson?' Bradley asked.

'According to reports recently received from the same European resistance groups that originally informed us about the Peenemünde rocket project, the rocket teams have recently been moved from the Baltic to underground sites in Nordhausen, and possibly nearby Bleicherode, in the southern Harz mountain ranges of Thuringia. Since those establishments are top secret and under the control of Himmler's most trusted SS troops, and since we are no longer talking about an occupied country – where you might expect assistance – but about Germany itself, it is felt that a parachute drop into Thuringia would be suicidal. It has therefore been decided that your time would be spent more profitably in mounting, staffing, and planning the specific aims of Operation Paperclip, which will come into effect once Europe has been breached.'

'That may be too late,' Bradley said in growing frustration. 'If Wilson's already helped the Nazis to build remote-controlled rockets, God knows what else he has in the pipeline. We have to stop him *before* the invasion starts, since he might come up with something even worse than the reported Peenemünde rockets.'

Wentworth-King simply shrugged. 'Can't be helped, old chap,' he said. 'For a start, we simply can't have anyone parachuting into Germany at this particularly sensitive point in time. Second, it *is* believed that Wilson, whilst contributing to the V-1 and V-2 rocket projects, was never actually a member of von Braun's team and is therefore probably still at Kummersdorf – which makes it even more sensible for you to follow the invasion troops into Berlin, once the invasion is underway. Either way, you are staying here, old son, until Operation Overlord commences.'

'And when will that be?'

'It's all down to the tides, old man,' Wentworth-King said, 'and here in England they *can* be unpredictable. In the meantime, I suggest you collect who you want for Operation Paperclip and otherwise enjoy your time in London. Anything else?'

'Go to hell,' Bradley said.

He walked out of the lieutenant-colonel's office with the bulky envelope under his arm, on the one hand bitterly disappointed and even outraged, on the other hand surprisingly, helplessly relieved that at least he could see more of Gladys Kinder, who had given him back the will to live.

She was a huge consolation.

Chapter Twenty-Six

'We *must* talk to them,' Wilson said as Ernst drove him from the BMW plant in the Berlin suburb of Spandau, back around the dreadful ruins caused by increasing Allied bombings, and then south toward the research complex at Kummersdorf. 'As you've just seen, the new multidirectional jet propulsion system for the flying saucer works beautifully and can be installed any day now. Once we do that, we can arrange a test flight of the saucer, but we must sort this business out first.'

'It's dangerous to go behind Himmler's back,' Ernst insisted, glancing out at the bombed suburbs, the skeletal houses and mountains of rubble, and deciding that he must persuade Ingrid, who was living with her parents in the nearby suburb of Wannsee, to move out of Berlin before it was too late. 'No one can be trusted these days. If they talk, we'll be shot.'

'They won't talk,' Wilson replied, looking straight ahead, thinking, his eyes bright with that icy intelligence that seemed not to know fear. 'Like you, they're becoming wary of Himmler's state of mind and think he's becoming unpredictable. They're also worried about how he'll react when the end finally comes – and they now know that it's coming.'

'*No one* knows that,' Ernst insisted, clinging stubbornly to a vain dream. 'The Allies haven't yet launched their invasion and might never do so.'

'They will and you know it.'

'We can use the rockets against them.'

'The rockets won't be enough to stop them. Now nothing can stop them.'

'Don't sound so pleased,' Ernst said.

'I *am* pleased,' Wilson confessed. 'Not because of my countrymen, nor because of the British, but because I want to go where I can work without feeling threatened.'

'Does *nothing* else matter to you?' Ernst asked him.

'No,' Wilson said flatly.

Ernst glanced to the side as they passed some blackened ruins and saw a one-legged child hopping along on crutches, surrounded by other children, all of whom were looking for valuables in the high mounds of rubble in which broken glass and twisted metal glinted in the light of the sun. The ruins were extensive, surrounding him on all sides, and he thought of the awesome power of modern technology and then glanced at Wilson.

He was seventy-four years old but looked perhaps sixty. Ernst knew that it was due not only to a lifetime of strict dieting and the ruthless application of mind over matter – Wilson's will was unyielding and he used it to recharge his energy – but also to the surgical operations he had recently been having in various SS hospitals. Operations on the stomach, on his varicose veins and joints, reportedly even on the heart, perhaps more than that. The experimental work had been done on humans, on the inmates of the camps, and then Wilson, when he thought the risk reasonable, had had them performed on himself, so far with remarkable results. Indeed, at seventy-four years of age he was more vigorous than Ernst.

And Wilson was different from other men in more ways than one.

Exactly what was he?

Ernst thought of him as a mutant, a creature not quite human, someone who had transcended normal emotions and embraced the god of pure logic, beyond kindness or cruelty. Ernst had tried to find out why – what childhood trauma had perverted him – but every record indicated that he'd had a lonely childhood, his parents strict but decent, and that the only explanation for his unique personality was his extra-ordinary intelligence. Such intelligence is beyond pity, feeding on logic, not emotion, and Ernst was now convinced that Wilson was an evolutionary accident, the product of pure reasoning, a human being for whom emotions were no more than unwelcome distractions. He was neither cruel or kind, good or bad, right or wrong: He was a creature impelled by the inhuman force of his mind – a mutant, without emotions, the personification of man's evolutionary drive toward mathematical absolutes.

His was the face of the future.

Ernst shivered involuntarily, gripped the steering wheel tighter, and was feeling decidedly uneasy when the ruins of Berlin gave way to open fields and eventually, as clouds covered the sun, to the barbed-wire fences and heavily guarded main gate of the research complex at Kummersdorf.

Waiting for them in Wilson's office in the main hangar were Hans Kammler, the blond, blue-eyed, former head of SS construction programs, now a brigadier and in charge of the Nordhausen Central Works in the Harz Mountains of Thuringia, and Artur Nebe, former commander of one of the notorious Action Groups in Russia, head of the dreaded *Kriminal Polizei*, or Kripo, the Prussian intelligence service, and now a full general of the SS, though his allegiances shifted with the wind and his actions were shadowy. Both men were wearing their SS uniforms and looking slightly annoyed.

'You're late,' Kammler said.

'I'm sorry, sir,' Ernst replied. 'We were observing a test at the BMW plant at Spandau and it took a little longer than expected.'

'I'm not interested in excuses,' Kammler said. 'My time is limited and I resent waiting for anyone, much less for an officer of lower rank.'

'Yes, sir, I understand, but—'

'How are things at Nordhausen?' Wilson asked in an unusual display of tact.

'Livelier than they are here,' Kammler said.

'The rockets are still being produced?'

Kammler practically sneered. 'Of course, American,' he said. 'A total of one hundred and forty V-2s were produced in January and February alone. Another one hundred and seventy were produced in March, and a further three hundred in April. With luck, we will soon be aiming them at London, and then—'

'They won't stop the invasion,' Wilson said. 'They'll just cause a nuisance.'

'And your flying saucer will do better?' Nebe asked skeptically.

'Yes,' Wilson said.

'So far it hasn't even flown,' Kammler said.

'The saucer we've been openly testing is Rudolph Schriever's adaptation of my work. The saucer I'm talking about, the *Kugelblitz*, is the one we've constructed at Spandau without Schriever's knowledge. We've just tested the new jet engines today and now know it will fly.'

General Nebe, who was a lover of intrigue, leaned forward in his chair and said, 'What's the difference between your saucer and Schriever's? And why haven't you told Schriever about yours?'

'Because I don't trust Himmler,' Wilson said boldly, 'and Schriever is Himmler's man.'

Ernst felt a tremor of fear, but willed himself to show nothing. He caught Kammler's searching glance and looked away, too nervous to meet it.

'We are *all* Himmler's men,' Nebe said softly.

'Himmler is not the man he once was,' Wilson replied. 'It's rumored that he sees the end in sight and is starting to crack up . . . just like the Führer.'

There was a long, dreadful silence, as if everyone was in shock, then Kammler, coughing into his fist, said, 'Continue, American.'

'As you know, it was Himmler's dream to create a colony of SS elite under the ice of Neuschwabenland in the Antarctic and protect it from the world with highly advanced weapons, including my saucer.'

'Yes,' Nebe said, 'we *do* know.'

'Then you must also know that the first of the underground accommodations has been constructed, that some of the finest SS troops, some scientists, and the necessary slave workers have already been shipped there, and that an escape route has been organized for those of us who wish to avoid imprisonment or death here in Germany.'

'Yes,' Nebe said. 'We do. And we also know that your flying saucer is supposed to be the ultimate weapon, but now you tell us these stories. I repeat: I want to know about you and Schriever. Why the deception?'

'Because it's my belief that Himmler has forgotten the Antarctic and thinks only of using the saucer to fight the Allied invasion, when it comes.'

'And if, as you say, your saucer works, what's wrong with that?'

Wilson turned his gaze on Kammler, who had spoken with icy sarcasm. 'Because to stop the invasion we'd need a great number of flying saucers and there's no way we can construct them in time. And that in turn means that if Himmler's paranoia keeps him in Germany, the war, the Antarctic colony, *and* the saucer will all be lost to the Allies – and all of us – me and Captain Stoll here, you, Brigadier Kammler, and you, General Nebe – will undoubtedly be tried as war criminals, found guilty, and hanged.'

There was another uneasy silence, a brief trading of questioning glances, then Kammler, his blue eyes clear beneath the blond hair, said, 'So we make our escape to the Antarctic . . . with your flying saucer . . . without Himmler . . . Which gets us to Schriever.'

'You're a clever man, Brigadier.'

'I don't need your compliments,' Kammler replied. 'Just tell us your plan.'

Awed by Wilson's icy control, but also terrified of where it was leading, Ernst glanced across the large hangar, saw Schriever's saucer on its platform, yearned for a cigarette but was frightened of lighting one, so returned his gaze to the men in the small, spartan office. Kammler and Nebe were an odd couple – one blond and blue-eyed, the other dark and unreadable – and Wilson, with his silvery-gray hair and lined face, was as unfeeling as stone.

None of these men is truly human, Ernst thought, *and I have sold myself to them.*

It was a dreadful admission . . .

'If Himmler gets any worse,' Wilson said, speaking softly, seductively, 'he'll change his mind completely about the Antarctic and refuse to let us go there. He'll want us to make a last stand in Germany – to go down with the Führer.'

'Yes,' Nebe said. 'He will.'

'Our first job, then,' Wilson continued, 'is to make him forget Projekt Saucer and turn his attentions elsewhere.'

'Understood,' Kammler said.

Wilson nodded. 'Since for the past couple of years I've only been testing the Schriever saucer – which will fly, but not much – and letting Schriever take most of the credit for it, Himmler now trusts Schriever more than he trusts me. However, he's already turned away psychologically from the project and instead is pinning most of his hopes on the V-2 rocket program.'

'Which is exactly why he placed me in charge of it,' Kammler noted.

'Correct,' Wilson said. 'Which is all to the good. We can't trust Schriever, who knows nothing about the Antarctic, so we have to get rid of him while keeping Himmler happy and giving us the freedom to prepare our escape without interference.'

'We are listening,' Nebe said.

Ernst sucked his breath in, feeling tense, and saw Wilson's quick glance. Then, to his amazement, Wilson smiled, almost victoriously, before turning back to Kammler and Nebe.

'The prototype for the real flying saucer,' he said, 'is a small, saucer-shaped, remote-controlled antiradar device, which I've dubbed the *Feuerball* because, when it flies, it turns white hot and becomes a ball of fire.'

'I know nothing about this,' Kammler said, looking upset.

'No,' Wilson said, 'you didn't, but now you do . . . Because now is the right time.'

'Please explain,' Kammler ordered icily.

'The *Feuerball* is an armored object powered by a special turbojet engine that is radio-controlled at the moment of takeoff. Then, attracted by the enemy aircraft's exhaust fumes, it will automatically follow that aircraft, automatically avoid colliding with it, and automatically short-circuit its radar and ignition systems. During the day this device looks exactly like a shining disc spinning on its axis – or a silver ball – but by night it looks like a burning globe – actually a fiery halo around the armoured device, caused by the exceptionally rich chemical mixture that overionizes the atmosphere in the vicinity of the target and so subjects it to extremely damaging electromagnetic impulses.'

'And if this *Feuerball* is faced with the guns of the aircraft it's pursuing?' Kammler asked.

'It will fly away automatically,' Wilson replied.

'Why?'

'A thin sheet of aluminum has been inserted under the armored plating of the *Feuerball*, and this acts as an automatic defensive switch. A bullet piercing the armored plating will automatically establish contact with that switch, trip a maximum acceleration device, and cause the *Feuerball* to fly vertically out of range of the enemy aircraft's gunfire.'

'Sounds wonderful,' Kammler said. 'But what's the difference between the small so-called *Feuerball* and your large flying saucer, the *Kugelblitz*?'

'Schriever's saucer is in fact a crude form of flying saucer, constructed from ordinary metal and using primitive propulsion. The *Kugelblitz*, on the other hand, is a piloted version of the *Feuerball*. It has the advantage of being constructed from a special metal and also using the most advanced form of jet propulsion that's yet been invented.'

'I'm not an engineer,' Nebe complained.

'The *Feuerball*,' Ernst explained, directing his words to Kammler, who like him was an engineer, 'is a perfectly symmetrical disc, devoid of all surface protuberances. Nevertheless, even with the *Feuerball,* the boundary layer limits its speed. In order to get rid of the boundary layer completely – and in order to make use of the dead air, not only for acceleration, but for maneuvering as well – what Wilson required was a porous metal that would act like a sponge, remove the need for air intakes altogether, and create what our famed engineer Schrenk called *frictionless airflow.* Such a metal was recently created by our scientists at Göttingen and Volkenrode – a compound of magnesium and aluminum, called *Luftschwamm,* or aerosponge. Wilson used it for the construction of all his flying saucers, thus solving the problem of the boundary layer and, thus, all previous limitations on speed and maneuverability. The *Feuerball* and the *Kugelblitz,* then, are extraordinary aircraft.'

'You've already described the *Feuerball,*' Kammler said, looking more interested. 'So apart from its size, why is the *Kugelblitz* even better?'

'The *Feuerball,*' Wilson said, 'not only spins around its vertical axis, but automatically follows its target, makes its target's radar and ignition malfunction by filling the immediate vicinity with a gas that, when burning, creates a damaging magnetic field, and also flies away automatically when attacked. Yes?'

'Yes,' Kammler said.

'Now let us enlarge this flying fireball,' Wilson said, as if giving a lecture in a classroom. 'The larger disc, the *Kugelblitz,* will also spin on its own axis, but with the addition of gyroscopic stabilization, a pilot's cabin can now be placed on that axis, with the main body – or engine – of the disc spinning around the steady cabin. We then add to the enlarged, pilot-carrying disc a form of radio that can cancel at the pilot's discretion the return signals, or blips, from the enemy's radarscope and so render our flying saucer undetectable. Next we have electromagnetically or electroacoustically controlled firing weapons, we have cannons that spit igition-damaging gas instead of shells, we possibly have various laser or pulse-beam weapons – in development right now – and we have devices that ensure that our flying saucer will automatically retreat from enemy attacks. Add to all this the fact that the disc is made of an alloy – courtesy of the Riva del Garda complex – that can withstand enormous pressure and a temperature of one thousand degrees Centigrade and that, being porous, can take the air in like a sponge and then use it to increase its own propulsion to almost unbelievable speeds.'

Still an engineer and unable to hold in his excitement, Ernst found himself leaning forward in his chair to say excitedly: 'Add it all up and what have we got?'

'The *Kugelblitz*,' Nebe said quietly.

'Yes!' Ernst exclaimed. 'The enlarged and enhanced offspring of the *Feuerball*. A *piloted* machine in which a single mass of wing, tail, and fuselage has been formed into the one gyroscopically stabilized, vertical-rising, soon-to-be supersonic flying disc.'

'That's our strength,' Wilson said.

'So how do we protect it?' Kammler asked.

'We're back to Schriever,' Nebe said.

Yes, Nebe enjoyed intrigues – they were food and air to him – and Ernst looked into the dark light of his gaze and saw the blood that had formed it. Nebe would take new life from this conspiracy and become its strong arm.

'Yes,' Wilson said, 'we're back to Schriever. Now that Himmler trusts Schriever more than me, we must confirm him in his faith by telling him that I'm trying to impede Schriever's progress, that for that reason we should be parted, and that Schriever should be given his own research center elsewhere – somewhere less accessible either to me or to the Allies – to enable him to continue his work without interference.'

'Which in fact means that *you'll* be able to continue your work without interference,' Nebe said, enjoying this, 'and that the escape route to the Antarctic can be organized without Schriever's spying eyes.'

'Precisely,' Ernst said, surprised to hear himself sounding so enthusiastic, but unable to help himself.

He had wanted to be a scientist, after all, and this was pure science.

However, Kammler simply stared coldly at him, before turning to Wilson. 'I will do it,' he said. 'Clearly there is no choice. It will be your task, over the next few weeks, to let Schriever steal – for want of a better word – the credit for the *Feuerball* and to convince him that its basic principles can be used to enhance his own saucer. When you have done that, he will undoubtedly take the *Feuerball* to Himmler and I, being in charge of the project, will be informed. I will then do as you've suggested and recommend an area near Prague, in Bohem, as the new location for Schriever's project, which will ensure that he's not in Berlin when the Allies get here.'

'And if the Allies get here,' Wilson said, 'they will also get me.'

'Correct,' Kammler said. 'So, since I'm also in charge of the rocket program at Nordhausen, I will also request that your project be transferred to Kahla, a small village near there, where, as I will tell him, I can keep my eye on it, ensure that any innovations you may come up with are passed on to the more important rocket program, and protect both projects more easily from the Allies as they advance. I think he will fall for this.'

'So do I,' Wilson said.

'And from there, in the Harz Mountains,' Nebe said, 'we can make our escape when the time comes.'

'So be it,' Kammler said.

Ernst glanced at Wilson, saw the shadow of a smile, and knew in that instant, beyond doubt, that he would get what he wanted.

A few hours later, when darkness had fallen, as English bombs fell from the sky and Berlin blazed and crumbled, Ernst made loveless love to Brigette, burying himself in her slick thighs, and accepted that any future he might have would be mapped out by Wilson.

Berlin burned all around him.

Chapter Twenty-Seven

Bradley awakened late in the morning to the familiar sound of broken glass being shoveled out of the gutters in the street below. Slightly hungover from the previous evening's pub crawl with the indefatigable Gladys Kinder, and not helped by a restless night in which new, disturbing sounds had been added to the German bombings, he groaned melodramatically, rubbed his eyes, then sat up on the bed.

It was nearly eleven o'clock. The sun was shining in between the curtains, illuminating the empty space beside him in the bed, where he wanted Gladys to be, though he sometimes said otherwise. She had been there for drinks and he had often walked her back to her room in the Savoy Hotel, but beyond good-night kisses and the silent touching of foreheads, he and the notoriously bold-tongued Gladys had done nothing at all.

It made him feel like an adolescent, which was not a bad feeling.

He climbed out of bed, pulled the curtains back, and looked down into the street just off Shepherd Market. A bomb had fallen nearby, a few streets away. While the buildings opposite had been untouched, the blast had shattered the windows and the broken glass was being shoveled up into a garbage truck by men in navy-blue coveralls.

That familiar sight made Bradley think of the previous night's air raid – which seemed to have lasted throughout the early morning – and reminded him that in his restless, drunken state of semiconsciousness, he'd been convinced that the sounds of the raid were different from normal.

I'm hallucinating, he thought ruefully, shaking his head from side to side – and was about to go into the kitchen to make some coffee when the telephone rang.

'Hi,' Gladys said. 'It's me.'

'Who's *me*?' he asked, teasing her.

'Don't even bother trying,' she replied. 'Are you at least out of bed?'

'Just about, Gladys. I don't think I can keep up with you. All those years mixing with hard-drinking service guys have made you immune to hangovers.'

'You have a hangover?'

'Yep. And that air raid didn't help me, either.'

'It wasn't an air raid,' she replied.

'What?'

'It wasn't an air raid. Not one German plane was seen. We were attacked by the long-rumored German secret weapons – pilotless planes or remote-controlled rocket bombs, depending on which report you accept. Either way, those pilotless things were buzzing down on London and the south of England all night and exploding all over the goddamned place.'

'Jesus Christ!' Bradley whispered, hardly believing his ears. His thoughts instantly turned to the rocket program at Peenemünde and Wilson's unofficial involvement with it and other unknown projects.

'A shock, eh?'

'Yeah,' Bradley replied. 'Right.'

'Wanna join me for breakfast, Mr Bradley?'

'I'd love to, but I think I should go straight to Baker Street and have words with my stubborn British controller.'

'You think you can use this to make him send you to Europe?'

'I don't see how he can refuse now.'

'He's British – that's how he can refuse. They're very good at refusing. Very quietly . . . very politely . . . but not budging an inch.'

'He doesn't have a leg to stand on now.'

'The Brits are notoriously good at balancing acts.'

'You're such a goddamned pessimist.'

'I don't want you to go, that's all.'

'That's nice to hear, Gladys, but you know I have to do this.'

'Yeah, Mike, I know. So what about lunch before you leave?'

He laughed at that. 'I won't be leaving today, that's for sure, so your idea sounds great.'

'There's a Lyons Corner House near Piccadilly Circus. Let's meet there.'

'Terrific. Twelve-thirty?'

'Don't get lost.'

'I'll try not to.'

'My day is made,' she said with a throaty chuckle, then the line went dead.

Putting the phone down, Bradley checked the calendar. It was June 13, 1944, exactly one week after D-Day, the invasion of Europe, which he had bitterly regretted having missed.

The thirteenth, he thought as he cast off his pajamas and hurried into the bathroom. Unlucky thirteenth. He ran the water in the old-fashioned bath, climbed in, and thought of the progress of the invasion as he hurriedly bathed himself.

He had wanted to go with the troops, to be one of the first to step onto the soil of Europe, but the urbane Lieutenant-Colonel Wentworth-King had refused him permission, insisting that he remain in London until the Allies had overrun Germany. Bradley had been furious, but there was little he could do about it, other than keep track of the known movements of the German scientists, contact European resistance groups regarding Wilson's whereabouts, and, when not thus engaged, spend his time with Gladys Kinder, with whom he was now undoubtedly in love in a pleasantly gentle, middle-aged way that so far was devoid of *angst*.

Nevertheless, while he would dearly miss Gladys, he was becoming increasingly excited by his belief that now Wentworth-King would be unable to refuse him permission to travel to Europe and begin the real search for Wilson.

If remote-controlled rocket bombs were already falling on London, God knows what other secret weapons the Germans, doubtless with Wilson's help, were about to use against Britain and, possibly, the Allied troops in Europe.

After letting the water out of the bath, he dried himself, dressed quickly and carelessly, then hurried out of the apartment and headed for Baker Street. By now he was used to the broken glass on the sidewalks, the fresh piles of smoldering rubble, and the scorched, jagged holes in the walls of the buildings, revealing the rooms inside, like stage sets, some untouched, some in chaos, all somehow naked and pitiful. The barrage balloons were still overhead, swaying like beached whales, and antiaircraft gun emplacements stood in the many small parks and squares, the gun barrels being polished by the crews while they waited for night to fall. Yet life continued – the roads were filled with buses and taxis – and as usual, the newspaper vendors shouted out the day's headlines, which today were about the 'miracle' weapons.

Bradley thought of Wilson, hidden somewhere in Germany, and wondered what he would spring next.

'Ah ha,' Lieutenant-Colonel Wentworth-King said brightly when Bradley entered his cluttered office in SOE headquarters in Baker Street. 'My American friend!'

'Morning, Mark,' Bradley greeted him, then pulled up a chair and faced the soles of the lieutenant-colonel's boots, which were up on the desk.

'Can I order you up some tea?'

'No, thanks,' Bradley said.

'I don't suppose I have to ask why you're here,' Wentworth-King said with a slightly mocking smile.

'No, I don't suppose you do. What have you learned so far?'

'As we suspected, the rockets are V-1s, being flown, as far as we can ascertain at this point, from bases in the area of Pas de Calais. They're not pilotless aircraft but flying bombs, powered by petrol and compressed air, coming in at low altitude at an approximate speed of four hundred miles per hour, steered by a gyroscope and designed to explode on impact. So far, our antiaircraft guns are proving to be fairly ineffective against them, though hundreds of ack-ack units are being rushed to the south coast, where even more buzz bombs, or doodle-bugs, as they're already being called by the populace, are falling.'

'Christ!' Bradley exclaimed.

'Here, in London, the flying bombs have scored direct hits on a church, a convent, a hospital, and a house in South London, with considerable loss of life. Outside of London, the situation is even worse, with a veritable deluge of bombs falling on Southampton, Kingston, Sevenoaks, and Bromley and, indeed, still falling this very minute. Apparently the ground of southern England is shaking as if in an earthquake, and whole areas are now covered in a pall of smoke. Are you *sure* you wouldn't like a cup of tea?'

'No, thanks,' Bradley said. 'It doesn't settle *my* nerves. Any comment on the bombs from across the water?'

'German radio is describing the flying bomb as a, quote, miracle weapon, whereas Dr Goebbels is repeatedly using the name "V-1," which suggests that other secret weapons are in the pipeline and about to be unleashed.'

'Wilson,' Bradley said.

'I beg your pardon, Colonel?'

'That son of a bitch Wilson's behind them.'

'I really don't think so. They're part of the Peenemünde project, headed by Wernher von Braun. Wilson has nothing to do with it. We're convinced he's still at Kummersdorf.'

'Wilson was working at Kummersdorf when von Braun's rocket project was also located there. I'm not saying the rockets are all his. What I'm saying is that he doubtless contributed to them – and God knows what he's working on right now. If Goebbels is hinting about *other* secret weapons, we should take him seriously.'

'Dr Goebbels *is* a genius at propaganda.'

'But I don't think he's lying. The V-1s are a sign of that. We also know that they wouldn't keep Wilson on at Kummersdorf if he wasn't working on *something* valuable. And if the V-1 rockets are going to be followed by something worse, it could come from him.'

Wentworth-King pulled his feet off the desk and began to tap his perfect teeth with a pencil while smiling knowingly at Bradley.

'I know what you're going for,' he said. 'You're going to use the flying bombs as leverage to force me to let you parachute into Germany.'

'Right. Even you'll have to accept that the flying bombs are a sign that our time may be running out. If they use those bombs, or something worse, against our troops, the tide could be turned against us.'

'If we survived the Blitz, we can survive the buzz bombs, I'm sure.'

'But what if they follow them up with something worse?'

Wentworth-King simply shrugged. 'We'll take our chances,' he said. 'Meanwhile, since the invasion is still in its early stages, I'd rather not let you, or anyone else, parachute into Germany.'

'Then let me go to France now, to at least follow the troops into Germany.'

'No, I can't do even that. I don't have the authorization. My only brief, regarding my own organization as well as OSS, is to wait until Germany is almost captured before moving over there.'

'Shit,' Bradley said.

'Orders, dear boy,' Wentworth-King responded. 'And unless you can come up with someone higher than me, I'm afraid you're doomed to remain here.'

'And what about the OSS project to track down the German scientists?'

'That also has to wait until the troops get there first. I'm afraid I can't budge on this, old son.'

'You're just keeping it all for your goddamned British Secret Intelligence Service buddies. You want it all for yourself, bud.'

'You said it yourself, Bradley, we're more experienced, so please let us handle it.'

'I'm going to get around you somehow,' Bradley said, standing up and not hiding his frustration.

But Wentworth-King just sighed. 'Unless you get someone with more authority than myself, I'm afraid you'll be staying here.'

'You goddamned Brits!' Bradley exclaimed in disgust, then turned away and walked out.

He heard Wentworth-King laughing.

'That son of a bitch,' he said to Gladys in the Lyons Corner House by Piccadilly Circus, where it was business as usual. 'He's gonna make sure his SOE buddies get all the glory and leave us out in the cold. So much for the OSS pursuit of the Nazi scientists – Wentworth-King has that tied up.'

Gladys lit a cigarette, inhaled, and blew a cloud of smoke. 'Why the hell should you care?' she said. 'You only want Wilson.'

'Yes,' he admitted, 'that's true enough; but I think Wilson's more important than the rocket scientists, if only because we *don't* know what he's up to.'

'And what do you *think* he's up to?'

'You know I can't tell you that, Gladys,' he said, thinking of the extraordinary, saucer-shaped machine he had found in that hangar near Mount Pleasant, Iowa.

Gladys grinned laconically. 'No, of course not. All the officers say the same when I ask what's going on, though I often know more than they do.'

'How?'

'They all talk when they're drunk.'

'Or in bed?'

'Yes,' she said, blowing a cloud of smoke in his face and staring steadily at him. 'There as well, Mike.'

'Recently?'

He was shocked to hear himself say it, as he certainly hadn't planned to, but she responded with the same steady gaze and slight, mocking smile.

'Maybe,' she said. 'Maybe not. Why? Would it bother you?'

'Yes,' he said, taken aback by his sudden, fierce jealousy, and thinking of her life in war-torn London with a resentment he had not felt before. She had led a good life here, he knew, ever since she left New Mexico, first writing a European column for her old newspaper in Roswell, then becoming more well known when her work became syndicated nationwide. Her list of contacts, mostly high-ranking officers of the armed forces, had grown with her reputation, and she had certainly not been short of male company throughout the frantic, sexually liberated war years. She had told him all about it and he had previously enjoyed the stories, but today, for no reason at all, he felt quite the opposite.

'It didn't bother you before,' she reminded him.

'Maybe I just didn't show it. And besides, I had no reason to lay claims on you.'

'You still don't,' she said. 'We're just good friends, after all, as we constantly remind ourselves.'

He recalled his first air raid, when she had told him she loved him. He'd been too shaken to reply and hadn't reminded her of it since, but he knew that what he was feeling was more than friendship, though he was frightened of saying so.

'Yes,' he said, 'we're just good friends.'

She smiled and blew some smoke rings. 'Come on,' she said, 'you know it's more than that. Why don't you admit it?'

He shrugged helplessly. 'I don't know. I'm not sure of what I feel. I feel foolish even talking like this, because I'm practically fifty.'

'That's not old.'

'It's not young.'

'It's young enough for adult relationships.'

Amused by that, he replied, 'Adult relationships can often be childish, and I don't trust myself.'

'You don't trust what you feel?'

'No – at least not always. I've spent a lot of years thinking about us – about your letters – and while I always enjoyed getting them and kept them and reread them, I felt guilty about it – before Joan's death *and* after – and also felt that we couldn't possibly be in love after only two meetings. In other words, I sometimes felt that I was kidding myself – that maybe both of us were romancing. And having thought of myself as a mature man, that made me feel foolish. I *know* how I feel about you, Gladys – I'm just not sure why.'

Gladys propped an elbow up on the table, cupped her chin in her hand, blew a smoke ring in his direction, then shook her head ruefully.

'God, I love you,' she said. 'I've never doubted it for a second. And I knew it when we first met, inside about ten minutes. I knew I was in love with that wonderful combination of maturity, common sense, and inhibition. I knew it when I sensed that you were startled by what you were thinking.' She chuckled and shook her head again. 'And what were you thinking, Mike? You were thinking I was attractive and attracted to *you* – oh, yeah, you saw that! – and you were excited and scared all at once, as well as hopelessly guilty. A real married man, right? And one with morals and principles. Yeah, that's what I saw inside minutes when we first met – and I loved it and it made me love you – and I did – and I do. Now what do you say, Mike?'

He glanced around the crowded tea room, at all the women in their wide hats, the men in drab suits and hats, the waitresses hurrying to and fro in their black skirts and white aprons. He studied them too intently. It was something to do. His heart was racing and he was blushing like a kid, and that made him speechless. Then he looked out the window, at the statue of Eros, and had to smile. He lowered his gaze to the traffic crawling around the central island. There the bobby was blowing his whistle and waving his arms as the citizens of this beleagured, majestic, defiant city went about their daily business in a perfectly normal manner.

'The goddamned Brits,' he said, turning back to Gladys. 'You've really got to admire them.'

She raised a skeptical eyebrow. 'Is that your answer, Mike?'

'Dammit, Gladys, you know damned well I love you. I just can't say these things.'

'You've just said it.'

'Have I?'

'Yep. You've just said it. I've certainly heard more *passionate* outbursts, but I've never felt happier.' She reached across for his hand, kissed the back of his wrist, squeezed his fingers, and refused to let go. There were tears in her eyes. 'You're going to leave me, aren't you?'

'I have to go, Gladys. I have to stop that son of a bitch Wilson before he goes too far.'

'What do you think he wants?'

'I don't know. You tell me.'

'I will,' she said, drying the tears from her eyes and gazing down at the table. 'I don't think he was after power. At least not for personal gain. I think he'd made science his god and worshipped it blindly. He didn't care about human beings and despised their most common feelings; he was convinced that our only purpose on earth is to serve evolution. Not mere *procreation* – no! even the animals can do that – but to form a bridge between our irrational past and a perfectly rational future. He hated irrationality and mistrusted all emotions. For him, what divides man from the beast is intelligence – not emotion, not *feelings*. He believed only the mind, the application of logic, the quest for absolute knowledge, which he seriously confused with truth.'

'I'm not sure I understand.'

'That's why you're frightened of loving me – which you do, God bless you! Because love is an emotion that flies in the face of logic – yet it endures while one scientific absolute after another is disproven and replaced with something new. Wilson didn't understand that. Not the Wilson I knew. He was convinced that what we value, our dreams and feelings, belong to the caves. He doesn't believe in human beings – he believes only in science – and because science is the sole road to truth, it's all that concerns him. What he wants, then, isn't power – at least not as we know it – but freedom to do what he wants without normal restrictions.'

'The son of a bitch is working for the Nazis,' Bradley said.

'Yes,' Gladys replied, unconcerned by his flash of anger. 'But not because he's a Nazi or believes in the Third Reich. Probably because they were the only ones willing to finance his work, whatever that is. He'll use them – as he used me and everyone else – and he may go down with them. But whatever it is he's doing with the Nazis, he's not doing it *for* them.'

'How could you be his mistress?' Bradley asked, before he could stop himself 'If he's that bad – if he's really as cold as ice – how could you sleep with him?'

'Does that thought hurt you?'

'Yes, dammit, it does!'

'Then you really *do* love me!' she exclaimed.

'That isn't an answer.'

She picked his hand up again, stroked his fingers, kissed his wrist. 'Because I was wounded,' she explained. 'Because I'd recently lost my husband. Because I didn't want emotional entanglements and he was perfect that way. He wanted only my body and I wanted only to lose myself, so we literally climbed into bed together and had few disappointments. To be truthful, it was perfect – we both got what we needed – but in the end, like most women, I confused satisfaction with love, and was mortally wounded when he left me without looking back. That's in the nature of woman – it's in the nature of *human beings* – but it's nothing that Wilson would understand, which in the end made me loathe him more.' She kissed his hand again, stroked his fingers, and stared steadily at him. 'And now you loathe *me*, don't you? For confessing my sins. You loathe me for sleeping with the man who's taken over your life.'

'No,' he said without a moment's hesitation. 'I just love you more. But that Wilson – goddammit! he's like a man without a center. And he's brilliant and totally mysterious and I have to look in his eyes. Do you understand that?'

'Yes, I think so . . . And so you're going to Europe.'

Which brought Bradley back to the real world and plunged him into depression. 'Not according to Lieutenant-Colonel Wentworth-King. As far as *he's* concerned, I'm here for the duration – probably until the war ends.'

'Go around him,' Gladys said.

'I can't. That's not allowed.'

'What if someone with more authority approaches you?'

'That's allowed, but unlikely.'

'Do you love me?'

'Dammit, yes.'

'Without doubts?'

'You know that now.'

'I don't know why I'm doing this. I really don't. I don't want to lose you.'

'What the hell are you talking about, Gladys?'

'I'm going to get you to Europe.' She stubbed her cigarette out, waved at the waitress, then said, 'Okay, you pick up the check. It's the least you can do.' When he had done so, she led him out of the café and headed toward Leicester Square. 'Can you meet me in the bar in the Savoy this evening?' she asked.

'Yes,' he said. 'Sure.'

'About—?'

The question hung in the air, because at that moment they both heard an awful roaring, buzzing sound, a nerve-jangling sibilance that passed overhead and suddenly cut out, leaving an abrupt, unnatural, chilling silence.

Bradley saw everyone in the street looking up at the sky, as if frozen where they stood, then, in that fifteen seconds of eerie silence, they threw themselves to the ground.

The V-1 rocket, the buzz bomb, the doodle-bug, exploded in the next street just as Gladys pulled Bradley to the ground.

He felt the ground shake, heard the explosion, and rolled into Gladys. He clung to her as more rockets buzzed overhead and lay there as they went silent – the sound everyone already dreaded – then exploded fifteen seconds later, some nearby, some faraway. The attack didn't last long, but it seemed to take forever, and when it ended, Bradley helped Gladys up and then glanced about him.

A pall of black smoke was rising above the rooftops. When

Bradley heard the sirens of the fire brigade, he knew that more fires were burning and more people dying.

'About nine o'clock this evening?' Gladys asked him, as if nothing had happened.

'Sure,' he said. 'I'll be there.'

Gladys kissed him fully on the lips and gave him a hug. 'Right,' she said, then waved good-bye and hurried off, heading straight for the ominous pall of smoke that now hung over Soho, to remind him, as so many things did these days, that Wilson was still somewhere out there, being far too creative.

The buzz bombs continued to rain down all day on the southern parts of England and were still falling on London that evening when Bradley made his way to the Savoy Hotel. As he walked along the Strand, he saw a pall of black smoke hanging over St Paul's Cathedral and the rooftops of the city, and even as he turned into the hotel, more bombs exploded.

Though most of the servicemen were now fighting in France, the party in the American bar was in full swing and packed with army, navy, and air force personnel from Britain, America, Canada, France, Belgium, Czechoslovakia, and even Poland. Most of them were either working in operation centers in London or preparing to join the advance through France. The men and women, most in uniform, were spilling out of the bar and into the lobby in a haze of cigar and cigarette smoke, red-faced and in good cheer, while a large group near the bar, obviously drunk, was singing in ragged chorus, 'We're gonna hang out our washing on the Siegfried Line . . .'

Gladys was seated near the entrance, well away from the noisy singers, beside a US army major-general, and she waved Bradley over as soon as she saw him. Bradley wasn't going to kiss her in front of the unknown officer, but she jumped up and embraced him and kissed him full on the lips.

'You didn't get a doodle-bug on your head, then?' she asked jokingly, though with visible relief.

'No,' he replied. 'They're falling mostly over the City, so I was okay.'

'Here, pull up a chair,' Gladys said, then, when he had done so, said, 'This is a dear friend, Major General Ryan McArthur, who's about to take off for France and could be of help to you. Ryan, this is the guy I told you about, my fine man, OSS Colonel Mike Bradley.'

Bradley and the silver-haired, sophisticated McArthur shook hands.

'No relation, I take it,' Bradley said with a grin, 'to General . . . ?'

'No,' McArthur replied, anticipating the question. 'No relation at all. Can I get you a drink, Mike?'

'Scotch on the rocks.'

'Right.'

When McArthur was at the crowded bar, Gladys, who was sitting beside Bradley, took hold of his hand. 'Still love me after all these hours?'

'Yes,' he said, 'I guess so.'

'Okay, Mike. If you truly love me, I'll put your mind at ease. While it's true that I've had a good time here in England, I haven't been involved with another man since you turned up in London. I've been faithful and living on hope – and you're my only man now.'

A lump came to his throat and he covered her hand with his own, then squeezed her fingers.

'You didn't have to tell me that,' he said.

'Yes, I did, Mike. As for McArthur, he's just an old friend and I *do* mean a friend, no more and no less.'

'Okay, Gladys. Thanks.'

'Do you love me just a little bit more for that?'

'I can't possibly love you more than I do.'

She grinned and winked. 'That's my man.'

Bradley released her hand when McArthur returned to the table, carrying three glasses of Scotch between his two hands. They took their drinks and he sat down, sipped some Scotch, grinned at Bradley.

'So,' he said, 'you're with OSS.'

'Right.'

'You're working here with the British Secret Intelligence Service?'

'I wouldn't exactly call it working. I'm supposed to be trying to track down a renegade American scientist—'

'Wilson.'

'Right. How did you know that?'

'I work for General Groves, director of the Manhattan atomic bomb project, and since we're also keen to track down the German scientists, we got in touch with OSS and found out about Wilson. Naturally we then found out, through your filed records, that Gladys had also known him, which is how I came to know Gladys.'

'Wilson appears to have a talent for introducing a lot of people to one another.'

McArthur grinned at that, then went serious again. 'You want Wilson in particular?'

'Yes.'

'Any special reason?'

'I have reason to believe he's been working on projects far more advanced than the German rocket program.'

'And you think he might be trying to complete it in time to use it against the Allies?'

'I'm not too sure *what* his intentions are, but I sure in hell want to find him.'

'So why aren't you in Europe?'

'According to my controller at SOE, I'm not allowed into Europe until the Germans have practically surrendered.'

'By which time Wilson, as well as a good many rocket scientists, might have disappeared or been captured by the Russians.'

'Or by SOE, which is what my controller wants.'

'Lieutenant-Colonel Wentworth-King?'

'Right.'

McArthur was amused. 'A regular British public schoolboy – and very smart with it. Yes, he'll want the Brits to get there first, which is why he's holding you back.'

'Can you do anything for him, Ryan?' Gladys asked.

'Sure.' McArthur turned back to Bradley. 'On behalf of the director of the Manhattan atomic bomb project, I'm sending a bunch of ALSOS agents into Europe, to stick with the advancing Allied troops and go all the way with them into Germany. When I say *stick* with the advancing troops, I mean just that: The ALSOS agents will be with the fighting troops, right in the thick of it, to ensure that they're present when anyone of value to us – mainly scientists – is captured. Would you like to come with us?'

'Damn right, I would, Major General.'

'Okay. Because in this matter I happen to overrule the bright son of a bitch, I'll get in touch with Lieutenant-Colonel Wentworth-King and tell him I'm grabbing you.'

'Terrific. When do we leave?'

'This Friday. Which gives you a couple of days to tidy up here. We'll be in touch before with details of our departure – but right now, since you two are obviously keen to be alone, I'm off in search of debauchery.' He stood up to take his leave. 'I'll see you on Friday, Bradley. As for you, Gladys, I'll see you when I see you.'

'In Paris.'

'Let's hope that's true,' he replied, then touched his fingers to his peaked cap in a mock salute, grinned, and made his way out of the bar, through the packed, noisy revelers.

The drunks near the bar were now singing the maudlin 'We'll Meet Again,' made famous by the British forces' favorite lady, Vera Lynn, who certainly sang it much better. Yet the words, which Bradley already knew, struck straight to his heart.

Another lump came to his throat when he turned back to Gladys.

'Thanks,' he said.

'Not at all, Mike. I don't want you to go – I want you here – but I know how important it is to you.' She shrugged forlornly. 'So go.'

'We still have a couple of days,' he said.

'Tonight and tomorrow night,' she corrected him. 'You'll be

leaving on Friday. Goddammit, I think I'm gonna cry. Goddamn *you*, Mike Bradley!'

She pushed her chair back, stood up, and rushed out. Bradley followed her, forcing his way through a sea of bobbing heads and flushed faces, all of which were hazed in smoke and exuding aromas of alcohol. Gladys didn't look back, but instead hurried across the lobby and straight up the stairs. Bradley went in hot pursuit, thinking of how familiar this great hotel must seem to her, as she had now lived in it for so long. It was an odd thing to think, but it was based on pure jealousy, for he also thought of all the men she had met here throughout the war years. He felt a spasm of pain, a flash of resentment for all those men, then he raced up the stairs. He eventually caught her in the corridor, right outside her room, and tugged her around and into his arms as she was opening the door.

Gladys Kinder was crying.

Bradley kissed her tears away, surprised to find himself doing so, and rocked her trembling body in his arms and eased her into the room. He kicked the door closed behind him, licked her eyelids, kissed her cheeks, stroked her spine as he kissed her on the lips, and then held her away from him. She was shaking and the tears had streaked her cheeks and made her look a lot younger.

It was a small room and the bed was right behind her, but he didn't know what to do.

'It's been so long,' he said. 'I don't know where to begin. I'm too old for this. I don't have the knack. I hardly know where to start.'

Gladys smiled through her tears, wiped the tears away with one hand, tried to control her heavy breathing, and said, 'You've already started, Mike, and you did it well. For God's sake, don't stop now.' And she put her hands on his shoulders and pulled him to her and kissed him, then let him press her back onto the bed where it would happen or not.

Bradley lost his senses then. That was God's blessing upon him. He somehow managed to strip Gladys and remove his own clothes and get under the sheets of the bed without thinking about it. When they made love, which came naturally as well, they were tuned into the cosmos – and Bradley, nearly fifty years old, was returned to his youth.

Her bed felt like home to him.

The next day, satiated with love, Bradley reported to SOE headquarters on Baker Street, where Lieutenant-Colonel Wentworth-King frostily informed him that orders from above had removed him from the jurisdiction of SOE and were placing him under the command of the director of the Manhattan atomic bomb project, for which he would implement Operation Paperclip immediately.

'Here are your marching orders,' Wentworth-King said, pushing across a thick envelope. 'Good-bye and good luck.'

That night, all night, Bradley made love to Gladys in his bed in the small apartment in Shepherd Market while doodle-bugs rained from the sky and exploded all over the city. He found new life in the midst of death, saw the light of hope in darkness, slept the sleep of the blessed, and awakened just after dawn.

The space beside him was empty. Gladys was gone. When he went into the bathroom, he saw her message on the mirror, scrawled in lipstick in a shaky, emotional hand.

'I can't bear the thought of seeing your eyes when we have to say good-bye, so I'm saying it now. I love you. I . . .' But the writing ended there, tapering off in a jagged line, and he knew that she had then started crying and hurried out of the room.

He put his hand out, touched the lipstick, traced the words with his fingers.

'Take care,' he said.

Chapter Twenty-Eight

Wilson awakened, as he had planned, at six o'clock in the evening and found himself thinking about himself

He had slept through the afternoon because the journey to Thuringia was going to be made under cover of darkness. Now, as he lay in bed, rubbing the sleep from his eyes and hearing the news on the radio in the living room, doubtless turned on by Greta, he wondered if this thinking about himself, which was unusual, had been caused by the temporary change in his sleeping habits.

He hadn't thought about himself in many years and was very surprised. He had always looked outward, not inward, and this introspection was troubling.

He was remembering Iowa, the days of his childhood, the parents whose goodness he had always viewed strictly as weakness. Now, when he closed his eyes, he saw himself as a blond-haired boy, his skin golden from the sun, and the sun itself an immense, silvery orb in a dazzling blue sky. He had stood alone in the field of wheat, the stalks shoulder high around him, and looked across that yellow sea to where green fields met blue sky, then squinted into the sun's striations, which were silvery and ravishing. He had looked but not been ravished, been blinded but not dazzled, and responded to it, even at ten years old, with one simple question:

When would the sun die?

That question turned him into a scientist. His religion became the pursuit of knowledge. He realized that the sun would die eventually, taking with it the earth's heat and light, and that long before it happened every form of life on earth would be extinguished. Man's time on earth, then, would be short if he simply followed nature's course. Still an animal, he would die off like the dinosaurs as his life-giving sun died.

Something had to be done.

Thus Wilson, at ten years of age, had found something to live for: the changing of man's destiny through science and, incidentally, the creation of a new kind of man as a means of continuance.

He had never strayed from that path.

Even then, as a boy and adolescent in Iowa, born of religious parents but unable to accept God, he had been convinced that mankind would eventually have to leave earth and inhabit another, less endangered planet. To do so, he would have to create an extraordinary technology; he would also have to transcend his still-primitive nature and escape the physical limitations of his weak, mortal body.

Man would have to turn himself into a Superman and then reach for the stars.

Now, sixty-five years later, as he sat up in the bed in his apartment in Berlin, Wilson was made aware of his own frustrating mortality, but also reminded that he had at least begun the process of turning Man into Superman.

He had the beginnings of the technology in the shape of his flying saucer, a protected base from which to operate in Neuschwabenland, Antarctica, and a demented ideology that, if not to his personal taste, could be used to give him the work force necessary for survival in an inhospitable terrain, isolated under the ground from the rest of mankind.

He would use Himmler's disillusioned followers to get him to the Antarctic and there, over the years, let science gradually transform them into his kind of people: neither dedicated soldiers nor fanatical mystics, but men ruled by the desire for knowledge as an end in itself, supported by a docile work force deprived of freedom and will, and all living together in perfect, enforced harmony, well away from the corrupting influences of a still-primitive, self-destructive mankind.

And eventually, when the technology used for the *Kugelblitz* saucer had advanced enough, his successors would leave the dying earth behind and fly to the stars.

Those chosen to make that epic voyage would have to be Supermen – but he, who had made it all possible, would not be one of them.

He would die before that came to be.

Mortality was what prevented men from becoming Supermen – life was too short for real achievement. Although Wilson had begun experiments on organ replacement, prosthetics, and general longevity, and had already delayed his own death with the recent operations on his heart and stomach, he knew that the medical and surgical experimentation begun in the camps would not be advanced far enough, soon enough, to prevent him from dying of old age. Nevertheless, his successor, whomever he might be, *would* benefit from the experiments, and eventually the more valued members of his Antarctic colony would have a much longer life span. Because of that, they would gain the time needed for their biological and mental transformation into Supermen.

In that sense, Wilson thought as he stood up and stretched himself, my life will not have been wasted and my death will have meaning.

From here he could hear the radio announcer blandly informing the citizens of the Third Reich that the Allied invasion of Europe, initiated sixteen days ago with a bloody assault along more than a hundred miles of the French coast, was being successfully resisted by the valiant soldiers of the Thousand Year Reich.

The announcer did not mention the Allied liberation of Rome, the US bombing of the Japanese mainland, the loss of the Cotentin peninsula, the increasingly hopeless position of General von Schlieben's surrounded troops, General de Gaulle's triumphant return to the liberated areas of France after the capture of Bayeux, General Montgomery's inexorable advance on Caen, or the fact that only yesterday the Allies had seized two German V-1 launch sites on the Cherbourg peninsula and were closing in on the historic town itself. Nor did he mention that Berlin, suffering Allied bombing raids every night, was being razed to the ground.

He was carefully silent on those facts.

It will soon be over, Wilson thought, no matter what we're told. No wonder we're fleeing to the Harz Mountains. It's just a matter of months now . . .

Not wishing to face Greta until he was ready to leave, he went straight from the bedroom to the bathroom, had his bath, dried himself and put on his civilian clothing, then returned to the bedroom. He had packed his suitcase the previous evening, when Greta was out with friends; now he pulled it out from where he had hidden it under the bed. Then, feeling little emotion, he walked into the main room.

Greta was anxiously turning the dial on the radio, trying to pick up a British station. She was smoking a cigarette, scratching her auburn hair with her free hand, and looking as worldly as ever, though she had aged greatly recently.

Since the bombs had started dropping on Berlin she had not been the same.

Looking up when he entered the room, she saw the suitcase. The news on the radio was replaced by Wagner as her eyes started widening.

'I'm leaving,' Wilson said, anticipating her question, 'and I probably won't be coming back. The apartment is yours to keep.'

'What?'

He knew she had heard him but did not want to believe him. The average person's unwillingness to face facts had never ceased to depress him.

'You heard me,' he said, setting the suitcase on the floor and noting the shocked light in her eyes. 'I said I'm leaving and probably won't be coming back. However, the SS always look after their own and in this case are treating you like my wife. In other words, you can keep the apartment and they'll provide you with a decent monthly income. They'll soon be in touch with you.'

She was smoking a cigarette, a habit he despised, and this time, when she sucked in the smoke, she did so as if drowning. 'I'm not sure I understand,' she said, glancing at his suitcase and letting the smoke drift out between her lips. 'I mean, we've been living together for so long, and now you just . . .'

'You always knew this would come,' he said, as he had said to so many. 'Our arrangement was always based on the knowledge that it would end sooner or later – and now the time's come.'

'Just like that? Without warning?'

'I couldn't give you any warning. The SS swore me to secrecy. I wasn't allowed to tell you until I was leaving – and that's just what I'm doing.'

'I don't believe that for a second.'

'Believe it – it's true.'

'You're going to leave me here all alone?'

'I'm being moved out, with the other scientists and engineers, but I can't tell you where.'

'Why can't I come with you?'

'It's not permitted, that's why.'

'You mean, the others are all going without their wives? Is that what you're telling me?'

'No, I'm not saying that. The others *are* taking their wives and children. But the others are Germans married to Germans – whereas I happen to be a foreigner here by their good graces and living with a woman not my wife. I asked if I could take you along, but they refused absolutely.'

'I don't believe that.'

'It's true. And who knows their motives? This war's coming to an end, the Third Reich is going to fall, and when that happens, they may decide to execute me – maybe that's why you can't come.'

It was a deliberate lie, offered simply to keep her calm, but he knew, when he saw her brightening gaze, that she hadn't believed him. She was an experienced woman, after all, particularly wise in the ways of men, and what he now saw in her normally hard eyes was a mixture of rage and fear.

'So I'm just being left here?'

'You have the apartment and will get an allowance. Believe me, you'll be better off than most. I'd count my blessings, if I were you.'

'Blessings?' she retorted. 'Being left here in Berlin? A city being bombed night and day, and soon to be conquered! What good's this apartment if it's bombed? What good's the allowance when the war is lost? What happens to me if I manage to survive the bombings, but the Russians get here first?'

'I'm sure you'll do okay,' he said. 'You're not a child, after all.'

He had said something similar to that other woman – Gladys Kinder? – about twelve years ago and now, as the memory of her passed briefly through his thoughts, thus reminding him of Goddard and those early rockets in the desert, Greta's mounting fear and rage set fire to her eyes.

'You can't do this,' she said, sounding strangled and shaky. 'You owe me more than this! You just can't pack up and walk out and leave me here in this hell. You've got to take me with you. You've *got* to! *For God's sake, don't leave me here!*'

'You're an experienced woman,' Wilson replied, taking note of her rising hysteria and therefore picking up his suitcase. 'You should manage okay.'

But she jumped to her feet, grabbed his shoulders, shook him violently, crying, 'No, Wilson! For the love of God! I'm too old now! The Russians might – *Don't leave me, Wilson!*'

Suddenly she looked old, her face ravaged by shock and dread, and he felt disgusted by her naked, primal emotions and pushed her away from him. She stumbled back into the fireplace, shaking her head, her gaze dazed. He left without saying another word, not looking back.

An SS car had been assigned to take him to Kummersdorf, and the driver was waiting for him when he emerged. Darkness had fallen and when the car had moved off he gazed out the window, saw the dreadful ruins and hillocks of rubble silhouetted against a starlit sky, and knew, given the clarity of the night, that the Allied planes would soon be flying overhead to drop more bombs on the city.

He closed his eyes, recalled Greta's outburst, and considered once more, as he had done so often, how the glory of man's mind could be perverted with primitive emotions. He had never felt such emotions, though he knew that most people did, as he also knew that there were many who thought his lack of so-called normal feelings was inhuman.

Was this so? He didn't think so. Instead, he took it for a sign of genius. He had always felt himself to be different from his own kind – even from his good parents, other children, his women – and had viewed the blatant emotions of others as the aberrations of weakness. Man's emotions belonged to the cave; his mind was his glory.

And he, this individual named John Wilson, was ruled by his brilliant mind.

It had always been so. Behind his closed eyes, he relived it. He saw his parents in the fields, their backs bent under the sun, then himself, a mere stripling, kneeling beside them in the church of Montezuma, where he kept his eyes open. They were decent, simple folk, introverted, even distant, and although they had always treated him well, he viewed their virtue as weakness. They made him read the Bible, but he thought it a book of myths. When they prayed, either at home or in church, he translated their worship as a form of awe no more rational than the primal fears and superstitions of the cavemen.

He felt that man was not made to worship gods, but to attain godlike stature.

He was not like his parents. Nor was he like other children. His parents didn't notice the difference, for they were too involved with themselves, but at school he was considered odd, because he didn't like playing games and was ferocious at studying. He always wanted to be alone, to live through his books, and that made him different.

Then he decided to become a scientist and devoted himself

to that. At twelve, he was practicing vivisection and was caught by his parents. They were shocked by his cruelty, which he viewed as pure research, and they punished him by sending him to his room for a whole week, which merely gave him more time for his reading and intense contemplation. It didn't stop his experiments – he just continued them in secret – and by the age of fifteen, when at high school in Des Moines, he knew more about biology and science than his teachers could teach him.

He was also convinced, by then, that the only thing dividing man from the beast was his ability to think – not the heart, but the mind; not emotions, but reasoning. Once he had accepted that as truth, he learned to distrust what were widely regarded as man's 'finer' feelings.

Man was but a tool of evolution; the human mind was its instrument. And because most human emotions were dead weight, Wilson, from an early age, took pride in not having them.

He was a genius, a completely rational being, and that made him unique.

Nothing else mattered.

When the SS car slowed down, he opened his eyes again and saw the beams of the searchlights crisscrossing one another as they swept over Kummersdorf, erratically illuminating the tall hangars, prefabricated offices, wooden huts, barbed-wire fences, and high, ugly watch towers, where the helmeted troops sat behind machine guns and kept guard all night. Though normally empty, the compound in front of the experimental center was now filled with troop trucks, all bathed in the steady glare of overhead lamps. A lot of the troops were carrying equipment and papers from the hangar to the parked vehicles, while other trucks roared into life and headed toward the main gate.

After leaving the car and entering the hangar, Wilson saw the Schriever saucer still sitting on its raised steel platform. It looked enormous in that enclosed space, its smooth surface giving off a silvery glint in the overhead lighting. Looking in vain for Flugkapitän Schriever, he crossed the floor and entered his own office, which was now bare of its filing cabinets and wall charts. There he found Ernst Stoll, SS Brigadier Hans Kammler, and the dark-eyed, dangerous SS General Artur Nebe sitting up in hardbacked wooden chairs, all smoking, drinking what looked like brandy, and clearly waiting for him.

'So,' Wilson said, 'the move's begun already.'

'Yes,' Kammler said. 'The first trucks are already at the station and you can leave any minute now.'

'What are the arrangements?'

'I have to remain here to oversee the V-1 and forthcoming V-2 rocket launchings against England. However, General Nebe and his finest troops will accompany you throughout the journey, for protection, and Captain Stoll will also go along, to ensure that you settle into Kahla without problems. Once things are running smoothly at Kahla, which will be administered jointly with the nearby Nordhausen Central Works under the jurisdiction of Captain Stoll, General Nebe will return to Berlin to organize the eventual time and means of escape from Germany; while Stoll will divide his time between Thuringia and Berlin, which will enable him to look after your project *and* keep his eye on our increasingly unpredictable Reichsführer.'

'What about Rudolph Schriever and that' – Wilson paused to glance through the window at the flying saucer in the middle of the hangar – 'that *thing* out there?'

'A week from today,' Ernst Stoll solemnly informed him, 'the remaining staff of Kummersdorf, with Schriever in charge, will be moved, with the saucer, to a secret location near Prague. Thus, while Schriever's progress will be watched closely by Himmler, you will be able to complete your *Feuerball* and *Kugelblitz*, protected by General Kammler, under my jurisdiction.'

'And what reason have you given Schriever for the move?'

'The same as we gave Himmler. Namely, that your work has become erratic, you can no longer be trusted, and so you're being moved to Nordhausen, to be placed under our supervision, now that Wernher von Braun has been moved back to the rebuilt factories in the development works, on the old site of Peenemünde East.'

'Excellent,' Wilson said.

'And now we better go,' General Nebe said softly, his face as unemotional as a rock, which gave Wilson comfort. 'We want at least to get out of the station before the Allied bombers come again.'

'Good thinking,' Kammler said.

The day before Wilson had supervised the dismantling and packing of the separate parts of his *Feuerball* and *Kugelblitz* in the BMW plant at Spandau for transportation to the railway station. Today he was pleased to follow the others out of his office for the last time. Just as they were leaving, Flugkapitän Schriever, Habermohl, and Miethe emerged from the former's office and stopped right in front of them. Schriever, thinking he was now in charge of Projekt Saucer, gave Wilson a broad, superior smile.

'So,' he said, 'you're going to Nordhausen.'

'Yes,' Wilson replied.

'Naturally, I'm sorry to be losing you.'

'I'm sure you are, Flugkapitän.'

'I have naturally recommended your work to Himmler—'

'Thank you.'

'– and while obviously he appreciates your contributions to Projekt Saucer, he feels it's now time that we Germans take it over completely.'

'I understand,' Wilson said.

'Once we get to Prague, I'll have the saucer flying in no time, I can assure you, Wilson.'

'I hope so, Flugkapitän.'

Schriever offered his hand. Wilson took it and shook it, then Schriever gave the Nazi salute and led his two men away. Stoll smiled thinly at Wilson, nodded toward the exit, then led him and the other two Nazi officers out of the hangar.

Wilson didn't look back. There was nothing there to interest him. He took his seat in the SS car, made room for Stoll beside him, and kept his eyes open as they drove out of Kummersdorf toward Berlin. The night sky was bright with stars, the moon gliding behind thin clouds, but he soon saw a red glow in the sky, far ahead in the darkness. Then he heard the sound, the distant *crump-crump* of explosions, and knew instantly that the glowing in the sky was from the flames of an air raid.

'They come nearly every night now,' Ernst said. 'The swine never stop.'

'Remember the Blitz on London,' Wilson replied, 'and you won't expect them to stop.'

'My family live in Berlin, Wilson.'

'I'm sorry,' Wilson said, though he didn't give a damn.

'My wife left me,' Ernst continued like a man in a trance, 'but she's living with the children in her parents' house in the district of Wannsee, which they bomb all the time.'

'Not good,' Wilson said, bored.

'I worry about them more when they're away – and now we're off to Thuringia.'

'It's important, Captain Stoll. *Very* important.'

'Yes,' Ernst said. 'I know. I just can't help but worry.'

Luckily, they did not have to return to Berlin, but instead turned away from it, to a station in a small town that Wilson didn't recognize, though he knew it was on the route to Brandenburg.

The station was heavily guarded, surrounded by armed SS troops, and the midnight silence was broken by the barking of Alsatian dogs and the awful sound of men bawling through megaphones. Flashlights shone on white faces, searchlights swept across packed trucks, and Wilson had to follow Stoll through massed ranks of armed troops, none of whom looked too happy, and into a small railway station that was the stage for a nightmare. Prisoners from the camps were there, under-nourished, terrified. They were forced to run the gauntlet of snarling dogs and cracking whips, then herded up into the boxcars, where they were packed in like sardines. There were not many left – most of the boxcars had been closed already – but Wilson saw enough to have a clear picture of what was happening.

It seemed chaotic, but it wasn't – it was very well organized – and when Wilson saw General Nebe near the last of the open boxcars, his face impassive but his dark eyes always restless, he understood why.

Nevertheless, Wilson was glad to get out of it and into his carriage, which, as he discovered when the train pulled out shortly after, he was sharing with Ernst Stoll, Brigadier Kammler, General Nebe, and their most favored officers. Nebe let them all relax, smoking and drinking, playing cards, and soon the distant sounds of the bombing of Berlin had faded away with the crimson sky, leaving only dark flatlands outside and the train's clickety-clacking.

'We are on our way at last,' Ernst Stoll said. 'Thank God for that at least.'

'Yes,' Wilson replied. 'The sooner we get there, the sooner you can return to Berlin and your family.'

'*If* they're still there,' Ernst said.

'If they are not,' Kammler said icily, 'you will have made your personal sacrifice for the Third Reich. Would you not consider that an honor, Captain Stoll?'

'Naturally I would, sir.'

'You seemed a little bitter, Captain.'

'No, sir. I'm just tired, that's all.'

'We all are.' Kammler sneered, then lit a cigarette, blew a cloud of smoke, and engaged Nebe in whispered conversation, which only served to make Ernst more nervous, as Wilson carefully noted.

Turning his attention to Kammler and Nebe, sitting together on the seat opposite, he wondered at the caliber of human being he had been forced to deal with.

Kammler, he knew, had been responsible for the planning of various concentration camps; had personally supervised and confirmed the plans for the enormous subcamp at Birkenau, part of Auschwitz, with its four gas chambers and crematoria; was impatient, ruthless, completely amoral, and, though Himmler's present favorite and ostensibly devoted to him, was consumed by no more than self-interest.

General Nebe, on the other hand, was a more shadowy figure, one of shifting allegiances, someone known to be a practiced survivor and no stranger to bloodshed. He rarely smiled, fondled his pistol a lot, and kept his conversation to the bare minimum. A good man to have on your side; a man to dread if your enemy. To Wilson, such men were animals – but they had to be used.

It was a truly depressing thought.

Closing his eyes, he tried to sleep, but instead thought about how divorced he was from his fellow men, unable to share their petty concerns and narrow ambitions. They wanted the here and now, the love of woman, man's esteem, but failed completely to see just how short life was and, therefore, how important. Though born to be the tools of evolution, they still lived like cavemen.

Their evolution would not come naturally. At least not in time to save them. The continuation of the human species could be guaranteed only if men took matters into their own hands and re-created themselves.

And as most men could not even conceive of that, the exceptional few, like Wilson, would have to lead the way.

I will do it, he thought, trying to sleep, but failing dismally. I will re-create myself, with my willpower and surgical assistance, and in so doing become the first of that race that will fly to the stars.

I will become a biological mutation with my mind unimpaired. I will not find immortality – no, it's too late for that – but the operations I've had, which have so far been successful, are merely the first steps on the road to man's transformation, physical and mental . . . Those who follow me, on the operating table and with my philosophy, will evolve, as their regressive fellow men die off, into the Superman.

This will be my achievement.

Thinking about it, he smiled. He was still traveling, after all. He had left his home in Iowa, left his friends, then his country, and now he was on the road out of Germany.

He was going to where the air was clean and mankind could be reborn.

Not immediately, however. He was still in the real world. He was reminded of that fact when the Allied bombers returned, growling low overhead, and the darkness outside the noisy train became a fabulous tapestry. There were ballooning balls of white light, jagged yellow flames, clouds of black smoke, then the luminous, scorching heat of the explosions lent the darkness a crimson hue. Sparks fountained to the sky, decorating moon and stars, and the buildings of the town outside the train collapsed into more beauty. It was the singular beauty of death, the awesome radiance of destruction. Wilson saw the walls exploding, the smoke billowing up from the flames, and knew, even as the noise erupted and clawed through him, that the beauty and horror of life on earth were one and the same.

The train screeched and shuddered, then ground to a halt while the SS officers crowded up against the windows and looked out at the night.

'Why are we stopping?' Kammler asked, glancing at Nebe.

'I don't know,' Nebe replied, then stood up and crooked his finger at Ernst Stoll. 'Come with me, Captain.'

The train had stopped on the outskirts of town. The darkness outside was filled with sheets of yellow flame and geysering sparks. Smoke billowed up from the buildings, obscuring the moon and stars, and the steady droning of the Allied bombers seemed to make the air vibrate. Nebe stopped and glanced out, started forward again, then stopped when an SS sergeant rushed into the carriage and gave the Nazi salute.

'Why have we stopped?' Nebe asked.

'Some of the prisoners are panicking, sir. They're hammering on the doors of the boxcars and might start a riot. We don't know what to do.'

'What we do is set an example,' Nebe said softly. 'Captain Stoll, come with me!'

Wilson watched them departing, followed closely by

Kammler, then he pulled his window down enough to stick his head out. The noise of the air raid was deafening, hammering at him like a huge fist, and he saw collapsing buildings, more showering sparks, billowing smoke, and glanced backward along the train to where armed troops were covering one of the boxcars, the dogs straining at the end of their tethers, barking and snapping.

Nebe, Kammler, and Stoll were there, standing in front of the boxcar. Nebe was removing his pistol from his holster as his troops opened the door. Bombs were exploding nearby, the ground roaring and erupting, and even as earth and debris showered back down, Nebe took aim with his pistol. The first prisoner was dropping. Nebe shot him and he fell. Another prisoner jumped out as Kammler and Stoll unholstered their pistols and started firing. The prisoners were shot as they jumped out, screamed and jerked and collapsed. Then the women inside started wailing as the SS troops, encouraged by their leader, fired into the boxcar.

The noise was atrocious, a savage, staccato roaring, adding to the crescendo of the aircraft growling overhead, the bombs exploding on all sides, and the sibilance of the tracer bullets crisscrossing the sky above the boiling black smoke.

No more prisoners jumped down, but Wilson heard the women wailing. That dreadful sound was shut off when the boxcar doors were closed again, locking in the subdued prisoners, then Nebe led Kammler and Ernst Stoll back to the carriage.

The train moved off again as they returned and took their seats, Kammler and Nebe facing Wilson, the pale-faced Stoll beside him.

Wilson noted Stoll's shocked appearance. It was something worth remembering. Stoll obeyed orders, but not without distaste, and that virtue, which Wilson viewed as his weakness, was what would make him useful.

Wilson closed his eyes again. He fell in and out of sleep. The train traveled through the night, through more air raids and long silences, passing smoldering ruins and columns of troops on the roads and villages still remarkably untouched and silhouetted in moonlight. The ruins gradually disappeared, giving way to pine forests. The forests rose and fell over the hills of Thuringia, shielding picturesque villages, nineteenth-century houses, and the remains of fortified castles that stood majestically on the crest of the hills, overlooking the babbling brooks and rivers that crossed lush valleys.

The train climbed up through the forests. There were no air raids here. The sun rose beyond the hills, a pearly light through starlit darkness, then the gray light turned into silvery striations that gave the trees back their color.

The trees covered the hills and mountains, hid the great caves hacked out of them. The train, which had been climbing more slowly by the hour, finally stopped in a cleared area by the old walled town of Kahla, in the region of the southern Harz Mountains, on the same line that led on to the underground Nordhausen Central Works.

Wilson looked out. The pine trees soared all around him. The old walled town of Kahla could not be seen from here, but the train lines branched off into a tunnel that led inside the forested hills.

In there lay his destiny.

Chapter Twenty-Nine

After spending a nightmarish week in the Harz Mountains, supervising the resettlement of Wilson and his flying saucer project, Ernst returned to Berlin to do the same for the ungrateful and increasingly arrogant Flugkapitän Rudolph Schriever, though in this case the move was to Prague, Czechoslovakia.

After settling Schriever, his two trusted engineers, and other assistants and slave workers in the research complex just outside the city, where the naive scientist had been looking forward to testing the flying saucer before the Soviets advanced too far, Ernst returned to a bomb-shattered Berlin. He felt older than ever and no longer was able to sleep at night.

When he made his report to Heinrich Himmler, the Reichsführer, who had once seemed so icily calm, now was oddly distracted. His eyes behind the glittering pince-nez roamed restlessly left and right.

'Four days ago,' he said, before Ernst could utter a word, 'the Russians took Minsk and captured one hundred thousand German soldiers. One hundred thousand,' he repeated slowly, like a man in a trance. 'It is something to think about.'

Embarrassed, Ernst didn't know what to say, so he simply remained standing in front of Himmler's desk, looking down at his chubby, pale face and surprised by the change in him. Eventually, as if remembering what Ernst was there for, the Reichsführer looked up and said, in a less distracted manner, 'So, you have completed the resettlements. I myself have recently visited the new site at Prague, but haven't been to

Nordhausen since last there with you. What's it like there?'

'Very good, Reichsführer. The Nordhausen Central Works are, as you know, hidden deeply in the Kohnstein Mountain. As of this moment, more than three thousand prisoners from the concentration camp at nearby Buchenwald are being used as slave labor and housed in a new subcamp named Dora. It is anticipated that by October this year, the whole of the Dora subcamp will have been transferred underground and also increased to a total of over thirteen thousand slave workers. Another camp for the prisoners is being set up in a mountain valley to the south, less than a kilometer from the entrance to Nordhausen's tunnel B.'

'The prisoners are disciplined and work well?'

'Yes, sir,' Ernst said, thinking of how the unfortunates were driven to work with sticks, worked exceptionally long and exhausting hours, and not allowed to rest for a single moment.

'How are they disciplined?' Himmler asked, for such matters always interested the bureaucrat in him.

'Naturally they're supervised at all times with SS guards armed with pistols, automatic weapons, bullwhips, and sticks. When not working, many of them are shut up in the tunnels of the underground complex. When they refuse to work on the V-1 or V-2, they are shot or hanged in full sight of the other prisoners – either in the underground corridors or in the rollcall ground of the open camps.'

'Excellent, Captain. It is always best to carry out disciplinary measures in full sight of the other prisoners. It is always good to remind them of the consequences should they too commit an infraction.'

'Yes, sir,' Ernst said. The nightmares generated by his week in Nordhausen and the other underground factories in the area, including the one at Kahla, were the cause of his inability to sleep.

'And the underground factories are definitely invisible from the air?'

'Yes, Reichsführer.'

'Good.' Himmler offered a smile that seemed to. be turned

inward upon himself. 'As you know,' he said, clasping his hands under his double chin and returning to his former distracted manner, 'as early as 1941, I personally set up an SS proving ground near Blizna, a small village located by the confluence of the rivers Vistula and San, in southern Poland.'

'Yes, sir, I remember it well.'

Himmler nodded again and smiled in a dreamy manner. 'Toward the end of 1941,' he continued, 'after the villagers had all been evicted, Soviet prisoners-of-war were sent there and killed off almost to a man by hard labor and starvation, in order to get the proving ground completed. When they had died off, we sent political prisoners and eventually built a concentration camp for them. Since then we have razed the original village to the ground, camouflaged the whole area, and built a new, mock village over the proving ground, to fool Allied aircraft and their photographers. Cardboard cottages and outbuildings were sent there from Germany; dummies of men, women, and children stand around; and even flowers and other shrubbery have been planted. From the air, the illusion of an inhabited village is complete – and I like to think of it, Captain,' he continued, looking up at Ernst and smiling, 'as the prototype for all the camouflaged, underground factories built since then . . . My personal creation.'

'And an excellent one, sir.'

'Thank you, Captain.'

Ernst, feeling weary and slightly unreal, did not think it wise to mention the fact that according to recent intelligence reports, Polish partisans were already moving in on Blizna, with a view to capturing it and holding it until the Soviet army arrived, as it surely would any day now.

'And a similar situation exists at the Schriever complex near Prague, in Bohemia?'

'Yes, Reichsführer. Exactly the same. And Flugkapitän Schriever is hoping to test his flying saucer later this year.'

'Good. We need all the secret weapons we can get, if we're to defeat the Allied advance. What is the American, Wilson, doing in this respect?'

'Not much, I'm afraid,' Ernst lied, knowing that in fact Wilson was already planning to test his small *Feuerball* in the guise of an antiradar weapon and, if it was successful, to then implement the same ideas in the larger flying saucer he was intending to construct in Neuschwabenland. 'He's making various small contributions to the V-2 program but has otherwise turned out to be disappointing.'

'If the Soviets or Americans even get close, I want that man shot.'

'He will be, Reichsführer. In the meantime, I agree that it's wise to pin most of our hopes on the V-2 rocket program and, possibly, Schriever's flying saucer.'

Himmler nodded, accepting Ernst's compliment, then unclasped his hands. 'So, Captain,' he said, 'when are you returning to Nordhausen?'

'As soon as I see my wife and children, Reichsführer.'

'Ah, yes,' Himmler said. 'Now living with your mother-in-law, I believe.'

'Yes, sir.'

'I do not approve of the separation, but am pleased to note that you did, at least, do something about her lover. I assume now he is one of the hundred thousand German soldiers captured at Minsk. It is all he deserves.'

'Yes, sir. I agree.'

Himmler stood up behind his desk and stared somberly at Ernst. 'These are terrible times,' he said, 'and we must all remain courageous. I wish to thank you, Captain, for all you've done so far. Believe me, I'm proud of you.' Then, to Ernst's amazement, he offered his hand. Ernst shook it, found it oddly clammy, then saluted and walked out.

Berlin was barely recognizable, with once-familiar areas now razed to the ground, blackened ruins and piles of rubble as far as the eye could see, and a constant smell of fire in the air, instead of the summer flowers. There were few soldiers about, only old men, women, and children, a good many of them crippled, and Ernst became even more depressed and longed for escape.

He went straight to Brigette's apartment, wanting to have her one last time. He was relieved to find the building still standing, though the one beside it had been bombed, and he hurried eagerly up the stairs to ring the bell of her door.

However, before he could do so, the door opened, a Luftwaffe flight lieutenant stared at him in surprise, then grinned sheepishly, finished buttoning up his jacket, called *'Auf Wiedersehen!'* back over his shoulder and left by the stairs. Brigette appeared in the doorway, her red hair disheveled, a cigarette between her lips, still wearing her dressing gown. She was just about to close the door when she saw Ernst.

Startled, she froze for a moment, then grinned, stepped back, and waved him inside, saying 'Ah! My pretty kapitän! Come inside and be warmed!' A little shaken, Ernst stepped in, pushed the door closed behind him, and just stood there, feeling foolish, until Brigette pressed her lips to his and ran her hand down his spine. 'Did you bring me a present, my beauty, from wherever you've been?'

'Not this time,' Ernst said.

She stepped away from him and pouted, blowing smoke in his face. 'Nothing? Not one little thing? Is this how you treat the girls who suffer at home?'

Ernst was not amused by her flippancy, assuming she was trying to make light of the man who had just left.

'You don't seem to be suffering too much,' he said. 'You still have your boyfriends, I see.'

She grinned, adjusted the dressing gown to cover her breasts, then waved her hand in an airy manner, indicating the once-elegant apartment. 'Not suffering?' she asked in a theatrical, manner. 'But darling, just *look* at this place. It is *not* what it once was.' Which certainly seemed true enough; the furniture seemed faded and dusty, the drinks cabinet bare. 'No Russian vodka,' she continued. 'No cognac from France. No more pasta and salami, no more dairy products from Denmark, no more jewelry and furs from handsome officers flushed with victory and pride. Only *angst,* my darling, and the air raids and the long queues for food. Why *not* the odd boyfriend?'

Her mockery angered him, but he tried not to show it, as he still hoped to get into her bed before visiting Ingrid.

'I suppose I've no reason to complain,' he said. 'It was just a shock, that's all.'

'Why, darling? You've always known about my other men. You've always known that I like my little presents and can't bear to be lonesome.'

He wanted to slap her face, but managed to restrain himself, because what she had said was perfectly true. Indeed, she had often teased him with talk about her other men, and in those days, when Berlin was rich and he a golden young conqueror, he had taken the teasing in good part. That he couldn't do so now was a sign that things had changed radically . . . He was no longer a conqueror, she had visibly aged, and both the city and this faded, bare apartment reminded him of the forthcoming defeat. He felt that darkness descending . . .

'So what are you doing here, Ernst?' Brigette said, inhaling and exhaling cigarette smoke and turning away to take a seat on the worn sofa, where she crossed her long, still-elegant legs and swung one invitingly.

'You know what I came for,' he said, feeling a choke in his throat.

She smiled, then stubbed her cigarette out, and stretched both arms along the back of the sofa, thus forcing her breasts out. 'But you didn't bring me my little present, dear Ernst, and you *know* I expect that.'

'I know you like your little presents, but I didn't realize they were mandatory. I mean, I never thought of them as absolutely vital. It was my *pleasure* to give them.'

'You gave them *in return* for pleasure.'

'That's beside the point.'

'The point, dear, is that I never lend myself unless I'm offered a present.'

'I didn't know you were for sale.'

'Yes, you did,' she said calmly. 'I charged more than a common whore would charge – it just wasn't money.'

'Presents,' Ernst said bitterly.

'Exactly,' she replied. 'Some men, they can't admit that they're buying it, so one asks them for presents. *Little* presents. *Expensive* presents. Ones with high resale value.'

'You're a mercenary whore.'

'No, Ernst, darling, I'm a survivor. I've learned not to depend on men for anything, so I take what I can from them. To save for a rainy day, darling – which means when Berlin falls.'

'That's the talk of a traitor.'

'Are you going to report me, darling? After all, that's what you often said you were – no more than a policeman.'

The remark humiliated him, reminding him of his failures, but the thought that he might not have her this last time made him desire her all the more, which made him swallow his pride.

'I'm going away,' he said, despising the plaintive tone in his voice. 'I'm being posted away and don't know what will happen after that. I just thought . . .'

'One last time?'

'Yes,' he said, almost whispering. 'For old times' sake, at least.'

'For old time's sake,' she echoed sardonically.

'Yes,' he said, walking toward her. He stopped directly in front of the worn sofa and gazed down at her swinging leg. It was exposed up to the thigh and it made him take his breath in; then, when he raised his gaze, he saw her breasts thrusting against the dressing gown, the skin above bare and marble white. When he raised his gaze higher, he saw her sensual lips curved in a mocking smile.

'So you're going away,' she said, 'and leaving me to the tender mercies of the Allied troops or the Soviets – and still you want your little pleasure for old time's sake. Well, my dear, a girl has to survive and, when the city falls, will need more than her fading looks – so since we've always had a particular relationship, let's keep it that way . . . Which means that if I don't get my present, you won't have any fun.'

'I've been away for weeks,' he said, loathing the piteous tone in his voice and feeling his anger rising out of his humiliation.

'I've been worked night and day. I didn't have the opportunity to buy presents – not even for my wife and children, let alone you.'

'You're *separated* from your wife and children.'

'I still see them – and will this evening.'

'Perhaps they no longer expect presents – but I do, my dear. '

'I don't have one, Brigette. For God's sake, don't be—'

But she stopped him short by leaning forward on the sofa, taking hold of his wrist and turning it over to examine his watch.

'A gold Rolex,' she said.

He jerked his hand away. 'If you think—'

She leaned back on the sofa and stretched her arms along the back of it, simultaneously exposing her full breasts and swinging that long leg. 'A gold Rolex is worth a lot,' she said, smiling. 'And I still want my present.'

Ernst exploded, hardly knowing what he was doing. He grabbed her by the collar, jerked her to her feet, slapped her face, and threw her back down. He saw the torn dressing gown, a bared breast, blood on her lips, then bent over and slapped her again and dragged her onto the floor. She cursed and clawed at him, tried to roll away but failed, and writhed beneath him when he straddled her body and ripped the dressing gown off her.

He didn't feel lust – only violent, blinding rage – but when the dressing gown was lying in shreds around her, he tried to force her legs open. She didn't scream, but she cursed him loudly, trying to jerk her wrists from his hands, and when finally he let go to hold her legs apart, she frantically tried hitting him with her fists.

Surprised, he released her thighs and took hold of her wrists again. He jerked her hands away from her face and, still straddling her and breathing in spasms, looked at her as she stopped writhing beneath him and glared fiercely at him. When she stopped struggling, when her body became motionless, he released her hands and rolled off her, then stood up and straightened his jacket, feeling foolish and beaten.

'The Soviets will know what to do with you,' he said with as much contempt as he could muster, looking down at her, where she still lay on the floor, too careful to move. 'Good luck, Brigette. You'll need it.'

He made a point of not slamming the door in anger when he left for the last time . . . but her mocking laughter pursued him.

The lines for the tramcars to Wannsee had been blown up in an air raid, so he took a taxi through the darkening light of the early evening, trying not to look out at the crippled children and old people who were clambering over the piles of rubble or exploring the charred ruins, hoping to find something they could barter for money or food.

Yes, Berlin was unrecognizable, the gaunt remainder of a lost dream. He was glad when the worst ruins disappeared from view and were replaced with the relatively less devastated areas overlooking the Havel River. Not that there were no ruins here, but they were fewer and more spread out, and he was even more relieved to find his in-laws' elegant old house still standing in its gardens overlooking the waters of the Wannsee. He asked the taxi driver to wait for him, then rang the doorbell.

Ingrid's mother answered the door, looking shockingly aged. Her hair was now completely gray and the skin of her handsome face, though tight on her cheekbones, was webbed with lines of tension and possibly hunger.

She stared in a confused manner at Ernst, then, recognizing him, murmured a greeting and pulled him into her arms. When they embraced, he kissed her cheek, which seemed cold, then followed her inside the house. She walked ahead of him, her body heavy and ungainly, saying over her shoulder 'The children will be so glad to see you. How long has it been now?'

Noting that she hadn't included Ingrid in her first comment, Ernst said, 'About eighteen months. Maybe two years. I'm not sure. How have things been?'

'Not so good,' she said vaguely. 'All the air raids . . . food shortages . . . the anxiety . . . Ingrid!' she called out as she entered the living room. 'You have a visitor, dear!'

She stepped aside to let him enter, hugged him again impulsively as he passed her, whispered, 'I think I'll leave you two alone,' then hurried away. Ernst stepped into the living room and saw Ingrid looking up from where she was sitting in an armchair, an open newspaper laying across her lap, her face still exceptionally pretty, but drawn, as if sleep had eluded her.

'Hello, Ingrid,' he said, walking across the room, which was, he noted, still filled with the excellent furniture, international bricabrac, and fine paintings that her father had collected before he died.

'What do you want?' she asked coldly.

Startled, he stopped in front of her, looked down at her, then glanced at the sofa opposite. 'Can I sit down?'

'Are you planning to stay long?'

'No. I have a taxi waiting.'

'Then you can sit down.'

He hadn't expected a warm welcome, but her coldness was truly shocking. He sat on the sofa and smiled at her, hoping to warm her.

'What do you want here?' she asked him, clearly not warmed at all.

'I'm being posted out of Berlin,' he said, 'and I don't know when I'll be coming back. I came to say good-bye – and also because I'm worried about you and the children.'

'Are you, indeed?'

'Yes.'

'Why?'

'Because of the air raids, for a start.'

'They've been bombing Berlin for a long time and you didn't worry before.'

'I did. It was you who left me. You *do* remember that, don't you?'

'Yes, Ernst, I remember. And I also remember why. It was

because I found out about your whoring and so turned to another man – a good man, Ernst, a *very* good man, whom you had sent to Russia.'

'At the insistence of the Reichsführer,' Ernst lied. 'He thought it best you were parted.'

'Damn the Reichsführer! And damn you for being a liar! Eberhard wasn't sent to Russia on the word of Heinrich Himmler. It was *you*, Ernst, who came up with that idea. You. You alone. You had him sent to Russia because you knew he probably wouldn't survive – and I haven't received a letter from him since the Russians captured our troops. Either he's dead or he's rotting in a Russian prison camp – and either way, I won't see him again. You're a bastard! *I hate you!*'

She turned away from him, picked up a packet of cigarettes, tipped one out into her hand, then reached out for the matches.

'You're exaggerating the whole affair,' Ernst said, though he knew that she wasn't.

'Please get out,' she responded, then struck a match, lit her cigarette, and exhaled a thin, nervous stream of smoke from shivering lips.

'No matter what you think of me,' Ernst said, struck by her beauty, cut by her vehemence, 'I'm seriously worried about you and the children. You've survived the air raids so far, but they're going to get worse – and sooner or later, either the Soviets or the Allies, maybe both, will march into Berlin. What happens then . . .' He tried to put it into words, could find none, so just shrugged. 'I simply don't know.'

Ingrid blew a cloud of smoke, watched it intently, then turned unhappy green eyes upon him and said, 'You haven't told me anything I don't know – except that if the Allies or Russians come, you probably won't be here.'

'I can't tell you where I'm going, but it's safer than here. We're still married, so I can probably take you with me, and I think you should come.'

'No, thanks.'

'Please, Ingrid. For the sake of the children, if not yourself.'

'You murdered the man I love – if he's not dead, he might

as well be – and I'm not going to share my future with you for the sake of the children. You're not the man I once loved. You're not the father I wanted for them. You *could* have been that man – you almost were – but then you threw it away. Now look at you, Ernst! A leading light of the SS. A man who fornicates with whores, collects the victims for the torture chambers, rounds up the unfortunates for the concentration camps, and generally lends his support to the bloodiest dictatorship on earth. And a man who once wanted to be a scientist – or at least an engineer! No, Ernst, you're not the man I married – and you're not the man for my children. I'd rather they died in an air raid than grow up with you. If you want to say good-bye to them, you may do so. But that's *all* you can do. After that, you can only leave.'

Ernst drank her in with his eyes, recalling what she had once meant to him, then filled up with unutterable grief at what he had lost. Though drawn and anguished, she was still lovely, and he had lost that as well . . . Ingrid . . . the children . . . His whole world. How had it happened?

He sighed. 'All right, Ingrid. Where are the children?'

'Upstairs in their rooms.'

'Can I go up?'

'Yes, but don't make it sound definite. As far as they're concerned, you're just off on another trip. Is that understood?'

'I *do* hope to be returning to Berlin,' he told her.

'Nothing's certain these days.'

He went up the stairs and found the children in the room they shared, Ula still blond and lovely, though now ten years old, Alfred nearly seven years old and no longer chubby. They greeted him warily, as they always did on his odd visits, but he welled up with emotion and clung to them so long he embarrassed them. Eventually he let them go, gave them some money, kissed their cheeks, then, sniffing back his tears and composing his face, returned to the living room to say good-bye to Ingrid.

Her mother had come back in and Ernst was shocked when he saw them both. Ingrid now looked like her mother had only ten years ago. There were streaks of gray in Ingrid's blond hair. Her bright-green eyes had darkened. She still had a good figure, but it had filled out in the wrong way, and Ernst noticed, with a shock, that she was wearing one of her mother's old dresses. Her face, though still beautiful, was closed against him.

'Will you reconsider?' he asked her.

'No,' she replied.

'For the sake of the children. For your mother's sake—'

'Don't bring them into this.'

Her mother looked embarrassed, staring down at the floor, and Ernst, not feeling angry but dead, walked up to the old woman, embraced her, kissed her cheek. Then, as her tears started falling, he simply nodded at Ingrid.

'I promise you, I'll make it back,' he said.

'Don't make rash promises, Ernst. None of us can make promises these days. We take each day as it comes.'

'I'll be back.'

'Good-bye, Ernst.'

He turned away and walked out. The taxi was still there, making a small fortune in these otherwise bleak days, and even as Ernst walked toward it, his boots kicking up gravel, he heard that distant, familiar rumbling and the eerie wail of the sirens. He looked toward Berlin, at the large moon in the starlit sky, and knew that the Allied aircraft were returning for another night of destruction.

There's nothing left for me here, he thought forlornly. Now I have only Wilson.

Then he slipped into the rear of the taxi and was taken back to the city, which, even as he was driven toward it, was turning into a furnace.

Hell is on earth, he thought.

Chapter Thirty

Bradley was in church. He was, to be precise, in an annex of the shell of the Church of St Pierre in the ruined old town of Caen, France, to which he had driven, one week after its fall to the Canadian and British troops, from the town of Saint-Lô, which had been captured by the US 1st Army.

Bradley had driven in a jeep from Saint-Lô to Caen through a landscape devasted by bomb craters, burned-out barns, collapsed houses, mountains of rubble, and putrefying dead animals, mostly cows. He had arrived in Caen, at the invitation of the British SOE, which was now being more agreeable to him, after the lovely old cathedral town, eastern bastion of the German defense forces, had been reduced to ruins by relentless Allied artillery and air bombardment. He had then been directed by some weary British 2nd Army infantrymen to the Church of St Pierre, which he had found simply by heading for the tower that was visible above the ruins of what had once been prosperous streets.

The tower had been damaged and was surrounded by more rubble, but luckily the interior of the church remained intact. It had become a refuge for hundreds of the townspeople who had lost their homes in the artillery and air bombardments. The refugees were still there when Bradley arrived, but within days they had been moved out to more hospitable quarters. Bradley at the invitation of the British Secret Intelligence Service, had set up a temporary office in this annex, where, with the assistance of members of the Manhattan atomic bomb project's ALSOS and OSS's Project Paperclip, he had begun an intensive interrogation of resistance members and local townsfolk as well as less cooperative collaborators, suspected and otherwise.

While the members of ALSOS concentrated on tracking down details of all German V-1 and V-2 rocket projects, Bradley and his fellow OSS sleuths were attempting to trace the whereabouts of those scientists and engineers known to have been involved in the construction of rockets and other secret weapons, including any aircraft remotely saucer-shaped and relating to Wilson.

Bradley was not having much luck.

What he had learned so far was that the Germans had built a frightening number of V-1 and V-2 rocket launching sites, most of them in the Pas de Calais area and the recently captured Cherbourg peninsula. What he had also learned is that after the devastating RAF bombing raids of 1943, Wernher von Braun's rocket team had been moved out of Peenemünde to an unknown destination, had been returned when the damage had been repaired, but reportedly was about to be moved again. Unfortunately, no one knew more than that . . . and no one seemed to know Wilson.

The American.

Goddamn him!

The more Bradley saw of the war's awesome devastation, the more he wondered how much Wilson had contributed to it and the more he wanted to find him and put a stop to him. He was still haunted by the memory of that saucer-shaped aircraft in the barn near Montezuma, Iowa, where Wilson had been born and returned to work in secret, and he was convinced that the V-1 rocket program could not have been so advanced without Wilson's help. Now, more than anything else, he had to find out.

Sitting behind his makeshift desk in the annex of the damaged church, he had come face to face with the best and worst faces of the war – female collaborators with heads shaved by their liberated former friends; male collaborators bruised and scarred from beatings by their fellow countrymen;

the pitiful victims of Nazi torture; old and young members of the French resistance, whose features had been shaped by deprivation and constant fear and courage. He was feeling overwhelmed and exhausted when he finally came up with something.

The man who sat facing him across the old, cluttered farm table the morning of July 20, 1944, was wearing the clothing of a French peasant – black jacket and baggy pants, open-necked white shirt and beret – but had strikingly handsome features and brown eyes filled with passionate conviction.

He had not been brought in, but had specifically asked to see the investigating officer. According to his papers, he wasn't French but Polish, and his name was Andrzej Pialowicz.

'I'm surprised,' Bradley told him, 'to find a Polish citizen in the French resistance.'

'I am a leading member of the *Polish* resistance,' Pialowicz replied in surprisingly good English, 'but am forced to flee the country when the Gestapo and SS round up and murder my group. When you finally get to Poland, and if you find your hands on the Nazi secret services documents, no doubt you will find me listed there.'

Bradley nodded. 'Why did you not just go underground in Poland'

'It is becoming too difficult in Cracow, where I operate, and when my group is captured and my lover tortured and sent to a concentration camp, I know that the last people I can trust are all gone – and if I stay in Cracow, it will only be a matter of time before I am caught.'

'Good thinking,' Bradley said.

'Also, Major Riedel of the SS is becoming obsessed with capturing me, which is a further motive to leave the country and go underground, where even my name will not be known. So, convinced that the Allies will invade Europe eventually, I come here and join the French resistance.'

'How did you get out of Poland?'

'I travel by night, usually cross-country, keeping well away from the roads. I also cover great distances by train, hanging under the carriages for hours.'

'That's a helluva thing to do,' Bradley said. 'One hell of a thing.'

'When we have to, we can do surprising things. You should know this by now.'

Bradley was certainly learning it. He was gradually getting used to the fact that many of the people he interviewed, who often looked so young and inexperienced, had lost their families and loved ones, been tortured by the Nazis, lived under the threat of death for as long as they could remember, and treated adventures such as that described by Pialowicz as perfectly normal.

He was getting used to it, but sometimes it still amazed him, though he tried not to show that.

'So you've been in France since . . . ?'

'June 1940.'

'Have you heard anything about your lover since?'

'No.' Pialowicz showed the merest flicker of emotion, then became stone-faced.

'You don't know which camp she went to?'

'No.'

'If you give me her name, I'll put her on the file. If she's found, we'll get in touch with you.'

'This I would appreciate. Also, she is the reason I come to see you.'

'Oh, who is she?'

'Her name is Kryzystina Kozilewski.'

Bradley wrote the name down in his notebook, after asking Pialowicz how it was spelled.

'So,' he said, looking up again. 'What's the relevance of Kryzystina Kozilewski?'

'One of my functions here in France,' Pialowicz responded, 'is to liaise between the French and Polish underground groups. It is one of those Polish groups that conveys to you through the French resistance, in 1942, that the Nazis are testing remote-controlled rockets near Peenemünde, in the Baltic.'

'The V-1 rocket.'

'Yes. Anyway, since I am the person liaising between that Polish resistance group and the Frenchmen who pass the information on to you, through SOE, London, I naturally know about your interest in the American scientist, John Wilson.'

Feeling his weariness slipping away from him, Bradley leaned across the table and prompted Pialowicz with 'Yes?'

'This is where my former mistress, Kryzystina Kozilewski, comes into the picture,' Pialowicz said, keeping his features carefully composed to mask any pain he might be feeling. 'When the Nazis overrun Poland in September 1939, I form a Polish resistance group and enlist the help of Kryzystina. Kryzystina has had a hard life, is experienced in the ways of men – I say this without rancor – and on behalf of the resistance, uses her charm and experience to gain the trust of German officers, obtain valuable gossip from them, and pass the information on to us.'

'Is that why she's in a concentration camp?'

'I think so, yes,' Pialowicz said.

At that moment, a great armada of Allied aircraft passed overhead, heading toward Germany. Pialowicz glanced up at the ceiling of the annex, then lowered his gaze again.

'Early in 1940 the Germans requisition the boarding house owned by Kryzystina and send its residents to a concentration camp. Kryzystina saves herself from this fate by engaging in an affair with the commander of the troops involved in the requisition – an SS captain named Ernst Stoll, who is under the command of my worst enemy, Major Riedel. And it is through her affair with Stoll that Kryzystina learns about the American, John Wilson.'

The noise of the aircraft passing overhead had reached a crescendo and Pialowicz stopped talking for a moment, waiting for the bombers to pass on . . . for the noise to die down. Bradley thought of the ruins of Caen, of all the other ruins he had seen in his journey and shuddered to think of what that mighty armada of bombers would soon do to Germany. The awesome power of modern technology was now ever-present . . . and if Wilson had progressed even further, God knows what would be coming.

When the noise of the aircraft had passed, Pialowicz said, 'To return to Kryzystina . . . According to what she tells me in 1940, this German who becomes her lover, this SS captain Ernst Stoll, is a former rocket engineer, deeply embittered at being denied membership of the VfR, or German Amateur Rocket Society and, later, General Dornberger's rocket program, which is placed under the command of Wernher von Braun, one of Stoll's old school chums, while Stoll is turned into a mere technical administrator. Disgusted, Stoll lets himself be persuaded to join SS intelligence, which at least gives him the opportunity to supervise certain secret weapons research programs at Kummersdorf, south of Berlin – and it is there that he becomes involved with the American, Wilson.'

'He actually worked with Wilson?'

'Yes. Wilson does not actually work with von Braun's rocket teams, but with a much smaller group at the other side of an old firing range at Kummersdorf West. However, according to what Stoll tells Kryzystina, while Wilson is to work on secret weapons other than remote-controlled rockets, many of his remarkable innovations are passed on to the rocket team, which certainly hastens the development of the rockets.'

Now Bradley was feeling really excited. At last Wilson's continuing existence had been confirmed. At last he'd been given shape, even if he still was faceless.

'Did Kryzystina find out what Wilson's project actually was?'

'Yes. One night when Stoll is drunk and particularly bitter, he lets slip that the program is called Projekt Saucer and involves the construction of a saucer-shaped, vertical-rising aircraft. How far it has progressed, he doesn't say, but he does also let slip that the project is highly secret, that it is Heinrich Himmler's personal passion, and that even Hitler is unaware of its existence.'

'What was this Wilson like?' Bradley asked, desperate to put a human face on his faceless quarry.

'Apparently a lot older than he looks,' Pialowicz replied. 'About sixty-five years of age.'

'In 1940.'

'Yes.'

'Which makes him about seventy now,' Bradley observed.

'Yes.'

'Anything else?'

'Yes. This Wilson is very strange. According to Stoll, John Wilson is a man obsessed. He cares for nothing but his work and has few scruples when it comes to doing it. That is one obsession. There *are* others.'

Pialowicz glanced around him, at the ruins of the church, saw nothing that he hadn't lived with for a long time, so returned to the subject.

'He does not smoke, does not drink, and claims that his exceptional youthfulness is due to some kind of lifelong diet. Also, he is obsessed with extending his life span and, according to Stoll, is convinced that any kind of extreme emotionalism, such as love or sexual passion, encourages the aging process. Regarding his own sexual drives, he claims to relieve them as functionally as humanly possible. And, finally, while not sharing Heinrich Himmler's mystical notions of an Aryan Super Race, he certainly believes and is striving for the creation of a race of geniuses, devoted to science – of which he will naturally be the leader. For that reason, he treats his own health and his work as the base material for research, medical and scientific. In other words, he is a man so objective, he is scarcely human at all . . . Very strange, yes?'

'Yes,' Bradley said. '*Very* strange.'

He glanced back through the arched doorway of the annex and saw other intelligence officers at other tables, interviewing other suspects, collaborators, and allies. The sunlight outside was beaming in through the stained-glass windows, which had remained unharmed, casting striations of many colors over worn, harassed, and sometimes jubilant faces. Big guns thundered in the distance and some people looked around. The battle for Europe had moved on from this destroyed town and was continuing elsewhere.

'So in 1940,' Bradley continued, 'Wilson was still located in Kummersdorf, south of Berlin. Do you know if he's still there?'

'No,' Pialowicz said, 'he is not. About three weeks ago Wilson's team are split up for reasons we have not yet ascertained. But according to our informants, Wilson and some others are moved by a train filled with SS troops and concentration-camp prisoners to somewhere in the southern Harz Mountains. Alas, we do not know where, though we *do* have reason to believe that the area around Nordhausen, in Thuringia, is littered with large, well-disguised underground factories where the Nazi secret weapons are produced with the help of slave labor from nearby camps. We believe Wilson is destined for one of those hidden factories.'

'And the rest of his team?'

Pialowicz shrugged. 'About a week after Wilson is moved out, the rest of the team, including Schriever, Miethe, and Habermohl, is put on board a train heading for Prague, in Bohem, in Czechoslovakia. We have no idea why – nor do we know their final destination.' Pialowicz shrugged again, then raised his hands in the air. 'This is all I can tell you.'

'It's a helluva lot,' Bradley replied. 'More than you realize.'

Pialowicz smiled for the first time, then stood up and said, 'For me you will please find Kryzystina?'

'We will,' Bradley said.

He watched the young man walk out of the annex, sat there for a few minutes in silence, trying to calm his excitement, then followed him out of the church.

Too excited for coherent thought, he walked around the shattered town, letting the sun shine on his face, observing the appalling ruins and the troops and civilians moving around them, passing tanks buried in rubble and overturned, scorched trucks and eventually arriving at another church, which also was damaged. Stepping inside, he had to adjust to the gloom. Then he saw hundreds, maybe a thousand or more, refugees on the floor, lying on mattresses, surrounded by bits of furniture, making coffee and soup on small paraffin burners, and attending to the wounded and the dying, for whom there was still no room in the remains of the hospital. Light beamed obliquely on them, illuminating motes of dust, covering them in a silvery haze that made them look slightly unreal.

It was a dream of life and death, of suffering and self-sacrifice, and Bradley had seen it too many times on his journey through France. Nevertheless, he was shaken, torn between faith and despair, and he turned away from it, from man's stupidity and nobility, and hurried back to the Church of St Pierre, to continue his work.

Chapter Thirty-One

Ernst's growing conviction that hell might be on earth was made concrete when, after his painful farewell to Ingrid, he returned to the Harz Mountains. For a week that seemed like a year, he divided his time between the nightmarish daily routine of the underground factories in Nordhausen and Wilson's flying saucer construction plant nearby, just outside the old walled town of Kahla.

Desperate to avoid the daily whippings, public hangings, and shots to the back of the head in the bunkers of Nordhausen, all designed to keep the V-1 and V-2 assembly lines rolling, he spent most of his time in the underground factory at Kahla, pretending to supervise Wilson, whom he knew had seen through his pretense and was quietly amused by it.

'You always seem so tense,' he said to Ernst. 'You must learn to relax.'

Ernst was fascinated by Wilson, fearing and admiring his old man's wisdom, but mostly drawn to his air of icy invincibility and fascinated by his plans and theories, which admitted no human doubts. He was completing his *Feuerball*, the remote-controlled antiradar device that looked like a flying saucer but was only three feet wide and was, so he said, a flawless prototype for the larger, pilot-controlled system still on the drawing board.

'If the *Feuerball* flies,' Wilson said, 'and responds to its commands, then the *Kugelblitz* will also fly when we have the time to complete it. In the meantime, every test that needs to be done can be done with the *Feuerball*. Very soon now I'll try it against the Allied planes and see how it performs. I don't doubt that it will work admirably.'

Humiliated by Brigette, deprived of Ingrid and his children, rarely able to forget that he had once been an engineer and now was merely *observing* the great achievements of Wernher von Braun and Wilson, Ernst leaned toward the latter, was ensnared in his web, and began to see his only hope for redemption in the dream of Antarctica.

'Not with Himmler,' Wilson confided. 'We can't trust him anymore. Personally, I never did for a second, but now I know I was right. Kammler and Nebe are talking. They see Himmler a lot. They say he hasn't been the same since the first great defeat in Russia – and like Hitler, he's losing control and falling back upon fantasy. Astrologers and occultists, quack doctors and mesmerists – Himmler and Adolf Hitler, soulmates, will eventually go the same way.'

'I could have you shot for saying that.'

'But you won't,' Wilson said, 'because you too have witnessed Himmler's changing moods and know what he's like.' Which was true enough, after all. Ernst thought Himmler was going mad. The more the Allies advanced, the more distracted and crazy Himmler became, albeit in his quiet way. The Reichsführer, the bureaucrat, the chicken farmer, was quietly falling to pieces. He had forgotten Neuschwabenland, had lost confidence in Wilson, and now pinned all his hopes on Rudolph Schriever's abortion of a flying saucer, on other obscure 'secret' weapons, and on his own demented plans for making a 'private' peace with the advancing Allies.

He was not the awesomely remote Reichsführer of the past, but a pitiful creature.

Not a man to trust.

'Yet I steal from him,' Wilson said. 'I steal the gold from his mind of mud. I don't believe in his mysticism, in his blond young gods of war, in his anthroposophy and theosophy and Rosicrucianism, in his bizarre dreams of Atlantis and Lemuria and the undefiled Aryan. These are the dreams of madmen, the visions of the demented; yet they do hold a kernel of truth:

the transformation of man. I too believe in this – though not in the same sad way. I believe in man's evolutionary drive toward the Superman – and I believe in biological mutation and mental enhancement.'

They sometimes walked out of the tunnels, into the day's clear light, and gazed over the forested hills of Thuringia to the summer's horizon. There were no whippings there. No hangings. No beatings. But somewhere out there, beyond the horizon, the world was at war.

'Forget Himmler,' Wilson told Ernst. 'He's just another Nazi lunatic. He's raised muddled philosophy and primitive dreaming from the slime to the tortured blood and bone of an insane ideology. Blood and bone are acceptable – we're all here to feed evolution – but his philosophy of ice and fire, his pitiful dependence upon Hörbiger, is enough to show us that he doesn't belong to the real world. We *will* go to Antarctica – but not to further an idiotic SS elite. We will go to further what you once had and lost: the belief in science as an absolute – the one hope for mankind. You can recapture that dream, Ernst – but only through me. Forget Himmler. Betray him – yes, you must! – and regain your faith where it matters: in a colony devoted to science and unimpeded by ephemeral, earthly concerns. It has already begun, Ernst. The factories and accommodations under the ice have been completed and already a few hundred people have been shipped there, to prepare for our coming. Cast off your past, come with me, and get back what you lost. All the rest is lost anyway.'

Which Ernst knew was the truth, because the truth was undeniable – the Allied advance through France, the Soviets forming a pincer movement, Berlin crumbling in flame and smoke, his wife and family endangered – even his mistress, his whore, defeating him and laughing at his retreat – everything now defeating him and mocking his youthful dreams – and so Wilson, who had once seemed so distant, now seemed very close to him.

'We need an escape route,' Wilson said, back in his workshop, over the *Feuerball*, his steady gray gaze focused on the three-foot disc gleaming beneath him. 'We need to get from here to Kiel in the Baltic, and from there to our friends in Argentina, then from there to Antarctica. Nebe can help us in this. He's a vulture, but reliable. But to do it, he has to disappear, and that makes things difficult. You must do this for us, Ernst. You must help him disappear. When he disappears, when no one is looking for him, he can lead us to freedom. Do you understand, Ernst?'

'Yes,' Ernst said. 'I understand.'

'Arrange that and you can travel with me to Antarctica and become an even better engineer – no, a scientist! – than you'd ever imagined you could be. Do that and . . . *you're free!*'

Ernst left Wilson in Kahla and returned to Nordhausen where, in the great tunnels, while the conveyor belts rolled, the SS guards cracked their whips, spines snapped at the end of ropes, gunshots ricocheted in the bunkers, and the German genius for organization was completely perverted. He had chosen this life – at some point he had decided – and so he swallowed his remaining guilt, cast shame aside for all time, and traveled back to Berlin by train and car for another meeting with Kammler.

He returned to a nightmare.

'There's been an attempt on the Führer's life,' Kammler told him in his office in SS headquarters. 'Lieutenant-Colonel Claus Schenk von Stauffenberg, the chief of staff to the commander of the General Army Office in Berlin, planted a bomb in a briefcase during a meeting in Führer Headquarters in Wolfsschanze. Miraculously, the Führer escaped with minor burns, but now all hell has broken loose. A planned military revolt in the city by Stauffenberg's co-conspirators has already been put down, Stauffenberg, generals Beck and Olbricht, and their two adjutants have been executed by firing squad in the courtyard of the Bendlerstrasse, other conspirators have committed suicide, and Himmler has already set up the machinery for an investigation of the uprising and is drawing up a death list containing hundreds of names.'

'They were all involved in the attempted coup?'

'Highly unlikely,' Kammler replied. 'But in situations such as this, guilt or innocence is often a matter of luck. Hundreds of men are going to die, Captain Stoll, and General Nebe may be one of them.'

'Nebe?'

'Yes, He has no alibi. At the time of the assassination attempt, you were in Nordhausen and I was in the Pas de Calais, supervising the rocket launchings – but Nebe was right here in Berlin, and, since Himmler has never trusted him, he's gone down on the list.'

'Does he know this yet?'

'No. I caught a glimpse of the list in Himmler's office only an hour ago. He was still filling in names.'

'What do we do now?' Ernst asked, feeling sick with fear.

'It's the perfect excuse for Nebe to disappear,' Kammler said with a self-satisfied air. 'In order to plan our escape route from Kahla to Kiel and collect troops truthworthy enough, and willing, to be our armed escorts during the journey, Nebe was always going to have to go underground. Our problem before was that his disappearance would have raised too large a question mark. However, now, if he disappears, it'll be assumed that he simply fled in fear of his life – as so many will. So now he will disappear. He'll go underground in Thuringia. We'll protect him there until all this fuss has died down – if necessary, I can confirm that he was executed by my men – and then, when the dust has settled, he can surface with new papers and quietly start organizing what we need for our escape before the Soviets or Allies reach us.'

'Excellent,' Ernst murmured, his thoughts clogged with dread. 'But who will . . . ?'

'I will arrange it,' Kammler said. 'I have the freedom of movement necessary. Meanwhile, you'll report directly to Himmler and become his right hand, thus ensuring that you remain above suspicion.'

Still haunted by the memory of the infamous Night of the Long Knives, and aware that a similar nightmare was about to be put into motion, Ernst felt sick to his stomach and said, 'I really would rather not—'

But Kammler stepped up to him and stared icily at him. 'You will do it, Captain Stoll. You will do whatever he asks of you. You will be his right hand, his loyal subject, no matter what is asked of you. Do you understand, Captain?'

'Yes, sir,' Ernst said.

He reported to the Reichsführer. The nightmare closed in upon him. The death list was completed and the rounding up began and the days and nights after were filled with beatings and entreaties and roaring guns and blood-soaked, riddled corpses. They were shot in their homes, in floodlit courtyards, in their beds and in cars and in fields where the wind howled and bent the grass.

Ernst had to be part of it, prove his worth, show his loyalty, and he managed it by denying it, by pretending it wasn't happening, or by convincing himself that those begging and screaming deserved what they got. The innocent died with the guilty, the same way, without mercy; and the ghastly climax was held in the great courtroom of the Kammergericht, where, for the cine-cameras, the most notable of the defendants were humiliated even as they were sentenced.

They were brought in in old clothes, haggard, unkempt, some deprived of their false teeth, all forced to hold their beltless trousers up, and then, when sentenced, were led out of the courthouse and into Plötzensee Prison where, in a small room, they were stripped to the waist and hanged from meathooks with nooses made of piano wire.

Ernst and his fellow officers were obliged to look on, all sweating in the bright lights required for the cine-cameras that were taking moving pictures of the stripped bodies writhing in agony.

That's when it ended, when Ernst was reprieved, and he returned to his bed in the SS barracks and slept the sleep of the damned, haunted by nightmares.

Meanwhile, the western front had collapsed, the fate of France had been sealed a few days before when General

Patton's divisions poured through the gap at Avranches, and the Allied bombing of Berlin was now reaching new heights of appalling efficiency. The ruins stretched as far as the eye could see; the sky was a constant pall of smoke.

Ernst was called to Kammler's office and went drugged from lack of sleep. He was informed that General Nebe had gone underground in Kahla, in Thuringia. Nebe had been listed officially as missing, possibly dead in the recent mass executions, when many bodies had been buried unnamed. Ernst was to return to Kahla, to keep a close eye on Wilson. He was to leave the next morning.

Feeling haunted and lost, dispossessed of his soul, he returned to the barracks and started packing . . . and then heard the wailing of the air-raid sirens.

The noise seemed to cut through him, lacerating his stripped nerves, and something collapsed inside him, the final remnants of his will. He lay on the bed and closed his eyes and begged the planes to turn back. Naturally, they ignored him, were soon above him, making the room shake, and then the darkness outside erupted and filled up with hellish noise. He covered his ears with his hands. It didn't help at all. The noise seemed to fill his head, a vast symphony of destruction, and his bed shook and rattled as a brilliant light washed over him and the men in the other beds cursed and jumped up and ran for the door.

Ernst hurried out through clouds of dust, felt waves of heat, saw fire and smoke, then was struck by a dreadful premonition that could not be denied. He thought of Ingrid and the children, of that old house in Wannsee, and sensed, even as he visualized it, that something had happened.

It was there and would not budge – the conviction that they were dead – and he commandeered an SS car and drove out of the barracks and raced through the blazing, erupting city, heading for Wannsee. This time he found no respite – the pattern of bombing was widening – and a cloud of smoke and dust covered the river and the houses around it. Ernst glanced up at the sky, saw the crisscrossing searchlights, the Allied bombers as thick as flies in the paler light of the full moon and stars. It was a lovely August night – only mankind had made it hellish – and as he drove through the gateway of the house in Wannsee, he knew that he had been part of it.

He squealed to a halt in a cloud of smoke, climbed out into scorching heat, and rushed toward the flames that licked up from the rubble. It had been a direct hit – most of the house had collapsed – and he was beaten back by the heat. He fell to his knees in hot ash and looked up at the flames licking over the exposed beams and beating at the broken walls. Then he screamed like an animal, out of the deepest well of his old self, as another wall collapsed, causing more geysering sparks and smoke, and he covered his face with his hands and shed the last of his tears.

Ingrid and his children were dead.

Now he had only Wilson.

Chapter Thirty-Two

A V-1 rocket had been found intact. It lay near an enormous bomb crater in a field not twenty yards from the southern wall of the immense main building of the launching site in the Pas de Calais in liberated northern France.

'It's nearly twenty-six feet long,' explained US Army Major General Ryan McArthur, 'has a wingspan of about seventeen point five feet, a body diameter of approximately two point five feet, and a launch weight of four thousand eight hundred and sixty pounds. Its warhead weighs eighteen hundred and seventy pounds and its fuel, twelve hundred pounds. She's some baby, right?'

'Right,' Bradley said, suitably impressed. He had not seen McArthur since being introduced to him by Gladys Kinder in London, three months ago. Now, as he followed McArthur across the bomb-cratered field near the launch site and its silos, he couldn't stop thinking of her.

'And this,' McArthur said, stopping where an even bigger rocket, approximately twice the size of the V-1, was being hoisted into the air by a British-controlled Straho crane, 'is, we think, one of the enormous sons of bitches that devastated parts of Chiswick and Epping a few days back.'

'The V-2,' Bradley said.

'Yeah, we think so. And this mother is nearly fifty feet long, has a body diameter of five point five feet, a weight, *empty*, of seven thousand-odd pounds, and a fuel weight of twenty thousand one hundred and fifty pounds, compared to the V-1's meager twelve hundred. How'dya like *that* on your head?'

'A homburg hat will do fine, thanks.'

McArthur laughed and slapped Bradley on the shoulder. They stood side by side on the cold, windswept field, watching the enormous rocket being hoisted up off the ground by the crane, prior to be taken somewhere safer for a thorough examination by a team of Allied scientists. Bradley had driven here from Caen, after the recent capture of Antwerp. Major General McArthur's invitation had surprised him.

In fact, while Bradley had been interrogating people in Caen, McArthur's ALSOS agents had been swarming all over the liberated areas of France, particularly the Pas de Calais and the Cherbourg peninsula, where, it had been discovered, most of the V-1 and V-2 rocket launch sites were located. Over the past two days, then, since Bradley's arrival, McArthur had been taking him on a tour of the major captured rocket sites, which were, in their sheer size and design, something more than impressive. This particular site was located on the edge of the forest of Eperlecques, three miles north of the village of Watten, on the canal network between the sea and the Belgian border.

'It's our belief,' McArthur now said as he walked Bradley away from the V-2 rocket and back toward the site's huge main building, 'that this was intended to be one of the largest rocket sites of all. Mercifully it was put out of action by the repeated bombing raids of the B-17 Fortresses of the Eighth Air Force of the good ol' US of A.' He stopped a good distance from the towering, concrete-bunker-styled building in front of them. 'Just look at it,' he said. 'That was the reception building for V-2 trains arriving from Germany. It contained offices and staff accommodations. Over there,' he said, waving his right hand, 'is the railway station, with the lines two feet below floor level and the roof five feet thick – though it *has* been penetrated by one of our bombs that didn't explode. Over there,' he continued, pointing past the damaged wall of the enormous bunker to a tower rising out of the windblown grass, 'is the launch control, approximately sixty-three feet by seventy-three feet and fifteen feet high – no small silo, believe me – and the launch silo, which is thirty by fifty, though now filled with water.'

He led Bradley into the enormous main building. Constructed from reinforced concrete, it was three hundred feet long, one hundred and thirty-eight feet wide, and had work levels going two hundred and sixty feet belowground.

'We believe it was their intention,' McArthur said, 'to construct a building that could be demolished only by a bomb so large that it'd be impossible for an airplane to carry it. That's why the ceiling above you,' he said, pointing up to the eighty-foot-high roof, 'is made from reinforced concrete twenty-three feet thick. Theoretically speaking, to pierce it you'd need a bomb weighing about twelve tons and striking the ceiling at Mach One, the speed of sound – but we don't have that yet.'

Bradley looked up. Above the northern entrance, at the junction between the ceiling and the north wall, an explosion had blown off a large piece of concrete and forced out a mess of steel reinforcing bars. A second explosion, near the center of the roof, had detached another large piece of concrete and caused a fine web of cracks.

'*Something* obviously damaged it,' he observed.

But McArthur shook his head. 'Not our normal bombing raids,' he said. 'In fact, what you're looking at is very minor damage, right?'

'Right.'

'Well, it wasn't caused by our beloved Flying Fortresses during the course of normal operations. In fact, to test the strength of the structure, *after* we'd captured it, we deliberately tried to destroy it with a couple of twenty-two thousand-pound Grandslam bombs– and this is all the damage we managed to inflict. This goddamned place is damned near impregnable – and so are most of the others.'

'How was it constructed?' Bradley asked him as they walked around the enormous, empty, silent building, looking up at its towering walls and high ceiling.

'Forty-nine-thousand tons of steel were needed to build that roof alone,' McArthur said. 'According to intelligence reports, based on the interrogation of locals, hundreds of jacks were used to raise the roof slowly, inches at a time, with the walls being built up beneath it, as it was raised. The enormous amounts of steel, cement, sand, and gravel needed were brought in from Watten on that standard-gauge railway track you saw outside. So far we've estimated that the site took six months to construct and used about thirty-five-thousand slave workers, who came from the two prison camps located about a mile and a half from here. At any one time there were always three to four thousand men at work, which went on around the clock on twelve-hour shifts. The slave labor, or *Sklavenarbeiter,* was controlled by armed members of the black-shirted SS *Totenkopfverbande,* who didn't hesitate to execute anyone too ill or exhausted to work. This place, then, is an extraordinary achievement . . . but the price . . . Jesus Christ! You don't want to think about it! Come on, let's get out of here.'

They went outside again, into the shadow of the towering wall, and were whipped by the wind howling across the bleak, bomb-blasted fields, where once livestock had roamed. Now the fields were covered with soldiers, British, French, Canadian, and American, as well as concrete silos and the usual debris of war: armored half-tracks, overturned trucks, the blackened remains of burned-out tanks, melted tires, and scorched earth.

'I *have* to think about it,' Bradley said as McArthur walked him toward his parked jeep. 'I have to fix firmly in my head just what they were capable of.'

'The Nazis?'

'Right. When you hear the stories you can't believe it – they're too incredible to be true – vast underground factories hidden deep in the mountains; the assembly lines run night and day with slave labor – and then you see places like that, the sheer enormity, the work behind it – and you have to accept that they could do it and that he must be part of it.'

'Wilson?'

'Yeah. He's always been a man to hide things. He hid his

own life, hid his work in Iowa, hid his hangars in the wilds of Illinois, then went to hide himself in Nazi Germany, to create God knows what. We saw those rockets, right? We know how advanced they are. And even though that's frightening enough, they're just the tip of the iceberg. Wilson's in the Harz Mountains. We don't know exactly where. We only hear about vast underground factories and the use of slave labor. Was it possible? I didn't think so. Not until I came here. Now, having seen what you've shown me, I know that it is ... The Harz Mountains ... Factories hidden *inside* the mountains ... Yes, they could do it ... And that bastard is using it.'

'Why?'

'I don't know ... and that's exactly what frightens me.'

McArthur smiled gently, patted him on the shoulder, then climbed into the driver's seat in the jeep and cocked a finger invitingly. When Bradley had climbed in beside him, he turned on the ignition, drove carefully around the bomb craters, and said, 'Thank God, Paris has been liberated – a few days there will do you good.'

'I don't want to go there,' Bradley replied. 'I don't have the time.'

'I think you'll *make* the time,' McArthur said with a lopsided grin, "cause Gladys Kinder is there. Now, do we go there or not?'

'Faster!' Bradley said. *'Faster!'*

Almost convulsed with laughter, McArthur maneuvered around the last of the bomb craters, bounced off the high verge, then drove along the straight, tree-lined road that would take them to Paris.

The bar in the Ritz Hotel in the place Vendôme was packed with British Tommies, American GIs, young men and women wearing armbands of the French Forces of the Interior – FFI – or Red Cross, and more than a few journalists, including the famous, and famously loud, bearded American novelist who, five days before Paris was freed, had entered Rambouillet where he had, according to what he was now loudly stating to those crowded around his bottle-strewn table, acted as an unofficial liaison officer between the 5th Infantry Division and the French partisan patrols. The roar of the conversation that came out of the swirling cigar and cigarette smoke was punctuated by the tinkle of glasses, the popping of champagne corks, the metallic clatter of M-1 army rifles, tommy guns, joggling hand grenades, and other weapons; and Gladys Kinder, looking flushed, was leaning sideways in her chair to take hold of Bradley's hand and tell him, 'It'd be a lot cheaper in the correspondents' mess in the Scribe Hotel, but this is, after all, a once-in-a-lifetime event and the Ritz is the *only* place to experience it.'

In this atmosphere of celebration, Bradley was almost sorry to have missed the previous day's victory march from the Arc de Triomphe and along the Champs-Élysées and on to Notre-Dame, but being here so unexpectedly with Gladys was doing his heart good.

'I'll never forget yesterday as long as I live,' Gladys continued while stroking Bradley's sweaty palm. She wasn't embarrassed by the presence of Major General Ryan McArthur, who in any case was looking around the crowded bar with a broad grin on his face. 'There were thousands of people lining the Champs-Élysées all the way up to the etoile. General Leclerc's division, including elements of the US 82nd Division, marched between the cheering thousands, to repeated shouts of '*Viva la France!*' De Gaulle, on the reviewing stand in the place de la Concorde, surrounded by other dignitaries and a couple of US generals, was stiff as a board and proud as punch. And after that, when the parade disbanded, it was hugs and kisses all afternoon, with God knows how many glasses of Calvados and champagne and wine – and I'm *still* not hung over!'

'It's the excitement,' Bradley said. 'You'll probably be as high as a kite for days, then come down with a bang.'

'We'll all come down with a bang when this war ends. That's a terrible truth.'

'It sure has its excitements,' Bradley replied with no great deal of pride, thinking of the death and destruction he had witnessed on the march through France, yet unable to deny that he had never felt more alive than he had felt these past few weeks. 'I can't deny that. But right now, the most exciting thing in the world is seeing you again, Gladys.'

'Aw, shucks,' she said, beaming, then kissed him on the cheek. 'You sure know how to please a gal!'

McArthur turned back to them, raised his glass of Calvados, and said solemnly, 'Ladies and gentlemen, lovebirds, a toast to the liberation of Paris.'

'I'll drink to that,' Bradley said, raising his glass.

'And so will I,' Gladys said, touching his glass with hers.

'You've been drinking to it for two days solid,' McArthur observed, 'but you're looking good on it. So, let's drink!' They all emptied their glasses. As McArthur was refilling them from the bottle on the table, a drunken young member of the FFI kicked his chair back, stood up, and raised his glass above his flushed face. '*Vivent les Americains!*' he declared in a ringing tone. He tossed down his champagne in one long gulp while the others at his table cheered and various British, Canadian, and Dutch troops booed and catcalled. The young FFI man, with a broad, sweaty grin, bowed theatrically to the packed room and fell back into his chair.

'Victory is sweet,' McArthur observed, 'but can lead to more fighting.'

'Let's hope not,' Gladys said. 'So what have you two been up to since we last saw each other? Still in pursuit of rocket bombs and mad American scientists?'

'We're not allowed to discuss it,' McArthur said, 'particularly to journalists.'

'This journalist has a personal interest in the case. Besides, this conversation's off the record. I just wanna know, kids.'

Bradley grinned. 'McArthur here's been showing me the V-1 and V-2 rocket launch sites, which have already been photographed for the newspaper – so no big secrets there.'

'And what did you think?'

'I think the Krauts are more advanced than we'd imagined

– and in more ways than one. I think that no matter how big the project, they'd know how to hide it.'

'Such as Wilson's project, for instance.'

'You got it, Gladys. Bright girl. If Wilson's trying to build a new kind of aircraft, we're talking about a *big* project – but no matter how big it is, I now think the Krauts could keep it well hidden.'

'Where?'

Bradley glanced at McArthur, who simply smiled and nodded. 'Underground,' Bradley said, turning his gaze back on Gladys. 'In great tunnels and factories hacked out of the interior of mountains. I think that's where our man is.'

'Where?'

'You've already asked that.'

'I mean, precisely.'

Bradley shrugged. 'We don't know exactly, but we *think* it's somewhere in the Harz Mountains, probably south, in the area of Thuringia.'

'And is that where you plan to go, Mike?'

'Yes,' Bradley replied.

'You're going to follow the advance?'

'Yep. As far as I can go.'

'With the fighting troops?'

'Yes.'

'I don't want you getting yourself killed.'

'I'll try not to,' Bradley said.

Gladys stared steadily at him, her face showing concern. He was touched and wanted to kiss her lips, but was too shy to do so, because McArthur, filling up their glasses again, was grinning broadly at both of them. 'Ladies and gentlemen,' he said, 'let's drink up and fall down!'

They touched glasses and drank as a combo started playing a Cole Porter medley. The American novelist, all belly and beard and drunken bellowing, stood up and lurched out of the bar, trailed by his admirers. A French woman crossed the room, giving address cards to the men. She stopped in front of Bradley, glanced at Gladys and McArthur, smiled and gave

McArthur a card and said, 'Call anytime,' then gracefully passed on. McArthur studied the card thoughtfully, slipped it into his shirt pocket, and said, 'A night of love in Paris at a price. To the victor the spoils.' Gladys chuckled and McArthur grinned, his eyes scanning the noisy room, then he raised his eyebrows and said, 'Well, well! We have an unexpected visitor!'

Bradley looked up in surprise as his urbane, friendly adversary, Lieutenant-Colonel Wentworth-King of SOE, London, emerged from the crowd around the bar, carrying a glass in his right hand, a swagger stick under his left arm, and looking dashing in his British army uniform and peaked cap. He stopped at their table, grinned, and said sardonically, 'I *thought* I recognized you, Bradley! What on earth are you doing here?'

'Just celebrating the liberation of Paris. Nothing more, nothing less.'

'I'm sure . . . And in the presence of Major General Ryan McArthur, of the Manhattan atomic bomb project – accidentally, no doubt.' He smiled guilelessly at McArthur and said, 'Good to see you again, sir. Mind if I join you?'

'Pull up a chair,' McArthur said. 'It's party time in the Ritz.'

When Wentworth-King had taken a chair, Bradley introduced him to Gladys. 'Ah!' he exclaimed softly, shaking her hand. 'Gladys Kinder, the well-known American journalist. I've read your articles in *Collier's* and elsewhere. Your work is spread far and wide.'

'What I write is widely syndicated,' Gladys explained. 'I don't really write that much.'

'I enjoyed your regular London column,' Wentworth-King said. 'It made me feel quite heroic. Not that you mentioned me *personally*, but you were kind to the British.'

'I've won a heart,' Gladys said to Bradley. 'Where have you been hiding this lovely man? You must invite him more often.'

Wentworth-King beamed and McArthur chuckled while Bradley tried to hide the spasm of resentment that unexpectedly shook him. Wentworth-King was charming his lady and he didn't like that.

'So what are *you* doing in Paris?' he asked Wentworth-King, after throwing an angry glance at Gladys.

'I came in this morning,' Wentworth-King replied, 'to set up a base of operations and grill a few Frogs. Still chasing your rocket engineers, are you?'

'Yes,' Bradley said tersely.

'Then you might be interested in knowing that the Russians have captured Blizna, in Poland, including Himmler's mock village and disguised rocket proving ground.'

'Any reports on anything unusual?'

'So far, no. But then the Russians don't talk a lot. We only know that since it's a proving ground, they certainly found a few rockets.'

'A great help,' McArthur said.

Wentworth-King grinned, unperturbed, then smiled charmingly at Gladys. She returned his smile, then, catching Bradley's accusing glance, hid her face in her glass.

'Can I take it,' Wentworth-King said, returning his attention to Bradley and McArthur, 'that you chaps are still convinced that Wilson is working on something more advanced than the V-1 and V-2 rockets?'

'I'm convinced of it,' Bradley said.

'Well, just to prove that I'm a decent chap at heart – no hard feelings and so forth – you might be interested in knowing that the most *unusual* reports have recently been coming into SOE headquarters in London.'

'Unusual?'

'Yes. A few days before I left to come here, we started receiving reports from Allied pilots, saying that when flying over Germany they were harassed repeatedly by strange lights that tailed their aircraft and appeared to make their engines malfunction.'

'Strange *lights*?' McArthur asked.

'Yes,' Wentworth-King said, 'Lights . . . or balls of fire. One report described an encounter with a, quote, enormous ball of fire, unquote, that made the aircraft's engine cut out. Another report talked about ten *small* balls of reddish fire that were, according to the report, flying in formation, at amazing speed. In both cases, the so-called balls of fire, or "Foo fighters," as they've been dubbed, reportedly flew away when fired upon, but usually returned afterward. The balls appear to have been systematically tailing the aircraft.'

'What areas?'

'All over Germany, but mostly in the vicinity north of Nuremberg.'

'Have the reports been analyzed yet?' McArthur asked.

'Yes,' Wentworth-King said. 'And according to analysis, if the so-called balls of fire weren't some kind of atmospheric or electrical phenomenon, they could have been solid objects that were glowing red-hot. And if that *is* the case, they'd have been no more than three or four feet in diameter, remote-controlled, and, most oddly, shaped like discs or . . .' He paused to shrug his shoulders and raise his hands in a gesture of disbelief. 'Like saucers . . . *flying* saucers.'

To contain his excitement Bradley stared stonily at Gladys, who simply smiled back sweetly, then turned to Wentworth-King and said, 'Isn't this information confidential? Or is it just *me* you trust?'

Wentworth-King was amused. 'The information's already been published in the British press, so I think it's okay to discuss it now. Not that I've got anything else to add – I merely pass the information on to my American friend here, Bradley, whose imagination is clearly more vivid than mine. And now, alas, duty calls and I have to be off.' He finished his drink, stood up, and offered Gladys his hand. 'It was an absolute pleasure meeting you,' he said. 'We must do it again sometime. You'll find details of our Paris HQ tomorrow in the correspondents' mess in the Scribe Hotel. *Do* give me a call.'

'I will,' Gladys said.

'*Au revoir,*' Wentworth-King said, kissing her hand and letting it go with what seemed like great reluctance. 'And to you, Major General,' he said finally. 'And you as well, Bradley. No doubt I'll see you when I see you. Travel safely. And good luck.'

'Same to you,' Bradley said curtly. He didn't look at Gladys again until the urbane lieutenant-colonel had left the room, skipping around a uniformed member of the French 2nd Armored Division and a British lance corporal who were arguing heatedly about something or other. When he had gone, Bradley asked McArthur, 'Well, what do you think?'

'I think it's Wilson. What's north of Nuremberg?'

'Thuringia . . . the Harz Mountains,' Bradley said, feeling more excited, though still angry with Gladys.

'Exactly,' McArthur said. 'We better run a check on those reports and see what we come up with. Right now, however, I have to get back to the ALSOS office and see what's cooking there, which should make you two lovebirds happy, though you don't look it right now.' He stood up with a broad grin on his face, finished his drink, then gave them the thumbs-up and left the bar.

'Alone at last with my man,' Gladys said, 'but he's no longer smiling.'

'I'm fine,' Bradley said. 'I'm just surprised you didn't go chasing after that upstanding British officer, Wentworth-King, who so clearly charmed you.'

'Oh, ho!' she responded, smiling. 'The fires of jealousy! I'm having a wonderful day!' She reached out for his hand, squeezed it affectionately, and said, 'A lady my age is easily charmed, Mike, and I *do* like to flirt. But come on! I was only doing it to tease you – because I want you to want me. *Do* you want me? Do you want me right now? Here and now, in this grand hotel?'

'What's your room like?' Bradley asked her.

'Come up and see,' she said.

They made love under the pink satin coverlet of the twin bed in a dove-gray room filled with elegant Empire furniture and overlooking the rear gardens of the Ministry of Justice. They no longer made love with the vigor of young people, but with the tenderness of two souls united as one, bonded by common experience and a lack of illusions. Bradley took to her body like a lemming to the sea, returning to that place he could fondly call his own, and received all the pleasure he could obtain by simply giving her pleasure. All his love for her returned, pouring out of him like a river, leaving him cleansed and renewed, at peace in her arms. He then slept in those arms, as she slept in his, and when they awakened they made love again, even less vigorously, though as tenderly, as before, then dressed and went for a walk through the darkening city.

'I love Paris,' Gladys told him. 'It's a city made for lovers. I loved it before the war, when I used to visit it a lot from London, and I nearly always thought of you when I walked its streets – my married man, my secret, platonic lover, far away in America. Finally I've got you here with me. Isn't it nice?'

'Yes,' Bradley said. 'Very nice.'

Already familiar with the city, Gladys led him by the hand down the passage that ran alongside the Ritz, from the place Vendôme to the rue Gambon, pressing her nose to the elegant shop windows, which she could see in the moonlit darkness, and showing him all the things she would buy before leaving Paris. She took him into the rue de Rivoli, around the place de la Concorde, then along the broad, tree-lined avenue of the Champs-Élysées, which in the moonlight was wonderful.

'It'll all be over soon,' Gladys said.

'Yeah, I guess so,' Bradley replied.

'Do you think you'll be able to find Wilson?'

Bradley sighed. 'I don't know.'

'If you don't find him, you'll go crazy.'

'I just might at that. Of course now that I've got you, it won't be too bad – but I *do* want to finish it.'

Gladys chuckled softly and slid her arm around his waist. 'You've only got me for the moment,' she said. 'When will you move on?'

'Tomorrow,' Bradley said. 'I have to find myself an army. Probably General Bradley's 1st Army, since they're heading for the Rhine. And you?'

'I might see you in Berlin.'

'And when it ends? Will you return to America or stay here in Europe?'

'I'm not too sure. I mean, I'll have to think about it. I love living here – I mean in London, of course – and I don't really have anything to go home for. I've been gone a long time, Mike. Maybe too long now.'

She had led him off the Champs-Élysées, down past the Grand Palais, and now they were coming to the river Seine, its water stippled by moonlight, curving away toward the distant Eiffel Tower, silhouetted against the sky. Tracer bullets were looping upward around the tower like a fireworks display.

'The German planes must be coming,' Gladys said. 'They won't give up that easily.'

Bradley heard the big guns firing, then a series of explosions, and saw that familiar red glow filling the sky, a good distance beyond the Eiffel Tower, in what he thought were the suburbs.

'They're going to have to give a lot up,' he said, 'so they better get used to it.'

Gladys smiled and tugged at his hand, leading him across the Cours la Reine, then back along the river, toward where they had come from.

'Say, Mike, do you really love me?'

'Sure, Gladys, you know I do.'

'Then how can you even *think* of giving me up? What kind of man are you?'

'What do you mean, Gladys?'

'Give me a reason for going back.'

'What reason?'

She sighed in exasperation. 'Goddammit, Mike, you're dumb!'

'You think so?'

'Yeah.'

'Would you marry a dumb man?'

'Yeah.'

'And would you let him take you back to America?'

'Yes, dammit, I would. Have you proposed?'

'I think so.'

'I accept. Yes, I do!'

She turned into him, her hair blown by the river's wind, and he kissed her, clung to her, choked up and inspired. Then she stepped away, gave him a smile, and raised his hand to her lips – but she didn't quite make it.

Her back was turned to the river, to that fireworks display in the distance, but before she could raise his hand, the river rushed up to swallow her. Bradley saw the geysering water, a flash of light, a stream of smoke; then heard the explosion, the plane passing overhead, and felt himself being picked up and slammed down into silence.

The silence became a ringing – a jarring sibilance in his ears. His lips were pressed to the pavement, so he rolled onto his back and saw Gladys covered in the blood that was spurting out of her head. He tried to sit up and collapsed, looked at Gladys, saw the blood, groaned aloud, not in pain, but in despair, then passed out again.

He was awakened by the sound of a siren and the screeching of brakes. Then someone told him he was going to be okay and helped him sit upright.

They were rolling Gladys onto a stretcher and her head was all bandaged.

'Oh, God!' Bradley groaned.

He clambered to his feet, swayed dizzily, found his balance, then hurried forward as the men with the Red Cross armbands hoisted Gladys up on the stretcher to put her into the ambulance. Her head was bandaged, her leg was in a splint, and she was covered in blood.

'Jesus, no!' Bradley said, then reached out to touch her, but was foiled when the Red Cross men slid the stretcher into the ambulance. Bradley, shocked in more ways than one, started clambering up after her. When he was in the back, kneeling beside the stretcher, Gladys looked up and smiled at him.

'Hi, partner!' she said.

Bradley picked up her hand, passionately kissed it, his tears flowing, then one of the medics clambered in beside him and said, 'She'll be okay.'

'What?' Bradley asked, stupidly.

'She'll be okay,' the medic repeated. He looked about eighteen years old and had the smile of an angel. 'She got hit on the temple with a piece of the pavement and fractured her leg – apart from that, she's okay.'

Bradley looked down at Gladys. She was soaked in her own blood. The bandage around her head was bloody and she was as white as the sheet they had wrapped around her. 'But the blood . . .' he began, fascinated and frightened by the sight of it, though Gladys was smiling.

The medic slammed the ambulance door closed, then placed his hand on Bradley's shoulder. 'Steady on there,' he said. 'We're taking off. I don't want you to fall on her.' The ambulance roared into life and moved off with a jerk. The medic grinned and kept Bradley steady, then also studied the blood covering Gladys.

'She was hit on the temple,' he explained. 'That always causes a lotta blood – but it's deceptive, believe me. She'll only need about two stitches and then she'll be right as rain. As for the leg, it's only broken. It may hurt, but it ain't serious. She'll be in a French hospital for a week or two, then she'll be up and about. No problem at all, bud.'

Bradley almost wept with relief, then was filled with exultation. He bent over to kiss Gladys on the forehead, on the bloody bandage, then held her hand in his lap and smiled like a happy fool. Gladys, getting her color back fast, smiled broadly and winked at him.

'You two are married?' the medic asked.

'Yeah,' Bradley said. 'Right.'

He stayed with Gladys all the way to the hospital, all the way to her bed, ensured that she was tucked in like a baby, then kissed her good-bye.

'I love you,' he said. 'It's as simple as that, Gladys. If I don't see you in Berlin, I'll catch you in London. I still have your address.'

'You take care,' she told him.

He nodded and kissed her again, then walked out of the ward, treading lightly and not looking back because his tears would embarrass her.

'Hallelujah!' he whispered.

Chapter Thirty-Three

Wilson awakened at dawn as he had planned, immediately switched on the light, then looked around his spartan room. Apart from clothing and technical books, it contained no personal items. Like the rest of the complex, his room was located underground, but it had at least been built into the breast of a hill and therefore offered a magnificent view of the forested valley. Wilson lay on for a brief while, letting himself feel slightly excited, then swung his legs off the bed, worked his bare feet into his slippers, and walked across to the desk.

A red circle had been drawn around today's date: February 16, 1945. Wilson picked up a pen and scored through the date, then dropped the pen and went to the window to look over the valley. At the other side of the valley was the old walled town of Kahla, but Wilson's modest research complex, really an underground launching site, was well hidden in this hill, within its sheltering pine trees. Here, today, he would supervise the first test flight of the *Kugelblitz,* which had progressed much quicker than expected.

He did not feel nervous, because he had nothing to fear. The *Kugelblitz* was merely an enlarged version of the antiradar *Feuerball* – and the latter had been tested last year, to everyone's satisfaction.

From August to December, Wilson had sent the three-foot-wide, saucer-shaped, remote-controlled *Feuerballs* hurtling skyward from this underground launching site near Kahla, to harass the Allied aircraft, cause their engines to malfunction, and fly out of range before they could be attacked. Some of the *Feuerballs* had blown up in flight, others had malfunctioned in various ways, but each failure had been examined as minutely as possible and its causes corrected in the following prototype. Eventually, by November, Wilson had had nightly launches for a month without any failures. Then, confident that his design was foolproof, he had canceled further launches, ordered the destruction, by high explosives, of the remainder of the prototypes, and begun applying the same principles and designs to his nearly completed, pilot-controlled larger model, the *Kugelblitz*.

But now his time was running out.

According to what Ernst Stoll had told him, news of the relentless Allied advances on all fronts had even reached the ears of the inmates of the concentration camps that were supplying Nordhausen Central Works and Kahla with forced labor – in fact, now sabotage by the prisoners was a very real threat. Indeed, only three months earlier, in November, a large number of prisoners from the Nordhausen underground camp had been arrested, shut up in the bunkers, and forced by torture to confess to sabotage. A group of those who had confessed had even made a failed bid to escape, which only hastened their deaths. All in all, according to Stoll, about three hundred prisoners had been executed – some hanged in the roll-call ground, some in the factory corridors, and some shot in the back of the head while still in the bunkers.

A foul business, Wilson thought, and one not likely to encourage the prisoners to be merciful when the Allies came to their rescue.

Thinking of that possibility only reminded him again that his time was running out. Even more pleased, then, that the *Kugelblitz* was to be tested this morning, he pressed the bell to call his breakfast and went for his shower in the adjoining bathroom. He returned to find his meal on the table, placed there by his servant who, like all the rest of the workers, came from one of the camps. It was his usual frugal breakfast of cereal and fruit juice, and when he had finished it, he left his room and went down to the hangar.

Ernst Stoll, who now had the eyes of the walking dead but otherwise looked handsome in his SS uniform, was already waiting for him in his glass-walled office, looking out at the hangar.

'You've come straight from Berlin?' Wilson asked, surprised. 'You must have traveled all night!'

'No, Wilson, I didn't. I arrived here yesterday evening with General Kammler, but spent the night in Nordhausen Central Works.'

'Kammler's still at Nordhausen?'

'Yes. He's just checking things out. He'll be here on time.'

'I haven't been to the Central Works since Christmas. How are things there?'

'Busy,' Ernst said. 'There are now about forty thousand political prisoners and civilians working there. And Camp Dora and the many other subcamps in the area are expanding tremendously. Production of the rockets proceeds at full speed, the underground passages are being enlarged, as requested by Himmler, and four new factories are being undertaken: one as a refinery, another for liquid oxygen, and two for Junkers jet engines.'

'So much ambition at the end of the road!'

'It keeps Himmler happy. Bear in mind that the original plans were drawn up in much better days – and if we don't stick to them now, we'll arouse great suspicion. Besides, it's good experience for where we're going. For instance, in the town of Bleicherode, about twenty kilometers from the Kohnstein Mountain, there's an old potassium mine where we'd already begun to bore new tunnels, galleries, and accommodations at a depth of seven hundred meters, with the idea of reaching sixteen hundred kilometers. The plan was to tunnel through to another potassium mine nearby, in Neubleicherode, and there install more factories for work on the V-2 and smaller antiaircraft rockets. Not far away, in a cliff face near the town of Lehestein, a tunnel is still being bored, intended to end in a large cave in which we were going to install a liquid oxygen plant and quarters for rocket crews . . . and so forth. Naturally we no longer have use for these places, but they keep the work force busy, allay the suspicions of Himmler's Nordhausen spies, and incidentally prove that what we're planning for Neuschwabenland can actually be accomplished.'

'And today, after testing the *Kugelblitz*, we'll start planning to leave. How much time do we have left?'

'Not much,' Ernst replied, gazing out of Wilson's glass-walled office at the large, pilot-controlled flying saucer that was resting on a hydraulic steel platform in the center of Kahla's biggest underground hangar.

The saucer looked exactly like the Schriever saucer, except for the smaller, less visible, but infinitely more powerful, adjustable jets around its rim, as well as its more seamless surface. This was made from *Luftschwamm*, or porous metal, thus allowing the saucer to fly at least as fast as the much smaller *Feuerball*, and probably faster. The saucer's top body rose up to the central pilot's dome, made of unbreakable Perspex.

'The war is being lost and a lot of our leaders are breaking down,' Ernst continued. 'The Führer's permanently on drugs supplied by his quack, Dr Morell, and is also rumored to be suffering from syphilis and going insane. Himmler spends most of his time in his sanatorium in Hohenlychen, one hundred and twenty kilometers north of Berlin, where he talks to his astrologer and discusses the possibility of arranging a private surrender to the Allies. I myself was visiting the rebuilt Peenemünde in October when Marshall Göring was shown a successful launching of a V-2 rocket. Göring's eyes were tired and his face was very puffy. During the rocket launching, he swallowed a lot of pills; then he pulled his pistol from his holster and kept tossing it in the air and catching it, as if in a trance, until his aide-de-camp gently took it away from him.'

Never before had Wilson heard Stoll talk with such weary contempt about his masters. Now he knew that he could finally get the SS captain to do whatever he wanted.

Wilson was pleased: Disillusioned romantics always made the most fanatical converts.

'And how goes the war?' he asked.

'Most of France and Belgium are liberated. Soviet divisions have taken Warsaw. Italy is virtually lost. Most of Germany is in ruins. Our air force has no fuel. Our industry has been wiped out by Allied bombs. Our rocket attacks came too late.'

'It's only a matter of months, then?'

'Yes, Wilson. No more than that.'

'And Kammler?'

'Since last July, when the attempt on the Führer's life turned him against the Wehrmacht and encouraged him to place the whole rocket program in the hands of the SS, meaning Kammler, our recently promoted brigadier has been making an admirable public display of crisscrossing the country to take charge of the rocket firings – which means he has freedom of movement and is absolutely above suspicion. I still don't like him, but he's certainly no fool and knows just what he's doing – though now that most of the launching sites have been captured, he has less to do there.'

'Do you think *he's* still dependable?'

'Yes. His sole desire is to avoid being captured and hanged as a war criminal – which means he wants to go with us.'

'When is he coming here?'

'Any minute now,' Ernst said. 'He wants to witness the test flight of the *Kugelblitz*. It's not something he'd miss.'

Glancing across the hangar, the doors of which would soon open to reveal the southern Harz Mountains of Kahla, Wilson saw that the German workers, under the supervision of the engineers, were already starting to raise the hydraulic platform under the saucer.

In that gloomy space, the saucer looked even larger than its seventy-five meters in diameter. It was resting on retractable shock absorbers, had an almost seamless, perfect aerodynamical shape, and even the pilot's cockpit, located at the machine's center of gravity, could be retracted during high-speed flight, thus making the machine look like a perfect disk, with no surface protuberances of any kind.

It was, to Wilson's way of thinking, something worth seeing.

Just as the whining, clattering steel platform came to rest on its adjustable wheels and went silent, Kammler and Nebe entered the hangar by the rear door and marched past the saucer into Wilson's office. Looking as handsome and cold as ever, Kammler sat on the edge of Wilson's desk. Nebe, as dark and unreadable as always, stood near the door of the office with his hand on his pistol.

He feels naked without that pistol, Wilson thought. *The man is a predator.*

'Welcome,' Wilson said, addressing his words to Kammler. 'How are things going?'

'Excellent,' Kammler said. 'At the end of January, Himmler placed me in complete control of the rocket program. I've just returned from the Hague, from where the V-1s and V-2s are being fired. We'll keep firing them from there until Antwerp falls, which it surely will, and then we'll be firing them no more, since we'll have run out of launching sites. When that time comes, it will be time to move from here – let's say March or April – certainly not much longer, since as from yesterday, Allied troops were massed along the Rhine on a sixteen-kilometer front, prepared to launch themselves into Germany. In other words, our time is running out, so let's hope this test flight succeeds and we can start making arrangements in the knowledge that we have a workable saucer to take with us.'

Even as he spoke, the large doors at the far end of the hangar were being opened. Sunlight poured in and revealed an immense open space that ran out to the base of a steep, densely forested hill. The smooth, metallic gray surface of the *Kugelblitz* took on a brilliant, silvery sheen that clearly reflected the images of the men around the platform. Then the engine of the hydraulic platform roared into life and the platform, now on its raised wheels and manipulated by a combination of remote-control console and jib and crane, started moving slowly out of the hangar into the open air.

'Oh, my God!' Ernst murmured, awe making him seem more alive. 'It's absolutely superb!'

Wilson could not resist a smile, then nodded at Kammler

and Nebe and led them, with Stoll, out of his office and across the concrete floor of the hangar, toward the open doors and the still moving *Kugelblitz*.

'Has the escape route been organized yet?' he asked Nebe, who had fallen in beside him.

'Yes,' Nebe said in his flat, passionless manner. 'The matter of when and how we leave will be complicated by the Soviet offensive, which is moving rapidly toward Peenemünde. Because of that, Wernher von Braun and five thousand of his workers are being moved this week to the new research station still under construction in the Bleicherode mine. Because the technicians and their families are going to be housed in the surrounding villages, as requested personally by Himmler, we're going to have to keep this place secret and leave at night, when we won't be observed.'

'When the time comes to evacuate,' Kammler said, 'I'll ensure that von Braun and his team don't know about it. In the meantime, while they're living in the Nordhausen area, I'll keep them under close guard and make sure that none of them comes this far. In short, they won't know you exist.'

'Fine,' Wilson said as he led them out of the hangar and into the freezing wind of the cleared area, 'but how will we go?'

'The same way von Braun and his team are coming here,' Nebe replied. 'By train, truck, private cars, and even barges. To ensure that at least *some* of us get through, we'll be split up into groups and make the journey on three separate nights by different routes. The first will go to Rostock, then round the coast of the Baltic Sea; the second also to Rostock, but then on to Lübeck; and the third and last to Hamburg, via Hannover, then on to Kiel from there. A meticulous schedule has been arranged for each group; each journey will be made by a combination of vehicles to confuse anyone trying to track our movements; and each stop, or change-over point, along the way will be in a secret location heavily guarded by my most trusted SS men – all of whom, like me, had to go underground after the failed July plot against Hitler. In other words, they're all men who've everything to gain and nothing to lose by coming with us. In that sense, at least, they'll be trustworthy and reliable.'

'It all sounds very organized,' Wilson said.

'It is,' Nebe replied.

The engines of the mobile platform in the clearing went dead, the wheels were raised to let the platform rest on the flat earth, and the *Kugelblitz* bounced lightly on its shock absorbers, then steadied again.

Out there, in the open air and sunlight, it was a thing of great beauty.

Wilson walked up to the pilot, who was waiting by the concrete observation bunker in the shadow of the high wall of the hangar. The man was wearing a Luftwaffe flying suit and seemed totally fearless.

'Are you ready to go?' Wilson asked him.

'Yes,' he said.

'Good. Then let's do it.'

Wilson escorted him across the clearing and up onto the steel platform, finally stopping at the curved rim of the *Kugelblitz*, their heads in line with its ring of tiltable jet nozzles. From there, the raised pilot's compartment seemed to tower high above them, at the top of the ladder sloping upward to it. The pilot climbed up and Wilson followed to help him in. When the pilot was strapped in, Wilson checked that all seemed well, then climbed down and let an engineer climb up to secure the Perspex hood. When that was done, the engineer climbed back down, pulled the collapsible ladder after him, gave the thumbs-up to the pilot, then marched with Wilson back to the concrete bunker in front of the open doors of the hangar.

Kammler, Nebe, and Stoll were already there, gazing through the protective, tinted glass in a long slit in the bunker's wall. Because the *Kugelblitz* was being flown by a pilot, there was no remote-control panel, as there had been with the *Feuerballs*, though there was a man sitting by a radio console, prepared to talk to the pilot.

'All set?' Wilson asked him.

'Yes, sir.'

'Then there's no point in waiting.'

The man at the simple radio console relayed Wilson's permission to take off to the pilot. Kammler smiled and crossed his fingers. General Nebe remained impassive. Ernst took a deep breath and licked his lips, then bit his right index finger.

Wilson heard the birds singing, the wind moaning through the forest, the babbling of a brook beside the hangar, where the land rose protectively. He thought of his first prototype, the *Flegelrad*, or Wingwheel, which had been a crude affair based on the principles of the wheel, with its many wings radiating out to the rim and revolving around the pilot's cockpit at the center of gravity. Impossible to control, its balance destroyed by its vibrations, it had been superseded by a later model, in which balance was achieved with a new stabilizing mechanism and the earlier Rocketmotor was replaced by an advanced turbojet engine. That second model flew, but not much better than a helicopter, so Wilson had experimented with his smaller, remote-controlled model, the *Feuerball*. Finally this, the *Kugelblitz*, the perfect aeronautical machine, would allow for frictionless air flow and defeat the former limitations of the boundary layer. Thus, he was giving the world a saucer-shaped, jet-propelled aircraft of extraordinary speed and maneuverability.

And at last it was taking off. Tilted downward, the adjustable jet engines roared into life, spewed searing yellow flames at the earth, and created a circular wall of fire around the saucer, between its rim and the ground. The flames beat at the blackened earth, roaring down, shooting up and outward. The saucer shimmered eerily in the rising heat waves and then took on a crimson glow. It shuddered violently for a moment, swayed from side to side, bounced up and down on its shock-absorbing legs, then lifted tentatively off the ground.

It hovered in midair, floating magically on a bed of fire, then roared louder and ascended vertically, thrust upward by the flaming jets, and was distorted in the shimmering heat waves. It turned to a silvery jelly, then became a lava flow, red and yellow and glaring white, then hovered magically once more, about ten meters up, before roaring demonically, the noise shocking, almost deafening, and suddenly disappearing – though in fact it had shot vertically skyward, to be framed by the rising sun.

It stopped there, bouncing lightly in the sun's shimmering, oblique striations, then shot off again, this time flying horizontally, to disappear beyond the horizon in the wink of an eye.

Wilson heard the applause around him, then the pilot's voice on the radio – distorted by the static but obviously exultant – confirming that he was flying beyond the limit of his airspeed indicator, higher than the upper limit of his altimeter, and already could see the Elbe River, winding toward Hamburg. He soon saw the curved horizon, the Baltic Sea, the port of Rügen, then he turned back and was soon crossing Magdeburg and reappeared as a flash of light above the green, forested hills of the majestic Harz Mountains. That flash of light became a silvery coin, a flying saucer, a glowing disc – then, abruptly, the *Kugelblitz* was right above them, hovering high up in thin air, again framed by the rising sun. It descended vertically, perfectly, on pillars of yellow flame. The flames scorched the earth and flew outward in all directions and formed a bed of fire and smoke, then the *Kugelblitz* settled down on the steel platform, which its flames had made red-hot. It subsided onto its shock absorbers, bouncing lightly, swaying gracefully, then its engines cut out, leaving a sudden, shocking silence, and the flames died out and the smoke drifted away and the flying saucer was visible.

It was resting on its shock-absorbing legs, gleaming silvery in the sunlight – a technological object of rare beauty, an extraordinary achievement.

'We've won,' Wilson said with quiet pride. 'Now let's blow it to smithereens.'

Chapter Thirty-Four

The landscape that Ernst drove through on his way to
Himmler's unofficial headquarters in Dr Gebhardt's sanatorium at Hohenlychen, 120 kilometers north of Berlin,
resembled the interior of his own mind – a place of ruins and
mounting rubble, a cold, bleak terrain.

He had felt that way since the death of Ingrid and the
children – first grief, then guilt, then despair, then a feeling
like death – and he now sensed that he would never feel better
as long as he lived. He understood that this was why he'd
decided to throw in his lot with Wilson. He needed the
American's icy confidence, his air of calm invincibility, but he
also needed to hide away in a place like the Antarctic the way
other men, disillusioned with or frightened by life, hide
themselves in isolated monasteries, wanting only the silence
of the day and the night's lonesome wind.

He wanted escape.

Reaching the sanatorium, he wasn't surprised to find it
surrounded by trucks and heavily armed SS troops – just as
the Führer's bunker in the Chancellery had been. Even though
wearing his uniform, Ernst had to show his papers to an
unsmiling guard at the main gate, then was escorted inside
the building, past other guarded doors, and into Himmler's
personal study. The Reichsführer was at his desk, leaning
slightly forward to look down through his pince-nez at a large
astrological chart, but he looked up when Ernst entered and
offered a wan smile. Ernst saluted and murmured 'Heil Hitler!'
– because this ridiculous formality was still kept up – then

Himmler, who rarely invited his guests to sit, actually told him to do so.

Ernst sat in the chair facing the desk as Himmler said, 'You have come from Berlin, Captain?'

'Yes, sir,' Ernst replied. 'After flying in from Nordhausen. I was expecting to find you in the Chancellery, so I naturally went there first.'

'I'm not feeling too well,' Himmler said testily, 'so I came here for a much-needed rest.'

Ernst did not choose to argue, though he knew that Himmler had in fact come here to get away from the bombings and the general madness overtaking Berlin, now that his envisaged Thousand Year Reich had shrunk to the area confined between two rivers, the Rhine and the Oder, and was about to be annihilated completely with enemy attacks from the east and west. Also, since January, when he had been given the responsibility of stopping Marshal Zhukov's advance to the Oder River but failed lamentably to do so, his position of trust with Hitler had been lost. Now, along with Göring and Speer, he was a rejected former favorite, forced to watch the fanatical Martin Bormann gain the trust of the increasingly paranoid Führer and become arrogant with it.

'And how were things in Berlin?' Himmler asked, as if he had not been there for months.

Ernst sighed and shrugged. 'The same. There are air raids every day and night. Our courageous Führer insists on staying in the Chancellery bunker and refuses to give in.'

'Most admirable,' Himmler said.

'Yes,' Ernst replied. 'Indeed.' Not mentioning that Hitler's bunker, deep beneath the Chancellery garden, had more than once been badly damaged by Allied bombs and was a most depressing sight, with air vents covered in cardboard, the rooms now barren of their former paintings, tapestries, and carpets, rubble on the floors, planks thrown across gaping holes filled with water from burst mains, and an almost daily breakdown of water and electricity. Hitler himself had appeared to be in a dreadful condition, with a limp left arm, an incapacitated right hand, a general lack of muscular coordination, obvious breathing problems, and an embarrassing tendency to absentmindedness and outbursts of paranoid anger. Because of this, there were armed SS troops standing guard at every door, in every corridor. The bunker was filled with rumors about suspected plots, coups, and assassination attempts that, if nothing else, distracted everyone from the bombs raining down almost nonstop.

In short, a nightmare.

'Did you speak personally to the Führer?'

'No, sir. I only saw him in the Chancellery air-raid shelter, when he was conversing with some of his officers.'

'Did you hear my name mentioned?' Himmler asked anxiously, twisting his snake ring around on his finger.

'No, Reichsführer,' Ernst lied.

'You don't think he's heard about . . . ?' But his voice trailed off into an uneasy silence, as if he couldn't even mention the subject that was, even more than his recent rejection, gnawing away at him.

Ernst knew what his deeper anxiety was about.

The past couple of months had seen the disaster in the Ardennes, the terrible bombing of Dresden, the Soviet crossing of the Oder River, and the Allied advance to the bank of the Rhine where they were, this very day, massing for their advance into Germany.

Not oblivious to this dreadful turning of the tide, and encouraged by his masseur, Felix Kersten – a dubious character and doctor without a medical degree – as well as by his chief of espionage General Walter Schellenberg, Himmler had earlier in the month held a secret meeting right here with Count Folke Bernadotte of the Swedish Ministry for Foreign Affairs, in an attempt to negotiate a separate peace. The attempt had failed, but now Himmler was terrified that the Führer would find out what he had been up to behind his back – even more so because his former personal adjutant and current SS chief in Italy, General Karl Wolff, had also been negotiating behind the Führer's back, first with Allen Dulles, the OSS representative in Switzerland, then with two Allied generals in Ascona, Switzerland.

Himmler was convinced that if Hitler found out, he would be executed without further ado. No wonder he was a dramatically changed man, his pale face now sweaty.

'No, Reichsführer,' Ernst replied, keeping his face composed. 'I don't think he's heard anything at all. In fact, I don't think he hears much about anything except the war's progress, which of course is disastrous.'

'That's the talk of a traitor!' Himmler snapped with a sudden, surprising burst of energy.

'I apologize, Reichsführer,' Ernst said quickly. 'I meant no offense. I merely point out that even the Chancellery is being bombed every day and the enemy is closing in from east and west and will soon be heading for Berlin.'

Visibly sagging again, Himmler looked down at the ring he was twisting on his finger, studied it for a moment, then looked up again with a hopeful gleam in his normally distant gaze.

'We might still be able to stop them,' he said, 'with our new, secret weapons.'

'I'm afraid most of the rocket launching sites have been captured,' Ernst informed him. 'So even if we produced more advanced rockets, we could not—'

But Himmler waved his hand impatiently to cut him short. 'I don't mean the rockets,' he said. 'I know all about the rockets. I'm thinking, instead, of Rudolph Schriever's flying saucer, which he insisted he would be testing soon. Have you been to see him in Prague?'

'Yes, Reichsführer. I was there a week ago. Schriever is still confident that he can have the saucer flying before the Soviets get that far. I was certainly impressed with what I saw there, and I think he can do it.'

'Good,' Himmler said.

Nonsense, Ernst thought. He had indeed visited Schriever in his research complex outside Prague. Although his saucer might fly, it would be little help. It was an obsolete model, using Wilson's old gas-turbine rotors – not much more advanced than a helicopter and without decent weapons. In truth, it was a joke, designed to keep Schriever engaged and Himmler's mind off Wilson. Even if Schriever *did* get it flying before the Soviets got to him, it would hardly do much damage to the Soviet or Allied advance. In fact, it would probably be shot out of the sky as soon as it took off.

'I knew I was right in depending upon Schriever,' Himmler observed. 'He is a German, after all. I only wish I'd had the sense to do it a lot sooner, rather than waste all that time on Wilson. How *is* the American?'

Ernst had been waiting for the question. Though prepared for it, he could not stop a tremor of fear from passing through him. He had rehearsed this many times, with Wilson, by himself, and though he knew it would probably work, the thought of failure was frightening. He was going to lie to his Reichsführer – it was a major lie, and a dangerous one – and when he recalled those high-ranking officers writhing in piano-wire nooses strung from meathooks in that small room in Plötzensee Prison, he didn't relish what would happen to him if he made a mistake.

'I'm afraid you were right about Wilson,' he said. 'We put him to work in Nordhausen, helping the rocket engineers, but he was clearly too old and senile to be of much use to them. As for his so-called flying saucer, it was a poor imitation of Schriever's. When test-flown, it hardly got off the ground before blowing up.'

It had indeed been blown up, but deliberately, by Wilson, after having performed superbly during its test flight. Wilson had done it with no flicker of emotion. He didn't want to risk flying it until the war had ended (he didn't want it to be observed) and, also, the components for many models had already been shipped to Antarctica. He himself would take the drawings for this final, successful prototype there, when they sailed out from Kiel.

Wilson, then, was still very much alive . . . but well hidden in Kahla.

'Naturally that failure,' Ernst continued, 'combined with

409

Wilson's increasingly senile behavior in the Nordhausen Central Works, encouraged us to do what you had suggested and put him to death. He was executed in one of the bunkers and his body then burned as part of the mass cremations at Buchenwald. Then all the papers regarding his Projekt Saucer were set to the torch.'

'You did the correct thing,' Himmler said. 'Good riddance to bad rubbish. We should have known that an American would not have served us well in the end. And now all of our resources can be directed toward the Schriever saucer, which *must* be successful.'

'It will be, Reichsführer.'

Himmler nodded, scratched his nose beneath the pince-nez, then glanced down at his astrological chart and spoke to the desk. 'Wernher von Braun and his five thousand technicians are now safely housed near Nordhausen?'

'Yes, sir. The new research station has almost been completed in the Bleicherode mine. Von Braun and his technicians have been accommodated there and in the other villages in the general vicinity of Nordhausen.'

'They discovered nothing about Wilson and his Projekt Saucer?'

'No, Reichsführer. We executed Wilson and destroyed all evidence of his project a few days before von Braun and his team arrived.'

'Good,' Himmler said. 'The Allies and the Soviets will both want our scientists, so failing all else, we can use them as bartering points if it comes to surrender. Make sure they are kept under guard and be ready to move them at short notice.'

'Yes, sir,' Ernst said.

Himmler nodded thoughtfully, still gazing down at the astrological chart, which had, Ernst knew, been given to him by his 'masseur,' Felix Kersten.

How the mighty have fallen, Ernst thought. This pit has no bottom.

'Nevertheless,' Himmler said distractedly, 'I have good reason to believe the tide will turn again and leave us victorious.' He looked up at Ernst, smiled in a dreamy manner, and tapped the astrological chart with his knuckles. 'My charts,' he said. 'I study them often. The charts tell me that we'll be saved at the last minute with some secret weapon. Perhaps our new jets or the atom bomb project . . . But most likely Flugkapitän Schriever's flying saucer . . . I place my faith in my stars.'

'Yes, Reichsführer,' Ernst said, too embarrassed to say anything else, but standing up and getting ready to take his leave. 'I'm sure that's the case.'

'You are returning to Nordhausen now?'

Ernst nodded.

'Good. When do you next plan to visit Schriever?'

'When he calls me for the test-flight of his saucer, which should be in a month.'

'According to my charts, that should be enough.'

'I hope so, Reichsführer.'

Himmler stood up, adjusted his jacket, then straightened his spine and gave the Nazi salute. He waited until Ernst had returned it, then said, 'Thank you, Captain. These are trying times, but you have behaved commendably so far. I trust you won't let me down in the future.'

'No, sir, I won't.'

'Good-bye, Captain. Heil Hitler!'

'Heil Hitler!'

The words had a hollow ring in the large, gloomy study, reminding Ernst of the life he had wasted for the dream of such madmen. He walked out with relief, as if escaping from prison, and drove back to Berlin through the evening's descending darkness, reaching Reinickendorf Airport as the bombs started falling.

He saw the fires all over Berlin as he climbed out of his car, heard the explosions growing louder as they came closer to the airport, and strapped himself into the seat in the plane as the darkness just beyond the airport became a hell of explosions. The plane took off through a brilliant web of languidly looping tracers, flew through exploding flak, and managed to make its escape without being damaged.

Ernst settled into his seat, feeling nothing, not even fear. He thought of how everywhere he went these days there was only destruction. Then the young navigator emerged from the pilot's cabin, stopped in front of him, and handed him a written message.

Reading it, Ernst learned that earlier that morning Britain's General Montgomery had launched his assault across the Rhine; that two airborne divisions – one British and one American – had dropped on the German side of the river to support the infantrymen; and that 240 kilometers upriver, General Patton's US 3rd Army had done exactly the same.

Fully aware that the news signified the beginning of the end of the Thousand Year Reich, Ernst simply crumpled up the message and let it fall to the floor.

He was almost relieved.

Chapter Thirty-Five

Bradley was so tired, he thought he was dead. He was sitting behind another makeshift desk surrounded by rubble and four broken walls, with no roof, in the remains of what had once been an elegant house in what was now left of the city of Cologne, which had been bomb-shattered and torn by the dreadful fighting of the past few days.

The ruined building in which Bradley was sitting was being guarded by filthy, weary, armed soldiers from the 104th Infantry Divisions of General Omar Bradley's US 1st Army, with whom Bradley had made the bitterly won advance from Aachen, on the Siegfried Line. When he glanced at them, which he could do with ease, because few of the building walls still stood completely, he was reminded of just how hard they had fought and how far they'd come.

Sitting at his makeshift desk – the ruined house's kitchen table – and waiting to begin what he thought would be his most important interrogations on behalf of Project Paperclip, he could hear the continuing sounds of battle from beyond the battered city, as the Germans were pushed back to the Rhine. Nevertheless, irrespective of the constant noise, he still managed to fall in and out of a delerious half sleep, in which he thought of nothing but what he had experienced over the past couple of months.

'The pilot's on his way,' his assistant, Sergeant Lew Ackerman of the US 3rd Armored Division, whispered into his ear. 'He'll be here any minute.'

'Thanks,' Bradley said.

He had meant to open his eyes and smile, but instead drifted into another half sleep and recalled the Hürtgen forest, snow and mud erupting around him, the infantrymen moving forward through that hell of exploding shells, swirling smoke, chattering machine guns, and screaming wounded, their blood splashing on the muddied white of the snow, their bodies crumpling into it. Bradley had survived it (he had hugged the ground a lot), but then found himself farther south, advancing toward the heavily fortified village of Schmidt and the Roer reservoirs. The resistance was fierce and many men died in the mud, but the village was taken, then the west bank of the Roer. Then the Germans flooded the river by blowing up the dams and Bradley found himself helping to form a bridgehead in the early hours of the morning. The men of the US 1st and 9th forced a difficult crossing and assembled a temporary bridge for the others to follow. The moon was bright and many of them died – but Bradley survived again, soaking wet but not with blood, and helped drag some of his dead friends from the river before moving on.

It wasn't excitement that stuck in his mind, just constant noise and permanent exhaustion – and Bradley remembered that sitting at his table in this ruined house in the ruined heart of the city of Cologne, now one great heap of rubble.

He remembered being deaf and cold, being exhausted and cold, and then recalled, more specifically, the march eastward to Düren, the city's complete destruction, another river crossing – someone said it was the Erft – and finally, in a hell of noise and smoke, the outskirts of this city. Allied aircraft bombed it constantly, the big guns leveled what was left, then the US 1st Army moved in, taking the town street by street. Bradley was right there, with the 104th Infantry divisions, clambering over the rubble, choking in dust and smoke, firing his M-1 rifle at those murky figures in the dust-wreathed ruins, throwing his hand grenades into rubble-filled basements, running forward and ducking and running forward again, and dragging dead, bloody bodies out of his way to start all over again.

He had played his small part in the capture of Cologne and couldn't help feeling proud of himself. He was too old for this, after all, and was not obliged to do it. The function of OSS was intelligence gathering – to *follow* the advancing armies and set up headquarters in their wake – but Bradley had wanted this last adventure, a final testing of his courage, and he had to confess that doing it had made him feel young again. It was confirmation of that awful truth – that men throve on risk-taking – and it helped him to understand what drove Wilson on his weird personal journey: the need to risk everything he had to create his own world.

What would be frightening about Wilson, Bradley suspected, would be the world he was hoping to create – clearly one in which normal human feelings had little weight.

It helped to think about Wilson. It made Bradley feel more alert. He rubbed his eyes and yawned and stretched himself on the wooden chair. He was pleased to note that a jeep had just pulled up outside and his ALSOS assistant, Major Arnold Grieves, was leading a US Air Force pilot through the remains of the front doorway, past the armed guards, and through the rubble-strewn passageways to his open-air office. A cold wind was whipping up the dust and forcing Bradley to shiver.

'Hallelujah!' he whispered as Sergeant Ackerman stepped over a broken wall, holding a tray containing what looked like four mugs of steaming coffee.

'I brought us all coffees,' he confirmed, placing the tray on the table. 'It'll help keep you warm.'

'You're a treasure,' Bradley said. 'I will never forget this act. Look me up after the war and I'll give you a kiss.'

'No, thanks,' Ackerman said, taking the chair beside Bradley and raising his steaming mug to his lips as Major Grieves, small and portly and reportedly brilliant, stopped in front of the table with the pilot beside him. The pilot was in his flying uniform, was roughly handsome and unshaven, and was actually puffing on a cigar, just like in the movies.

'Hi, Mike,' Grieves said informally. 'This is Lieutenant Edward Schlesinger of the 415th Night Fighter Squadron.

Eddie, this is Colonel Mike Bradley of OSS and his administrative assistant, Sergeant Lew Ackerman of the US 3rd Armored Division.'

'Hi,' Schlesinger said, exhaling a cloud of smoke and pulling up a chair without being asked. 'Howya doin'?'

'Fine,' Bradley said, as Arnold pulled up the last chair. An enemy shell came screeching in toward them and fell in the ruins of a house in the adjacent, debris-strewn street. The explosion threw up more debris and a ballooning cloud of smoke, but neither Bradley nor anyone else at the table took any notice. Instead, Bradley glanced down at his notes and said, 'You're a pilot with the—'

'He's just told ya,' the pilot said, nodding in the direction of Major Grieves. 'The 415th Night Fighter Squadron, flying bombing raids over the Rhine.'

'Originally out of England?'

'Right. But now out of a French airbase near Paris. One hell of a city.'

'I agree,' Bradley said with a grin, amused by the pilot's lack of respect for rank. 'But the incident you're going to tell me about actually happened when you were flying out of England.'

'Right. Aston Down, Gloucestershire. A Limey base.'

'How'd you get on with the Brits?'

'That's a joke, isn't it? They thought we were overpaid, oversexed, and over there to steal their women.'

'Which you were.'

'I guess so, Colonel. No argument there. Are those coffees for us?'

'Yes,' Ackerman said.

'Terrific.' Schlesinger picked up one mug, Grieves picked up the other, they both drank, then Schlesinger inhaled on his cigar and exhaled some more smoke. Because the smoke from the last explosion was drifting over them, the cigar smoke went unnoticed.

'Apparently this incident occurred on the night of November 23, last year, during a bombing run over the Rhine.'

'Right. November 23, 1944. 1 have the date branded in my brain and won't ever forget it.'

'What happened, exactly?'

'It was a pretty normal bombing run,' Schlesinger said, 'with nothing out of the ordinary until we got to about twenty miles from Strasbourg.'

'When you say "nothing out of the ordinary," what do you mean?'

Schlesinger spread his hands. 'Nothing!' he said. 'Just another routine bombing raid. No problems over France, a bit of flak over the Rhine, then another untroubled period until we started gettin' near Strasbourg. That's when it began.'

'You were harassed by some kind of flying object.'

'A Foo fighter,' Schlesinger said.

'That's the word you guys are using for this particular kind of unidentified flying object?'

'Right. We call them Foo fighters.'

'Why?'

'Just a joke name. It comes from the Smokey Stover comic strip. You know? The popular phrase, "Where there's foo, there's fire." It's as simple as that.'

Bradley chuckled and shook his head in amusement, then got back to business. 'So you'd heard about the Foo fighters before you made that particular flight.'

'Yeah, right – but that don't mean I imagined the sons of bitches. Everyone in the crew saw the same objects – and one of our B-25s went down because of the harassment. No, sir! They were real, all right!'

'So what happened?'

'We're just approachin' Strasbourg with not a thing in the goddamned sky – no enemy aircraft, no flak, no tracers – nothing! Then, without warning, these goddamned Foo fighters appeared – about a dozen of them – and started tailing certain of our aircraft, mostly the bombers. They ascended from the ground – most of us saw them coming up. They looked like balls of fire – an orange-yellow fire, sometimes flaring white, with a tail of fire streaming out behind it – but when they flew beside my plane, a B-25, I could see that they had a dark, inner core, which was probably solid. That core was shaped like a disc, or saucer, and most of us agreed it was no more than three or four feet wide.'

'And you think they were actually tailing your aircraft.'

'No doubt about it, Colonel. Those goddamned things were controlled. With that orange-yellow fire around them and their unusual shape and size, they certainly seemed a bit weird and even unreal – but they were under control.'

'What makes you think that?'

'Because they flew right at our airplanes as if about to crash into them, then turned abruptly and tailed us, sticking really close to us. Then, each time we fired our guns at them, they flew out of range at incredible speed – and in every direction.'

'How fast?'

'Faster than any plane I've ever seen.'

'Why did you fire at them? They were only *tailing* you, after all.'

'Because as soon as they started tailing us, or at least flying in formation with us – since they were usually right beside us – they appeared to cool down a bit, giving us a clearer impression of the dark core inside. Then they definitely looked saucershaped, probably made of metal – at times they *glinted* – and they seemed to be spinning rapidly on their own axis. When they were spinning like that, they made a whipping, whistling sound – like they were whipping up the air around them. And when *that* happened, our radar *and* engines malfunctioned and our planes started failing . . . It was weird. Really frightening.'

'And you're sure that the malfunctioning of the engines was directly related to the spinning of the fireballs?'

'Absolutely. I'm sure – we were all sure – because as soon as we fired on the Foo fighters, they flew away from us – the second we started firing, in fact – and as soon as they flew out of our range, our engines kicked on again. So that's what was happening, see? When they came close to us, our engines malfunctioned and we started going down; when we fired at them and they flew away, our engines kicked back into life and we were able to level out and keep flying. So they came at us and were chased away, returned and were chased away again, and our engines were cutting in and out, and we were falling and then leveling out again. This happened repeatedly until we gave up and turned back to England . . . which we only did when Tappman's B-25 went down for the count.'

'Lieutenant Victor Tappman . . . the fatality.'

'Right. Good old Vic. Out of Denver, Colorado. One of the best pilots we had – and even he couldn't handle it.'

Another shell fell nearby, exploding a few streets away, but Schlesinger merely turned his head to glance at the rising smoke, then inhaled on his cigar and shook his head ruefully.

'His B-25,' he continued, 'like all of the others, had been cutting in and out, going down and leveling out again; but then it cut out for too long, fell too far to be leveled out, and then went into a nosedive that he couldn't control. I think his engines came on again, but then the aircraft was in that spin, and so the plane was forced quicker toward the earth and eventually crashed. I heard Tappman on the intercom, shouting about the goddamned fireballs. *"They're killing our engines!"* he shouted. *"They're not planes!"* I heard his gunner cry out. *"They're balls of fire!"* The gunner also emphasized that the balls of fire were *climbing* – so they weren't natural phenomena – and then Tappman screamed, *"We're going down! Pull her up!"* Then he gave one, long drawn-out cry of the word *"Foo!"* which is where it all ended.'

'You mean, the Foo fighters flew away after Tappman crashed.'

'No,' Schlesinger said, taking another drink of his coffee and putting the mug back down. 'We all turned back when we saw Tappman crashing – and only *then*, when we were actually heading home, did the Foo fighters fly away . . . And those sons of bitches *did* fly away, Colonel, they didn't just disappear. They ascended vertically above our aircraft, stayed above us for a short while, then, when they were certain we were heading home, they flew away horizontally and finally, when a good distance away, descended *in formation* toward the ground. They were controlled, Colonel. *Definitely!*'

'It could only have been remote control,' Bradley said.

'Like the V-1 and V-2 rockets,' Grieves offered, 'so it's certainly possible.'

There was silence for a moment. Bradley heard the distant battle.

'This is some office you got here,' Schlesinger said. 'Real cozy, in fact.'

Bradley smiled. 'We make do with what we have.' Schlesinger nodded, straight-faced, and said, 'Can I go now?'

Bradley also nodded. 'Sure. And thanks a lot. You've been a great help.'

Schlesinger grinned, pushed his chair back, and stood up. 'Anytime. No sweat.'

Grieves stood up with him. 'Are you going to that hospital right now?'

'Yes,' Bradley replied. 'I want to catch up with the 1st Army. I can't hang around too long.'

'Any messages for HQ in Paris?'

'Not yet,' Bradley said.

'Okay, Colonel, I'll see you in Berlin.'

'I sure as hell hope so.'

Grieves grinned at him and left, taking the pilot with him, and Bradley stood up and stretched, then said to Sergeant Ackerman, 'I'll take the jeep and be back in an hour or so. Can you hold the fort?'

'I'm not expecting many visitors,' Ackerman replied laconically, his gaze taking in the ruined walls and missing roof of the house.

'I'll bring you back a hot blonde,' Bradley said.

'You do that, Colonel.'

Bradley left the ruined building, passing the armed guards, then climbed into his jeep and drove through Cologne, or what was left of it. The devastation was appalling – no street was untouched. He drove past skeletal buildings, imposing hillocks of rubble, the blackened remains of exploded tanks, overturned trucks, and mangled half-tracks. People still lived in the ruins, their pitiful possessions grouped around them, and children kicked up clouds of dust as they clambered over charred wooden beams and jumped off the remains of walls. Occasionally shots rang out – the army was cleaning out German snipers – and Frenchmen with FFI armbands and women armed to the teeth were kicking collaborators – the men bruised, the women with shaved heads – along the streets and into basements and rubble-strewn rooms to mete out rough justice.

Bradley tried not to see that, for he disapproved but could do little to stop it. He was undeniably relieved to arrive at the hospital. Though it was still standing, it had also been severely damaged and was surrounded by rubble.

He parked as some Flying Fortresses growled overhead, heading toward the Rhine and the German cities beyond it, and thought of the balls of fire, the so-called Foo fighters, that had been harassing and sometimes destroying Allied bombers for months now.

Saucer-shaped objects, he thought. *It could only be Wilson.*

And he had to admire Wilson, while also feeling a touch of dread. Bradley was more determined than ever to find him as he entered the hospital.

There was a jagged hole in the roof just above the reception desk and the floor below it was covered in broken plaster and a dirty white powder. Uniformed MPs were on guard, checking for malingerers, but they snapped to attention and saluted when Bradley stopped at the desk. He asked for Major General Saunders, the OSS officer who had called him there. When Saunders arrived, he forgot to salute, but offered his hand.

'Major General McArthur told me about you,' he said with a casual, relaxing smile. 'He told me what you were after. This woman, we think she knew the man you want, and she's eager to talk. No love lost there, I think. Come on, Colonel, this way.'

'How is she?' Bradley asked as Saunders led him through the nearest door and into a corridor.

'Not too good,' Saunders replied. 'She copped a bomb in this very hospital. She was working here as a nurse for the Germans when we bombed it to hell. She was buried in rubble, broke a lot of bones, and will possibly be paralyzed for life. But she can talk. She's coherent. She came here from Berlin, where she'd lived in the Kürhessen district with an SS engineer named Helmut Kruger. According to her records, which we found in the hospital files, she came here to work under the auspices of the SS and was otherwise being favored with all the privileges of an SS dependant or wife. Since, according to those same records, she and Kruger had not been married, we wondered why this was so and decided to ask her about it. We were surprised, then, when she told us with some bitterness that the name "Kruger" was a pseudonym for an *American* engineer, John Wilson, who had worked at the rocket research center at Kummersdorf, just fifteen miles south of Berlin. I conveyed this information to Major General McArthur and he told me to contact you. Your special baby, he said.'

He led Bradley along some more corridors, few of which were undamaged, then into a ward where the beds were crammed tightly together and the roof, which had collapsed, was temporarily covered with canvas sheets. Most of the windows were also covered in canvas, and the wind drummed against it.

Saunders led Bradley to the bed of a woman whose steady, fearless gray gaze emerged from a swathe of bandages that covered her head and hid most of her features. Her arms and legs, protruding from a white sheet, were in plaster casts.

'Mrs Bernecker,' Saunders said, 'this is Colonel Bradley, from the American intelligence service, OSS. Mike, this is Mrs Greta Bernecker.'

'Hi,' Bradley said, feeling awkward because of the woman's injuries.

'Hello,' the woman replied in good English. 'You wish to know about Wilson?'

Taken aback to hear Wilson mentioned so casually – like a living person – Bradley took a deep breath and said, 'Yes.'

'So . . . ask your questions.'

Bradley took another deep breath, surprised by his nervousness. He glanced at Saunders, who smiled back and said, 'I don't think you'll need me anymore, but if you do, you can find me through our temporary office right here in Cologne – and you know where that is. Okay?'

'Okay,' Bradley said. He watched Saunders take his leave, walking past the other beds, sometimes nodding and waving at the patients he knew, then, when the OSS officer had gone, he turned back to Greta Bernecker.

'You were living with Wilson in Berlin, is that right?'

'Yes.'

'He was called Kruger at the time?'

'No. He was only listed officially as Kruger. The SS confiscated his American documents and gave him those of a dead German named Kruger. I gather it was because they didn't want uninformed government clerks and administrators learning that an American, Wilson, was working for, and being supported by, the Third Reich. Officially, then, he existed as Kruger – but those who knew him, or worked with him, called him Wilson.'

'He was working at Kummersdorf at that time?'

'Yes. He was actually working at Kummersdorf West, at the other side of the old firing range, well away from the real rocket research center.'

'The one run by Wernher von Braun.'

'Correct, Colonel.'

'And when Wernher von Braun left to go to Peenemünde?'

'Wilson took over the larger hangars at Kummersdorf.'

'Do you know what he was working on?'

'Some kind of highly advanced, radical aircraft.'

'Did you find out anything about it?'

'No. He sometimes talked about it, but I didn't understand what he was saying. He was an engineer, an aeronautical scientist, and such talk just bewildered me. He was after an aircraft that could go straight up and down, like a helicopter, but could fly a lot faster. He said it was shaped like a saucer – I remember that much. In fact, the research program was called Projekt Saucer, which confirms what I say.'

Bradley thought of the hangar in Iowa, then of the Foo fighters, and knew he was traveling in the right direction.

'Did von Braun know anything about Wilson's project?'

'I don't think so. It's possible, but I doubt it. I know from what Wilson told me that he'd contributed considerably to von Braun's rocket program – by passing on certain of his technical innovations – and I think that because of that, von Braun thought that Wilson's experiments were related solely to the V-1 rocket program.'

'Who *did* know about Wilson's work?'

'The people who worked with him: an old Italian, Belluzzo, two German engineers, Habermohl and Miethe, and a Luftwaffe engineer, Flugkapitän Rudolph Schriever, who was obsessed with pleasing Himmler and tried stealing the credit for Wilson's work. While at Kummersdorf, they were all under the supervision of an SS officer, Lieutenant Ernst Stoll – now a captain, I think.'

'Is Wilson still at Kummersdorf?'

'No. Conflict between him and Flugkapitän Schriever, with Schriever gaining Himmler's trust, led to the research team being split into two groups. One group, headed by Schriever, Habermohl, and Miethe, were sent to somewhere in Bohem, in Czechoslovakia, and the other, headed by Wilson alone, went to the Harz Mountains.'

'Whereabouts in the Harz Mountains?'

'I don't know exactly. He mentioned a place called Nordhausen, though I don't think he was actually going there, but to somewhere close to it.'

That made sense to Bradley. British and American aerial reconnaissance and local resistance intelligence had already confirmed that some kind of huge rocket production center was located underground, near Nordhausen, in Thuringia. As that area was also part of the Nazi's planned Last Redoubt, it was logical that anything related to secret weapons would be transported there.

Trying to hide his excitement, he forced himself to look at the heavily bandaged Greta Bernecker and asked, 'Is what when you and Wilson separated? When he was moved to Thuringia?'

'Yes,' she replied bitterly. 'We weren't married and only SS wives could go – so I was left in Berlin.'

'Yet ended up in Cologne.'

'Yes,' she said, still sounding bitter. 'The SS offered me a pension or the chance to work in one of their hospitals. Since the pension was laughable, I accepted their offer of work here. And this *was* an SS hospital, Colonel, before you people came here.'

Bradley studied the woman carefully – or what he could see of her. Her visible features were hard, the lips sensual, slightly cruel, and her gray eyes, though hardly filled with warmth, were admirably fearless. She might be paralyzed for the rest of her life, but she was not seeking pity. You had to admire that.

'How did you come to be living with Wilson?' he asked her.

'I was working at the time as a nurse in a secret, experimental hospital just outside Berlin, and Wilson went there more than once to have some operations.'

'What do you mean by an "experimental" hospital?'

'It was devoted to Himmler's so-called anthropological experiments, mostly under the auspices of the *Ahnenerbe,* the Institute for Research into Heredity. Normally, the experiments were carried out – often under appallingly crude conditions and without anesthetic – on inmates from the concentration camps; but Wilson was obsessed with extending his life, and as soon as an experiment produced results, he made personal use of it, no matter how painful. He used himself a lot, in fact – gave his blood and urine and shit and even semen; underwent numerous tests and experiments. He had operations on his failing heart, on his stomach and joints; he even had some basic plastic surgery to make him look younger. He was a man obsessed, Colonel.'

'And no longer like a seventy-five-year-old.'

'No, the pig looked much younger.'

The vehemence was startling, but Bradley knew he could use it. 'Why did you move in with him?' he asked.

'Because he asked for me,' she said. 'It was an SS hospital and he had a lot of influence, and I wanted to have a few comforts so I went with him.'

'Why did he want a woman at his age?'

Greta Bernecker, swathed in her bandages, actually managed a smile. Bradley didn't like her, but he had to admire her guts. The combination of bandages and courage reminded him of Gladys in the ambulance in Paris. Thank God, she was now back in London – and writing letters again.

'It wasn't romance,' Greta said, 'if that's what you're thinking. No, he needed a trained nurse – one who understood his needs – and since I'd been looking after him for so long, I was an obvious choice . . . He was a vigorous man, Colonel – those operations had done him good – but he wasn't interested in normal sex. What he wanted was his own semen – for the experiments, nothing more – and since I had already done it for him, he wanted me to masturbate him and bottle his semen and arrange for its delivery to the hospital. I did the same with his piss and shit and blood. It was a job and I did it.'

'Did he treat you well?'

'Yes. In the sense that he wasn't cruel. He was neither cruel nor kind – he just didn't have such emotions – and as long as I did what he asked, he let me have what I wanted. But I thought he cared for me at least a little . . . It's a human conceit.'

'But he didn't.'

'No. Not a bit. When the order came for him to move out, he just moved out and left me. I meant nothing at all to him.'

'Did anyone mean anything to him?'

'Not that I noticed. I think he was dead from the neck down. He had no heart, no soul. He was all brain – a mathematical machine, above human emotion. I've never met a man like him.'

'Is there anything else you can tell me?'

'No. I don't think so. He left me and went to the Harz Mountains and is probably still there. I want you to find him and hang him. It's all he deserves.'

'Yes, Frau Bernecker.'

'Now I'm tired and wish to go to sleep. Good-bye, Colonel.'

'Good-bye.'

Unable to move anything else, Greta Bernecker closed her eyes. Bradley, elated and disturbed at once, walked out of the ward.

By nightfall, Bradley had left his makeshift office in the ruins of Cologne and was resting on one knee, like Davy Crockett, with his M-1 rifle in his right hand. The sky above him was filled with black clouds of bursting flak, phosphorescent streams of tracers, descending parachutists, and fat-bellied Allied bombers and gliders. All combined to make a noise that could strip the senses bare.

Bradley gazed across the river, along the length of that enormous bridge, and saw the water geysering up all around it and roaring dramatically. There were infantrymen bunched up all around him, behind him, in front of him, and as the ones in front jumped up and yelled obscenities and rushed forward, the distance between him and the bridge decreased all too rapidly.

He moved forward at a crouch, holding his M-1 like a woman. He heard the shouting and the roaring and the rumbling of tanks and half-tracks and thought that he was living a dream too intense to be borne. Then he was all alone there – not one soul in front of him; just the river and geysering water and that enormous length of bridge, plus a dizzying drop down into the river, where dead bodies were floating.

American bodies, he thought, and started shaking. I can't do this. It's too much.

'Go, dammit! *Get going!*'

Someone grabbed him by the shoulder, shook him violently, and threw him forward. He jumped up and ran like the wind, straight onto that damned bridge. The wind was worse out in the open, carrying all the noise to him, and the German shells were looping down all around him and the water was roaring. He was drenched, but kept going – he had no choice. When he glanced around him, he saw geysering water and more men falling off the bridge. Shocked, he looked away, raising his eyes to the heavens, where he saw the bombers and bursting clouds of flak and tracers painting the night. Death in war could be so beautiful – always lighting up the darkness – but it was still blood and broken bones and burning and it made him feel nauseated.

'Keep going, goddammit!'

Which he did, as he had no choice. Running above death and destruction. Advancing beneath a night sky rendered exotic by modern technology. He ran and fell down, jumped up and ran again, while the water splashed over him, fell away, and bawling men, some of whom were his friends, jerked frantically and fell down. He couldn't stop to check their pulses. Once you started, you couldn't stop. You just had to keep going, through the hellish noise and chaos, and pray to God, as he was doing right now, that you'd somehow get through it.

'Goddammit, fuckin' German sons of bitches! Goddammit, we've made it!'

Bradley didn't know who was shouting. All the voices seemed the same. They were filled with exultation and dread and a childish defiance. He just followed the other men, still running, crouched low, his M-1 bouncing, and raced through raging water into more hellish noise and emerged to a stretch of solid ground that was erupting in flame and smoke. He jumped off the bridge, bringing his M-1 up, taking aim, but the wave of men filing up behind him forced him onto the scorched ground.

It was earth and it was black and torn asunder by bomb and shell and his buddies were spreading out across it and heading into the darkness.

INCEPTION

Bradley stopped for a moment, briefly blind and deaf, drenched, then realized that he was standing on the soil of the Thousand Year Reich.

He held his rifle at the ready and marched forward, straight into Germany.

To Wilson.

Chapter Thirty-Six

The move began on the first day of April. Kammler had arrived back from the Hague at the end of March, after firing the last of his 1,050 V-2 rockets on London. He had immediately informed Ernst that as the American army was rapidly approaching Nordhausen, the whole complex was to be evacuated forthwith.

'As you know,' he said, seated in his office in the Nordhausen Central Works, his back turned to the panorama of forested hills and sky framed by the large window behind him, 'it is Himmler's intention to use Wernher von Braun and his five thousand technicians as pawns in a possible trade-off with the Allies. While I personally disapprove of this, I cannot argue with the Reichsführer, who is increasingly neurotic. I therefore had to agree to personally move them to a safe place in Oberammergau, in the Bavarian Alps. I plan to do that in four days' time. While I am thus engaged, I expect you personally to supervise the evacuation of the labor force from Camp Dora and back to Buchenwald, Bergen-Belsen, Neuengamme, Ravensbruck, and similar camps around Brunswick and Hannover. Brook no resistance. Execute those who either cannot or refuse to go. Make sure the evacuation is completed by the fourth of April, when the evacuation of the Kahla complex is due to begin. Understood?'

'Yes, sir,' Ernst replied. Although he had formerly detested Kammler's icy efficiency, he had to admire it now. 'But I fail to see how you can make it back here from Oberammergau by April 4.'

'I won't be coming back,' Kammler said. 'As soon as I've settled von Braun and his men there, where they'll be placed under guard, I'll take a plane to Kiel and join you there. Once I'm there, I'll remain with Wilson and his team until you return to Berlin to pacify Himmler.'

A tremor of fear passed through Ernst at the thought of returning to Berlin, let alone seeing the increasingly demented Himmler. '*Pacify* Himmler?' he asked tentatively.

Kammler smiled with cold, mocking amusement. 'When I saw Himmler yesterday in that quack's sanatorium in Hohenlychen, he expressed his concern that the much-discussed Schriever saucer be test-flown as soon as possible and insisted that I send you to see him, to give him a full report. To avoid any kind of suspicion, you must do just that.'

Knowing that escape from the besieged Berlin was becoming more difficult every day, Ernst did not feel too happy. He was ashamed of the tremor in his voice when he said, 'But I may not get out of Berlin in time to rejoin you in Kiel before you leave for Argentina.'

Kammler chuckled maliciously. 'You'll get out, all right,' he said. 'I've personally arranged for an SS plane to fly you out of Reinickendorf Airport on the night of April 10, which should give you plenty of time to see Himmler, sort out what he wants you to do regarding that idiot Schriever and his saucer, and make your escape before Berlin falls. Any more questions?'

'No, sir.'

Ernst saluted and left Kammler's office; then he went to work with no great enthusiasm, but considerable efficiency. No longer revolted by what he had to do, he arranged for the first of the Camp Dora inmates to be moved out that evening. He personally supervised the movement of some groups to Bergen-Belsen; some were driven there by truck or train; others were made to go on foot, forced along by the snapping dogs and cracking whips, usually without food or water. If they lacked the strength to go on, they were killed, their bodies dumped in the ditches. Even here, Allied aircraft flew constantly over the roads and railway lines, bombing the lengthy columns of prisoners and increasing the chaos. By normal standards, it was a nightmare, but Ernst took it in his stride. He was disgusted not because of any moral outrage, but because he was risking his own life to escort this ragged column of Jewish scum and other useless human rubbish to what would be their final destination.

Yes, he knew that they were marked for extermination before the Allies arrived.

He went to bed late and awoke feeling groggy. He was more alert later when Kammler's special train, with its sleeping cars and dining car and many well-armed SS guards, left with Wernher von Braun and about 500 of his V-2 experts and their families, on the first leg of the journey to Oberammergau.

Once they'd gone, Ernst paid a visit to the Kahla complex, where he found Wilson, silvery-haired but lean and remarkably fit, supervising the packing of the last of the components and drawings for the *Kugelblitz*. Because the workable model had been blown up a few weeks before, the hangar outside Wilson's office looked vast and cold.

'Will you soon be finished?' Ernst asked Wilson.

'Yes. Today, I think. Most of the components have already been boxed. Copies of the drawings and notes have been placed in three separate, portable safes and will be taken with each group, to ensure that if one lot is lost, the others will make it. Those in charge of the papers have been instructed to destroy them if there's the slightest chance of Soviet or Allied forces capturing them. And since the *Kugelblitz* itself has been blown up, there'll be no evidence left here regarding what we were doing.'

Ernst smiled. 'Good,' he said. 'Wernher von Braun's men did something similar with their papers. I gather that two of his engineers, Dieter Huzel and Bernard Tessman, hid the archives of the Peenemünde research station in the disused iron-ore mine near the village of Dorten, not far from Bleicherode. All over Germany, in disused mines and evacuated caves, the Third Reich is hiding its scientific secrets. We're the only ones who are burying ourselves with our secrets – hopefully in the Antarctic.'

'We're not burying ourselves,' Wilson corrected him. 'We're creating our own world.'

'I hope so,' Ernst replied.

He didn't see Wilson for the next two days – he was too busy supervising the continuing evacuation of Camp Dora and ensuring that those in charge of the ragged columns of prisoners would not be merciful to anyone too ill to march. As before, they were moved out at night, by truck and train or on foot. Driving back and forth in his jeep, between the trucks and the trains, along the roads filled with those marching, he heard the snarling dogs, cracking whips and gunshots, and saw bodies in the ditches or lying beside the railway tracks, their crumpled forms illuminated by moonlight and stars, or by the incandescent flashing of the exploding bombs from the planes growling overhead.

On the horizon, where the starry sky met black earth, the Allied big guns also flashed constantly, moving forward inexorably.

By the fourth day, both Camp Dora and the Nordhausen Central Works had been cleared of all prisoners. Then Ernst could begin moving out the technicians and troops. By nightfall the caves were empty, the great tunnels echoing eerily, the railway tracks leading into a darkness in which nothing stirred.

Ernst drove back to Kahla, leaving Nordhausen to the Allied troops, and found Wilson, his technicians, and the SS troops ready to leave. They went in three groups, one on each successive night. On the third night, Ernst joined Wilson and his team on the last train from Kahla.

The Allied guns sounded much louder when the train pulled away.

General Nebe was in charge and shared a car with them. His face was impassive, but his dark eyes were restless, first studying his fellow officers, then examining his pistol, then gazing out of the window at a darkness fitfully illuminated with distant explosions.

'The Americans are rich and have an endless supply of

aircraft and bombs,' he said. 'No wonder they're winning.'

After that rare observation Nebe contented himself with his restless roaming – from one carriage to another, going outside when the train stopped, checking the boxcars containing the components or the workers they had decided to take with them to help with unloading.

Occasionally there was trouble – usually a prisoner in revolt. At such times Nebe moved with calm efficiency, usually by dragging the recalcitrant, ragged figure from the boxcar, making him or her kneel by the tracks, then putting a single bullet through the back of the victim's neck and kicking the body down the incline or into the brush.

That night brought another problem, near the station of Wolfsburg. A group of resistance fighters or possibly escaped prisoners attacked the train where it had stopped to change tracks. There were perhaps a dozen men, all wearing civilian clothes, firing rifles and pistols through the windows as they leapt up from the dark field and ran alongside the train. Nebe knew what they were doing – trying to capture the engine. While his men fired on them, he hurried though the linked cars to the engine and personally protected the driver until the train had pulled out again. When it did so, Ernst saw many of the resistance men sprawled dead in the dirt.

None of this bothered Wilson, though he said, 'Nebe enjoys the smell of blood in his nostrils. I'm glad he's on our side.' Other than that, he kept to himself, snatching sleep when he could and spending his waking hours with his notebook and pen, playing with mathematical formulas to distract him from the smoldering ruins of Germany outside the train.

They were bombed before dawn, just as Ernst was about to sleep. The sudden roaring almost split his eardrums as he dived to the floor. The bending tracks shrieked and he thought of Wilson and his crates. The whole car climbed up and crashed down and then rolled onto its side. The noise was deafening. Ernst slid along the floor, hit a wall, and rolled over Wilson. He turned around and saw the windows above him, glass shattered and glinting. Men screamed or bellowed

curses as Wilson crawled toward the nearest door. A bloody
corporal formed a stirrup with his hands, Nebe planted his
boot in it, then the corporal heaved him up through a window.
More bombs fell and exploded around the train as Ernst found
a cleared space. He pulled himself up through the window. The
night roared and spewed flames. He crawled away from the
window, rolled off and crashed down to the ground outside.

'Get the crates!' he heard Wilson shout.

He saw Wilson hurrying alongside the car, which was
practically on its side. Men were dropping through the
windows and crashing down and rolling away from him. Ernst
followed Wilson, crouched low. A silhouette was bellowing
orders. Ernst clawed two or three men from his path and then
saw the boxcar. General Nebe was already there. Six or seven
trucks were near the train, and a dozen men were laboring
under Wilson's crates with smoke billowing over them.
Another bomb fell nearby. Nebe stepped forward and barked
an order. The men heaved the crate up into the truck, then
some knelt down to rest. General Nebe's jackboot glistened.
He kicked one of the lolling men. All the men jumped up,
grabbed at their weapons, and climbed into the truck. Wilson
was in there with the crates, so Ernst climbed up beside the
driver. Nebe climbed in beside him, barked an order, and the
truck started moving. The bombers passed overhead. A gray
dawn began to break. Ernst saw a truck ahead, another behind,
and was surprised to be still alive.

The dawn that broke over the devastated land was smoke-
filled. All that remained were charred trees, smoldering
buildings, and dusty columns of refugees, the latter heading
in the opposite direction, away from the Soviets. They were
gone soon enough, and the countryside became anonymous.
Eventually the trucks stopped on a hill just outside Kiel,
offering a view of the Baltic Sea beyond a broad, windblown
field.

They were at a military station, surrounded by SS guards.
An enormous bunker, half buried in the ground, its sloping
roof covered in earth and grass, dominated the middle of the

field. Presumably it could not be seen from the air.

'That's where we'll stay until the submarines arrive,' Nebe explained with a shrug. 'It's as safe as we'll find.'

The remaining workers from the concentration camps unloaded the train and carried the crates and boxes into the bunker. When they were finished, Nebe said to Ernst, 'Now we have to get rid of them. My SS men will help us load the submarines – and we have no room for this scum. Take care of the men in the bunker and leave this lot to me.'

Ernst did as he was told, glad to wash his hands of the matter, and merely looked on as Nebe's men forced the prisoners up onto the waiting trucks and then drove them away, to another field well away from the sea. He caught Wilson's glance, but the American said nothing. When they heard the distant, savage roar of the machine guns, they turned away from each other. The trucks came back empty, and when Nebe climbed down, stroking his pistol, he simply nodded at Ernst.

Another day passed. Ernst had to wait for Kammler. The SS troops passed the time by playing cards and reading magazines, while their leader, General Nebe, sat in a chair all day to breathe in the fresh sea air. The docks could not be seen from there – only a gray swathe of the Baltic – but Nebe seemed to be content to just sit there and let events take their course. Wilson, on the other hand, was as restless as ever, didn't like being in the bunker, and as usual passed the time by solving mathematical equations and toying with scientific formulas.

'Don't you ever just relax?' Ernst asked him.

'I *am* relaxed,' he replied.

Beyond the noise of the sea, it was quiet. The Allied bombers hadn't come this far yet. It was the first peace and quiet Ernst had known for a long time, but he was still glad when Kammler finally showed up to give him something to do.

'It all went well,' he said. 'The rocket team is now off our hands. Von Braun and his men were housed in army barracks in Oberammergau, behind wire and under SS guard, and will soon be joined by General Dornberger. Now you better get back to Berlin and keep Himmler happy. I'll expect you back here on the tenth. Good-bye – and good luck!'

Ernst was driven from the hidden bunker to a small, heavily guarded SS airfield nearby, where he boarded a plane. He spent the whole flight scanning the sky for Allied aircraft, but his luck held that day and soon, when he cast his gaze down, he saw the ruins of Berlin.

A pall of black smoke covered the city and was thickened with dust. The devastation was boundless.

'It's the end of the world,' Ernst said aloud, to no one in particular.

The plane touched down in hell.

Chapter Thirty-Seven

The sheer size of it was overwhelming. Bradley and Major General Ryan McArthur were inspecting the Nordhausen Central Works in the Harz Mountains, occupied the day before by the US 1st Army. The rocket production works, consisting of a series of tunnels, each approximately one mile long and joined together at regular intervals by other corridors, were located in the base of forested hills around a verdant valley; but where Bradley and McArthur were walking, in the middle of one of the gigantic tunnels, they could see only the railway tracks glinting dully in the overhead lamps and gradually disappearing into a darkness that led to a pinpoint of light – the outside world – a good half-mile away.

The tunnels were not quiet, because the army's engineers had already moved in, but Bradley's voice still echoed eerily when, stopping beneath the enormous shell of a V-2 rocket, he said, 'There's no doubt about it. Wilson had a lot to do with them. These bastards have been based on the rocket designs of our very own, shamefully neglected Robert H. Goddard, whom the German rocket engineers revered. And we both know who worked with Goddard just before he came here.'

'Wilson,' McArthur replied.

'Wilson,' Bradley agreed. He ran his hand wonderingly along the base of the enormous rocket above him – it was hanging from a jib and crane – and said, almost reverently, 'The most notable features of this baby's propulsion unit are the shutter-type valves in its fixed grill, the fuel-injection orifices incorporated in the same grill, the combustion chamber, spark plugs, and nozzle – all of which are found in a Goddard patent, issued on November 13, 1934, and reproduced in full in the German aviation magazine, *Flugsport*, in January 1939. The Germans copied the designs for their early Peenemünde rockets, then Wilson came along and contributed his own, much wider knowledge of Goddard's work to the subsequent V-1 and V-2 rocket program. Eventually the rockets attained about a hundred times more thrust than Goddard's reached back in New Mexico, when Wilson worked with him.'

'That's some achievement,' McArthur said. 'The V-2s that dropped on London are believed to have had a thrust of fifty-five thousand pounds, attained a velocity of six thousand four hundred feet per second, and could soar to an altitude of sixty-eight miles.'

'Right,' Bradley said. 'Practically on the way to the moon! And just think of the other similarities we've found so far between this baby and Goddard's original rocket. Both rockets have the same motor-cooling system; the same pump drive; the same layout front to rear; the same stabilizer; the same guidance and fuel-injection systems. The only differences are that Goddard's rocket motors used gasoline and oxygen, whereas the V-2 uses hydrogen and peroxide; Goddard's rocket fuel was liquid oxygen and gasoline, whereas the V-2 uses liquid oxygen and alcohol; and, finally, Goddard's rockets were a lot *smaller* than the V-2. So the Nazis, with Wilson's help, simply did what the US government refused to do – they took Goddard's work seriously.'

'And you think Wilson's taken it even further.'

'Yeah,' Bradley said. 'Definitely.' He stroked the V-2 one last time, then started walking McArthur along the tunnel, toward that dime-size circle of light that represented the outer world. 'The war's not even over yet, but already we've discovered a helluva lot about what the Krauts were up to, scientifically speaking. So far, Germany's scientific papers have been found hidden in tunnels like this, plus caves, dry wells, plowed fields, riverbeds, and even cesspits – and we know that the weapons we've found so far – not only these rockets, but heat-guided ground-to-air missiles, sonic-guidance torpedoes, Messerschmitt jet planes, rocket planes that fly even faster, highly advanced electrical submarines, and even the beginnings of an atom bomb project – yes, we already know that these weapons are more advanced than any *we've* got. Also, for the most part, they are based on the work of Robert Goddard and – in my estimation – on the furtherance of that work by Goddard's pupil, that goddamned traitor, John Wilson.'

'You've never called him that before,' McArthur said. 'I thought you almost admired him.'

'Yeah,' Bradley confessed. 'I do. Though I hate myself for it.'

'A genius,' McArthur said. 'A perverted genius. A mutant. . . . No wonder you can't give up the chase. It's like pursuing an alien.'

'Right. He's not real. He's a part of my dreams. And to shake him loose, to get back to the real world, I've just got to face him.'

'You'll have to face something else soon,' McArthur said. 'And I don't think you'll like it.'

Bradley was going to ask him what he meant, but was distracted when they emerged into the light at the end of the lengthy tunnel. There they viewed the grandeur of the valley below: lush green, ribboned with sparkling streams, surrounded by the densely forested hills of Thuringia, and, rising above them, the majestic, rolling peaks of the Harz Mountains.

It was certainly beautiful, a pastoral vision . . . but one scarred by spiraling columns of smoke, great fleets of Allied aircraft, marching troops and advancing trucks and tanks, and pale-brown clouds of dust – a victorious army.

'You don't believe it,' Bradley said, 'but it turns out to be true. All over Germany there are places like this – great factories and laboratories and camps hidden underground – immense, but invisible from the air, their existence once unknown. This place here – it's vast, but it's only one of many.

And what I want to know is, where was Wilson? Where is he now? And what has *he* hidden away?'

'Let's talk to someone,' McArthur said.

He led Bradley across the cleared area in front of the immense tunnel, past tanks and half-tracks and trucks disgorging more troops, under the great rockets hanging from cranes directly above, and into his jeep, which was parked by the road that led back to Erfurt. When Bradley had climbed in beside him, he drove down toward the valley, past columns of marching US troops. All the troops, Bradley suddenly noticed, looked terribly young.

God, he thought, *for the first time in years, I sincerely want this business to be over. I want Wilson to disappear* . . .

What he wanted, he then realized, was to be what Wilson was not – an involved human being.

'Where are we going?' he asked impatiently. 'I've no time for joy rides.'

'It's no joy ride,' McArthur replied. 'You're going to hell.'

He drove Bradley through Erfurt, a picturesque Renaissance town, dominated by its cathedral and fish market and old quarter, with its quaint burgher houses, Gothic alcoves, and timber-framed walls. Then on to the fields beyond, very green, though not sweet-smelling, then into the Buchenwald concentration camp, which was not quite so pretty.

The dead lay in neat rows, staring skyward, emaciated, and the living, though sometimes on their feet, did not look much better. Some of the living were dying – they had lived too long to want life – and the stench of the dead and the dying permeated the smoky air.

Bradley saw the raised gallows, the delousing rooms, the crematoria, and steeled himself to get out of the jeep and walk through hell's basement. He stuck closely to McArthur, feeling cowardly, and was glad when they had stepped up from the mud and entered a clean, cluttered office. A US Army captain was sitting on the edge of his desk, staring out through his window. He was smoking and drinking a glass of something and looked drained and haunted.

'Hi, Cap'n,' McArthur said lightly. 'How are things in the funny farm?'

'Not funny at all.'

The captain turned to face them, his eyes crimson from lack of sleep, and when Bradley saw the way he gazed at McArthur, he knew they shared the same grief.

'I've only been here two days,' the captain said, 'and it seems like two years . . . A goddamned, motherfuckin', two-year nightmare. I just can't believe this shit.' He shook his head from side to side disbelievingly, then looked up at Bradley. 'You're the guy wants to talk to my man,' he said.

'What man?'

'The guy from Kahla. The one who worked for your Wilson. An *American* was involved in all this shit? I just don't believe it!'

He shook his head again.

'Involved how?' Bradley asked him.

'Your Wilson used a lotta the people from this camp. All these scarecrows, they swear to it. Hold on, I'll go get my man. McArthur said you were coming.'

The man he brought in was rag and bone inside striped pajamas. His eyes, which seemed too big for his head, were disconcertingly bright.

'This is Colonel Mike Bradley,' McArthur's friend, Captain Shaw, said to the apparition who stood meekly by the desk. 'He wants to talk to you about Kahla. Here, take a seat.' When the corpselike individual had sat down, Shaw lit a cigarette and said, 'Colonel Bradley, this is Alex Overbeck. He's been in Buchenwald for two years and somehow survived it. He already knows who you are. Fire away, Colonel.' Then he gave the cigarette to Overbeck and kicked a chair toward Bradley. 'Sit down, Colonel.'

Bradley felt that he had to.

He opened his mouth to speak, glanced despairingly at McArthur, received only a forlorn shrug of his shoulders, then looked back at Overbeck, whose eyes, which still seemed too big and too bright, were steady upon him.

'I understand,' Overbeck said, his voice as light as a feather. 'It is difficult to talk when I look like this, but it's not your fault, Colonel. I worked for the American at Kahla. Shall we take it from there? What would you like to know?'

Bradley coughed into his fist and said, 'I didn't even know that Kahla existed. You better . . .'

The gaunt creature smiled. 'Oh, yes, sir, it exists. It is an old walled town, approximately halfway between Erfurt and Nordhausen, and the Nazis constructed another underground factory there, using labor from this camp, the closest to it.'

'We don't have a damned thing on it,' Bradley said, gradually getting used to Overbeck's appearance and feeling less ashamed.

When Overbeck inhaled on his cigarette, his cheekbones looked devoid of flesh.

'I had the impression,' he said, 'that even those at Nordhausen didn't know about it. The complex at Kahla was constructed in great haste, at a great cost in human life, and guarded by the SS Death's Head elite. The man in charge of it was SS General Hans Kammler. Next in charge was an SS captain, Ernst Stoll. When Himmler visited Nordhausen, he never came near Kahla – and it's widely believed that the other scientists, from Peenemünde, didn't even know that it existed. It was a *special* place, Colonel.'

'Are you suggesting that even Himmler might not have known about it?'

'I cannot confirm that fact, sir, but I certainly suggest it. That belief was widely held among the Buchenwald inmates who worked at the Kahla complex.'

'And the American, Wilson, was there.'

Alex Overbeck, having survived a living death, was still able to smile – and to make it sardonic. 'Yes,' he said, 'the American was working there. I was amazed, but there he was. At first I couldn't believe it – it just didn't seem credible – but though occasionally, sometimes jokingly, he was referred to as

Kruger, those who worked most closely with him addressed him as Wilson. I noted, further, that though his German was grammatically perfect, it retained a trace of an American accent. Also, though he often wore an SS uniform, it was clear to anyone but a fool that he wasn't a military man – and never had been. Besides, he was too old – that was the biggest joke of all. He looked about sixty – an extremely healthy, vigorous sixty – but there were rumors that he was much older than that, maybe even by fifteen years. Whether or not there was any truth in those rumors, he was certainly no German soldier, let alone a member of Himmler's SS Death's Head.'

'What did you do in Kahla?' Bradley asked.

Overbeck just shrugged. 'What we all did – I worked.'

'Doing what?'

'Anything they ordered me to do.'

'Let me rephrase the question: What work was the *American* involved in? What was he constructing?'

'A secret weapon,' Overbeck said as if it was self-evident. 'Not much different from the work going on at Nordhausen – rockets, submarines, jet planes . . . all sorts of highly advanced weapons.'

'And Wilson's? Specifically?'

'A disc-shaped aircraft. Jet-propelled, I think. We all made jokes about eating off the saucer – we were so poorly fed, you know. Anyway, that's what he was working on, this saucer-shaped, jet-propelled aircraft that rose straight up in the air. I hated him – to me, he was just a Nazi – but his machine was breathtaking.'

'You saw a test flight?'

'I helped wheel it out of the hangar.'

'And it made a vertical ascent?'

'Yes. Then it hovered in the air – not moving, just hovering – then shot off horizontally – so fast, I hardly knew where it went.'

'How fast?'

'Too fast to calculate. And since I couldn't judge even an aircraft's speed, I wouldn't hazard a guess.'

Bradley smiled. 'What did you do before the war, Mr Overbeck?'

'I was a priest,' Overbeck replied.

Bradley didn't know where to look. The man's strength made him feel weak. He coughed into his fist again, felt foolish, then cleared his throat. 'No wonder you can't judge the speed of aircraft.'

Overbeck blew a cloud of smoke and smiled again, his cheeks prominent. 'Anything else?' he asked.

'Yes. Is Wilson's flying saucer still at Kahla?'

'No,' Overbeck said. 'It was blown up a few days later. I think they did it to keep you or the Soviets from getting your hands on it. Which is why, when they evacuated the site, they executed everyone who'd worked there and took everything with them. I'm a lucky man, Colonel.'

'Sounds like it. How did you escape?'

Overbeck spread his hands in the air and glanced up at the ceiling, as if speaking to God. 'I wasn't at Kahla that day,' he said. 'I normally worked there – but not that day. One of the wives here – the wife of an SS officer – wanted help in the house, and since the prisoner who normally did it fell ill and was therefore shot, I was dragged out of the queue waiting for transport and given to her instead. It's as simple as that.'

Bradley studied the floor. It had the look of something solid. He needed it because his head was swimming in a whirlpool of madness.

'When did they leave?' he asked.

'Early this month,' Overbeck replied. 'Apparently Kammler went first, taking the scientists from Nordhausen—'

'Who?'

'The scientists from Peenemünde.'

'But not Wilson?'

'No. Then Camp Dora was evacuated and the prisoners returned to their former camps. And finally, on the fourth, fifth, and sixth, the scientists from Kahla departed, one group each night.'

'Do you know where they went?'

'Prisoners working at the railway stations can confirm that the three trains, one each night, were all heading for different destinations – the first one marked to terminate at Rostock, the second for Lübeck, via Rostock, and the third and last for Hamburg, via Hannover. Since all of those places were in the line of the Allied advance, it can be assumed that they were only halfway houses and that the final destination would be on the Baltic.'

'Peenemünde?' Bradley asked.

'No,' Overbeck said, stubbing his cigarette out with obvious unhappiness, then breathing deeply, as if yearning for another. 'Since the Soviets are advancing at great speed toward Peenemünde – and were even then – the only other possible destination would be a port of escape, most likely Kiel.'

Bradley straightened up in his chair. This priest who looked like death was smart.

'Can you tell me anything else?' he asked.

'Just go to Kiel,' the priest said.

Bradley glanced through the window, saw the gallows and a stream of smoke, shivered, and pushed his chair back and stood up to leave.

'Thank you,' he said.

'My pleasure,' Overbeck replied, his smile exposing his pain.

Bradley nodded at McArthur and they both left and walked back through Buchenwald. Bradley kept his gaze focused on the ground and prayed to God for deliverance ... deliverance from hatred.

His new hatred for Wilson.

'I'm going to Kiel,' he said.

Chapter Thirty-Eight

Berlin was hell on earth. The black-charred ruins stretched away as far as the eye could see, the air was thick with smoke and dust, people were queuing hopelessly for food and even water, bombs fell constantly from the Allied planes overhead, and from a mere thirty-two kilometers to the east, the guns of the Soviet army roared ominously.

Ernst's final visit to the Führer's bunker made him feel that he had entered an insane asylum. Goebbels had encouraged his unfortunate wife and six children to come and die with him and his beloved Führer when the city fell. Göring had fled to Karinhall, where his butler was waiting with fourteen carloads of treasures and expensive clothing. Bormann, after demanding the execution of Göring as a traitor, had telephoned his wife at Berchtesgaden, to inform her that he had found a hiding place for them in the Tyrol, that she was to pose as a director of refugee children, and that he had kidnapped six youngsters from the kindergarten in Garmisch to make their escaping group look more plausible. And, finally, the Führer was still babbling about secret weapons, accusing everyone of trying to betray him, ordering the arrest of that traitor, Göring, discussing the distribution of cyanide tablets with his frightened mistress, Eva Braun, veering wildly between chalk-faced exhaustion and outbursts of paranoid anger, and hoping to prolong the battle for Berlin until at least May 5, because he could then die on the same day as Napoleon.

All of this was taking place beneath the garden of the

Chancellery, upon which Allied bombs were falling with the consistency of rain.

Himmler had been to the bunker that very morning to pay his respects to the Führer on his birthday, but had then left to return to Dr Gebhardt's sanatorium. Ernst made the 120-kilometer drive to Hohenlychen, passing columns of marching German soldiers and trucks and tanks that were being bombed relentlessly by Allied aircraft.

Eventually he found himself in Himmler's study, which was practically dark. The Reichsführer was tapping his front teeth with his fingernails and looked glassy-eyed.

'I have not given up on negotiating peace,' he babbled without prompting from Ernst. 'I have instructed my masseur, Felix Kersten, to fly to Eisenhower's headquarters and discuss an immediate cessation of hostilities. I myself braved the pouring rain to meet with Norbert Masur, the representative of the World Jewish Congress, in an attempt to solve the vexing Jewish problem, explaining that I have already turned the camps at Bergen-Belsen and Buchenwald over to the Allies, have arranged the evacuation of nearly forty thousand prisoners from the camp at Sachsenhausen, and have authorized the release of another one thousand Jewish women from Ravensbrück – and still the *Schweine* was not impressed!'

He glanced wildly around the room, as if expecting to see Soviet troops bursting through the walls, then tapped his front teeth with his fingernails again and took a deep breath.

'Nor have I forgotten Count Bernadotte, of the Swedish Ministry for Foreign Affairs, with whom I am still having consultations regarding a peace-making formula. I met him yesterday and will be meeting with him again. Failing that, I will arrange a personal meeting with Eisenhower, who may be more reasonable.' He removed his pince-nez, rubbed his glassy, dazed eyes, blinked and put the spectacles on again, and glanced nervously about him.

'It is not fair,' he whined. 'Everyone wants something from me. Kersten and Schellenberg want me to overthrow the Führer with a coup d'etat. Von Krosigk has begged me to seek peace through the Pope. Meanwhile, I'm supervising secret negotiations elsewhere – and now the Führer and those *Schweine* surrounding him in the bunker suspect me of treason. Have they arrested that imbecile Göring yet? I hope so. They should shoot him!'

He pushed his chair back, paced the floor, stopped to tap his front teeth with his fingernails, then sighed and sat down again.

'All hope is not lost,' he said. 'We still have our secret weapons. My stars tell me they'll be ready just in time to turn the tide in our favor.'

Ernst heard the Soviet guns. They were only sixteen kilometers from here. He wondered how Himmler could have managed to convince himself that his secret weapons, even if they existed, could be produced in time, and in sufficient quantities, to hold back the Soviet and Allied advance, let alone turn the tide.

'I'm afraid, Reichsführer,' Ernst began, hoping to offer some common sense, 'that the secret weapons—'

'Schriever's saucer! He said it was almost finished. What news do you have of it?'

Himmler's eyes gleamed with hope – the forlorn hope of the truly mad – and Ernst, who had once feared this man, now almost pitied him.

'I'm afraid, Reichsführer, that Schriever's flying saucer won't help us now. Even if it works, it's come too late to do us much good.'

'Nonsense!' Himmler exploded, almost jumping out of his chair. 'The very sight of it will terrify the Soviets and make them turn back! As for the Allies, though they clearly are not so primitive, they will most likely do the same. I want that flying saucer to be finished! *I want to know if it works!*'

He stared wildly at Ernst, who hardly knew what to say, then drummed his fingers on the desk and took a few deep breaths. 'According to my astrological chart,' he said, sounding calmer, 'something extraordinary will occur toward the end of this month, just in time to turn the tide in our favor. I believe that's a reference to Flugkapitän Schriever's flying saucer, so I want you to go straight to Prague and find out what's happening.'

'The Soviets are advancing on Prague,' Ernst reminded him.

'You can get there before the Soviets do – so do it, Captain. For me! Do it for your Reichsführer.'

'Yes, sir,' Ernst replied, as he had in fact been planning to go there to complete Wilson's plot, but preferred to do it with Himmler's permission, to avoid suspicion. 'But what if the Soviets reach Prague before Schriever escapes with the completed saucer and his technicians?'

'In such circumstances you must destroy the flying saucer and hide all the papers relating to it. Then, when the tide turns in our favor, we can rebuild the saucer.'

'Very good, Reichsführer,' Ernst said, now having permission to do what he had planned to do anyway.

'Nevertheless, that should not happen. The Soviets are still a good way away. I see no reason why you cannot get to Prague and back here again before the end comes – and I expect you to bring me good news.'

'I will, Reichsführer. I promise.'

'Good-bye, Captain. And good luck.'

'Heil Hitler!'

'Heil Hitler.'

Ernst saluted, then walked to the study door. He opened it, started out, then glanced back to take a last look at his once-frightening, all-powerful Reichsführer. He was already slumped over his desk, studying his astrological charts, neurotically tapping his front teeth with his fingernails and making loud, sighing sounds. He was all alone in that gloomy room, a shadow-figure, a mirage, a man disappearing into himself, to be lost in his own dream.

He was covering his face with his hands when Ernst quietly closed the door.

The car journey to Prague took nearly eight hours, was further hindered by more Allied bombing raids and roads filled with columns of troops, and was not without a great deal of tension.

Bypassing Dresden in the dead of the night, Ernst saw the darkness illuminated by the flashing of the Soviet guns, where they were firing from the Oder River. The Soviet army was very close indeed. It had already captured most of Pomerania, Poland, and Hungary, and Ernst was thankful that it was closer to Berlin than to where he was going.

He arrived at Prague in the early morning. It smoldered just like Berlin. Ernst heard bombing and the continuing roar of the Soviet guns, and realized that it was only a matter of days before Prague fell also.

The war was practically over.

Indeed, the first news he received upon reporting to the SS officer in charge of security at the BMW plant on the outskirts of the city – placed in charge, as he was soon informed, because of fears that the plant would be overrun by groups of Czechoslovak patriots – was that by dawn that very morning, Berlin had been completely encircled and its last free airports overrun by the Red Army.

Now there was no way in or out. The fate of the city was sealed.

'You can't go back there,' the SS commander, Lieutenant Günter Metz, informed him. 'You might as well stay here. Wait until we see which way the Soviets are moving, then make your escape.'

Ernst had no intentions of remaining in Prague, but he complimented the officer on his keen thinking and then asked to be directed to Flugkapitän Schriever. He was escorted to the well-guarded East Hall of the great factory. There, remarkably, with a lack of realism fully the equal to that of Himmler and the rest of them, Schriever was still racing to complete his flying saucer, which was resting on its mobile steel platform and surrounded by engineers.

When Schriever saw Ernst walking toward him, he could not hide his frown.

'Captain Stoll!' he exclaimed, trying to recover, though not too successfully. 'What a pleasant surprise!'

Still smarting, even after all these years, from the knowledge that he had been passed over by the German scientific fraternity to make way for second-raters like Schriever, Ernst realized that he was going to enjoy doing what he now had to do – which was to check that Schriever had not, by some combination of luck and thievery, made any unexpected advances with his design and ensure that what he *did* have was destroyed before the Soviets reached here.

'I have been sent by Himmler,' he said without preamble, 'to check on the progress of your flying saucer. Is it actually flying yet?'

'Unfortunately, no,' Schriever replied, wiping his oily hands on a rag, 'but we should have it ready any day now – and then we will test it.'

'You *do* realize, do you not, that the Soviet Army is advancing on a front that extends from Görlitz to Vienna and will soon be marching right into Prague?'

'Yes, Captain, I know; but a drastic shortage of components – ball bearings for the ring plates, new heat-resistant wing discs – led to a bigger delay than anticipated – and then the Soviets captured Breslau, where Habermohl was working, and since we then had to do his work as well, we were held back even more. Nevertheless, we've replaced the original gas-turbine rotors with jet engines – and the saucer you see before you, if test-flown, will not let us down.'

What Ernst was looking at was one of Wilson's crude, earlier models: a wide-surface ring that consisted of adjustable wing discs that could be brought into the appropriate position for vertical or horizontal flight while rotating around a fixed, cupola-shaped cockpit. Now powered by Schriever's addition of adjustable jet engines, it would, in Ernst's judgment, rise vertically a few feet, but then, once the angle of the jets was adjusted, go out of control – just as Wilson had said it would.

Although pleased that Schriever had made no unexpected progress and was still deluding himself with this piece of aeronautical rubbish, Ernst still knew that it was imperative that the Soviets did not learn about any aspect of Projekt Saucer – at least not until Wilson wanted them to know, which would be in the future. He therefore said what had to be said – and took pleasure from doing so.

'It has to be destroyed,' he told Schriever, 'before the Soviets arrive.'

'What?' Schriever exclaimed, shocked.

'You heard me the first time,' Ernst said, thinking, *How sweet is vengeance!* 'We have to destroy it.'

'But it hasn't even been test-flown yet!'

'We still have to destroy it.'

Schriever's assistant, Miethe, arrived, also wiping his hands on an oily rag. Schriever glanced at him with widening eyes, then turned back to Ernst.

'Why?' he asked.

'To prevent it from falling into the hands of the Soviets, of course,' Ernst told him as flatly as possible.

'But we can arrange a test flight almost immediately!'

'You may be too late. The Soviets are advancing fast. We're also concerned about Czechoslovak patriots who already are causing trouble in Prague and may have men planted here, just waiting for the Soviets to get close.'

Schriever started to look desperate. 'But without even a test flight . . .'

'I'm sorry. We can't think about that now. We must destroy the machine.'

Looking increasingly suspicious, and even aggressive, Schriever glanced automatically at Miethe, who was cleverly keeping his mouth shut, then turned back to Ernst and said, 'I've been receiving instructions direct from Himmler's office – not from Nordhausen – so why are you suddenly taking over?'

'Nordhausen was evacuated and Himmler sent me to arrange the same thing here.'

'We're evacuating now?'

'Do you wish to shake hands with the Soviets?'

'Why can't we take the saucer with us?'

'The risk is too large. We might get captured. We don't want them to get it.'

Schriever looked even more suspicious. 'Do you have written authority, Captain Stoll?'

'No. Of course not. Officially, this project doesn't exist. No project – no papers.'

'Then why did Himmler's office not contact me?'

'Berlin was being encircled,' Ernst lied blandly, 'and Himmler's phones were cut off. The city, as you know, has since been cut off – so you can't ring through to them. Now please do as I say, Flugkapitän Schriever, and stop all this nonsense.'

'Himmler *may* have ordered the saucer to be destroyed, but not without a test flight. I *insist* on a test flight.'

'When can it be arranged?'

'By tomorrow morning. Ten o'clock sharp.'

'Fair enough,' Ernst said.

He went straight to the commander, the young lieutenant, and gained his trust by sharing confidences with him, as if with an old friend.

'He can't be trusted,' he told Metz. 'We've had problems with him before. Himmler asked me to ensure that this project was obliterated, but Schriever, if his test flight is a failure, will insist on more time. We have to destroy it, no matter what, and I need you and your men. Will you help?'

'Of course, sir!'

Ernst did not sleep well that night. He rarely slept well anymore. His sleep was haunted by nightmares of death and destruction, by dreams of Ingrid and his children and all his other failures and betrayals.

It was dreams and nightmares, but also constant noise: the bombers growling overhead, the exploding bombs, the wailing sirens, the Soviet guns belching in the distance, but sounding closer each hour.

You couldn't tell how close they were – you never saw them; you just heard them – and Ernst, who had once dreamed of glory, was glad to get out of bed.

It was just after dawn. He wandered around the East Hall. He saw the sun burning through mist and the pall of smoke from the bombing raids, the smoke drifting from the city to the fields that were pockmarked with shell holes. He tried to think of another world – a normal world, without war – but every image in his head contained violence, destruction, blood and tears, flame and smoke – all created by a dream of omnipotence, the perversion of science.

He had helped to create it.

He was hungry but couldn't eat, so he lit a cigarette instead, and smoked it while gazing across the destroyed fields at the ruins of Prague. He smoked a lot that morning, just kneeling there, waiting, and then stood up when the doors of the East Hall opened and the engineers walked out.

Ernst went to a telephone in the hall and phoned SS lieutenant Günter Metz.

'Bring your men down,' he said.

Schriever arrived with Miethe, nodded at him, then ordered the saucer to be wheeled out of the hall. While this was happening, Lieutenant Metz arrived with a demolition team and a squad of seasoned SS troops, all carrying weapons. They spread themselves around the sunlit clearing outside as the retractable wheels of the steel platform were being withdrawn to let it become the saucer's launching pad.

Schriever, when he saw the demolition team, became flushed with anger.

He climbed into the saucer and strapped himself in, then Miethe replaced the Perspex lid on the cupola and made sure it was locked. Then he climbed back down the ladder and pulled it away. Schriever started the saucer when Miethe had returned to the safety of the concrete bunker.

It roared into life. Yellow flames spat at the platform. The flames shot back up and spread out obliquely to form a great fan of fire. The flying saucer roared and shuddered. It lifted off the platform, hovered just above it, making the steel turn redhot, then it ascended a few more feet and swayed dangerously from side to side. It roared even louder, belching flame and smoke in a fury. Then, unable to go higher, Schriever tried to go horizontally – but the minute the jets on one side were raised, the machine tilted over. It hit the ground and rocked wildly like a dropped coin, then its engines cut out.

There was a brief, shocking silence.

'Destroy it,' Ernst said.

Miethe ran to the saucer, clambered up its tilted side, released the locks holding down the canopy, and helped Schriever out. Looking shocked and angry at once, he slid down the body on his backside, dropped to the ground, and rubbed his chin with his right hand, then saw the SS demolition team walking toward his precious creation.

'No!' he bawled. 'Damn you, *no!*' He hurried across to Ernst, fists balled, eyes blazing, while Miethe and the other engineers fanned out behind him.

They were going to protect the saucer, to keep the demolition team at bay, but when Ernst unholstered his pistol and aimed it at Schriever, Lieutenant Metz's squad of SS troops raised their submachine guns and took aim on the hapless engineers.

Schriever froze where he stood, about four feet away from Ernst, and the engineers behind him did exactly the same.

'Let the demolition team through,' Lieutenant Metz said, 'or suffer the consequences.'

The engineers looked around them, at that circle of submachine guns, then parted to let the demolition team walk up to the saucer. Schriever glanced over his shoulder, saw them unwinding the plunger cables, then looked back at Ernst, his dark eyes appalled. 'My life's work! We have to at least have the chance to correct what's wrong. One more day . . . a few days at most . . . It's too important . . . *You can't do this!*'

'Shut up,' Ernst said. 'You damned fool.' Then he cocked his raised pistol.

We want no witnesses of any kind, Wilson had said, *unless they're in the Antarctic . . .*

That meant Schriever and Miethe and all the rest of these engineers. When the Schriever saucer, though relatively seless, was blown up, they would all disappear as well.

Schriever's eyes became wider.

'You wouldn't!'

'We would and we will. The whole business ends here.'

He glanced over Schriever's shoulder at the demolition
eam and saw the man in charge of the plunger preparing to
ean on it.

'Good-bye, Schriever,' Ernst said.

The flying saucer exploded. No, it didn't – something else
lid – an eruption of silvery light and boiling smoke and
eysering earth . . . right *beside* Schriever's saucer.

Confused, Ernst hesitated. He saw Schriever ducking,
queezed the trigger, fired too late, and saw the man running
way as the ground erupted around him.

The shells were whistling in from the east – Soviet shells,
rom the big guns. Then the soldier fell on the plunger – was
hrown forward, in fact, on a wave of erupting soil – and
chriever's saucer disappeared in a ball of fire and spat debris
verywhere.

'Shit!' Ernst hissed as the engineers scattered and the SS
uns started chattering. Then he sprinted straight into the
haos, trying to take aim at Schriever as he ran away.

The SS troops were spreading out, firing wildly from the
ip – not at the engineers, who were running across the field
ast the smoldering debris of the saucer, but back in the
irection of the East Hall, toward which Schriever was
unning. They were not firing at him but at the other men
ouring out, most of them wearing civilian clothes but
eturning the gunfire.

Schriever saw them as well – he was in fact running toward
hem – and he turned left and cut across the hangar doors and
ıst about made it.

A Soviet shell saved him – exploding right behind him,
etween the men who were running out of the East Hall and
he SS troops firing at them.

Ernst managed one shot but missed. He was blinded briefly
y flying soil, cursed and rubbed his stinging eyes, then saw

the men who were wearing civilian clothes still running at him and firing.

Czechoslovak patriots! he thought. *Coming out of the factory. The Soviets must be in Prague!*

Then he saw Schriever, cutting back across the field, heading with the other engineers in the general direction of Prague. The ground was erupting between them, shells exploding around the factory, but Ernst went after him anyway because, given the Czechoslovak patriots, it was the only direction left.

The SS troops were holding their ground, spreading across the remains of the saucer, firing their submachine guns at the advancing resistance men while being cut down by bullets or blown apart in explosions.

A burning light erased all of it. An appalling roaring filled the world. Ernst was slapped by a wave of heat, the breath was sucked from his lungs, he was picked up and spun wildly in the air, and then grass and earth rushed at him. He plunged into a silent darkness, losing his senses. Later he heard a ringing sound . . . Eventually he opened his eyes to find himself on the ground, lying on the rim of a smoldering shell hole near a parked SS truck.

The battle had moved away from the East Hall. It was ending in the shell-torn field with the SS troops being massacred by the greater number of Czechoslovak patriots. The engineers, including Schriever and Miethe, were still running, much farther away, toward Prague.

Let Schriever talk about his flying saucer, Ernst thought, sitting upright and shaking his head to clear it. *It will become just another red herring. Another aid to confusion. It will suit us just fine.*

He glanced carefully around him, looking for other resistance fighters, but saw only a clearing filled with the bodies of dead Czechs and Germans. After climbing to his feet, he checked himself for broken bones, found himself to be fit, then clambered up into the troop truck, which still had the key in the ignition. He turned the engine on, then drove across the grassy field to get away from the factory, which was almost certainly now overrun. He managed to get to the road without being stopped.

From there he drove to the nearest Luftwaffe airfield, which was luckily still held by Germans. He pulled rank in order to commandeer a light plane, then ordered the reluctant pilot to fly him to the SS airport near Kiel.

When the plane had ascended, he looked down through the clouds at the pall of smoke hanging over Prague. Moving in on the city, like ants advancing in numerous lines toward their anthill, were long columns of Soviet tanks and men.

It was something to see.

Chapter Thirty-Nine

Bradley was scared. He had been well trained for this by OSS, had rehearsed it so many times, even making the goddamned jumps, but now that it was real and he was doing it with the professionals – worse, in pitch darkness and in the middle of a war zone – he was not as confident as he had been during his training.

He glanced at his watch. Five minutes to go. His heart missed a beat and he looked along the aircraft, through that dim light, and saw the men of the 82nd Airborne Division facing one another in the belly of the plane, looking bulky with their parachutes and helmets, not frightened at all.

Well, certainly not showing it, as he was convinced he was doing. His heart was racing and he was sweating, though his hands felt too cold, and he knew that the urge to have a piss was also due to his fear.

He was fifty years old, for Chrissakes, and shouldn't be doing such things!

He tried to forget what was going to happen by thinking instead of Gladys, who had continued to write him her wonderful, witty letters from her sickbed in a hospital in London. Apparently she had been shipped back to London from Paris, was making a good recovery, and would soon be walking again, but she badly missed having him in bed beside her. She had also informed him, by letter, that she had scribbled his name about fifty or sixty times on the plaster cast on her broken leg and all the nurses, doctors, and visitors now knew who he was.

Goddammit, he loved her.

She certainly made him feel good. Thinking about her made his heart race. It raced even more when he looked again at his wristwatch and realized that the jump would soon be starting.

Closing his eyes, he breathed deeply, trying to steady his racing heart, and saw, as he had so often since that one visit, the gallows and crematoria of Buchenwald, the priest's gaunt, haunted face.

He had gone back to the priest, feeling trapped in a web of horror, and had learned a lot more from him about life in the concentration camps and underground factories. The priest had told him about the beatings, about the all-too-public hangings, about the shots to the back of the neck and the daily gassings and burnings. He had also told him about worse things – most notably the medical and surgical experiments, performed on men, women, and children, often without anesthetics.

Apparently the Nazi doctors had been trying to learn what could not be gleaned from experiments on animals: the limits of human suffering; the effects of extreme heat and cold, of starvation and sleeplessness; the possibility of survival without certain vital organs; artificial insemination; the swopping of healthy limbs; the potential for extending the human life span by medical, biological, and mental mutation – all of which meant unimaginable pain and horror for the unfortunates used . . . And Wilson, whether or not he had been involved directly, had not only shown an interest in the dreadful experiments, but had willingly used the people in the camps as part of his work force.

The man was a monster.

Or, as Major General McArthur had said, some kind of mutant.

Bradley shivered in his harness, then checked his wristwatch again. When he saw that he had one minute left, his stomach almost turned over.

What the hell was he doing here, with the 82nd Airborne

Division, about to parachute into the darkness?

He was searching for Wilson.

He had left Nordhausen with the US 1st Army, with which he had traveled so far and seen so much action. He had gone as far as Paderborn with them, but there they had parted company, because he was intent on reaching Kiel before the Soviets took it. He had commandeered a jeep and driven himself through a landscape of appalling destruction, along roads filled with advancing Allied troops and fleeing refugees, past enormous open-air prison camps that stretched as far as the eye could see, to the town of Minden on the Weser, which had recently been occupied by the US 9th Army. There Bradley had attached himself to the British 2nd Army, which, reinforced by the US 82nd Airborne Division, was about to launch itself on the drive toward Lübeck, the doorway to Kiel.

Just before the attack was launched, Bradley had learned that a British SOE headquarters had been set up in Weser. When he paid them a visit, he found himself face to face with his old friend Lieutenant-Colonel Mark Wentworth-King.

'Kiel?' Wentworth-King said in reply to Bradley's query. 'Difficult to say who'll get there first, old chap – General Montgomery's 2nd Army, now closing in on Hamburg, the 1st Canadian Army, now closing in on Oldenburg, or the bloody 2nd White Russian Army, now spreading right along the Baltic Coast. If the Russians get there first, you won't get your man, so you'd better move sharpish. I suggest, dear boy, if you have the heart for it, joining a contingent of your very own 82nd Airborne Division, which, to avoid our own guns, is about to parachute down just beyond Neumünster, near Kiel's ship canal. From there they're hoping to fight their way into Kiel. What age did you say you are?'

Now here he was, fifty years old, preparing to jump out of his plane and parachute down into Germany . . . Maybe because Wentworth-King had goaded him into it, the smart son of a bitch.

Goddamned Brits! he thought.

'Hitch up!' someone bawled. '*Hitch up!*'

The door was pulled open and an angry wind howled in. The paratroopers connected their ripcords along the length of the plane. Bradley did the same, standing up like all the rest of them, feeling shaky and not sure if he could make it, but trying to hide that fact.

With the hatch open, the noise was dreadful – a combination of rushing wind and the roaring engines and whipping canvas flaps – but the men shuffled inexorably toward the opening, taking Bradley there with them. The flight sergeant was bellowing instructions laced with obscenities – and Bradley thought he heard other noises outside, though he couldn't be sure. The plane was shaking badly, as if about to fall apart, and he fought the urge to sit down again. Then the flight sergeant bellowed again, a man ahead shouted, the queue moved, and Bradley realized that the first man had jumped out and the others were following,

'Jesus Christ!' he said softly.

The men went out one by one, some bellowing just like the flight sergeant. Bradley swallowed, licked his lips, and wanted to be sick – and was shocked at just how loud the noise was three men away from that open hatch.

Two men.

One man.

The man disappeared through the hatchway, leaving Bradley exposed. The wind almost floored him, roaring at him beating around him, but he stepped forward, was *jerked* forward – yes, the flight sergeant had grabbed his shoulder – and he saw his open mouth, the glint of fillings, heard him bellowing. 'Fucking jump!' were the words he heard as the roaring wind sucked him out.

He was swept back and up, his stomach somewhere in his throat, and saw spinning lights, maybe stars, perhaps the moon, and heard the roaring of engines and the magnified rush of wind and then plunged down. He was falling! His parachute hadn't opened! Then he was jerked up violently, a puppet on a string, and suddenly he fell down a black well of silence and saw darkness around him.

Darkness? No. He was falling through clouds. He saw other figures falling all around him on the end of their parachutes. They looked ghostly in the clouds, silhouetted in a gray mist, above and below and all around him as if in a dream.

Then he dropped down below the clouds and was dazzled by dawn light.

More than that . . . the whole world.

Or so it seemed to him. He thought he could see its curved edge. It was actually the horizon, far away, beyond the land's end, a strip of gray stippled by rays of sunlight and spitting fountains of water. It was the Baltic Sea. The fountains of water were explosions. The sky above the sea was filled with black dots – Allied bombers – and the land, now below him, all around him, racing upward, was divided by streams and roads and endless, shifting black lines that, he realized with a shock when he saw the tracers and billowing smoke, were columns of refugees and soldiers passing each other, going in opposite directions, while the war raged about them.

The ground rushed up at Bradley as he fell down through the streaming smoke and noise of the continuing battle.

He braced himself for the landing.

Wilson saw the parachutists through his binoculars and knew they were at least an hour's march away. He turned away from them, scanning east and west, and saw the smoke of battle in both directions as the Soviets and Allies advanced. Then he looked at the Baltic Sea beyond land's end, a few miles away, and saw that the sky was filled with Allied bombers now pounding the port of Kiel.

'We have to leave right now,' he said to General Nebe.

'I *know* that,' Nebe replied. 'We've already loaded the trucks. I'm taking just enough men to help us unload at the harbor and the rest are being left here to hold off the enemy.'

'Do they know what you're asking of them?'

'These are SS troops, Wilson. SS troops are trained to obey and take pride in doing so.'

'Lucky us,' Wilson said, then glanced at Ernst Stoll. The SS captain had made it back from Prague in the nick of time, bringing with him the news about Schriever and the latest troop movements. Now, because over the past few days he had actually *seen* what was happening, he was obviously keen to move.

'Let's go,' he said.

Wilson nodded. Stoll led them out of the bunker, away from the officers quarters and past the troop accommodations, along bleak concrete corridors with reinforced, low ceilings and machine-gun crews at each open window, then around the weapons room and ammunition dumps and storage huts, up the sloping ramps, and outside. There the trucks were parked in the covered, camouflaged garage, with the troops that were actually guarding them clambering up inside.

One of the trucks was special, because it carried the crate containing the remaining components of Wilson's saucer. Wilson insisted on riding in that, instead of in Nebe's staff car. Shrugging, Ernst Stoll climbed in beside him, saying 'Why not indeed?' They sat side by side, the large wooden crate looming over them, then the trucks coughed to life and moved out in column.

'I've thought about it,' Wilson said.

'About what?' Ernst replied.

'This Schriever business. The fact that he's still alive. I don't think it matters that much – and may even help us. If, after the war, Schriever starts talking about his flying saucer, it will lead everyone in his direction. They'll check out his drawings and conclude, correctly, that the saucer he constructed was unworkable. After that, if anyone reports seeing *our* flying saucers, they'll almost certainly be treated as cranks. Once that happens, we can create a smokescreen of confusion and fly our own saucers with impunity. What do you think?'

'I think you're right,' Ernst said.

Wilson smiled and patted him on the shoulder. The German had lost everything in the world and now only had him.

'Good,' Wilson said.

The trucks traveled down to Kiel. A fine mist veiled the

dawn. Aircraft growled overhead, shells exploded on land and sea, and the big guns were thundering in the east, west, and south. Wilson pressed his hand against the rocking crate and then they came to the docks.

The truck squealed to a halt. The crate shook and then was steady. General Nebe's dark eyes emerged from the drifting mist and he motioned them out. Wilson clambered down first and was surprised at how dark it was. The black water reflected the lamps beaming down on the submarines. He glanced toward the warehouses. Nebe was murmuring to his troops. The men formed up in a neatly spaced line against the wall of a hangar.

'I'm going to take a demolition team,' Ernst informed him, 'and get them to lay a trip-wire across the road we've just come down, to blow up anything coming after us.'

'Very good,' Wilson said.

He almost felt proud of Stoll – this new Stoll was his own creation – but as pride was a destructive human weakness, he concentrated elsewhere.

Some men were unloading his precious crate – slowly, very carefully – and eventually, when they got it out of the truck, they hitched it up to a crane.

The crane started groaning.

Wilson glanced at the submarine anchored just below him: U-977. There were men on the deck, arranging themselves around the hold. Chains rattled and Wilson saw his precious crate dangling over the water. There was a moment's hesitation. The crate jerked up, then started spinning. Hands reached up and guided it down and then it dropped out of sight.

General Kammler appeared on deck, accompanied by the commander of the submarine, Captain Heinz Schaeffer, whom Wilson had previously met in the Harz Mountains when Schaeffer was inspecting the new XX1 electric submarines. Both men climbed up the ladder to the quay and walked straight to General Nebe.

Kammler talked in a low voice, glancing repeatedly along the docks. His shadow trailed out along the wet stones and touched Wilson's feet. Nebe turned away and murmured something to his sergeant. Kammler took a flashlight from his pocket and flashed it three times.

Wilson glanced along the dock, where another truck was approaching. The truck shuddered as it started to slow. Kammler walked up to Wilson and introduced him to Schaeffer. They shook hands as the truck driver changed gears and turned in toward them.

The SS troops remained silent – a line of men along the hangar, all of them with their weapons in their hands slanted over their chests. They were as still as they were silent. Their discipline was remarkable. The sergeant stepped back and bellowed an order, and the troops performed a precise about-turn and froze facing the wall. Wilson heard their guns rattling. Their snapping boot heels left an echo. The truck stopped, overlooking the harbor, and its ramp was thrown down.

A shocking noise split the silence, almost deafening Wilson. The soldiers lined up along the hangar wall were suddenly jerking and screaming. Wilson glanced up at the truck and saw a barrel spitting flame. The machine gun was roaring and rattling as the men died and fell. When Wilson blinked, there was silence. A gray smoke drifted lazily. The high wall of the hangar was filled with holes and splashed with fresh blood.

All the men lay on the ground, sprawled across one another, their pupils reflecting the lamps beaming down on their faces.

Schaeffer turned away, but Kammler looked almost bored. Nebe took his pistol from its holster and then cocked its hammer. He nodded to his sergeant and they both approached the pile of bodies. Nebe fired the first shot. His sergeant fired the second. They took turns, bending over the bodies, the gunshots reverberating eerily while the morning light brightened. The coup de grace seemed to take a long time, though it didn't take long at all. When it was finished, Nebe turned away and gently waved his free hand.

Some men jumped out of the truck. The machine-gun barrel clanged. Nebe returned his pistol to its holster and walked away from the bodies. There was no sweat on his brow. His dark eyes were unrevealing. He simply nodded at Kammler and Schaeffer, and they walked down to the submarine.

Wilson waited until Ernst Stoll had returned, wanting to check his reaction. Stoll glanced at the pile of bodies, at the blood on the walls and ground, then said -unemotionally, 'Now there are no witnesses to the number of the submarine. We've also wired the road leading onto the quay. I think we should go now.'

'We *are* going,' Wilson said, 'but you have to destroy the evidence. The submarine's leaving now, since the light will show us up, but we're going to wait just outside the harbor until you get to us. Will you do that?'

'Yes,' Stoll said.

Wilson, who knew a disciple when he saw one, just nodded and turned away, then climbed down the ladder to the submarine.

Having landed in one piece, Bradley marched for an hour with the 82nd Airborne Division and arrived at the camouflaged SS bunker as sunlight bled through the mist. He ran across a windblown field, crouched low, a survivor – then all hell broke loose. German machine guns and bazookas opened up, and he found himself right in the thick of it.

It was a brief but bloody battle, because the Krauts refused to give in, but eventually the paratroopers succeeded by sheer dint of numbers to take control of the bunkers.

Bradley was still with them, very glad to be alive, but he didn't forget what he had come for and asked to question the prisoners. There weren't all that many – the fields and bunkers were strewn with corpses – but that simply made it easier to find out what he wanted to know.

'I don't know what we were guarding,' the first SS prisoner said. 'I can only state that I was disgusted to be asked to risk my life to protect an American scientist. I thought that was too much.'

'And where did the American scientist go?' Bradley asked.

'With all the others,' the SS sergeant said in disgust. 'With all the runaway generals and traitors – to the harbor of Kiel. To the submarine dock.'

'When?'

'Half an hour ago.'

'Oh, my God!' Bradley exclaimed, then turned to the commander of the 82nd Airborne Division. 'We've got to get down there right away. That son of a bitch is escaping.'

'My orders were to capture and *hold* this bunker,' the commander told him. 'I've been given no authority to go to Kiel. Sorry, Bradley. Can't help you.'

'I could go out there and steal a goddamned jeep.'

'I'm not looking, Colonel.'

Bradley hurried outside, feeling as if he were going mad, impelled by the need to fit a face to the man who had haunted him. It had been nearly fifteen years – so long that he'd turned gray and lost his wife and found Gladys . . . and fought a war he was too old to fight and become an obsessed man.

Yes, obsessed – just like his quarry, though in a different way. As he climbed into the jeep and turned the ignition on, he was convinced that he'd go out of his mind if he didn't get to the end of this.

He had to fit a face to the man whose dreams had made him inhuman.

A genius.

A mutant.

Bradley still could not accept it. As Gladys had said, he was a moral man. He believed that man was both good and evil, a creature of moral choice, and he had to know if someone like Wilson could be as natural as air.

He had to know if Wilson's lack of humanity had been formed in the womb – perhaps by his intelligence – if Wilson's inhumanity, his extraordinary lack of feeling, was as innocent as sunlight or rain, as helpless as a child being born, as alien as Mars.

He had to know if Wilson mirrored his own darker side.

'Goddamn you!' he said aloud as he drove away from the

bunkers. 'I won't let you stay invisible any longer. I'm gonna make you real.'

Then he drove down to Kiel, down that steep, narrow road, seeing the boats out at sea, the water geysering up around them, the bombs falling from the fat-bellied planes flying out of the clearing mist. It was the same everywhere – the whole world was at war – and the beautiful earth, its clean air, was being ruined for all time. Death and destruction, smoldering ruins and flame and smoke – Man's genius, his creativity, his science, had sowed what was now being reaped. Not Man, but men – individuals – those like Wilson – and the rubble of Europe, the conflagration of this mighty conflict, was the product of scientific genius used without moral constraints or commonplace feelings.

This was Wilson's inheritance.

Bradley had to see his face, to know if evil was innocent, and he drove like a lunatic into the docks.

He only saw the wire stretched across the road when it was too late to stop.

The wire snapped and flew past him on a sheet of scorching flame as the distant Baltic Sea turned upside-down and his body exploded. He saw whirlpools of light, heard his heartbeat in silence, returned through a sibilance, a ringing, and saw the world turning over. The sea, which had been the sky, became the Baltic Sea again, and he saw the wrecked ships, the other debris of the many air raids, then rolled onto his belly and felt the pain devouring his skin.

'Oh, God.' he groaned. 'Jesus.'

He was hurt pretty badly, but refused to give up. Black and blistered, burning hot and cold, in anguish, almost crying, he crawled away from his upturned jeep, from the fierce, scorching heat, toward the water glittering blackly in morning light. The smoke billowed around him, stung his eyes, choked his lungs, and each time he coughed, he was whiplashed by a spasm of pain. He was hurting so bad he wanted to die, but he just couldn't stop. He simply had to see what he had come for and that kept him going.

'Goddammit!' he gasped, keeping himself aware, fighting

the urge for oblivion. 'Think of Wilson! *Remember!*'

So he managed to crawl forward, along the quay, by the docks, the stones covered in expelled shells and reeking of cordite – and wet, as he suddenly realized, not with rain, but with blood.

Whose blood?

What the hell . . . ?

He shuddered and gasped and put his head down, trying to think, listening to the bombers rumbling overhead, the gunfire in the distance. The war was still raging, coming closer to its bloody end, and he couldn't believe how far he had traveled to arrive at this nightmare.

The stones beneath him were wet with blood.

Whose blood?

'Goddammit,' Bradley whispered to the wet stones. 'Gimme a break here!'

The pain whipped him again and he sobbed and then gritted his teeth. When he raised his head, he turned slightly to the side and looked out to sea.

There was a submarine out there.

At first he thought he was imagining it, but then he saw it more clearly, still on the surface, just outside the harbor, obviously preparing to go to sea but not yet submerged.

Bradley knew who was on it.

He sobbed with frustration, clenched his fist, and hammered the wet stones.

Then, when he heard approaching footsteps, he looked up again.

An SS officer was walking toward him, holding a pistol in his right hand, his shadow stretched obliquely across the quay in the morning's pale light. He stopped by Bradley's head, looked down at him, then knelt beside him and took hold of his hair to jerk his head up.

He placed the barrel of his Luger pistol against Bradley's temple.

'Who are you?' he asked.

'Mike Bradley. An American.'

'It's an American uniform, I grant you, but your German is excellent.'

'I'm an American. Believe me. I'm a member of OSS.'

'The Americans haven't got this far yet, so what are *you* doing here?'

Bradley started to reply, almost blacked out with pain, recovered and pointed weakly at the distant submarine. 'Is he out there?'

'Who?'

'You know who. That son of a bitch, Wilson.'

'Your compatriot.'

'No!'

'Your friend. Your national hero. The man we Germans now revere. You want Wilson. You've come here alone for him? You must want him a lot.'

'I do.'

'Tell me why.'

Bradley didn't know what to say. There was no way to explain it. Besides, this handsome, civilized SS officer was going to blow his brains out.

'He's a traitor,' Bradley tried.

'Not enough,' the German replied. 'You have the look of someone obsessed, so tell me why you want Wilson.'

Bradley, who thought he was dying, needed to confess. 'I have to see his face,' he said. 'I've wanted to see it for years. I have to fit a face to the man to know what he's about. It's as simple as that.'

He thought he heard the German sighing. He looked up and saw him smiling. The German removed the pistol from Bradley's temple and aimed it at the warehouse.

'You want to know what Wilson's about?' he said. 'Then look in there, my friend.'

Bradley managed to raise his head. He looked into the warehouse. At first he couldn't see – it was pretty dark in there – but then his eyes adjusted to the gloom beyond the doors, and he saw an open-topped German truck, piled high with some rubbish.

No, not rubbish.

Piled high with the bullet-riddled, bloody corpses of uniformed SS troops.

'Jesus Christ!' Bradley whispered.

He shuddered with revulsion and a touch of disbelief, then the German jerked his head up again and waved the Luger in front of him.

'Bradley?' he asked, confirming the name. 'Mike Bradley of OSS?'

'Yeah,' Bradley said. 'Right.'

'And you've been pursuing Wilson for a long time?'

'Nearly fifteen years,' Bradley said.

The German gave a low whistle. 'That's a long time, Mr Bradley. And although you're in a very bad way, you still look determined.'

'I am,' Bradley told him. 'I won't give up on this, believe me.'

'We'll remember that, Bradley.'

'Goddammit,' Bradley said. 'I've got to see that bastard. Take me out there, then throw me overboard. I want to see him that bad.'

'Your tenacity is admirable, Bradley. You will not be forgotten.'

The German holstered his pistol, released Bradley's head, then stood up and walked away a few feet and knelt down again. He took a cigarette lighter out of his tunic pocket, lit something on the ground, and when he stood up, Bradley saw the fuse cable running back toward the warehouse. Set alight, it spluttered and sparkled as it started its journey.

'Oh, my God.' Bradley groaned.

The German walked back, knelt beside him, and smiled at him. He looked handsome in his SS uniform, but his smile was a dead thing.

'I have to go now, Mr Bradley. Mr Wilson awaits me. My name is Ernst Stoll – Captain Stoll, of the SS – and if you manage to survive the explosion, I hope you'll remember me. Naturally, I will tell Wilson about you . . . and he has a long memory. *Auf Wiedersehen.*'

Captain Ernst Stoll stood up and walked casually across the quay, where four other SS officers, all lieutenants, had been waiting for him. They let him climb down the ladder, obviously to a boat below, then they followed him down, one by one, leaving Bradley alone.

He glanced at the burning fuse. It was racing toward the warehouse. He looked back at the harbor, saw the submarine in the distance, then noticed a rubber dinghy heading toward it, carrying five men.

Obviously Stoll and his officers.

Bradley almost wept with frustration. He was so close yet so far. He thought of Wilson and cursed, thought of Gladys and nearly smiled, then turned his head to look at the burning fuse. It reached the warehouse, then the truck piled with corpses.

My last memory on earth, Bradley thought. Wilson's truckful of corpses.

He held his breath and prayed silently.

Wilson stood with Nebe and Kammler on the deck of the submarine and thoughtfully watched the men on the distant quay. Apart from Stoll, there were only four men. They worked long and very hard. They piled the bodies of their comrades onto the back of the truck and then drove the truck into the hangar. The docks seemed very quiet. The lamps beamed down through the mist. There was an explosion near the road at the end of the docks, and a man who was most likely Stoll walked along there to check. He knelt down for some time, stood up, walked back and forth. Allied planes rumbled overhead as Stoll's four men emerged again.

They were not in the truck, because they had left it inside the hangar. Stoll joined them and they clambered down the ladder and dropped into the dinghy. The oars splashed in the water. The distant lamps showed desolation. After what seemed like a very long time, the men arrived at the submarine. They were all helped aboard. Stoll seemed steady as a rock. Wilson stared across the water at the docks and saw the clouds of mist thinning.

The explosion was catastrophic. The whole hangar disintegrated. The flames shot up in jagged yellow lines that made the thin mist look silvery. The noise was demonic. A black smoke billowed up. The flames swirled and turned into crimson tendrils that embraced one another. Then the smoke drifted sideways, revealing great piles of rubble. The flames leapt across the charred, broken beams and stained the quay with great shadows.

The flames burned a long time. The harsh wind made them dance. They were still burning brightly when Stoll nodded at Wilson and they went belowdecks. The hatch above them was closed and the submarine, with much moaning and groaning, submerged in the Baltic Sea.

The real journey began.

EPILOGUE
Roswell, New Mexico
July 2, 1947

'The space age is beginning,' Bradley told Gladys. 'It began when we shipped the first captured German V-2s to New Mexico in 1945 and when, in March the following year, the first US V-2 launches began at the White Sands Proving Ground under the direction of our old friend, Wernher von Braun, now under contract to the United States. Since then about fifty V-2s have been launched, most of them successfully. Meanwhile, the Soviets, who got Peenemünde and to whom we kindly handed over Nordhausen shortly after capturing it, have started a similar rocket development program and are preparing to launch their first V-2 from a range near Volgagrad, better known to us as Stalingrad. And apparently, back here in the good ol' US of A, improved rocket motors, using liquid self-igniting fuels and based on the V-2 research, are about to go into production with civilian aviation organizations given USAF contracts . . . And all that in two years!'

'Give it a rest, Mike,' Gladys said. 'Let me fill up your glass.'

'A man's gotta have a hobby,' Bradley replied. He handed Gladys his glass and glanced out of the window at the desert, flat under a starlit sky. They were living not far from the late Robert H. Goddard's Mescalero Ranch and his old rocket launching site, Eden Valley, and Bradley often felt inspired by the location, given what he was doing.

They'd moved here when they got married, shortly after Bradley's release from the hospital, and now, when he was not involved in the drafting of contracts between the many US Air Force and civilian aeronautical establishments in the area, he was conducting his own investigations into Wilson's whereabouts and his possible connections with the recent spate of sightings of so-called UFOs, or flying saucers.

It kept him busy. It helped him forget the pain. As they had told him in the hospital, he would have to live with the pain for a long time. He owed Wilson that as well.

Gladys handed him the refilled glass, kissed his forehead, then took the chair facing him. Her hair was getting grayer every day, but her smile was still radiant. He loved her and loved being married to her; he'd gained that much, at least.

'Feeling okay?' she asked him.

'Sure.'

'When are we going to New York to see your kids? I sure like those visits.'

Bradley shrugged, then winced. Even shrugging could hurt like hell. 'Christmas,' he said, remembering the submarine in the harbor of Kiel, the icily sardonic SS captain, the fuse spluttering toward the truck piled with corpses, then the stupendous explosion . . . 'We'll go see them at Christmas. They're looking forward to seeing you again. We'll have a real family holiday.' He'd awakened hours later, pulled back to life by pain, and found himself half buried under rubble with a lot of bones broken. He'd been rescued, of course – the Allies and Soviets had met in Kiel – but he'd spent the next six months in a US Army hospital in Frankfurt, then been shipped home, to New York, for a long and painful convalescence.

All that, and he still hadn't seen Wilson, didn't know what he looked like. It was hard to take.

'What are all those notes?' Gladys asked him, indicating the pile of papers on his desk.

Bradley had a sip of whiskey. 'I'm just finishing off my research on the members of Projekt Saucer . . . on what happened to them.'

'Anything interesting?'

'So so. It's known that Rudolph Schriever and his team were trying to construct a flying saucer in the BMW plant near Prague, were hoping to test it in 1945, but had to destroy it in the face of the Soviet advance. When the Soviets took Prague, the saucer team all went their separate ways. As far as I can gather, Habermohl was captured and has disappeared into the Soviet Union; Miethe surrendered to the Allies and now works for the A.V. Roe Aeronautical Company in Malton, Ontario; and Schriever managed to make his way back home and has recently, from the safety of his home at Hökerstrasse 28 in Bremerhaven-Lehe, been telling the press that the flying saucers now being seen all over the place are based on his original Projekt Saucer designs.'

'Schriever doesn't mention Wilson?'

'Nope. Not a word.'

'And the others have vanished from the face of the earth.'

'More or less,' Bradley said. 'My only clue is that damned German submarine, *U-977*, which docked at Mar Del Plata, Argentina, on August 17, 1945. According to its commander, Captain Heinz Schaeffer, it had put out from Kiel harbor in late April 1945 and arrived in Argentina after an epic voyage of nearly four months. According to the Argentine authorities, their inspection of the submarine had revealed nothing unusual; however, given Perón's fondness for Nazis, we have to treat what they say with some skepticism. Captain Schaeffer *was* later handed over to an Anglo-American commission for intensive interrogations, during which he was asked if anyone of, quote, political importance, unquote, had been aboard his submarine during its final voyage. Naturally he denied all knowledge of everything.'

'But you have your doubts.'

'Well, we certainly know that an awful lot of fanatical Nazis have been given sanctuary in Argentina and Paraguay. So if Wilson *was* on that submarine – which he certainly was *if* it was the same submarine that *I* saw leaving Kiel harbor – it's possible that he disembarked at Mar Del Plata and went on to his final destination, wherever that might be, under the protective cloak of the Argentine government. And certainly there are rumors that a former Nazi named Ernst Stoll is currently living in seclusion in Paraguay.'

He glanced out the window again at that flat, dark desert stretched out under a starlit sky, and thought of Goddard's first rocket tests all those years ago, not too far from there. He shook his head, mystified by his own questions, then drank some more bourbon.

'You know,' he said, 'it sometimes really scares me. In April 1945 Wilson disappears with his designs for a highly advanced saucer-shaped aircraft, then, on June 24 this year, a part-time pilot, Kenneth Arnold, reports seeing nine saucer-shaped objects flying over Mount Rainier in Washington State. Since then similar objects have been observed all over the place – but mostly over New Mexico, right here where we live. Why?'

Gladys gave that familiar, laconic grin. 'One theory is that they're of Soviet origin,' she said.

'Well, the Soviets *did* capture the Peenemünde facility and a lot of its documentation and products – and they *did* ship more than six thousand German technical specialists of all kinds to various research centers throughout the Soviet Union – so we certainly know that they're working with the V-2 rockets and other advanced German secret projects.'

'So the theory,' Gladys continued, 'is that the flying saucers originate in the USSR and have been sent here to spy on our top-secret installations.'

'Which theoretically explains the preponderance of UFO sightings in New Mexico.'

'Exactly,' Gladys said. 'Right now New Mexico contains more of our postwar defense installations than any other part of the United States, including atomic research, aircraft, missile and rocket development, and a lot of highly advanced radar-electronics and stratospheric flight experimentation. The top-secret Manhattan atom bomb project is in Los Alamos. The White Sands Missile Range and Proving Range at Alamogordo is the most important of its kind in the United States. And we even have the only combat-trained atom bomb group in the world at this time: the 509th Bomb Group of the US Army Air Force Base, right here in Roswell, where Goddard flew his first real rockets. So, yes, if those flying saucers are spying on us, they'd certainly want to come here.'

'The Soviets or Wilson's group,' Bradley said dreamily. 'It sure as hell makes you think . . .'

He was just about to have another sip of his whiskey when the telephone rang. He picked it up and gave his name.

'Bradley,' a familiar voice said tersely, 'you better get your ass over here.'

Bradley immediately recognized the voice as that of First Lieutenant William B. Harris, Flight Intelligence Officer of the Roswell Army Air Base. 'What's up?' he asked, glancing automatically at Gladys.

'We've just been informed that a saucer-shaped aircraft crashed on the plains of San Augustin, between Magdalena and Socorro, New Mexico, about forty minutes ago.'

Bradley glanced at his wristwatch. It was just going on ten-thirty p.m.

'It's probably just a Rawin weather balloon.'

'No,' Harris said firmly. 'There are none up tonight. Besides, we tracked this thing on radar until it went down and it was certainly no weather balloon. Also, the flight controller at the private airfield at Carrizozo, about thirty-five miles southwest of the crash site, called a few minutes before the crash to inform us that a saucer-shaped aircraft had flown over at an altitude of approximately four to six thousand feet, at a speed of about four hundred miles per hour. Some goddamned farmer's already been out there and called from his home to say that what crashed is some sort of metallic, saucer-shaped object about twenty-five or thirty feet in diameter. He also said that there are dead bodies in the wreckage.'

'Jesus Christ!' Bradley whispered.

'And right now,' Harris continued, 'at the insistence of General Hoyt Vandenburg, deputy chief of the air force, an intelligence team from the 509th Bomb Group of the Eighth Air Force is on its way to the crash site to pick up the pieces. Once they get it, you can rest assured that it'll be flown out to either Carswell AFB, Forth Worth, or Wright-Paterson AFB in Dayton. So if we want to see what the hell it was, we better get out there fast.'

'Where'll I meet you?'

'Right outside the main gate.'

'I'm on my way,' Bradley said. Excited, he put the phone down and stood up, saying to Gladys: 'It's too good to be true. Something saucer-shaped has crashed near Socorro. I'm meeting Bill Harris at the main gate of Roswell Army Air Base, then we're going to drive the hell out there – so don't wait up, honey.'

'But I can't sleep without your battered bones beside me.'

Bradley grinned. 'Glad to hear it.' He bent over and kissed her full on the lips, then straightened up and looked down at her. 'I owe that son of a bitch Wilson one thing,' he said. 'I found you when I was trying to find him. That's a pretty good trade-off, right?'

'I'm glad you think so,' she said.

He grinned and waved his hand, then walked out of the living room, grabbed his coat, and hurried out to his car and drove into the night.

The land was flat and featureless, windblown, with the dust swirling eerily, but the sky above it contained an enormous moon and a spectacular display of stars. There were very few clouds – just some candy floss, here and there – but enough to cast shifting shadows on the desert floor.

Bradley drove fast, too excited to be careful, and enjoyed the feeling of power, of magical omnipotence, that came with being isolated from the world and moving through it at great speed. He loved the desert at night, its stark, lunar beauty; loved the play of shadow and lights on its barren floor, which made it seem like a living thing.

So, he was enjoying the drive and feeling excited ... Then he began to feel odd, no longer alone ... aware of some unseen presence.

'What the hell ... ?'

He spoke aloud to break the silence – or the silence contained within the beating wind – and automatically glanced at his rear-view mirror.

He saw only a cloud of billowing dust churned up by his wheels.

Nothing else ... just the darkness ... the stars seeming to move away ... the sky unfolding radiantly in his wake as the car barreled forward. Nothing else in the mirror.

Yet his heart started racing.

He glanced left and right, convinced that something was out there. He saw nothing and glanced up, where there was nothing unusual, and so concentrated on the road straight ahead, aware that he was sweating.

'Dammit, Bradley,' he said. 'Imagination – that's a dangerous thing.'

Talking to himself ... talking aloud to calm his nerves. There was nothing out there but moonlit darkness, starlit sky, shifting shadows ...

No, something *was* out there. What was *that*? Something moving. A flashing light. Growing bigger. Approaching ... Yes, dammit, *approaching!*

He saw the light, then it was gone, though it hadn't flashed on and off. It had flown from east to west at tremendous speed, then maybe shot upward – so fast it just disappeared.

Where was it now?

Bradley felt his skin crawling. His fear was an embarrassment. He was aware of something out there, couldn't see it, but could *feel* it, and his hands became slippery on the steering wheel when his heart raced in panic.

He tried to convince himself that he was imagining it . . . then, as his helpless fear deepened, something flashed in his eyes.

He almost swerved off the road, but blinked and straightened out. He squinted into the darkness, trying to see between the headlights. To the side, a pool of light brightened on the road beside the car, keeping abreast of it, speeding along and growing brighter and wider until it covered the whole road.

Bradley glanced up and was blinded by dazzling light. Then he lost control.

'Shit!' he exclaimed, his voice reverberating in his head as he fought with the wheel. The car swerved off the road, out of the light, then back onto the road and into the light again. 'Jesus Christ! What the—'

The light disappeared abruptly. The car barreled into the darkness. Its headlights had gone out and Bradley frantically worked the switch. Then a bass humming sound, an infrasound, almost *physical*, filled the car and tightened around his head as the engine cut out.

Bradley slammed on the brakes, went into a skid, straightened out, and was slowing down when something passed above, shot into the darkness ahead, then became an enormous, burning globe that froze right in front of him.

The car came to a halt. It just rolled to a stop. Bradley sat there, hardly believing what he was seeing, but too stunned to move.

He was looking at an enormous, glowing, saucer-shaped object that was hovering in midair along the road, almost as wide as the road. It had a silvery, metallic appearance, had no surface protuberances, and seemed to possess a perfectly seamless surface beneath that eerie green glowing.

Bradley sat in the car, too stunned to move, mesmerized by that *thing* out there. Then that thing, the flying saucer, sank lower and settled on the ground. It didn't appear to have any legs – it just settled down on its base – then the bass humming sound increased, tightening around Bradley's head, and he saw a panel opening up in the base of the saucer.

First one, then two, then three black-clad figures dropped down and spread out across the road and walked toward him.

Bradley was terrified.

He didn't know why – they were just people, after all. As they advanced deliberately upon him, he saw only that they were dressed completely in black, looked otherwise human, but were possessed of a frightening, calm intensity that seemed terribly unreal.

He wanted to get out of the car and flee, but he felt paralyzed.

Then the infrasound faded away and the tightness left his head. He immediately reached for the ignition key and turned it, but heard only a dead *click*. He dropped his hand as if he'd been scorched. His heart was still racing dangerously. He licked sweat from his upper lip and moved his gaze, taking in the three men.

One stopped right in front of the car, the other went to the far side, and the third walked around to stop by Bradley's door.

When he bent down to look through the window, Bradley wanted to scream.

'Roll the window down, Bradley.'

The man's voice was very soft. It was also oddly flat. It was the voice of a man with few feelings and a lot of authority. Bradley did as he was told. He didn't seem to have a choice. That voice, though quiet and unemotional, would brook no disobedience. Bradley rolled the window down, his hand shaking, then stared at the man.

He had silver-gray hair, unnaturally smooth white skin, coldly handsome features, and hypnotic blue eyes.

'You're Mike Bradley,' he said.

'Yes,' Bradley replied.

'You were with OSS during the war.'

'That's right,' Bradley said.

The man smiled without warmth. 'I believe you wanted to see me, Bradley. I'm told that your need to see me was an obsession that would not let you rest. Why was that?'

Bradley felt calmer now – not too good, but in control. He felt paralyzed, but the fear was less intense and allowed him to think.

'You're Wilson!'

The man smiled again, this time as if amused. 'Why did you go to such lengths to find me? What did you hope to find?'

'An answer,' Bradley said.

'An answer to what?'

'I had to know if such a genius could be human or was some kind of mutant.'

'Observe – I am human.'

'No, you're not – you're not like us. You exist on some plane beyond humanity, where feelings don't count.'

'Feelings aren't important. They belong back in the caves. Where we're going – where the human race must go – only logic prevails. Science, Mr Bradley, not emotion, is what will guide us to glory.'

'You're evil.'

'No, I'm not. To be evil, one must have feelings. *Extreme* feelings, I grant you – but feelings nevertheless – and since my mind has taken me beyond those, I cannot be evil. I am what I am, that I will be. I am nature's child also.'

'Nature can be brutal.'

'Nature *is*. There's no good or bad in it.'

Bradley studied Wilson's face. He wanted to find the evil in it. He saw nothing but blue eyes that were brilliant with intelligence; handsome, unrevealing features; skin too smooth to be natural.

Otherwise, there was nothing.

'Your world is dying, Mr Bradley – the world of wasteful emotions. The new world, my world, is approaching and can't be held back. It's a world of pitiless logic, of truth, and that's the way we must go. Science will take us there.'

He reached into the car and pressed his fingers to Bradley's forehead. 'Stop pursuing me,' he said. 'It will do you no good. You will only be treated as a crank and have a very unfortunate life, Think of your wife, Bradley. I know her, I believe. Consider your married children and don't make them endure your humiliation – since you can't stop me anyway. My flying saucers won't be hidden. They'll fly the world with impunity. Those who report seeing them will be ridiculed and, where necessary, silenced. Retire, Bradley. Think of your children. Enjoy your retirement. Now relax . . . *Auf Wiedersehen.*'

Bradley felt that he was dreaming. In his dream the fear returned. He kept thinking of his children, of that warning, and he knew he would stop here.

He would not go to Socorro. He would burn all his research. He knew, even as Wilson smiled and departed, that his search had come to an end. He would retire to guarantee his children's safety and let others do what they would.

Wilson walked from the car, between the other two men in black, and disappeared back into his flying saucer while Bradley just sat there. The hatch in the base moved up again, became part of the seamless body, then Bradley heard the bass humming sound, almost *felt* it – and as his head started tightening and his skin became numb, the flying saucer started glowing, its silvery body brightening magically, then became encased in a cocoon of pulsating white light and rose off the ground.

Bradley heard the noise, felt it, was surrounded by it and became part of it, as the saucer ascended slowly, gracefully, even majestically – then suddenly shot upward, but stopped again, as if by magic, to hover above him.

The infrasound cut out abruptly, allowing Bradley to move, and he climbed out and stood beside his car and looked directly above him. The saucer was high up, about

the size of a dime, and it seemed to be spinning on it
vertical axis and filling the sky with light. Then it shot u[
even higher, shrinking rapidly, but still shining, unti
eventually it merged with the stars and suddenly winke(
out.

Bradley saw the moon and stars, the vast web of th
cosmos, and he thought of Gladys and his children an
grandchildren, feeling fear for their future. Determined t
protect them, he climbed into his car, turned it around, an
headed back in the direction he had come from, throug
the dark, windblown desert.

He had the feeling that the flying saucer was stil
somewhere out there, gliding eerily through the night
keeping him under surveillance . . . and he knew that tha
feeling would haunt him for the rest of his days.

It was best to be silent.